DEEP BLACK

Andy McNab

CORGI BOOKS

DEEP BLACK
A CORGI BOOK : 0 552 15019 3

Originally published in Great Britain by Bantam Press,
a division of Transworld Publishers

PRINTING HISTORY
Bantam Press edition published 2004
Corgi edition published 2005

1 3 5 7 9 10 8 6 4 2

Copyright © Andy McNab 2004

Set in 11/12pt Palatino by
Falcon Oast Graphic Art Ltd.

Corgi Books are published by Transworld Publishers,
61–63 Uxbridge Road, London W5 5SA,
a division of The Random House Group Ltd,
in Australia by Random House Australia (Pty) Ltd,
20 Alfred Street, Milsons Point, Sydney, NSW 2061, Australia,
in New Zealand by Random House New Zealand Ltd,
18 Poland Road, Glenfield, Auckland 10, New Zealand
and in South Africa by Random House (Pty) Ltd,
Endulini, 5a Jubilee Road, Parktown 2193, South Africa.

Printed and bound in Great Britain by
Cox & Wyman Ltd, Reading, Berkshire.

Papers used by Transworld Publishers are natural, recyclable
products made from wood grown in sustainable forests. The
manufacturing processes conform to the environmental
regulations of the country of origin

DEEP BLACK

1

Bosnia, October 1994

From where I was hiding, the bottom of the valley looked like no man's land on the Somme: acres of mud churned up by tank and heavy vehicle tracks, mortar craters filled with dirty water. Here and there a dead hand clawed at the sky, pleading for help that had never arrived.

It was a grey and miserable day, not yet freezing, but plenty cold enough to have robbed me of a whole lot of body heat over the last three days. Even so I was still luckier than the scattered corpses, half buried in the mud. Judging by their state of decomposition, some had been there since the summer.

I was about a hundred Ks north of Sarajevo, dug into the treeline at the base of a mountain. My hide looked across the valley to what had once been a cement works, precisely 217 metres away. The problem for the owners was that it had been a Muslim cement works. The perimeter fence had long since been flattened by Serb tanks, and not a single part of the complex had been left unscarred by the bitter fighting. Most of it had been reduced to rubble. A three-storey building that I guessed had once been a block of offices was just about standing, heavily pitted by artillery and small-arm rounds. Black scorch marks framed the holes where there'd once been windows.

I'd counted maybe thirty or forty Serb troops through my miniature binoculars, and I could see they were as cold and pissed-off as I was. Smoke billowed from an annexe, mixing with the occasional burst of diesel exhaust; one or two of Mladic's boys were starting the vehicles, so they could get warm inside the cab.

I could only guess that, like me, they were waiting for the general's arrival. Ratko Mladic, the commander-in-chief of the Bosnian Serb Army, had been supposed to show up the day before, but that hadn't happened. Fuck knows why. Sarajevo had just told me to wait where I was, and that was what I'd do until they told me to lift off the target.

I was up to my ears in a Gore-Tex sniper suit, a big, bulky overall with a camouflaged outer and a duvet-type lining. It had kept me warm for the first few hours, but prolonged contact with the ground was steadily draining me. I had about two days' food left, but being so close to the target, I was on hard routine. I couldn't heat up food, or make a brew. Still, at least I was dry.

I raised the binos and scanned the ground again, controlling my breathing. It wouldn't take much of a vapour trail for someone to think I was having a cookout.

The coffin-shaped scrape I'd dug after moving covertly into the area was about two feet deep and covered with camouflage netting. I adjusted it again to make sure the objective lens at the front end of the LTD [laser target designator] had a clear field of view to the factory. When Mladic arrived to do whatever he was going to do in the middle of nowhere, I'd call it in. The Firm, getting shelled to shit by the Serbs back in Sarajevo, would green-light a fast jet loaded with a 2000-pound Paveway laser-guided bomb. About fifteen or twenty minutes later, depending on how long it took the platform, as we said in the trade, to deliver, there'd be a top-level vacancy in the Serb high command.

After the hit, I'd get the fuck out as quick as I could. The Serbs weren't fools; they knew these precision bomb strikes were man-in-the-loop technology and they'd be out looking for me.

Apart from the LTD and my daysack, everything from the sniper suit to the plastic bags of shit and petrol can of piss would stay in the hide. It wouldn't matter if the Serbs unearthed it: this wasn't the first time they'd been marked, and it wouldn't be the last. They knew who was doing it, but would blame the Muslims anyway. I'd rather have left the LTD as well, but there was a difference between the Serbs knowing they were getting designated and being able to prove it.

After extracting myself from the immediate area, I'd just hit a road and become Nick Collins, freelance reporter, again. I carried a Sony Hi-8 video camera and a Nikon 35mm SLR in my daysack. On the way in to the job I'd mixed with the local population here and there to make sure I had plenty of shots. If I was caught, I wanted to look the part.

Nick Collins had an Irish passport for this job. Irish or Swiss, they're the safest documents in the world. Who's ever pissed off with Dublin or Berne? With a name like Collins but a London accent, I'd have to say I came from Kilburn. Dad just never got round to taking Brit nationality when he finished working for McAlpine in the early seventies.

Freelancers like me were two a penny out here. Young guys, and the occasional girl, trying to make their fortune with bang-bang pictures and footage that might be good enough to be syndicated round the world. I'd joined a cast of hundreds who'd booked an air ticket then headed to Dixons in search of a decent SLR camera and a few hundred rolls of film. Once in-country, they asked where all the chaos was and made for it like bees to a honeypot.

Shouts were coming from the factory. I raised my head slowly and squinted through the dull, grey light. A group of Serbs were playing football again to warm themselves up. They were in a ragbag of uniforms. Some had camouflage; some were in what looked like German army-surplus parkas. Some were wearing wellington boots with thick, knee-high socks folded over at the top; some had decent calf-height boots. I'd seen better dressed and better organized Serb troops; maybe these were the cooks and bottle-washers. Whatever, they had a new football today.

I'd watched as these guys killed two Bosnian 'soldiers' the morning before – an old man and a boy of about fifteen. They'd taken them into the factory. Judging by the screams, they'd probably interrogated them, then brought them outside and shot them in the chest. I thought it strange at the time; why not in the head? That was what normally happened. I found out why at afternoon kick-off.

The whole thing over here was a fuck-up from start to finish – if there ever was a finish. I thought about the young girl I'd met a few days before, shivering at the roadside with a much older woman. She spoke a bit of English, so I asked their permission to take some photographs to fill up another roll of thirty-six for my cover story. She smiled shyly and told me her name.

'Where you going, Zina?'

She shivered again and motioned down the road. 'Sarajevo.'

What could I say? She was jumping out of the frying-pan and into the fire. The Serbs had had the place under siege for over two years. As well as constant sniper fire, they were lobbing about four thousand mortar and artillery shells into the city every day. The UNPROFOR troops who controlled the airport had their hands tied. About the only thing they could do was fly in aid for the half-million or so Sarajevans who were trapped. Thousands had been killed, but maybe this lot would be among the handful who made it through the Serb front line and into somebody's basement. I hoped so. If we both got to the city I might get my jacket back.

Even in this fucked-up place, some situations were more fucked-up than others. The old woman had been wearing a once-pink anorak many sizes too small for her. Her face was barely visible under the hood's fringe of white nylon fur, but I could see in her eyes that she was dying.

'Here.' I was still several Ks short of the cache – where the LTD and all the other kit I'd need had been dug in by the Regiment as soon as the cement works became a possible target – but I couldn't just leave the young girl like that. I took off my red ski jacket and gloves and handed them over.

She thanked me. Then, as if she had forgotten her plight for a few seconds, she struck a pose, right shoulder towards me, head flicked to the side as she zipped up her new jacket. 'Kate Moss, no?'

I brought the camera up to my eye but I couldn't bring myself to press the shutter release. Tears were suddenly streaming from very clear brown eyes and down her face. She was already back in the real world.

2

The football game had really warmed up now. Today's ball had mud caked on its matted grey hair and beard. I lowered my binos. I didn't want to see that shit. If they found me, the next head could be mine.

The ground below me was soft but sappingly cold. I wished the Regiment boys had left me a roll mat. Tensing my body, I wiggled my toes again and again, trying to generate some heat, but it wasn't working. Mladic had better turn up soon. I didn't have a picture of him with me because of opsec, but I'd burned one into my memory before I came out. I'd know his ugly fat face when I saw it.

The LTD was housed in a green metal box about the size of a breeze block. The tripod it was mounted on was extendable to about two feet, though I had it just inches off the ground. It had a viewfinder at the back, and a lens at the front, protected for now by a plastic cap, which would fire a laser about ten miles. There was also a laser range-finder, which was how I knew the target building was exactly 217 metres away.

The theory behind this kind of attack was very simple. A jet would come in from behind me, roughly in line with the beam from the LTD, but low, the other side of the mountain, out of sight and sound of the factory. When it was about nine or ten miles away, the on-board computer would tell the pilot to pull into a steep climb. At just the right moment he would let go of the Paveway, very much like bowling a ball underarm. By the time it had cleared the mountain, the jet would have turned and be on its way home.

The Paveway wasn't so much a missile as a standard 2000-pound lump of metal and explosive, with some fins strapped on its tail. Once it had been lobbed, the nose-mounted detector would look for the laser beam splashing on the target, lock on, and freefall to the target. This man-in-the-loop technology was all very well, but as I watched the soccer match, hoping I wasn't going to fuck up and become their next ball, I wished someone would hurry up and invent no-man-in-the-loop technology.

I had to be this close because of the mountains behind me. When the LTD fired its laser, the beam would break up at the point it hit the target, giving the splash the Paveway would be looking for. Had it been aimed down at an angle from high ground, there would have been less splash, and the Paveway might have trouble locking on as it came over the mountain. I had only one chance of getting Mladic. To maximize

14

the splash, I had to aim the laser at as near to a right angle to the target as possible, which meant being virtually on top of the factory – in fact, in tactical terms, close enough to spit on it.

I checked again that the alloy tripod was nice and solid. I had filled three plastic bags with mud and slapped them over the legs to keep the beam constant and stable. If Mladic was to get hit in the building, the Paveway's fuse would be set to delayed, to make sure it penetrated the brick-work before detonating. Paveway had what was called a 'circular error probable' – in other words, circumference of fuck-up – of about nine metres. If I was out by three, the bomb could be out by twelve, but pinpoint accuracy wouldn't matter too much today. The full blast of 945 pounds of tritonal would rain the steel casing down on him, and even I'd have to get my head down.

I'd taken a pair of badly made and cumber-some black nylon gloves from a body at the roadside. I pulled one off with my teeth and reached into the top pocket of the Gore-Tex suit for another two Imodium. I tried to time my bowel movements for the night.

The sound of engines rumbled up the valley to my right. I raised the binos again as a convoy of mud-covered wagons with canvas backs lumbered towards the factory. There were six of them, civilian vehicles. They all looked as if they had seen a few winters. As they got closer, I saw the drivers were in Serb uniform.

They drove into the compound and turned. I

saw heads, many in headscarves, bouncing from side to side, sandwiched between Serb guards. The prisoners weren't just men and women. There were children too.

3

The Serbs who'd been sitting in the back, AKs over their knees, jumped down, smoking and joking with each other. The Muslim civilians clambered out after them, scared and bewildered, wrapped in blankets and all sorts against the cold. Their breath hung around them in a big cloud as they huddled together.

The bottle-washers stopped playing football. There was a new game in town. They left the head where it was and ambled over towards their weapons.

More tailgates dropped and there was a lot more shouting. Children cried as they were wrenched from their mothers and herded out of sight behind the office block. The remaining men, women and teenagers were split into groups. It was not looking good.

This was the third job with Paveways I'd been on since the end of August. The theory was that if you wiped out the Serb command, the troops would dissolve into chaos and the Muslims might stand a chance against the fourth largest army in Europe.

The first two principals I'd hit were colonels in charge of ethnic cleansing brigades. I'd heard the horror stories. The Serbs moved in after the shelling and rounded everyone up. The men would get separated, then they'd get dropped. Then the women and children were brought forward and despatched alongside their husbands and fathers. Anyone unfortunate enough to be female and between the ages of about fourteen and thirty was raped, often repeatedly. Some were killed during the assaults. Many were held until they were at least seven months pregnant before being released.

Others were sold into the sex trade, exchanged for cash and drugs with the traffickers who follow all wars and do business with both sides. A white girl could be worth up to fifteen thousand dollars these days.

4

I checked my watch. It would take the Serbs a good half an hour to sort out the prisoners. If I called in the air strike right now, some of these people might stand a chance, if they survived the blast. It was worth a shot; as things stood, most of them were going to die anyway.

As I watched a 4x4 bouncing along the track towards the factory, I wanted to reach for the beacon big-time. But my hand didn't move. That wasn't the mission. I was here to take a life, not save it. It was not the best of choices, and I knew I'd be waking up in a sweat at three a.m. for the next few weeks, feeling a low-life for not having done anything but, fuck it, we all had to die some time. I just wished I wasn't the one with his finger on the button.

The segregation was almost complete, except for one boy's mother arguing with a soldier. The bottle-washers were kicking her, trying to pull her son away from her and put him with the men. She begged and pleaded, holding on to the boy for dear life. He didn't look much older than thirteen.

My view was blocked for a second by the arrival of the 4x4, an unusually shiny Landcruiser. The door opened, and out of it came a slight figure with a flowing beard, not very tall, who walked calmly towards the mother and son.

The man seemed to float across the mud. The Serbs couldn't take their eyes off him. There was no begging, no arm-waving, the newcomer just held his hands in front of him and talked. I studied him through my binos. He was in his early to mid-twenties, and wore a Russian-style fur hat and a heavy greenish coat. His body language was confident. The bottle-washers seemed almost subservient to him. They stopped kicking the woman. She stayed on her knees in the mud, clutching her child to her chest.

The bottle-washers looked like they'd been told off at school. I couldn't help feeling that the boy's reprieve would be short-lived.

Beardilocks helped them to their feet and took them back to the group of women. The Serb guards even parted ranks to let him through.

Then there was a shot, a stunned silence, and another shot. Two of the male prisoners crumpled to the ground.

As the truth dawned, the women and children began to wail and scream.

There were two or three more shots. Slow. Rhythmic. Methodical.

More cries. Just tens of metres away, husbands, sons, uncles, brothers were getting it in the head.

I got my head back down into the hide, mentally numb now, as well as physically. You had to be able to throw that switch or you'd be barking at the moon.

5

For the next ten minutes, all I could hear were screams and the rhythmic tap of single shots. Then I heard the sound of vehicles, gradually getting louder. I slowly raised my head, and pointed the binos down the road.

A convoy of seven this time, all civilian Toyota 4x4s, two with flat beds and .50 cal machine-guns mounted over the cabs, was moving fast up the valley. The vehicles were new, too good for squaddies to be messing around in, and they bristled with whip antennae. This looked like a command group.

As they swung into the compound, I checked each one, but the windows and windscreens were too splattered with mud to make anyone out. The only people I could see were the heavily wrapped-up gunners on the .50 cals, who were being thrown around on the back, but trying to look cool.

The convoy pulled up outside the office block. Soldiers and bottle-washers ran towards them and fell in at attention. This was looking promising. I felt warmer already.

Mladic got out of the second vehicle, dressed in American camouflage BDU [Battle Dress Uniform] and a Serbian pillbox hat. He was just like his pictures; fifty years ago he could have been Hermann Goering's double.

After a quick fuck-off salute, he was bonding big-time with the local commander. As he stood over the bodies, chatting to his junior officers, I turned on the beacon to get the platform stood to. It had only one frequency, constantly monitored by an American AWACS aircraft, circling the country some forty thousand feet above me.

I hit the send button. This close to the target, I couldn't risk speech.

I kept on hitting it, maybe six or seven times, before a soft American female voice came through the earpiece. That was a pleasant change: last time it had been a hard-nosed guy with the kind of East Coast accent that took no prisoners.

'Blue Shark Echo? Radio check.'

I hit the pressle twice. She would get squelch into her headphones.

She came back on, very quiet, very slow. 'That's OK, strength five, Blue Shark Echo. Do you have a target?'

I hit the pressle twice.

'Roger, Blue Shark Echo. Stand by.'

AWACS would be telling Sarajevo I had the principal. The whole detect, decide, destroy system was being bypassed because the decision to destroy had already been taken. All Sarajevo had to do was authorize the aircraft to stand to.

Because this job was known only to about a dozen people, there was no way the command set-up could have operated from the UN safe zone at Sarajevo airport. Instead, they were in an office above a café in the city, probably huddling under the table right now as another Serb artillery bombardment rattled their windows.

Maybe an American pilot on one of the carriers was striding to an aircraft. Very soon he or she would be circling above the Adriatic, waiting for the call to make their approach to target. Maybe it was a Brit Tornado based in Italy, less than the distance from London to Scotland but a whole different world away. The crew wouldn't even have time to get comfortable before they'd be heading home for hot coffee and a video. I didn't have a clue, but it didn't really matter. I wasn't going to hear the aircraft, let alone see it.

I was waiting for her to come back and tell me a time to target. I just hoped that Mladic stayed static long enough. On the last job, time to target had been fifteen minutes.

The bottle-washers were getting busy again. Two were blacking out the ground-floor door-frame and windows with blankets. Then foldaway chairs and trestle tables were dragged out of the 4x4s and taken into the office block, followed by baskets of food and armfuls of wine bottles.

I couldn't believe what came out next: a pair of candelabra, complete with candles. It reminded me of the cavalry officers I'd known before I'd joined the Regiment, who'd carry the regimental silver with them in their tanks on major exercises and set the table for dinner as if they were taking a break from the Charge of the Light Brigade. As an infantryman I used to honk about the crap hats and their fancy ways, green with envy as I opened my ration can of sweaty processed cheese.

Mladic just stood there with his hands on his hips, apparently oblivious to the carnage.

My new best friend was back on the net. 'Blue Shark Echo, over.'

I hit the pressle twice.

'I hear you fives, Blue Shark Echo. You will have a fifteen – that's one five – minute time to target. Copy?'

I did. I hit the pressle twice as I watched bundles of firewood being taken into the office. Smoke was soon streaming out of the cracks in the wall. With luck he would just have sat down to eat by the time I started easing the Paveway up his arse.

I pulled my glove off with my teeth then slowly reached out to the front of the LTD and lifted the little plastic cover from the objective lens. Next I dug around in the breast pocket of my sniper suit for some toilet roll and gave the glass a wipe from the centre outwards to clear it of condensation. Then I eased myself up a little so I could look at the sight picture in the viewfinder. I aimed the crosshairs at the ground floor, on the area of wall between the two covered window-frames. I moved them vertically up, aiming at the point where the first floor hit the front elevation. With nine metres margin of error, I wanted to make sure that there was no chance it would just plough into the ground. Now it didn't matter if it was nine metres high or left or right, it would still hit.

It looked as if pre-dinner drinks were about to be served. Mladic headed for the office block, his sidekicks in hot pursuit. The shooting continued as he disappeared inside.

There was nothing I could do now but wait. I couldn't afford to call the platform in just yet. He might take it into his head to come outside again with his G and T and go for a wander. With the amount of alcohol, food and candelabra on show there was no rush. Well, there was, but I couldn't cut corners.

I gave it ten minutes. Chances were he was staying inside now. I hoped he had seen enough dead bodies for the day.

I got on the net and hit the pressle five or six times.

'Is that you, Blue Shark Echo? Send again.'

I hammered the pressle another couple of times.

She came back. 'Do you have a designation?'

Press, press.

'Roger that, confirm you have designation.'

Press, press.

'Delayed fuse?'

Press, press.

'Confirm no change to attack profile.'

I pressed again. The platform was coming in on the same bearing.

She'd be giving the good news to Sarajevo, and they'd be passing it on to an aircraft orbiting over the Adriatic.

It was about thirty seconds before she came back. 'Blue Shark Echo, you have a platform. Time to target plus one five minutes. Five, four, three, two, one, check.'

I double pressed to acknowledge. That was it. Precisely fifteen minutes from now, the Paveway would make contact. All that was left for me to do was switch on the LTD in eight minutes' time, make sure I could hear the little motor start up, check the sight picture hadn't been moved from the building, then splash the fucking thing before ramming both index fingers in my ears and getting my head down.

I heard shouting and lifted the binos. Beardilocks had swung back into action. He must have torn himself away from the rest of the prisoners, because he was now at the door of the building, remonstrating with a guard. Not many seconds later, the blanket across the door was pulled aside. Mladic appeared, his features contorted by rage.

6

The general's BDU jacket was off, revealing an olive shirt with rolled-up sleeves. There was a towel in his hand. He combed back what was left of his grey hair and prodded Beardilocks angrily in the chest. The guy stood his ground, calm and collected. It was Mladic who was going apeshit. I was just waiting for him to take the pistol from his belt and discharge it into his head.

Beardilocks' hat fell into the mud as Mladic struck him, but he didn't even blink. He had a black skull cap underneath. He was either a very mad mullah or a very brave one.

He took the beasting completely calmly, just wiping the mud off his beard now and again with his right hand as he picked himself off the ground. Mladic was the frustrated one, still hollering and shouting, waving his arms about. His hair had lost its groomed look.

Mladic knocked the bearded man to the ground one final time, then stood, hands on hips, looking down at him. Finally he shouted something to one of the officers and, pointing at the track, disappeared back inside the building.

The officer moved over to a group of soldiers and barked a series of orders. They began to herd the prisoners together on the football pitch. An old woman bent and picked up the ball, cradling it in her arms. The bottle-washers just looked on, smoking, weapons hung loosely over their shoulders.

I got myself ready to hear the .50 cals open up to finish the job quick time.

Instead, something strange happened. Under Serb orders, the survivors started to shuffle back towards the trucks. Beardilocks stood by the door, waving for them to get a move on. Some paused to kiss his muddy hands.

I checked my watch. It was time. Whoever was driving those trucks had better get their foot down. I checked that the spring was holding the green cover on the objective lens in position. There was no need to worry about the sun giving away the hide today. I grabbed a sheet of toilet paper and wiped the lens again. I couldn't lean forward enough to see the glass; I just had to hope it was clean.

I checked the viewfinder one last time, then tightened the adjustment screw on the tripod. It didn't need it: it just made me feel better. We were set. I pushed the power button and listened for the gentle whine of the electrics. A small red LED told me the target was being splashed.

Just six minutes to go. The platform would be screaming in towards the mountain range now, keeping below the skyline, ready to pull up and lob its load.

I looked back at the building. The last of the trucks was leaving the compound. Two remained. They weren't needed: their passengers were all lying in the mud. Beardilocks was still by the door, his gaze fixed further inside the factory compound. I followed his line of sight.

One small group of prisoners had been kept behind; maybe twenty young girls with their arms outstretched, clutching at each other. Their bodies jerked with sobs as one final victim was added to their number.

This time I felt a surge of adrenalin and my heart thumped painfully in my chest. I might not have recognized Zina's face, but there was no mistaking my red ski jacket.

7

Beardilocks gobbed off at the blanket that covered the door, then climbed into his Landcruiser and followed the rest of the vehicles down the track. It looked like he'd got what he wanted. The group of girls was brought to the two trucks. I lay there willing the Serbs to kick Zina faster towards the fucking things.

I was wrong: not all of them were going to the trucks. Five were being kept back.

Serbs closed in on them. Two girls, no older than sixteen, were pulled away from the others and frogmarched towards the office block. Their legs slipped and slid in the mud as they tried to resist.

I got my binos on Zina. She was being held outside the building with another two girls. She didn't cry as she watched the trucks disappear down the track; she wasn't even looking frightened. She stood there with the kind of dignity I'd never had, or that I'd lost years ago doing this sort of shit.

There were screams from upstairs. Both girls had been dragged to the third floor. One was hanging out of a window-frame, her blouse stripped off, arms flailing. She turned her head, screaming and begging, her body jerking as the first Serb pushed himself into her. The other girl was getting punched and kicked for resisting.

I time-checked: three minutes to go.

Another loud scream from the third floor. I swung the binos up in time to see the first girl's body land on top of one of Mladic's 4x4s, mangled by one of the .50 cals. She didn't move again.

Mladic pushed his way through the blanket covering the door and strode over to the new vehicle, pointing animatedly at the blood running down the side panels.

Get back in that fucking building!

The bottle-washers scurried around; two jumped on to the flatbed and dragged the body away. Seconds later another appeared with a bucket of water and a cloth.

Two Serbs poked their heads through the upstairs window and Mladic laid into them, pointing at the state of the wagon as he disappeared back inside. Thank fuck for that.

Over the last few months, I'd seen women's bodies hanging from trees as the Serbs advanced. Suicide was often a whole lot better than survival.

Thirty seconds to go. I got my head down below the lip of the shell scrape, fingers in my ears, and started counting.

Five, four, three. I braced myself.

Two, one. Nothing. I counted another five seconds. Maybe I'd got my timings wrong. I checked my watch. Spot on. Maybe it was the LTD. I got my head up and checked. It whined gently. The red light was still illuminated. I checked the cap was still up – everything was right.

The target was designated. Where the fuck was the Paveway?

8

Two minutes passed, and still nothing.

I hit the pressle and her voice was waiting for me. 'Blue Shark Echo, radio check.'

I spoke quietly, I didn't whisper. Whispering always comes over as mush on the net, and in any case you always do it louder than you think; it's better just to keep your voice really low and constant. 'Blue Shark Echo. OK, I'm OK. What's happening? There's no strike. No strike, over.'

'That's a no strike, no strike.' It was like she was taking an order at McDonald's. 'Wait out. Wait out.'

She obviously didn't know what was happening either, but I couldn't wait long for an answer. I needed to conserve battery power on the LTD in case I was going to have to stay here and redesignate.

The pause was taking too long. It was six minutes now since the attack should have happened. Renewed screams and cries for help came from the office block. The voice sounded different. The girl must have been replaced.

I was just about to hit the pressle again when she came back on. 'Blue Shark Echo, Blue Shark Echo? Wait out, wait out.'

This wasn't good enough. 'Do I still designate? Do I have a platform?'

All she did was repeat, 'Wait out.'

What was I supposed to do? I kept the LTD running. Why the fuck couldn't Sarajevo get their act together?

I caught a blur of red in my peripheral vision and swung the binos.

9

Almost simultaneously, there was a yell from the right of my field of view. Zina was making a break for it. The remaining girl outside was on her knees, hands outstretched, screaming out to her. The Serbs just laughed and nonchalantly unslung their weapons from their shoulders. Their fun was just beginning.

I silently willed the Paveway to come tumbling out of the sky.

Zina scrambled across the open ground, slipping and sliding in the mud. The ski jacket was suddenly a sentence of death: it was going to make an easy target in the gloom.

Zina tripped and fell into a large puddle, then scrambled to her feet, face and hair dripping, and carried on running. She switched direction, making for the treeline. She was heading straight towards me.

The Serbs hadn't fired a single shot. Maybe she was still too close to them, not enough of a challenge. I could hear them laughing and joking with each other; it looked as if they were trying to work out who was going to have first pop.

She was getting closer to me. I could hear her sobbing.

The first shot rang out. It missed. I didn't see where it landed but I heard the thud somewhere in front of me.

Zina kept coming. There was another shot. Missed again. More laughter and jeering from the Serbs.

There was another shot, then another. They pounded into the mud in front of the hide. At this rate, it was only a matter of time before the LTD took a hit. Zina was no more than ten metres from me now, five. Then she saw me. Confused, she stopped, looked around, started to run again. There was another shot. She took it in the back and fell directly in front of me. Mud splashed through the cam net on to my face.

She managed to raise herself on her elbows and tried to crawl the last few feet towards me, her eyes begging me for help. I couldn't do anything but look back at her, hoping the next round would kill her and stop the pain before she compromised me. Another couple of rounds rang out in quick succession. She jerked forwards, almost landing in the hide. She gave a whimper, then a gasp. Blood trickled from her mouth into the mud just a few feet in front of me. The entry wounds in her back steamed in the cold air.

I heard clapping and a few mocking cheers. Someone had won the bet.

I wondered how long it would take them to stop the backslapping and come to check her out. All it would take was one of Mladic's boys getting busy with his binos.

I didn't move an inch. I felt her lifeless gaze bore into me.

There were no sounds of feet splashing through the mud towards me, just more laughter from the Serbs and more screaming from the girl in the upstairs room 217 metres away.

Another shot was fired and Zina's body jolted as she took the round. Good; it looked like they were going to save themselves the journey.

Then I realized one of her legs was splayed across the LTD's line of sight.

I couldn't hold the LTD: it had to be braced firmly on the tripod. I checked the field of vision to the right of the shell scrape, thinking I might be able to re-site it, but there were too many bumps in the ground. It had to stay where it was.

Besides, I'd run out of time.

I would have to clear the body.

10

I kept very still in case they were watching her, ready to take another pop. But I had to get my head up. The target had to be splashed. I raised my head millimetre by millimetre, and looked over the lip of the shell scrape.

Zina's blood had stopped steaming in front of me and was already congealing in the mud. Her leg was still blocking the line of sight of the LTD.

The Serbs' attention was back on the three surviving girls, two on the third floor and one still outside. Now was my chance.

I crawled out of the rear of the hide as the cries of anguish and despair continued from the top window. Taking care not to disturb the cam net, I inched forward to the left of the hide. Camouflage wasn't a problem: the sniper suit was already caked with mud.

After five feet of crawling I was able to reach Zina's leg with an outstretched hand and pull it towards me. Her skin was still warm. I had to be careful now: too much movement and one of

Mladic's boys might notice a difference in the body's position, even if it seemed they had other things on their minds.

I crawled back into the hide and checked the viewfinder. The LTD had a clear line of sight once again on to the target.

The exertion had warmed me a little, but now I was static again the cold renewed its attack. I picked up the binos.

The last girl was being dragged into the building. Mladic stood in the doorway, his ugly fat face creased in a grin. I longed to plant a high-velocity round right in the middle of his greasy forehead. After a while he turned and went back inside. Maybe it was time to push his way to the front of the queue.

There was nothing I could do but wait as the girls' screams and sobs rattled around the building. What the fuck was happening? Where the fuck was that platform?

I checked the viewfinder once more, but I had a sinking feeling deep in my guts. Who was I trying to kid? The strike wasn't going to happen. Mladic and the rest of his bastards were going to get away with this. And they were going to live to do it another day.

Zina's eyes stared back at me. They were no longer clear and bright, just vacant and drab like everything else around her.

Fuck the Firm, fuck Mladic. I should have called in the Paveway as soon as she'd turned up.

11

Washington DC
Thursday, 2 October 2003

'Fuck it, that was over nine years ago. It's all history now.'

Ezra sat back in his chair and studied me with one of those serious yet deeply understanding looks they probably teach at shrink school.

I shifted slightly in my own chair and the leather squeaked. I let my gaze wander along the wood-panelled walls, past the pictures and framed certificates. Ezra would probably say this was me looking for a way out, but I knew there wouldn't be one for another twenty minutes at least. I ended up staring through the window at the Arlington Memorial Bridge, fifteen floors down and a couple of blocks away.

'Was that the first time you felt betrayed?'

I looked at him across the low coffee-table. There was nothing on it but a box of tissues. In case I ever wanted to burst out crying, I supposed.

Ezra was maybe seventy, seventy-five, something like that. His hair was like a steel-grey helmet, and although the rest of his face had aged, his eyes sparkled as much as they probably had when he was thirty and knocking women shrinks senseless at conferences in Vienna. For all I knew he still was.

Why was he still working? Why hadn't he retired? I'd wanted to ask him that ever since I started with him nine months ago, but these sessions were strictly about me. He'd never tell me anything about himself. All I knew about him was that he was the one who got lumbered with the fruits who worked for George and needed sorting out.

He raised an eyebrow to prompt my answer. I was well used to his repertoire of body signals by now.

'Betrayed? No. Shit happens. It was more a turning point in how I thought about them. So many deaths, so many of them kids. Especially Zina. It's just, well . . .' I paused and looked back out towards the bridge. 'It doesn't matter now, does it?'

He didn't believe me and I heard myself filling the silence. 'Three hours I waited there. All that time, calling on the net, trying to find out what the fuck was happening. Meanwhile, Mladic filled his face, had his afters and left. And all that time his boys were upstairs with the girls. When I finally got back to Sarajevo I didn't even get told why the job was cancelled. Just to wind my neck in and hang around the hotel for the next one. Which never happened.'

Ezra just sat and waited.

'Who knows? Maybe if Zina had held on and

not done a runner she'd still be alive. Maybe if I'd called in the Paveway earlier she would have lived, or I would have put her and the others out of their misery. Fuck it – who cares? It's all in the past.'

Ezra tilted his head a little to one side. Even through the double-glazing I could hear an aircraft coming out of Ronald Reagan airport just the other side of the Potomac. I watched it lift into the sky, probably rattling the windows of my apartment block as it went.

'Then why talk about it so much these last few weeks, Nick? Why does it always come back to Bosnia?'

I didn't have an answer, and I knew by now that he wouldn't fill the silence himself. If it took the whole fifty minutes, he'd wait.

In the end I just shrugged. 'You brought it up.'

'No, Nick, I think you'll find that you did. But we always get to a certain point and then we stop. Why do you think that happens? It certainly feels to me that there's a lot more in there you want to let out. Could it be that your psyche is protecting you? Preventing you letting everything you feel come out?'

I hated it when he played the subconscious card. 'Listen, I don't know too much about the psyche shit, but I'll tell you this: I've been thinking about topping myself.'

'Because of Kelly?'

'Because it's hard to think of reasons why I shouldn't.'

'You know it wasn't your fault. You know

there was nothing you could have done to save her. So why would you do that?'

'I might as well. She's gone. What the fuck's left? Therapy with you twice a week for the next ten years? You might not last that long.'

I rubbed my fingers into my hair and smelt them. I was waiting for him to ask why I thought I did that. He normally did. Even though I bet he knew the answer.

He brought his right hand up to his face and stroked his chin. 'You know, Nick, if you really thought that way, you would have done it by now. I prescribed you enough drugs to open your own pharmacy.' He pointed at the window. 'You could try running away if you wanted to, just like Zina did. But the fact is, you continue to come here to carry on with our therapeutic relationship.'

I leaned forward and rested my elbows on my knees. 'I keep telling you, I'm not here for any sort of relationship. I'm here because George sent me. The whole thing is bollocks.'

It was like water off a duck's back to him. 'Why is it bollocks, Nick? It was you who thought therapy might help you cope with Kelly's death. Isn't that what all this is about – helping you overcome the trauma of losing her?'

'No, I'm here because George sent me. And everything I've said will be reported back to him, won't it? Maybe he's listening right now – what the fuck do I know?'

'Nick, you know that isn't true. How are we going to move forward if there isn't complete trust between us? You have nothing to fear. I understand the pressures you're under. I understand the sort of work you've been involved with. It's natural in your business that you would keep everything battened down inside. I've been doing this for people just like you since Vietnam, trying to help them overcome those feelings. But we're going nowhere unless we have complete trust.' He sat back slowly, giving me time to let it all sink in. The index finger went back to his chin. 'George understands the pressures and constraints you're under. He wants you back, fit and able to work.'

We were going round in circles. We must have had this conversation at least a dozen times. 'But being here won't help that, will it? I feel I'm trapped in some kind of *Catch 22* situation. If I don't conform, you'll keep me here until I admit I have a problem. If I do conform, I'm admitting there's a problem and I won't get out.'

'But you must still have some notion that you want to be helped. You've talked about having feelings of loneliness . . .'

'I didn't ask for help, I only agreed to it because I didn't know what the fuck else to do. I now realize I should have shut up and got on with my job. People all over the planet have their kids dying on them every day and they still go to work, they still get on with their lives. I should have said nothing and got on with it.'

Ezra leaned forward. 'But Kelly didn't just die, did she, Nick? She was killed – and, what's more, you were there. It does make a difference.'

'Why? Why does everything have to have a label? You can't be shy any more, you have to have social phobia. Try hard to succeed and you've got a perfectionist complex. Why can't I just get on with life and go back to work? What are you going to say now, that I'm in denial?'

He studied me again in that way of his that always got me pissed off. 'Do you think you're in denial, Nick?'

'Look, I know I'm fucked up a bit, but what do you expect? Who isn't? Can't you be happy with that diagnosis – "fucked up a bit"? You've got to be a bit Dagenham to do the job anyway.'

He raised an eyebrow. They must learn that at shrink school too. 'Dagenham?'

I nodded. 'Two stops short of Barking.'

'I'm sorry?'

'London joke. On the London Underground, Dagenham is two stations away from Barking. Barking? Barking mad. Dagenham, two stops short of Barking.'

He sort of got it but decided it was time to close that particular chapter. 'So, did you see Bang Bang yet?'

'Yeah. I'm not sure it helped. I didn't become a gibbering wreck or come out crying, if that's what you're asking.'

I got a smile out of him again, but I hated it when he did that: he looked as if he could see right through me. 'Nick, what you've really got to remember is that by doing your bit to help end that war, you probably did save a whole lot of lives.'

I lifted my hands. 'So what? The war was

bollocks. People got killed for nothing, kids got killed for nothing. Anyway, whatever. Over and done with.'

His eyes flicked towards the clock on the wall behind me. 'I see we've run over our time again.'

That was always my cue to get up and take my leave. Most times I'd have liked to wrench the door open and make a break for it. But I knew that would only mean the next fifty-minute session would be spent talking about why I'd done a runner, so, as always, I got up and put on my leather bomber slowly. I'd learned that I needed to take it off when I arrived, because if I didn't we'd end up talking about the reasons why I'd kept it on. Did it mean I didn't want to be here, and was hoping for a fast getaway?

He stood up with me and came to the door. 'I'm glad you finally went to Bang Bang, Nick. The psyche, you see – you can never rush it, it takes its time to work things through, to help you take the right decisions.

'I think Bosnia affected you more than you think. I think there's a connection between losing Kelly and the death of Zina. We'll get there eventually, when the psyche is ready to beam us in.

'But that can only happen if you feel comfortable with our therapeutic relationship. I'm not here to hurt you, I'm here to help you. All your life you've had to hold things inside and not show your feelings, so I appreciate it was never going to be easy to let all this emotion out. As long as you realize it's going to take some time . . .

'And, Nick, even if you were lied to, it sounds like you really did make a difference during that time.'

I stood on the threshold. 'Just like old Beardilocks, yeah? At least he had the bollocks to let a few die in order to save the rest.'

12

Friday, 3 October

My neck was stiff and my face was stuck to the leatherette. The sofa wasn't the most comfortable place to sleep, but that was what I always seemed to end up doing these days.

Forcing my eyes open, I checked Baby-G. It was a pink one – Kelly's fifteenth and last birthday present from me. There was still time, so I pulled the blanket over my head to block out the glare of the TV and the dull grey light just seeping through the blinds.

I pressed one of Baby-G's side buttons and watched the face glow a purple colour and the stick man do a break-dance. She'd thought it was a bit silly, but I liked it. Fucking hell, I missed her. I rubbed my hair and smelt the grease on my hand as I closed my eyes.

She lay so perfectly still, as I'd seen her lie so many times when she was asleep – stretched out on her back, arms and legs out like a starfish. Except that this time there'd been no sucking of her bottom lip, no flickering of her eyes under their lids as she dreamed. Kelly's head was twisted to the right, at far too unnatural an angle.

Why the fuck hadn't I got there quicker? I could have stopped the fucking nightmare . . .

As I'd leaned over her, my tears had fallen on to her hair-covered face. I checked for a pulse, even though I knew it was futile.

I'd dragged her to the edge of the bed and gathered her in my arms, trying to hold her as best I could as I stumbled back towards the doorway.

They would be coming up the stairs soon, respirators on, weapons up.

I'd lain down next to her, gathering her head in my arms and pulling it on to my chest.

And buried my face in her hair.

A voice from the TV told me tonight's hot ticket was going to be *Lost Dinosaurs of Egypt*. The TV had kept waking me during the night, but I couldn't be arsed to scrabble around for the remote to switch it off. In fact, last night I hadn't even been arsed to get undressed before channel-hopping for hours and eventually falling asleep. On an MTV night I could learn quite a lot about the latest bands out there. Kelly would have been proud of me.

It was no use. I was awake now. I felt about on the floor, knocking over a couple of empty mugs then running my hand over the remains of a toasted cheese sandwich. I finally got hold of the remote and flicked through the morning soaps and re-runs of *Jerry Springer* until I hit a news channel. Another two US soldiers had been killed in Iraq.

I planned my day, which didn't take long. It was going to be exactly the same as most of the other days I didn't spend sitting in front of Ezra. Or maybe not. I remembered promising myself I was going to open the windows today. It was getting so rank in here that even I could smell it. And, of course, there was another meeting with George.

I rolled off the sofa and threw the blankets back on top. The kitchen was a disaster zone. The stainless steel and glass had been clean and shiny when I took up the tenancy, but these days I seemed to be sharing the place with a gorilla. He came in every night while I was asleep and messed up all the cleaning I'd done. He dirtied all the plates, filled the bin to overflowing, then spilled coffee and tea on the work surfaces. To top it all, he chucked bits of stale bread and empty spaghetti-hoops cans about the place, and after trashing the kitchen he fucked up the rest of the flat. The last thing he always did before leaving, as far as I could tell, was shit in my mouth. It certainly tasted like it, this time of the morning.

I shoved the last couple of slices into the toaster and peeled the plastic from some processed cheese. A constant stream of aircraft headed into Ronald Reagan, and the TV next door blasted out that Channel Nine was going live to an armed siege in Maryland.

I fired up the kettle and wandered back in to watch, munching on the cheese. I never knew why I bothered taking the wrappers off: it all tasted the same.

I found myself watching a young black guy coming out of his front door in just a pair of jeans. His hands were in the air, but there was a pistol in one. The place was surrounded by police, one barking at him through a megaphone to put down the gun. It was hard to tell from his body language: was this guy drugged up or just pissed off?

I tried to unstick the cheese from my teeth and the roof of my mouth. The black guy shouted for them to shoot him, pounding on his chest with his free hand. The megaphone screamed at him to put down the weapon, and for a split second it looked like that was what he was going to do. He started to lower the weapon, but instead of laying it on the ground he turned the muzzle towards the group of police hunched down behind their cruiser, and that was the last thing he did. Six or seven rounds hit him at once and he dropped like liquid. The screen went black, then we were back in the studio, the anchors changing swiftly to traffic conditions on the Beltway. Another suicide-by-cop for us to watch live over our corn flakes.

The toast popped up. I went and shoved a fresh batch of cheese squares between the un-buttered slices and scraped the last bit of Branston from the jar with a dirty teaspoon. I'd been getting through three or four jars of the stuff a week. Ezra would have had a field day if I'd told him: I clearly had an unfulfilled yearning for the old country. Sliced white bread, cheese slices and Branston pickle – often three times a day, and lying on the sofa watching *Oprah*. No wonder my jeans were getting difficult to put on.

I turned towards the window, looking through the gloom in the direction of his office to have my daily mimic. 'Do you have any idea what that might mean, Nick?'

Chewing on the sandwich, I shoved what was left in the air at him. 'Shove it up your arse.'

'That's ass, Nick – you're an American now.'

I rooted round in the empty boxes on the worktop but with no luck. I was out of teabags but not out of pills. I had nine big bottles of the stuff Ezra prescribed me. I told him I was taking them but, fuck it, I didn't want that shit inside me. I had enough problems with the Branston.

I was going to have to haul my fat arse out of the flat and down to the Brit shop in Georgetown that all the embassy boys went to. All Brits hate the fancy teabags on a string they try to fob you off with in the States. They taste terrible and there's hardly anything in them anyway. What I wanted was monkey tea, the sort you can stand your teaspoon up in, the sort that comes out of a plumber's Thermos looking like hot chocolate. But, then, could I really be bothered? Probably not. Depending on what George had to say, I could be leaving today. Where would I plug in my kettle then?

I thought about taking a shower, but fuck it. I just ran the kitchen tap and threw some water on my hair to tame the Johnny Rotten look, and pulled my trainers on.

On the way to the Metro I grabbed a Danish and got it down me before I reached Crystal City station. Eating, drinking, smoking – you name it, you can't do it on the Washington Metro.

A few minutes later, as the pristine aluminium train rumbled under the capital, I found myself thinking about the guy on the news. Whatever problem he'd had, it was over now. He'd got it sorted.

I didn't care what happened to me, but Ezra was right: if I really thought that way, I'd have already done it. I would never take that route. I could still remember the feeling I got when other ex-Regiment guys killed themselves, and it wasn't envy, pity or anything else. It was just anger, big-time, for leaving someone else to pick up the pieces. Sometimes I'd had to sort out their kit before it went back to the next of kin. It was important there weren't any letters from girl-friends or anything else from their secret lives to embarrass the family. I remembered burning letters to one particular guy, thinking they were from a girlfriend. When I took the rest of his kit round to his wife she burst into tears. How could Al not have kept any of the love letters she signed off as Fizz, his pet name for her?

Then I thought about all the insurance policies that were invalid because some selfish fucker had taken an overdose. If you've decided to do it, and you're sane enough to stockpile painkillers or whatever, why not go out and do a couple of freefalls and just forget to dump the canopy on the third jump?

Worst of all was the effect on the kids they left behind. How could anyone be so selfish that they ignored the price their families had to pay? The guy on the TV, I wondered – had he got a wife, kids, parents, brothers, sisters? What if, like me, they'd watched the whole thing on TV?

If I took the easy way out, at least it'd make fuck-all difference to anyone else's life.

But I wasn't going to. I had other plans.

13

The sun was out at last, but I could still see my breath as I walked along Beach Street. It was ten to eleven and I was a couple of blocks south of the Library of Congress. That meant I'd have to slow down if I was going to be late. It was important for George to see everything was normal.

The other foot traffic eyed me as if I was driving at five miles an hour on the freeway. They rushed along in trainers with their office shoes in their bags, heads down and cellphones stuck to their ears so the world knew they were doing really important stuff. Everyone, men and women, seemed to be dressed in the same make of dark grey raincoat.

I sipped at the hole in the Starbucks lid. I didn't want to drink it all before I got to Hot Black Inc. because that, too, wouldn't be normal.

I reached the brick building in the centre of DC a couple of minutes before eleven. Dwarfed by modern, nondescript concrete blocks on either side of it, the Victorian original had been converted into office space long ago. Six or seven worn stone steps took me up to a pair of large glass doors and into the lobby. Calvin was waiting behind the desk. A huge black guy in a freshly laundered white shirt and immaculately pressed blue uniform, he'd either come with the building or was part of the Hot Black alias business cover, I never knew which. I went through the palaver of signing in, not having to show ID any more because me and Calvin had a sort of relationship going. I'd been in for quite a few meetings with George lately. But he still looked me up and down as usual, taking in my jeans, trainers and leather bomber jacket. 'Dress-down Wednesday, is it, Mr Stone?'

'Correct as ever, Calvin. The day after dress-down Tuesday, the day before dress-down Thursday.'

He laughed politely, as he had all the other times.

I rode the dark wood-panelled lift to the first floor, George's part of the US intelligence jungle. I had no idea who really called the shots here: all I knew was that since I'd been working for George the apartment was taken care of, and I picked up eighty-two thousand dollars a year. As an employee of Hot Black Inc., advertising tractors or whatever it was I was supposed to be doing, I also received a social-security number and even filed tax returns. I was a real citizen, in theory as American as George. After so many years of being treated like shit by the Firm, it had felt good. I was still treated like shit, of course, but at least it was done with a great big American smile and a lot more money.

I checked Baby-G. Not late enough yet, so when the lift pinged open I waited a bit longer in the corridor, like one of the white alabaster statues set in little alcoves along the shiny black marble walls. The cleaners had been busy: the air was heavy with that morning office smell of spray polish and air-freshener.

At exactly five past I entered the smoked-glass doors into the empty reception area. Nothing had been touched since I'd first come here over a year ago: the large antique table that doubled as the front desk was still unmanned, the telephone still unconnected; the two long, red-velvet sofas still faced each other across a low glass coffee-table devoid of magazines and papers.

The main office doors were tall, black, shiny and very solid. I was still a couple of paces away when they were pulled open.

George stood on the threshold, looking me up and down. 'You're late. Haven't you any other clothes? You're supposed to be an executive.'

Before I could answer, he turned back into his oak-panelled office. I closed the door behind me and followed him. He hadn't even taken his rain-coat off. It wasn't going to be a long comfy chat, then.

'Sorry I'm late. It's harder getting round the city, these days, with all the security.'

'Leave earlier.' He knew it was a lie. He sat down behind his desk and I took one of the two wooden chairs facing him. The fluorescent lights had at last been fitted with dimmers. George no longer had to worry that they were going to give him cancer.

As ever, he was dressed under his raincoat in a button-down shirt and corduroy jacket. Today he even had a pin through his chunky cotton tie. I wondered if he was Donald Rumsfeld's secret twin brother. All he lacked was the rimless glasses.

He nodded at the Starbucks in my hand. 'You still drinking that crap?'

It almost felt reassuring. 'Yep, two dollars seventy-eight.'

He watched with disgust as I knocked back the dregs. They were cold, but I'd wanted to save some just to annoy him.

He wasn't in the mood for beating about the bush. He never was.

I cleared my throat. 'George, I've thought about what you've been saying this last week or so. But I don't care about the war any more. I don't care what you think you've done for me – I earned it. I'm not coming back to work.'

He sat back in his chair, elbows resting on the arms and his fingers steepled in front of his mouth. Whatever he was thinking about, his face didn't give it away. The right index finger jumped away from the rest and pointed at me. 'You think you're ready for that world out there, son?'

'Yeah, I do. I also think that the therapy is bullshit. All of this is bullshit. I've had enough.'

The finger rejoined the others. 'You're the one with all the bright ideas.'

I shrugged. 'I was wrong: I'm ready. I've got over it. I'm going to buy a bike that works for once, and maybe get to see some of my new country.'

He pursed his lips behind the fingertips. 'You were hurting after Kelly was killed, son, and quite understandably so. A loss like that – a child. Must be a lonely time for you right now. It's going to be a while before you're back on your feet.'

'George, you hearing me? I've been telling you for fucking weeks now but it doesn't seem to register. That's it. No more. I'm finished.'

He leaned forward, fingers still together, elbows on the desk. 'No need for profanity, son. What if I said you can't leave? You know too much. That makes you a liability. What would you expect me to do about that? Motorcycles can be dangerous things, Nick.'

I stood up, leaving the cup on the carpet. 'You can't threaten me any more. What have I got to lose? Kelly's dead, remember? My whole world fits in two carry-ons. What you going to do? Rip up my favourite sweatshirt?'

'How about you coming back to work? I think you're ready, don't you?'

I turned to leave. 'I'll get out the apartment today, if you want. It's in shit state, anyway.'

'Keep the apartment. Use it to do some thinking in.' George was as calm as ever. 'This isn't how the story ends, son, believe me. You're just lonely right now. You'll get over it.'

14

I sat staring vacantly at the Metro map above the head of the woman opposite, who was doing the same at the map above me. There was the smell of old margarine which had nothing to do with the train. I looked around, and suddenly realized it must be coming from me.

George was right. I was a liability now, and he would never make an idle threat. Fuck it, so what? If he wanted me dead it would happen, I had no control over that. All I could do was get on with what I wanted to do – and that was to get as far away as possible from being treated like a lump of shit. As bad as it was only having Kelly in my head now, it had sort of set me free. They couldn't use her to threaten me any more. It was going to be a different sort of life now. I'd watched the re-runs of *Easy Rider*.

Dupont Circle was a few stops further on. Did Ezra know I hadn't told him the truth about going to Bang Bang Bosnia? There were a whole load of things I'd either told various levels of lies about or withheld from him completely. Like my decision to bin the job, or that today's session had been the last I was ever going to attend.

It made me wonder if shrinks just let you spout your bullshit, but have a good laugh behind your back at your self-delusion. Or maybe they did it over coffee and a sticky bun at shrink reunions in Vienna.

And then I thought: Why not go? It wasn't as if I had anything else to do, and I'd got a few hours to kill before the *Lost Dinosaurs of Egypt*.

The carriage was about a quarter full, mainly families with tourist maps and digital cameras hanging round their necks. The kids looked excited, the mums and dads content. Shit, this was all I needed. George was right. I was lonely. But what he and Ezra didn't appreciate was that I always had been, until Kelly had come along. Work – first in the infantry, then the SAS, then this shit – had seemed to fill the hole, but it never really did. It just helped me cut away from that feeling of exclusion I'd hated so much as a kid.

Now? I was back to feeling like a kid again. I had the same feeling every time I lay on the settee in the early hours of the morning, watching people on TV having relationships, families doing family stuff. Even the Simpsons shared something that I didn't have.

I felt the same now as I had as a ten-year-old, bunking on the Underground all day to keep out of the rain, putting off going home and getting a beating from my stepdad just because the arsehole enjoyed doing it. It didn't even get better if my mum saw him punching the shit out of me. She would simply deny it had ever happened and buy me a Mars bar.

What had hurt most was not having other kids to play with. I was the free-school-dinners, odd-socks-and-Oxfam-clothes kid. I used to spend days on my own just walking around, checking the coin returns in phone-boxes, waiting for when I was old enough to leave home without the Social coming looking for me.

Now I was back to square one. No work, no Kelly, and I'd closed the door on the only person I'd had to talk to, an ancient shrink with a helmet for hair. Anyone who'd ever come remotely close to being a friend had fucked me over or was dead. I looked down at Baby-G and played the break-dancer. At least now I had put a smile in my day.

I came out at Dupont Circle and wandered around trying to find the exhibition. This was supposed to be the gay area for DC, but all I saw were groups of Somalians and students from the university. In the end, I stumbled across it. Art Works had once been an upscale shop. Posters across the glass frontage advertised the show; I could see bright lights through the gaps between them, and a very hip-looking clientele studying wall-loads of photographs.

I pushed the door and went inside. One or two heads glanced in my direction. Very soon the main topic for the chattering classes of Dupont Circle was going to be the strong smell of margarine.

I counted maybe fifteen people, all looking as if the only clothes shops they knew were Donna Karan or Ralph Lauren. Everyone had what looked like an expensive catalogue in their hands. I thought I'd give that one a miss: I only had enough on me for teabags and a few jars of Branston.

No one was chatting. The loudest sound came from the air-conditioning unit that blew hot air down at me as I walked through the door. At a counter to the right, a woman dressed entirely in black was standing by a display of merchandise. Duplicates of some of the pictures were for sale. If you couldn't afford the originals, you could take home a not-so-cheap souvenir. It made no sense to me. Who would buy it? There was nothing comforting about these photos. Bang Bang Bosnia was a collection of shots too honest to have made it into the Sunday supplements.

Immediately in front of me I saw black-and-whites of men dangling from trees after being hanged, drawn and quartered. Dogs pulling meat from the bones of a human corpse. A group of Serb infantry looking like they'd come straight from the siege of Stalingrad, swathed in white sheets for camouflage as they fought from building to building in the snow. The faces were gaunt, covered with grime, blood and bum-fluff. The eyes had the same haunted, hollow stare of front-line soldiers from the Somme to Da Nang.

I wondered about the kind of people who came to look at this sort of stuff. Suffering sold as art. It felt voyeuristic, almost perverted. What the fuck had Ezra been on? This wasn't going to help me. Why would I want to see this shit? I felt myself getting angrier the deeper I walked into the gallery. But I couldn't stop myself looking.

Art Works' walls and ceiling were brilliant white. Small halogen lights played on each photograph, caption and price tag. I walked down the first pier of frames giving each picture a cursory glance. Villages getting burnt to the ground. Armoured vehicles driving over bodies. Some of the killing done by Serbs, some by Muslims or Croats. It didn't matter in Bosnia: everyone just slaughtered everyone else.

Maybe I was wrong. Maybe if more people did come and look at this stuff close up, they'd stop thinking of war as a PlayStation game.

The second pier was simply entitled 'Children'. I wondered if this was what Ezra had wanted me to look at. I studied the first black-and-white, ten-by-eight plate under its perspex frame. A young woman, probably in her early twenties, held a baby in her arms. She was lying in the snow and mud at the base of a tree beside a road. It was obvious she'd been shot. There were bloodstained strike marks all over her, and splashes against the bark. Her eyes were wide open. She'd probably been sitting against the tree at the time she got hit.

This particular execution had been carried out by Muslims. In the background was a group of women, some with small bundles of belongings, being helped on to a truck by a man. Somebody had painted a white arrow on the bark just above the blood splash, and daubed the words 'Chetnik Mama'. It was hard enough wondering why they'd shot her, let alone stopped to paint a message. What was even worse was that the Muslims hadn't killed the baby: hypothermia had. I kept my eyes on the girl, staring into her eyes for clues. Had she stayed conscious just long enough for her to know her kid was going to die as soon as the frost arrived that night?

I rubbed a hand into my scalp and smelt it, wondering if the mother had been able to smell her child's hair while taking her last breaths.

I moved down the aisle, drawn to a particular plate four or five shots along. A drab image, with a flash of red in it.

I stood in front of it and couldn't decide if I should laugh or burst into tears. It was Zina, smiling at the camera, her arms out as she showed off her new jacket while walking along a mud track with a group of older women. Everything else was grey – the sky, the buildings behind her, even the old women and their clothes. But not her: she was a splash of colour and her eyes were bright as they looked into the lens, perhaps smiling at her own reflection.

The caption simply said: 'The Poppy'. The photographer was Finnish.

Her full name was Zina Osmanovich, and the picture had been taken on her fifteenth birthday. Two days later she was grabbed by Serbs, it said, along with the rest of her village, and killed while trying to escape.

Fifteen. I glanced down at Baby-G.

I tried not to, but couldn't stop myself looking back and staring into her eyes. The last time I'd seen them they were dull and glazed like those of a dead fish, her mutilated body covered in mud. Tears started to well.

It had been nine years. What the fuck was wrong with me? I wanted to move, and yet I didn't. In the end I just stood and gazed at her. I thought about her life and Kelly's. How would things have turned out for them both? Would they have got married? Had kids of their own?

I should have done something. They would both have been alive still if it wasn't for me . . .

What? What could I have done?

I felt a hand on my arm.

'I'm not surprised you can't tear yourself away from it,' a voice behind me said. 'She's beautiful, isn't she?' There was a sigh. 'What I'd give to have taken a shot like that . . . Wouldn't you, Nick Collins?'

15

I spun round to find myself face to face with a grinning, clean-shaven Arab, who had the whitest teeth this side of the Oscar ceremony.

'Jeral!' I shook my head with surprise and what I hoped looked like delight. Pointless pretending I wasn't who he thought I was: we'd spent too long together in Bosnia.

We shook hands. His face was still creased in a huge smile. 'It's been a few years, hasn't it?'

Jerry still had a touch of Omar Sharif about him, even though he'd put on a few pounds. There were specks of paint in his hair and over his watch, as if he'd been having an argument with a roller. 'You haven't changed a bit, mate.' I glanced at the holes in his faded black jeans, and the black shirt that had obviously been ironed with a cold mess-tin. 'And neither has your kit . . .'

He rubbed the thinning patch on his head ruefully before giving me the once-over. He looked as if he wanted to say I hadn't changed either, but couldn't quite bring himself to tell that big a lie. In the end he just rubbed his head again and his expression became more serious. 'By the way, I'm Jerry now. Arabic names haven't gone down too well around here since 9/11. And things in Lackawanna don't help . . .'

He came from a steel town in upstate New York that had become part of the rust belt. His parents had been among the hundreds who'd emigrated from the Yemen to work in the factories, but were probably now existing on welfare. Lackawanna had been in the news quite a lot in recent weeks. Six Yemeni-Americans who'd been arrested for attending an al-Qaeda training camp in 2001 came from there – the first Made-in-the-USA Islamic extremists. If I had, I'd have changed my name too.

I'd liked Jerry immediately. There was something that set him apart from the two distinct camps of journalists I'd come across in Sarajevo – the manic, gung-ho kids who'd turned up from all over the world in the hope of making their name, and the establishment figures who rarely risked leaving the basement of the hotel.

The night I met him in Sarajevo, I was having a quiet beer at the bar of the Holiday Inn while waiting for another job. It was the only hotel still operating during the siege. I stayed there because it was where the media hung out, and I wanted to keep up my cover story.

Jerry was arguing with a group of newsmen. He'd just made it back from Serb-occupied territory while some of the people around him hadn't made it further than the front door. They just went down into the basement each morning, climbed into a UN APC, and hitched a ride to HQ. There they'd pick up a press release, take it back to the hotel, pad it out with a few quotes – usually from other journalists – and file it as from the front line. Jerry was one of the few guys I'd seen who chased the real stories.

He'd broken away from the argument and come and sat next to me at the bar.

'They got their heads up their asses, man.' He took another swig of cat's piss lager. 'This isn't one war – it's hundreds.'

I looked shocked. 'You mean there's more to this than Serbs versus Muslims?'

For an American, he was quick on the uptake. His face lit up. 'Just a little bit. I've heard there's a Muslim-Croat thing going on, and Croat versus Serb. And as for Mostar . . .' He let it hang. He was testing me.

It was my turn to smile. 'Versus the rest of the south. Tuzla?'

'Versus the rest of the north, man. Like I said, hundreds.' He extended his hand. 'Hi, I'm Jeral. You with the networks?'

We shook. 'Nick Collins. Anyone with a chequebook.'

Over the next couple of bad beers I'd discovered that, although he looked like Omar Sharif's kid brother, he was born and bred in the States and couldn't have been more apple pie if he'd tried. And he was the only fluent Arab speaker I'd ever come across who'd never been anywhere near the Middle East. Come to that, he'd not even been out of New York state until he was nineteen. He spoke Arabic at home with his Yemeni parents and some Saturday classes at the mosque, but English at school and in the real world.

Art Works was like a library. Jerry leaned closer to keep the noise down. 'Why you here? What's your story?'

'I was just passing and I saw the sign . . .'

There was a pause. Neither of us seemed to know what to say next. It had been nine years; as far as he knew I'd just been in Bosnia to take pictures, and that was how I wanted to keep it.

I was keen to get away from here and hoped he felt the same, but he just stood there, smiling at me. 'What are you doing nowadays? Still clicking away?'

I shook my head. 'That's all changed, mate. I've been doing some advertising stuff until recently. Boring, but it paid the bills. Now I'm just taking a break. What about you? Any of these yours?'

'Actually, they're good, but not that good, apart from that one.' He pointed over my shoulder at Zina. 'And one other.'

Two of the Donna Karan gang stood behind us, wanting us to move on so they could tick Zina off in their catalogue. They looked us up and down, and one of them sniffed rather pointedly into her handkerchief.

Jerry had more contempt for them than he could hide. 'Nick, come and have a look.'

'I've got to go, mate, stuff to do.'

I needed to get away from him. He belonged to Nick Collins, not Nick Stone. But he wasn't taking no for an answer. 'Come on, two seconds. This is the other one I wish was mine. It's going to be really famous one day.'

We walked back to 'Chetnik Mama'. He scanned the image, his face alive with admiration.

A woman wandered past, fanning her face with her catalogue.

'It's one hell of a photograph. But that's not what's going to make this famous. It's him.' He tapped on the perspex where the man was helping the women in the background. 'You know who this is? Go on, have a closer look.'

I moved in. It was Beardilocks, I was sure of it. Leaning forward, I studied his face, my eyes just inches from his. His pale skin was smooth, stretched over high cheekbones below deepset eyes. He needed to put on a bit of weight to fill out that shirt collar. What struck me most was that, even in the midst of all the death and destruction, his nails were perfectly manicured and his long dark beard neatly clipped.

'No.' I pulled back from the frame. 'Not a clue.'

'Exactly. But one day you will. His face will be on as many T-shirts as Che Guevara's. They wanted some of my stuff here, but fuck 'em, man. I've had two exhibitions of my own. I'll let them have what I want, what I think is important. Not just some stuff to fill this wall or that.'

One of the staff, a woman with blonde hair

over a black polo-neck, came over to us. 'Could you please be quiet? Images like these deserve respect, you know.'

Jerry shook his head slowly in disbelief. 'C'mon, Nick, you want fresh air?'

We walked outside into the sun. Jerry put on a pair of mirrored wraparounds. 'By the way, Nick, you look shit. But it's still good to see you, man. A beer for old times' sake?'

We turned left, looking for somewhere. I'd have one beer and go.

'You're married, then.' I nodded at the gold band on his finger.

The smile hit maximum wattage. 'We just had a daughter. She's three months old. Chloë. She's the most beautiful thing I've ever seen.'

I grinned back at him. 'I guess she must take after her mother . . .'

'Funny. You?'

I shook my head. I didn't want to talk about Kelly. That was private stuff. Even Ezra only got the abridged version. The full story was the only thing I had that belonged just to me.

We went into a designer bar with low lights and leather settees. There were soon two Amstel Lights on the table between us, and the conversation continued. I found myself enjoying it. He wasn't the sort of person I would normally get to know: he was a lot better than that.

He'd been just twenty-three when we met at the Holiday Inn. His plan had been simple enough. Fly to London, buy a Hi-8 video camera to join the 35mm his mother had bought him as a graduation present, then hitchhike to Bosnia and take pictures that told the truth. He was going to sell them, once he found out how. By the sound of it, he'd done both.

'You cover the Gulf?'

'You kidding? With skin this colour? The last thing I need is to get on the wrong end of some friendly fire . . .'

His big challenge now was how to balance work and family. I told him I wasn't exactly the world's leading expert on that, but knew it wasn't going to get any simpler.

Jerry nodded. The three of them had moved from Buffalo less than a month ago, and Renee was nesting big-time. 'Maybe another child next year, who knows?' He went a bit dewy-eyed again. 'Good things, Nick. Good things.'

He ordered another beer, and I heard myself doing so too. We got back to talking about the exhibition. 'You know what?' His voice wavered. 'I've spent all my working life managing to block out the horrors I see through the lens so I can project my message through the image, but since Chloë everything's changed. You know what I'm saying?' He swallowed hard. 'Like, the tragedy of that mother trying to protect her child, knowing that she herself had only seconds left to live. Hoping desperately that someone would look after it . . . Looking at my stuff, it takes on a new meaning now. What a waste . . .' He took a long swig. 'It's all bullshit, isn't it?'

I rubbed my hand into my hair again and wiped my face with it. I felt a sudden pain in the centre of my chest and hoped I wasn't making it too obvious. I guessed I felt the way he looked; he brushed away a tear that fell slowly down one cheek. 'You're right, mate, it's all bullshit.'

He stood up with me. 'Come home with me, come see Renee and Chloë. We're not far.'

'I'm sorry, I—'

He just wouldn't give up. 'Come on, my car's just round the corner. I'd like to show you some of my work. It got a whole lot better since the last time we met.'

I hesitated as we reached the door.

'Come on, man. Come home. I've told Renee a hundred times about that day . . . She'd never forgive me if I didn't bring you back.'

Short of me pulling a knife on him, there was no way he was going to let me just walk away. 'I make great coffee too.' We set off through the door. 'None of that Arabic crap.'

16

We headed out of DC towards Chevy Chase, along the main drag. Massachusetts Avenue took us past all the embassy buildings and eventually to row upon row of nondescript apartment buildings. By then he had finished telling me that Renee came from Buffalo, not far from Lackawanna, she was a freelance picture editor, and up until recently she'd stayed in her small apartment because he was always away. But soon after they married, Chloë came along and it was time to move. Why they were here in DC, he didn't get to say.

His last job had been covering the anti-government violence in Venezuela. 'I got some great shots of protesters going toe to toe with National Guard. You see them in *Newsweek*?'

We turned left alongside one of the apartment buildings, then down a ramp and into the underground lot. He closed down the engine, and turned to face me.

'Don't you want to stay at home now, Jerry? I

mean, if I had a child right now I think it would stop me bouncing along to wherever the shit's hitting the fan.'

Rather than answering, he fiddled with a set of keys as we walked to the elevator. 'Security,' he said. 'You need to unlock a lock just to get to the lock in this place.' He had a little trouble with what key went into the elevator, but at last we were on our way up.

'Just one floor.' Jerry was beaming like a Jehovah's Witness who'd just added a brand new member to his congregation. 'Hope she's in. We normally take Chloë to the park about now.' He turned towards me. 'Nick . . .' His voice dropped. 'I never really got round to thanking you once we got back to Sarajevo. I've replayed it in my head so many times. I just want to say—'

I put my hand up to stop him. 'Whoa, it's OK. It was a long time ago. Don't worry about it.' I didn't want to go into all that stuff right now. Better to let it stay in its box.

He was a little disappointed, but nodded all the same. 'Thanks anyway. I just wanted to tell you, that's all.'

The elevator stopped and Jerry played with his keys as we headed towards the apartment.

The white-walled corridor was lined with good grey carpet. The place was spotless. Most of the inhabitants probably worked in the embassies we'd driven past.

The moment he pushed the key into the door of 107, I was hit by the smell of fresh paint. He pointed along the passage. 'No stroller. Coffee?

We'll go in the lounge. Too many fumes every-where else. Sorry about the mess. You know how it is with moving.'

I didn't really. I hadn't been lying to George: my whole life fitted into two carry-ons.

The doors to two bedrooms were open on the right. Each had just a mattress on the floor, and piles of boxes and clothes.

The lounge was stark white. No curtains yet, but a TV, VCR and music centre with red illuminated LEDs. It didn't look as if they were planning to keep the old carpet: it was covered with fresh paint stains. Everything else was baby stuff, changing mats, nappy bags and the smell of talcum powder. In the corner stood a blue carrycot on a stand, a plastic mobile with stars and teddy bears above it.

I could see a parade of pictures of all three of them along the mantelpiece. There were even a couple of Polaroids of Chloë on her own, looking very blue and wrinkly. The normal thing proud parents did, I supposed. The pictures were probably the first thing they'd unpacked.

He opened a box containing reams of contact sheets and photographs, all carefully protected in plastic sleeves.

'You've been busy.'

'And then some. See what you think.'

He went into the kitchen, leaving me to it.

Jerry really had come a long way since the days he carried his mum's birthday present round his neck. He'd covered everything from the wars in Ethiopia and the refugee camps in

Gaza to the Pope weeping in what looked like a South American slum.

Jerry clattered away in the kitchen as I held contact sheet after contact sheet up to the light.

When the serving hatch opened and a tray of percolated coffee and mugs appeared, I held up a laminated front page of the *New York Times*. 'This Sudan picture one of yours?'

A tiny starving girl, no more than a bag of bones really, hunched naked in the dirt. Behind her, watching her every move, stood a vulture. It wasn't just the picture that was fucked up. Beside it was an ad for a multi-thousand-dollar Cartier watch.

Jerry leaned through the hatch. 'I wish. It's one of Kevin Carter's. He's dead now. He won a Pulitzer for it.'

As I stood to collect the tray, a key turned in the lock.

'They're back.' For the first time, he sounded just a little bit anxious.

I let him get on with family stuff and went over to the sofa, dumping the brew on a packing case. I could see into the corridor.

Renee wore jeans and a long, thick, hairy nylon coat, a sort of bluey-green colour. She shushed him as he went to kiss her. Chloë was asleep. As Jerry started to unstrap the baby from the stroller, she shrugged off the coat and came towards me. Her smile broadened but she kept her voice low. 'Well, hello!' She had a happy, homely face on a small skinny body. Her brown hair was gathered at the neck, and she wasn't wearing makeup. 'I'm

Renee.' She held out her hand. It was soft and stained with paint.

I hoped the fumes cancelled out the stench of margarine I carried around with me, and put on a big smile of my own. 'I know, he's told me all about you.' It was a corny thing to say, but I didn't know what else you did in these situations. 'I'm Nick.'

'I know all about you, too. The guy who saved Jerry's life in Bosnia.'

She led me proudly over to the carrycot as Jerry gently placed the baby in it and disappeared back into the kitchen. 'And this is Chloë.' I looked down but couldn't see much. She had a woolly hat on and was up to her ears in duvet.

The pain in my chest had disappeared as we drove here. Now it was replaced by a different feeling. Maybe it was jealousy. They had everything I thought I wanted.

It seemed time to whisper a few of the right noises. 'Aww – she's beautiful, isn't she?'

Renee leaned into the carrycot, her eyes fixed on the sleeping face. 'Isn't she just?'

We settled down with the coffee and she apologized for the mess. 'We keep meaning to get a table.'

I thought I'd better make an effort before I took the first opportunity to get through that front door and out of there. I gestured towards the packing case and smiled. 'Last place I moved into, I had one of those. I got to rather like it.'

Jerry joined us with another mug.

'So what do you think of DC?' I said. 'A bit different from Buffalo . . .'

'It's fine.' She didn't sound too convinced. 'Maybe in another month or two we'll get sorted out, and Jerry will get the job he's after at the *Post*.'

She passed me a black coffee. Her lip had started to quiver. I sensed there was tension in the air. 'But he's going off on one more crazy trip before that . . .'

Jerry was doing his best not to look her in the eye.

Whatever was going on here, I wanted nothing to do with it. This was my opportunity. 'I'm sorry.' I tried a sip and put the mug down. The coffee was too hot. 'I really should be going. I was a bit tight for time anyway when I bumped into Jerry.'

He had other ideas. 'Come on, Nick, stay a little longer. Chloë will be awake soon and maybe we could all go for something to eat.'

'No, really, I—'

Renee looked up at me. 'We've made you feel uncomfortable.'

'No, no. Not at all.' I hoped I sounded more convincing to them than I did to myself. 'But I do have to go. I was only popping into the gallery for five minutes. I'll get the Metro, it's fine.' I didn't have a clue where the Metro was, but it didn't really matter.

Jerry tapped me on the arm. 'Least I can do is walk you to the station.'

There was no avoiding it: I didn't want to

stand there all day arguing. I said my goodbyes to Renee and we left the flat.

Jerry was all apologetic in the lift. 'I'm so sorry about that. Things have been pretty vexed with the move . . .'

I nodded, not wanting to get involved. Their domestic stuff didn't interest me.

'Renee is right,' he carried on. 'I've got responsibilities now. I will go and work for the *Post*.' He paused, looking slightly sheepish. 'It's just that I haven't quite got around to applying for the job yet. There's one last thing I've got to do before I shoot beauty pageants for the rest of my life.'

I smiled at the thought of him bobbing around at a beauty pageant trying to project a message through the image.

The lift stopped in the lobby. We walked out on to the street and turned left. Jerry seemed to know where he was going. He was looking a bit more relaxed. 'Listen, Nick. I know you don't want to hear this, but I really want to thank you for what you did for me in 'ninety-four. I was young, I didn't have a clue what was going on, it was a total fuck-up. If those Serb fucks—'

I chose my words more carefully this time, to make sure he drew a line under it. 'I'm just glad that you're alive and happy, you've got a great family and things have worked out all right.'

'I know it, but still – I've got this one last thing to do.' He had that Jehovah's Witness look again. 'In Iraq.'

'Iraq?'

'It's just one final picture. The shot of my life. Remember the guy—'

I found myself going into a rant. 'How are they going to feel if you wind up with a bullet in the head? Or get it cut off, live online for Renee to watch? You've got to be there for them. Believe me, you never know what you've got until you lose it.'

I took a deep breath and tried to calm myself down. 'For fuck's sake, Jerry, grow a brain. You've got everything. Why risk losing it?'

Jerry looked away. 'You're right, man. But this isn't Bang Bang. This is Korda's picture of Che Guevara. Hou Bo's picture of Chairman Mao. The guy bending over "Chetnik Mama" – I want my picture of him on the cover of *Time*.'

17

I had to speak up to be heard above the roar of the traffic. 'What's he doing in Iraq?'

We started to cross at a junction. 'He's not there yet – gets into Baghdad this Thursday for about a week. He's going to give the Iraqis a wake-up call. He's saying that the Sunni and the Shia need to unite, start controlling their own destiny. Believe me, Nick, this guy's on his way to being Islam's answer to Mahatma Gandhi.'

'What's his name?'

'Hasan Nuhanovic. He's a cleric. Even the Serbs were worried about him. He survived the whole Bosnia thing, and he's still walking on water. But only just – a lot of the "give war a chance" brigade, on both sides, want him dead. He's very bad for business.'

I shrugged. 'Still don't know him.'

'Exactly!' Jerry beamed. 'That's the whole point. He shuns publicity. He's not a personality-cult kinda guy. But his message is good, and I really believe that the right kind of picture will get it on to the world stage. You know he went to Pakistan and started a Coke boycott? Thing is, doing stuff like that, he ain't gonna be breathing for much longer. I gotta be quick. I've been trying to track him down in Bosnia, but it would be easier to arrange tea with Karadic. In Baghdad he won't have so many gatekeepers.' He gripped my arm. 'One last job, Nick, that's all I want to do. Renee's dead set against it, but it's not a frontline shot. The picture of Chairman Mao was taken on a beach. Nuhanovic on the banks of the Tigris. No problem, no danger. A walk in the park.'

I wanted to tell him that I knew he was talking bollocks to sell the idea. But I was interested in Nuhanovic. There are some things you don't forget, no matter how often you try to cut away, and watching him front up to Mladic at the cement works was one of them. 'So what did this guy get up to in Bosnia?'

'Some of the stories are just, like, amazing. I heard that he managed to stop a massacre some place north of Sarajevo. He actually confronted Mladic. No one seems to know what he said, but it seemed to get Mladic spooked. He let a whole bunch of prisoners go free.'

'What's happened with Mladic?' I tried not to sound too interested in the Muslim. 'They ever capture him? I've lost track of what's going on over there.'

'Nope, he's still out there. Last I heard he was maybe holed up in a monastery in Montenegro. It's only a rumour, but I heard that the Brits were just this far away –' he showed me the minutest of gaps between his thumb and his forefinger '– from killing him during the war. That would have been kinda neat, eh? But get this – the International Court was about to be set up in The Hague, and they needed some high-profile players to put in the dock. That way everyone could feel that justice was being done after the war. Everybody would be happy – apart from the Bosnian Muslims, of course.'

I thought about Zina. I'd never forget the look on her face as she posed for me, just fifteen and daring to dream for a microsecond of being Kate Moss. Then I thought about her and thousands like her getting killed so justice could be seen to be done. Well, it wasn't my kind of justice, but this wasn't the time or the place . . . Fuck it, so what? That was over ten years ago. It's all history now.

We stopped by the news-stand outside the Metro. 'Good luck, mate. I hope you get to take your photograph, and when there's world peace I'll be blaming you for it.' I put my hand out to shake his.

He hesitated. 'You know what? Why don't you come with me?' He did his best to make me think the idea had only just occurred to him.

'No, mate. I don't do that sort of—'

'Ah, come on. We'll be there for a week at the most.'

I put my hand out again and this time he took it. 'I've got to go, mate. I hope it all works out for you.'

'I could do with a white guy out there, Nick.' He looked me straight in the eye, and held my hand in both of his. 'Think about it. Promise me that much. I'm going to London Saturday, got a deal going with the *Sunday Telegraph*. Then head for Baghdad Tuesday.'

He finally let go of my hand and pulled out his business card and a pen. 'Don't get me wrong, Nick, I'm offering you a job. How does ten per cent plus expenses sound to you?'

I didn't want his money. I didn't need anyone's money. It wasn't as if I had any more school fees to pay.

He gave me the pen and a second card and I wrote down my mobile number.

'Listen,' I passed the pen and card back, 'here's my number, but only so we can have another beer when you get back.' I turned to go into the subway, fishing in my pocket for some coins to buy a token.

He called after me, 'Think about it?'

I gave him a wave as I went through the barrier.

18

The Metro rolled smoothly beneath Washington with me and twenty-odd other people in the carriage. It sounded like Beardilocks had come a long way since the concrete factory. He'd moved on, but had I? Zina and the other poor fuckers who'd been dropped by Mladic's crew hadn't, that was for sure.

I'd never admitted this to Ezra, but I still felt guilty when I thought about that day. What if I'd called in the fast jets earlier? Maybe Sarajevo had only made the decision not to attack a minute or two before I eventually pressed the button. Maybe if I hadn't delayed the Paveway would have been dropped. Some of the Muslims would have got killed, but more would have survived. Zina might have been one of them.

Fuck it, as I kept telling Ezra, it was all history. And talking of history, Beardilocks might be spreading the good news for now, but he'd soon be dead as well. Look what happened to Gandhi.

I hoped Jerry got the shot: it might be the last one anyone took of him.

I got off at Georgetown and took the escalator to the heart of Fortress America. There seemed to be barriers and policemen whichever way you turned. The Brit shop near the mall was normally five minutes' walk, but today it took at least ten. I stocked up on Yorkshire tea, a couple of party-size jars of Branston, bread and the last four bricks of Cracker Barrel Cheddar, then headed straight back to the station.

I got out at Crystal City. The sinking feeling was back in the pit of my stomach. I knew what the rest of the day held, and the next. Long hours in front of the TV, cuddling a jar of Branston and a mug of monkey, working out when I was actually going to buy the bike and when to get on the thing and fuck off. George was going to let me use the apartment, but only until he had the wrong yoghurt for breakfast and decided to chuck me out. I needed to go soon.

My cell rang. Only three people knew the number, and I wasn't expecting a call from any of them. I put down the carrier and flapped about in my jacket pocket to drag it out and check the screen: number withheld.

It might be George, changing his mind and telling me to get out of the building. Maybe Ezra wanted to change our next appointment. That would be an interesting call. No, he'd have been told by now that I'd binned George and, in turn, him. So maybe he was checking that I hadn't swallowed the pharmacy and wasn't about to jump off the Arlington Memorial Bridge. I just hoped it wasn't Jerry.

'Nick?' It was a woman's voice.

'Yes?'

'It's Renee. Jerry's wife?'

This was much worse. 'Hi – how have you been since an hour ago?'

She laughed slightly awkwardly, then went serious on me. 'Jerry doesn't know I'm calling. He's painting the kitchen. Can we meet? I need to talk.'

'What about?'

'I'll tell you when I see you. I'm going to Costco now, at Crystal City. You know where it is?'

I could virtually spit at it from my apartment. 'No, but I'll take the Metro.'

She gave me directions from the station but I wasn't listening. The only thing I was thinking about was that I'd said yes without realizing it. 'It'll take me about forty minutes to get down there. So meet in an hour? I'll wait outside for you. It's really important to me.'

'OK.'

'Thank you, Nick. Thank you . . .'

I put the cell back in my pocket, and headed for the flat. What the fuck was that all about? I supposed I'd find out soon enough.

I got to Costco early and sat on a bench outside the entrance by the vending machines. The Pentagon was walking distance away, so the whole place was crawling with people in freshly starched and pressed camouflage BDUs, grocery basket in hand instead of an M16. It felt like the world's biggest Naafi.

I hadn't seen her arrive, but about twenty-five minutes later Renee was walking towards me. Chloë was slumped in a front-loading harness, surrounded by her mum's hairy nylon coat.

I stood up. 'Hello.'

'No problems getting here?'

'None at all.'

Chloë was sound asleep, her head to one side and dribbling. Weren't babies' heads supposed to be supported? Fuck, what was happening to me? I was turning into a German grandmother.

'Nick, I haven't got long. Do you mind if we shop and talk? I don't want Jerry getting worried up because I'm late back.'

She collected a trolley and we went inside. Chloë's head lolled from side to side but she didn't wake. Renee didn't know the layout of the aisles yet, but was soon throwing in nappies, baby lotion, bags of fruit. She didn't really have a shopping plan. It was just kit-in-the-trolley stuff. I knew it well.

'Jerry told me he asked you to go with him to Baghdad next week.'

'He sounds pretty excited about this guy. But I can't go.'

She threw in a six-pack of tuna. 'He's got it into his head that this could be the last chance he ever gets to take a great picture. It's like he sees the *Washington Post* as the end of the line.'

We moved along the aisle.

'Problem is, Nick, I want him to stay here and paint the apartment and do family stuff with me and Chloë, but at the same time I don't want him to feel I'm standing in his way.' She looked up and smiled about her predicament.

I was feeling uncomfortable. This should have been just between the two of them. It was their problem, not mine.

'I know he appears the cool guy, but he's incredibly vulnerable. This Nuhanovic thing has got him not seeing straight. I can't stop myself thinking about Chloë being an orphan. I wake up at night and—' The trolley was filling. She sniffed. She was on the verge of tears. 'I love him for it, but—' She stopped and stared straight ahead. 'I had this thought, you see . . .'

'What's that?'

'Go with him.'

I looked her in the eye, focusing beyond the tears. 'I don't know what he's told you, but I'm not really in that line of work any more.'

She smiled knowingly as one dropped on to Chloë's hat. 'Oh, c'mon, Jerry's told me a million times about the man who saved his life in Bosnia, and I'm pretty sure advertising isn't the business he's just got out of.'

'I don't do that other stuff any more.'

'I'll beg if you want me to . . .'

I lifted a hand.

She touched my arm. 'I'm sorry, Nick. Unfair of me, I know. But I'm going out of my mind here. When you turned up today I thought, well, maybe . . .'

She stroked Chloë's head as her eyes searched mine. 'I believe him: this will be the last job. But I want him back safely.'

19

I went through the underground shopping arcade at the Crystal City Metro and came out the other side. Dead ahead were the five tall grey concrete apartment blocks that I still called home. They were so drab they wouldn't have looked out of place in a Sarajevo suburb, which probably explained why the concierge of my block was Bosnian.

Jerry's offer had stirred up all kinds of stuff, and my head was like a washing-machine with a full load on. You usually regret more the things you don't do than those you do. Maybe this was one of those times. But then again, it could be a total gang fuck. I knew the best thing to do. Go shopping for the bike, pack and fuck off south. At least there'd be some sun.

I got into the lift. But it would be great to do some work again, wouldn't it? After all, I'd just be holding a photographer's hand as we drove to this ayatollah's hotel.

Back in the apartment, I put some bread in the

toaster, cut up a bit of Cracker Barrel, and made myself a big mug of tea. There'd be no harm in running a few basic checks on Jerry in case I met up with him again. I only knew what he'd told me, and words have always been cheap. I checked Baby-G – 15:14: nearly time for the afternoon talk shows but, just for a change, I was beginning to feel I had something better to do.

I got online as I shoved the first slice of toasted cheese into my mouth, and kicked off with a Google search on 'Jeral al-Hadi'. There were 418 results. Adding a photograph to the search brought it down to 202. The first few seemed to back up what he'd told me about his life since we last met. I'd go back to them if all else failed, but for now it was enough to know that Jerry's career curve had taken an impressively vertical trajectory since Bosnia days. His work had appeared in *Time* and *Newsweek*, and he'd just missed the Pulitzer short list in 2001 for his photo reports from Ground Zero.

I took a swig of my brew. It was a pity I couldn't be doing this officially, using Hot Black's facilities. I could have logged straight on to Intelink and got a shedload of background much more quickly. All the same, it's scary what anyone can come up with after just an hour or three on the net.

I did a new Google search, this time for 'people finder + USA'. What I wanted was a company that ran checks on social-security numbers, past addresses, even the names and telephone numbers of neighbours, in any of the fifty states. The first link I clicked looked perfect. On their home page, I entered Jerry's name and state, and immediately got a list of addresses, probably everywhere he'd lived over the last ten years. It even gave his age, thirty-three. I clicked the link against the most recent address, in Buffalo, and it gave a phone number. I wasn't surprised not to find the DC address at the top: they'd only just moved, and the database hadn't caught up.

So far so good, but there was a lot more I could find out. So why not? Various services were on offer, from basic background at $39.95, to due diligence with criminal search at $295. The more comprehensive the search, the longer it took. I checked the delivery times and signed up for the best I could get: the $59.95 advanced background search sounded good to me. It promised everything from aliases and bankruptcy proceedings, to boat ownership and criminal records. Everything, in fact, apart from his shoe size.

I keyed in my credit-card number and details, chose a user name and password, and was told to check my email box in two hours. I then forked out an extra $19.95 for the marital-records service, suggesting they started with Buffalo.

I then ran a name check for Renee al-Hadi but drew a blank. Some states had direct online marriage databases. They all got the al-Hadi question as I waited for the paid information to come through, including Nevada. But they hadn't run away to Las Vegas and got married by a Sikh Elvis impersonator at a drive-thru house of love. Shame, it sounded like fun. I'd just have to wait for the New York state records to come through, and take it from there.

I logged on to anybirthday.com and entered Chloë al-Hadi. There was only one, and it gave her date of birth as 9 May 2003.

If I could, I wanted to find something linking Jerry to the DC address. Telephone databases were most likely to be up to date; I went to any-who.com and keyed in the number on his card. Sure enough, the reverse number lookup gave me the new apartment.

Next Google search was for 'dating + background check'. I got another search company, this time one that helped run checks on prospective dates, maybe people you'd met through the internet. It looked like it was just as healthy to be paranoid in the dating game as it was in my ex-line of work. I wanted to cover all the angles, and if the results didn't correlate, I'd need to know the reason why.

I now had nothing to do but wait while they did their stuff and got back to me. I went into the kitchen and got more tea and toasted cheese under way. This was basic stuff I was doing, at the very bottom of the intelligence food chain, but it felt good to be doing something familiar at last. It beat going the best of three falls with my psyche in Ezra's office, or watching others do the same thing on *Gerald Rivera*, that was for sure.

It was only when I smelled the cheese burning

that I started to wonder what the fuck I was doing. It wasn't as if I was going with him, was it? Was I just checking him out because I simply didn't trust anyone any more?

20

With a mug of fresh monkey tea in front of me, I went back online. Google took me to a site called classmates.com. I registered as Donald Duck and tried the same for a Hotmail address. But it seemed a million and one others had had the idea first, so I made up some other shit and gained instant free access to the site. There seemed to be thirty-three schools in Lackawanna, from Baker Victory High to Wison Elementary. Guessing Jerry's date of birth as 1971, I went through them all systematically, searching from kindergartens in 1975 to high schools in 1990.

Within twenty minutes, I had a positive hit. Jeral al-Hadi had attended Victory Academy, and the school site gave a list of twenty-three classmates, complete with email addresses. They all wanted to get together and show their new baby photos and tell everyone how successful they were. If necessary, I could either email them or go back to anywho for their phone numbers.

Next, I dipped into the sex-offenders register

for New York and neighbouring states, an online service to comply with 'Megan's Law'. Jerry had a clean sheet. Did his story about moving quite recently to DC stack up? And when exactly had he moved? Why did this all matter anyway? I knew the answer, of course, but was trying to avoid it, hoping I'd find something that would make me not want to go with him.

I sat and thought a bit. I was sure I'd seen a VCR in the apartment. I went to infospace.com and hit the link called 'near an address'. I keyed in 'video store', then Jerry's address. Video Stock was the nearest video rental place, just 0.2 miles away. I went back to Google and entered 'Video Stock + DC'. There were twenty-four branches. I picked up the phone and dialled the one that looked furthest away.

A young guy answered. 'Video Stock, this is Phil, how may I help you?'

I gave him my best-mate voice. 'Yeah, hi, Phil – listen, somebody in your store was really helpful to me a few days ago. Fantastic service. Tallish guy, brown hair?'

'There's a lot of us here.'

'Well, you know, I want to write to the manager about it. Doesn't happen very much, these days, that kind of service. What's the manager's name?'

'Mike Mills.'

'That's great. Listen, I might write to your headquarters too. What's your store number?'

'One thirty-six.'

'That's great. And you're Phil, right?'

'Right.'

'OK, thanks, Phil, you've been a real help. You take care now.'

I put the phone down and dialled again, this time to the store near Jerry.

'Video Stock, this is Steffi, how can I help you?'

'Hi, Steffi, this is Mike Mills. I'm the manager at Renton, store one thirty-six. Listen, I could use your help. Our computers are down and we have one of your customers here who wants to rent but he doesn't have his card with him. Could you just verify his details for me?'

'Sure. Go right ahead.'

I gave her Jerry's name and address, and Steffi checked her computer. 'Yeah, I got him.' Then, without me even asking, she gave me his account number.

'No problems with him? No late returns?'

'No.'

'When did he open the account?'

'September.'

'This September just gone?'

'Yep.'

While I was on a roll, I thought I might as well push my luck. 'OK, I'll sign him up by hand here and enter it in the database when the computer's back up. He wants to charge this to the card he uses at your store – hey, yeah, one moment, folks – sorry, Steffi, I'm holding up a whole line of customers here. Read me the credit-card number and expiration date?'

And she did. The weakest link in any security chain is always a human being.

It might not be so easy coming by the next piece of information. I wanted to check that Jerry owned the Jeep, but I didn't know the registration: all I knew was that the Cherokee had looked about three years old. I couldn't just phone the Department of Motor Vehicles and ask. At least, not directly.

I went to docusearch.com and akiba.com, but a plate check would take one business day. I went to the DMV site for Washington DC, and checked their criteria for releasing information. They protected the privacy of individuals by closely adhering to the Driver's Privacy Protection Act. Therefore, they would release driver's records only to the following requesters: driver, with proof of identity; driver's representative (for example, a spouse), with written authorization from the driver and a copy of the driver's proof of identification, bearing a discernible signature; law-enforcement representatives, with documentation showing driver's involvement in an investigation; government entities, as part of an established activity requiring records (for example, security clearances, investigations, and recruitment); attorneys, with written authorization from their client to obtain records; individuals or entities requesting information through the Freedom of Information Act; or insurance company representatives, with written authorization from the driver as part of an established investigation. That last one would do. The only problem was, requesters had to produce the client's name, date of birth, and driver's licence or social-security number – and they had to produce it in person.

When people don't have a reason to be suspicious, it's easy to gain their trust. Next thing I did, therefore, was a Google search for Chrysler and made a note of the head-office telephone number and address, and the same details for dealers in Buffalo and DC. I then did another to get the number for the Motor Vehicles Department in DC. After a five-minute wait – during which I was told I was a valued customer, my call was important to them and I was moving up the queue – I finally got through to a human.

'Hi, I'm calling from Kane Doyle, Chrysler dealership in Buffalo, New York. We got a vehicle recall problem with some 2001 Jeep Cherokees, and I have an ownership issue I hope you can help me with. See, we have a customer just moved from Buffalo to DC and I'm trying to work out if the recall is our responsibility or DC's. I'll give you his address, if you could just verify ownership?'

'I need some sort of—'

'No problem, I'll give you the number here, Kane Doyle, Delaware Avenue, and you can call us back?'

'No, that's OK, I guess. What're the details?' Nothing like the threat of extra workload to get a civil servant to change his mind.

I gave him Jerry's name and address. He hit a few keys. 'Yeah, Jeep Cherokee.'

'Year of registration?'

'2001.'

'That's right. Tell me, is he still on Buffalo plates, or has he reregistered for DC? If he's switched plates I'll get the DC guys to deal with it.'

'Still on Buffalo plates.'

'Ah, well, guess it's my baby, then. Look, thanks for your help.'

It was that simple. Jerry's car checked out.

I sat back and took a long gulp of monkey. The next part of the session was going to be very interesting and quite a lot dirtier.

21

Seven twenty. It would be dark soon. For once it was going to be an advantage that I hadn't done any washing in ages.

I picked my keys and cell off the kitchen work-top. As I turned towards the window and caught sight of his office on the other side of the Potomac, I thought about Ezra.

I thumbed in his voicemail, my very own 911 number he'd given me in case I needed some emergency shrinkage. I couldn't be arsed to go into the living room for the landline, and that, I thought, was a good sign of normality returning. If I'd still been his patient, he would have been proud of me.

Still looking out over the river, I pictured him doing the business with yet another in the long line of George's fruits, going through the same fucking pantomime. 'We must have complete trust between us. Blah-blah-fucking-blah.'

The voicemail gave me about a hundred options before I could talk. 'It's Nick. You probably know this already – George will explain if you don't – but I won't be coming any more. You're right about the suicide thing. I won't be taking the pills and jumping off the bridge, so no need to worry. And thanks, I suppose.'

I wasn't too sure how that felt but, fuck it, no more Ezra.

Thirty minutes later I was on the Metro, heading back to Chevy Chase. In a carrier-bag I had a pair of washing-up gloves and a torch.

The road was just as busy when I got out as it had been when Jerry waved me off, but now it was dark. The street-lights glinted on the slowly moving traffic. Washington's worker-bees had their heads down determinedly as they made their way home. Most of them just wanted to close the front door, get the telly on and throw something into the microwave. It was etched in their faces.

Jerry's apartment block was easy to find. Just before I got to it I took a turning to the left that brought me round the back, into their communal garden. I sat on a bench as if I belonged there, a resident taking some air before the microwave went ping. I looked along the line of windows on the first floor. Two had no blinds or curtains, very bright white walls and a bare bulb hanging from the ceiling. I could even see Chloë's mobile turning just above the window-ledge.

The door into the hallway was open. There was no movement. I minced round the rear of the building and found the unlit admin area, where the entire apartment block's garbage was stored in big dumpsters, awaiting collection.

I put on the rubber gloves and switched on the torch. It had been years since I'd done any dumpster diving. I always got out of one of these things smelling like shit, sometimes real shit, but it was worth it for what you could learn about a target if you were prepared to delve among the banana peel, coffee grounds and the odd dead cat in a bin-liner. Most people don't give much thought to the letters, phone bills, credit-card statements, medical prescription bottles and even workplace memos they discard.

The first thing I looked for was some cardboard boxes. I pulled them out and set them aside. If anyone challenged me, I'd say that a friend was moving and I was just looking for boxes to help him pack. If they persisted, I'd come clean and say I'd thrown my wedding ring in the trash in the heat of the moment, but now I'd patched things up and wanted it back before my wife found out. With luck, they'd even help me look.

People like me weren't the only ones with their heads in trash cans. Police departments around the country routinely trawled through garbage, and every kind of criminal from Mafia dons to petty embezzlers had had their convictions based, at least in part, on evidence gathered from their rubbish. Intelligence agencies had been doing it for years. After the Iranian revolution in '79, the new government had bands of students gluing together all the documents shredded by the previous lot. It took them four years.

I did a quick sift first, checking all see-through bags for disposable nappies or other baby items. Then I moved to black plastic ones, opening them one by one. An hour later, I found a bag that had come from Jerry and Renee's apartment. There was a letter from a clinic, saying that the whole family were now registered, and their medical cards were enclosed.

I went back to the bench with wet milk stains and onion skin on my knees. Still no obvious movement in the apartment. It was nine thirty. I got my cell out, and Jerry's card.

At that moment, they both appeared at the window. Renee leaned forward and smiled, presumably checking the carrycot. When she turned to Jerry, the smile evaporated. They seemed to be in mid-argument. Maybe Renee had told Jerry about our meeting. I hit the cell keys.

Three rings and Renee picked up.

'Hi, it's Nick. Is Jerry there?'

She looked taken aback. 'I'll put him on.'

She handed him the phone.

'Hey . . .' It was his happy voice.

'Listen, I just want to say it was really great seeing you and the family today. I will think about the trip, OK?'

'That's great news. I'll meet you in London?'

'Hold up, I haven't said I'm going yet. I'll give you a call in the morning. I've got one or two things to sort out.'

'No problem. I'll be in all tomorrow. I'll wait by the phone. Good things, Nick, these are good things.'

'One question.'

'Sure, Nick, anything.'

'How are you so sure your man's in Baghdad? How do you know what he's up to?'

There was the smallest hesitation. 'It's like, I have a friend, a source, I guess. He's on one of the nationals. I can't give you his name . . . If anyone knew . . . You know how it is. But he is very definitely on our team, Nick. He'll try to help us once we get there.'

'Fair one. Later.' I closed the phone down but kept my eyes on the flat. He was smiling, and so, soon, was Renee. They kissed and hugged.

Jerry went over and picked up Chloë, held her in the air and flew her about. Then he brought her down towards his face and blew on her stomach, just like I used to do to Kelly when she was little.

I sat there for a while, just watching them do family stuff, and then I went back to what I laughingly called home to learn more about my new employer.

22

Hot water splashed over my body, and I lathered myself from head to foot for the first time in weeks. Judging by the colour of the stuff that was filling the shower cubicle, it was a wonder I'd been let on the Metro. Ezra deserved a medal for making it through a whole session without reaching for the smelling-salts.

With yet another mug of monkey at my elbow, I sat at the PC with a towel round me, hair drying, face freshly shaven.

The Deep Web is a vast store of searchable databases that are publicly accessible, but for technical reasons not indexed by major search engines. Google or Lycos can tell you what the page might be about, but cannot access the content.

When I was shown how to access the Deep Web, the instructor told me searching on the internet was a bit like dragging a net across the surface of an ocean. A great deal may be caught in it, but there are still whole trenchloads of information lurking deep on the ocean floor.

The intelligence community has used BrightPlanet's DQM (deep query manager) for years to identify, retrieve, classify and organize both deep and surface content. Its information store was five hundred times larger than that of the world wide web, according to the expert on late-night cable TV – 500 billion individual documents compared to the one billion of the surface web. There are more than two hundred thousand deep-web sites. Sixty of the largest contain more than forty times the information of the entire surface web.

Even search engines with the largest number of web pages indexed, such as Google or Northern Light, each index no more than sixteen per cent of the surface web. Most internet searchers are therefore only scanning one of the three thousand pages available. Or, to put it another way, once I'd logged on to bright-planet.com I had a long night ahead.

Three hours later, after exploring databases that, among other things, catalogued all of Jerry's published work, I checked my new Hotmail box. Both sets of results were in. I printed them and cross-checked each result against the other.

It seemed that Jeral Abdul al-Hadi had moved round quite a bit in the last ten years. I had eleven addresses in front of me, complete with telephone numbers, as well as the names and telephone numbers of his previous

111

neighbours. If the address was an apartment, I'd been given names and numbers for most of the block.

Marriage records showed that Jerry had married Renee in Buffalo in July 2002. The bride's maiden name was Metter.

I phoned a couple of the numbers at random. After apologizing for calling so late, I told them I was trying to get Jerry but his phone seemed to be out of order. It was an emergency, could they go get him? Very pissed off ex-neighbours told me Jerry had moved away. I did my idiot bit, which came very naturally, and moved on.

Jerry checked out. I wasn't too sure if it was good or bad news; I supposed I'd decide when I got to Baghdad.

What about Nuhanovic? Google threw up only a few links. I picked one which took me to a site that published translations of pieces from Pakistani newspapers, talking about the Coke boycott.

It seemed the journalist liked thirty-five-year-old Hasan Nuhanovic, proudly endorsing him as one of the Muslim world's most progressive and revolutionary thinkers. The Pakistani rumour mill had it that Nuhanovic was in the country, wanting to teach them a little US history. In 1766, the Americans had discovered a political weapon without which the revolution might not have been successful: the consumer boycott.

Even before America was a nation, I was told, it was already a society of consumers, two and a half million strong, scattered along eighteen hundred miles of eastern coastline. But the colonists had little in common besides a weakness for what Samuel Adams called the baubles of Britain.

In 1765, the Stamp Act had imposed a duty on papers used in everyday business and legal transactions. In retaliation, merchants in at least nine towns voted to refuse all British imports. Benjamin Franklin was summoned to London, where Parliament demanded that his people paid the taxes. Franklin reminded the House that his people were huge consumers of British goods, but this lucrative spending habit should not be taken for granted: the Americans could either produce anything of necessity themselves, or quite simply do without. A month later, the Stamp Act was repealed, and trade in British goods continued to thrive.

Just two years later, the British had forgotten their lesson. Parliament imposed the Townsend Revenue Act, taxing tea, glass, paper, anything essential. 'Franklin's threat became a reality,' the piece said. 'The boycott became a public movement. Just as important, it allowed women, small-town dwellers and the poor to become political activists. In Boston in 1770, hundreds of women signed petitions saying that they wouldn't use tea, and of course they eventually had a big party with a few boxes of the stuff out in the harbour.'

Cities issued detailed lists of all items that were taboo. Voluntary associations formed in citizens' support groups to make sure nobody was buying the boycotted goods, and attacking those who did. The Brits were being attacked where it hurt, in their pockets. America was becoming united against the mother country, and it very soon became the fashion not to buy British. It didn't matter if American goods were inferior; it didn't even matter if they didn't exist. It was a change of mindset.

And this, apparently, was exactly what Hasan Nuhanovic was trying to achieve: to encourage people to retake control of their own destinies from those who thought they had the right to dictate to other cultures.

That was it. Never any recent picture of him, never any interviews. No wonder he was camera-shy. As well as being a target for every religious fundamentalist and political extremist going, it seemed he hadn't exactly endeared himself to the powerful multinationals either. In a piece in *Newsweek*, one reporter who'd spent several months failing to get an interview had written: 'You could say it was like getting blood out of a stone – if only you could get past the legions of gatekeepers and through the impenetrable smokescreen of security. Compared with Hasan Nuhanovic, Osama bin Laden's a media tart.'

I clicked another link that sang the praises of new cola brands, owned by Muslims, and offering a real alternative for people concerned about the practices of some major Western multinationals who directly or indirectly supported Muslim oppression. Once again, street talk was that

Nuhanovic had slipped into Pakistan last year, to explain that Coca-Cola represented American capitalism and that by boycotting it consumers were sending a powerful signal: that the exploitation of Muslims could not continue unchecked. But the Pakistan government wasn't too impressed. Their population was about half that of the United States – a huge market. Two per cent of the country's revenue came from tax on Coca-Cola sales.

A spokeswoman for the London-based Islamic Human Rights Association said the war on terrorism had made all American brands a focus for resentment, and buying alternative brands made the Muslim community feel better. 'It makes us feel like we can do something,' she said. 'Coca-Cola has become a big symbol of America. It's a tangible symbol at a time when there is increasing unhappiness about US foreign policy.'

In response, Coca-Cola said that an unofficial boycott of US products in retaliation for Washington's support of Israel had really fucked with its bottom line in the region. Zam Zam Cola, the Iranian drink introduced after that country's Islamic revolution, had huge sales growth a few years ago when a prominent Muslim cleric ruled that Coke and Pepsi were 'unIslamic'.

Zam Zam was now exporting to Saudi Arabia and other Persian Gulf countries, shipping more than ten million bottles in the last four months of 2002.

Qibla Cola – named after the direction the

faithful face when praying – had plans to expand into the Middle East, Africa, southern Asia and the Far East. I couldn't help smiling at the prospect of adverts asking us to take the Zam Zam taste test.

23

Thursday, 9 October

The forty-seater Royal Jordanian turboprop had
hit turbulence several times during the hour-
and-a-half flight. I had my head against the
window, watching the blur of the prop. It was no
surprise that most of the world's major religions
were born in the desert. There was fuck-all else to
do.

Each time the aircraft bucked, it drew gasps
from passengers who were new to the game.
They probably thought we were being downed
by a SAM 7. The not-so-funny thing was that
they might soon be right.

I glanced over at Jerry in the aisle seat. He was
busy sorting out his camera bits and pieces, so I
turned back and stared out of the window again.
Below me, in the emptiness of the Western
Desert, I saw the strip of tarmac that connected
Jordan to Baghdad. It looked as remote as a
motorway across Mars.

Jerry had met me off the plane at Heathrow.
After a three-hour wait, we were on our way to

Jordan. The *Sunday Telegraph* wanted not just the picture but six thousand words on how Nuhanovic had been found, and what he had to say for himself.

We'd had to hang around in the Jordanian capital since Monday evening. There was only one flight into Baghdad each morning and every man and his dog wanted to be on it.

The only way of getting in earlier was chancing it on the hell-for-leather roads. There were three routes in: from Kuwait to the south, Jordan to the west, or Turkey to the north. At the moment, myth had it that Turkey was best, but it was still a nightmare. They'd been nicknamed the Ali Baba roads for a reason. Every gangster in the region knew that journalists carried big wads of US dollars. They held them up, then hosed them down. And if the hijackers didn't get you, the nervous young American soldiers would. They didn't like people overtaking their convoys.

Even if we had been robbed, it would still have been cheaper than flying. It was costing us over a thousand dollars each, but even pre-booking didn't guarantee a seat. We'd paid for our Tuesday flight, but still had to turn up every day and try to blag our way on board. There was a list of passengers for each departure, but that really didn't matter. You just had to line up and take your chances with the women on the desk. Each morning, I would point to our names on the manifest, and each time she would say something like, 'Yes, you are on the flight, but you can't go today.' Jerry did the translating, but it always just sounded like 'Fuck off' to me.

It had still been dark when we left our minging hotel every morning to start the day's bribery. We'd even tried to bluff our way on to the daily UN flight. It didn't seem very full. They'd pulled out of Baghdad after a bomb had killed their representative, Sergio Vieira de Mello, and a shedful of others.

Jerry had been going apeshit because he wanted time to sort himself out on the ground before Nuhanovic arrived, but now he was coming in on the same day. I leaned over to him, and nodded surreptitiously towards a bunch of heavily bearded characters at the back of the cabin. 'You sure he isn't on this flight?' That got a smile out of him. He'd been contacting his DC source every day, but there was still no int.

Most of our other fellow travellers seemed to be overweight businessmen, sweating buckets in their compulsory Middle East business suits – khaki fishing waistcoats, pockets stuffed with digital cameras so they could snap away and tell war stories afterwards. I'd heard a few German and French voices among them, but mostly they were American. Whatever the nationality, they all carried their laptops and other business stuff in macho, brand new daysacks.

A few rows in front of us was a guy called Rob Newman. At least, I thought it was him. I hadn't seen him since the early nineties, when we were both in B squadron of the SAS. I'd got out and worked for the Firm. It was only later that I'd heard he'd commanded the patrol that dug in the

LTD caches for me in Bosnia. Rob wasn't a new boy to the Middle East either, or Baghdad for that matter. We'd both been into the city during the first Gulf War, fucking about trying to cut communication lines. He'd spent what felt like a lifetime sitting on a sand dune, just like me. If it wasn't training some Arab special-forces group, it was trying to kill them. 'Maintaining the UK's interests overseas', it used to be called, but it had probably had a shiny and very cuddly PR makeover under New Labour. I shouldn't have been surprised to see him. After all, every man and his dog with a mortgage to pay off would have headed straight to Iraq.

I'd seen Rob at Amman airport every day, doing the same as us, getting fucked off the flight. But while Jerry was foaming at the mouth, Rob never lost it. He was deep and consistent: he always thought about things before gobbing off. His was always the voice of reason, and it was directly linked to a brain the size of the Rock of Gibraltar.

The other constant with him was his dress sense. His uniform was blue button-down shirt, straining a little round the gut these days, chinos, Caterpillar boots, and a fuck-off Seiko diver's watch the size of a Big Mac.

I didn't know if he'd seen me; we certainly hadn't had eye to eye. It was one of the unwritten rules. Even if you recognized each other, you wouldn't go up and say hello. One or both of you might be on a job; you might be putting him in the shit if his name wasn't Rob Newman today.

It would have been good to say hello, though.

24

The back of Rob's head was still covered by a mop of wavy brown hair that stuck out in all directions. I was happy to see a bit of grey at the sides, and that he'd put on a bit of lard – not that I could talk after a few months on the toasted cheese and Branston diet. He was taller than me, maybe six one or two, but I didn't mind because he also had the world's biggest nose. By the time he was sixty it was going to be bulbous and red, with pores the size of craters. He came from the Midlands somewhere and had a voice like a midnight radio DJ.

He was with a guy in his mid-thirties, with thick black hair and very pale skin whose slight build reminded me of the younger Nuhanovic. He hadn't been hanging around in the Middle East for long, that was for sure. In the aisle seat of the row behind them was the sky marshal, a tall Jordanian with severely lacquered hair and a big bulge under his cream cotton jacket. Next row back were two Iraqi women who hadn't stopped gobbing off at each other, and their two mates across the aisle, at a hundred miles an hour since checking in. Then there was us: both bored, knackered and gagging for something to drink.

Apart from the bouts of turbulence, it had been a pretty uneventful trip. No flight attendants running up and down with coffee and biscuits. Nothing below us but mile after mile of the Mars expedition training area. Our inflight entertainment came from the row behind. A Canadian woman was going to Baghdad to write a book on women's rights. Her mother was Iraqi, but she'd never been there herself. She was sitting next to an American who'd been working on her almost since take-off, and deserved an A for effort because at last he was getting some feedback. He looked like he'd stepped straight out of a Gap store window, in khaki cargoes, polo shirt and a diving watch even bigger than Rob's. If he didn't get a shag I was going to suggest he could always go forward a few rows and compare functions.

She was going to change the world, and he was sitting there agreeing with everything she said. He made sure he kept his voice down, which was a shame for the rest of the cabin: when it came to bullshit, this boy was first class. It was very strange, almost fate, them meeting. He was also interested in women's rights. He worked for the CPA [Coalition Provisional Authority] now as a civilian, but he'd been in special forces. Not that he was really allowed to talk about it.

Jerry leaned across to me. 'Yeah, right. He can't tell her because it's a secret!'

The Canadian woman seemed to be warming to Mr Gap. 'You know, being in Jordan was so, so – like karmic. I can't wait to get to Baghdad. I just know it's going to feel like my spiritual home.'

Jerry winked at me. 'I've had my mom ramming this shit down my neck since I was a kid, but it ain't no spiritual home for me.'

I smiled, but my mind was on other things. We were in Baghdad airspace, and the desert was giving way to the first signs of habitation. It was a grown-up city, its history stretching back thousands of years. It wasn't a factory-built, flat-pack affair like Riyadh: let's have a capital, all right, stick one in the sand here. Below us were buildings centuries old, interspersed with tower blocks and elevated freeways that could have been on the approach to Heathrow. Snaking through the middle of it was the Tigris, glinting in the sun. About six million people lived there. I hoped one of them, this week, would be Nuhanovic.

Jerry had finished stowing his camera and assorted shit back in his bumbag. First and foremost he was a fucking good action photographer. If he needed it, he'd need it quickly.

The pilot announced in Arabic and then English that we would shortly be landing at Baghdad International in the sort of tone you'd expect if you were about to run in to Málaga or Palma. But that was where the similarity ended. We didn't glide gently into the final approach.

We circled directly above it, just once, then went into an alarmingly fast spiral. Anyone on the ground who wanted to take a pop at us with a SAM 7 was going to find it hard to get a lock on today.

As we tumbled out of the sky, the pilot continued to give us all the pre-landing waffle as if nothing unusual was happening, but the businessmen had temporarily mislaid their machismo and the cameras had stopped clicking. Jerry leaned back into his seat. Behind him, Mr Gap was soothing the Canadian. 'It's OK, standard procedure. I come in and out of here every couple weeks.' She didn't sound fazed at all: if anything she seemed excited, but that wasn't going to stop him.

I noticed two burnt-out 747s alongside the terminal building, noses and wings scattered across the tarmac. It was really a huge military camp, with a maze of fence lines and enormous concrete barriers. Rows of armoured vehicles, helicopters, and green Portakabins stretched to the horizon. Desert-camouflaged BDUs and olive-green T-shirts hung on washing-lines between the buildings.

As soon as the pilot hit the brakes, we were joined by a two-Humvee escort, their mounted .50 cals trained, by the look of it, against possible attack from the aircraft. The businessmen enjoyed that. The cameras were out again.

'Fuck me . . .' Jerry couldn't stop laughing. 'They'll be out of memory by the time we get to Immigration.'

The Iraqi women were still going at it nineteen to the dozen, but my attention was on Mr Gap, willing him to get a result. He deserved to, if only through persistence. He was trying his hardest to meet up again once she was in Baghdad. 'Where are you staying? Maybe I could help you with your research – after all, I work for the CPA. I could introduce you to the top guys.'

That was obviously what she'd been waiting for. 'Yeah? You know what? That would be great. I'm staying at the Palestine.'

'Cool.' He was one happy hunter. 'We can arrange to meet some time.'

'That would be so nice.' I could just imagine the big smile on her face. She had him by the bollocks.

We taxied past the terminal and finally stopped by a hangar. A few American soldiers dismounted from the Hummers and started to walk towards the aircraft as the propellers slowed and the door opened.

We stayed in our seats for as long as possible before shuffling towards the exit behind the Iraqi women. The moment we got there we were hit by a wall of hot air.

25

I squinted hard as I rummaged for my cheapo market sunglasses. The stench of aviation fuel was overpowering and the noise was deafening. It felt like the entire US military was on the move. Helicopters took off and landed less than a hundred metres away. Heavy trucks hauled containers and water bowsers. American voices yelled orders at each other.

As the businessmen got out their cameras, a voice barked and a young T-shirted soldier sprinted up, M16 in hand and Beretta strapped to his leg. 'No pictures on base. Cameras away.' He was enjoying this, and he didn't care who knew it.

I stood with Jerry in the shade of a wing, watching the macho men slip their Olympuses obediently back into their waistcoats.

A military truck arrived. The American driver and a couple of Iraqis started to pull our bags from the luggage hold and throw them into the back.

Another soldier headed across the tarmac towards an enormous freight hangar, shouting, 'Follow me, folks,' and, like a bunch of sheep, we did.

Rob and whoever he was with were out in front, followed closely by the still jabbering Iraqi women. Jerry and I stayed in the shade as long as we could, then fell in behind. A couple more US squaddies brought up the rear.

Inside the grey steel building, a black guy in T-shirt and sunglasses appeared, the obligatory Beretta strapped to his leg. 'Listen up, people.' He waved a clipboard. 'When that transport arrives, I want you to grab all your bags and bring them to the table. They'll be checked before you move on to Immigration. Did you all get that?'

He got a few mumbles of assent, perhaps in recognition of the fact that he was the first soldier we'd seen who wasn't still looking forward to his sixteenth birthday.

The truck arrived and our bags were dumped on the concrete floor. People started retrieving them and filing over to the table. I hung back until Rob and his guy had collected theirs, then picked up my daysack. Jerry had scoffed at how small it was, but why carry a whole suitcase of stuff if you can buy everything when you get there? One change of clothes and a toothbrush, that's all you need. Everything else is excess baggage.

Rob turned and must have seen me, but we still didn't have eye to eye. In fact nobody was talking much, apart from the four Iraqi women. Everyone looked apprehensive as the soldiers dug about in their bags, made them spark up their laptops and tried to look like they knew what they were doing.

I reckoned they were poking around just for the fun of it. If you were going to bring anything illegal into this country, you'd go the Ali Baba route. There were hundreds of miles of un-patrolled desert that everyone, from drug traffickers to armed militants, was pouring across.

After the checks were complete we had to move round to the other side of the table and collect our bags before being led through the hangar. Logistics people sat at tables, tapping busily on their laptops. This being the US military, the bulk of the hangar was stuffed with racks and racks of shiny new equipment. The kit would be rushed to whoever needed it. In the British Army, there'd have been six quarter-masters guarding one ration pack, and even that couldn't be claimed without a requisition order signed by the chief of the General Staff.

We reached a corridor and things got smarter. US soldiers sat drinking cans of Coke on old, recently liberated, gilded settees. It looked like this area had been the front office for whatever the hangar had once been used for. Right now it was home to the all-new Iraqi immigration service. Several officials in friendly blue shirts sat at desks, each equipped with a PC and digital camera. Behind them sat a group of Americans, some in uniform, giving everyone the once-over as they went through.

Beyond the tables was a blur of people in uniforms and civvies. It was obviously the *ad hoc* arrivals and departures zone, but it looked more like the reception area at the UN building. A bunch of Koreans in American BDUs stood around with a group of Italians. Every nationality had their flag stitched on to a sleeve. The smartest-looking troops were the Germans, in crisply laundered black cargoes, T-shirts and matching body armour. Their flag was almost invisible, but with their brown boots, Mediterranean tans and blond hair, they won the best-dressed-for-war competition hands down.

I filed through, showing my Nick Stone passport. I bullshitted Jerry that Collins was my Irish mother's maiden name. I'd applied for an Irish passport, but I lost it in a move and hadn't needed it for years. Not that he believed me, of course, but what did it matter? There'd probably be worse things to worry about once we got into the city. An Iraqi took my picture, stamped my passport and waved me through.

Jerry wasn't so lucky. Either the Arab face on the American passport threw them a bit, or they were just trying to show off to their new bosses who'd given them such nice shirts.

I waited for him in the general area. It was hot and noisy, and most of the noise was Italian. They put the four women to shame, and their hand gestures were much better as well.

It wasn't just the soldiers who were armed.

The place was heaving with guys wearing body armour over their civvies and carrying AK47s, MP5s, M16s, pistols, you name it. It made me feel good. Even if I was just holding Jerry's hand, I was working, and I was back with my own kind.

This was where I felt comfortable; this was my world. Maybe I had done the right thing coming here.

26

Dazzling sunshine streamed through a dust-covered window. I peered through and wondered how we'd get into the city. There were no taxis because they couldn't get on to the base. We were in a fortified confine: all I could see were rows of unmarked 4x4s with darkened windows and a few guys standing around with body armour under the obligatory sand-coloured safari vest, sun-gigs hanging off their noses, shoulder-slung MP5s at the ready. To complete the effect they had boom mikes stuck to their mouths to help them look like they were on top of the job. They hardly needed to be: there were more soldiers on show here than there were in the entire British Army. I reckoned they were the official freelancers in town, probably protecting the American and Brit bureaucrats who ran the country, looking good so the CPA thought they were getting their money's worth.

In the midst of this chaos one thing was for sure: Rob wouldn't be queuing up for a bus. He'd have organized everything down to the last detail, and was probably already gliding towards Baghdad in an air-conditioned 4x4.

It looked like the Canadian had got herself sorted too. Gap Man was busy loading her bag into the boot of a white Suburban as she jumped into the back and the BG started the engine.

Jerry was still being questioned. I caught his eye and indicated that I was going outside. He nodded, then turned back to yabber some more to his new friend. Ever since we'd got into Jordan he'd been saying how strange it was speaking Arabic all the time. Apparently this was the first occasion he'd ever used it, apart from talking to his grandmother and his mum or going round to one of the corner shops in Lackawanna.

I put my sunglasses back on and walked outside. The midday sun drilled into me as I looked round for transport. I hadn't gone more than a dozen paces when a loud cockney voice bellowed behind me, 'Oi, shit-for-brains, how's it going?'

I recognized him at once, even with Aviators on. I hadn't seen him since leaving the squadron, but there was no mistaking Gary Mackie. No discreet stuff for Gaz: it had never been his style to obey the written rules, let alone unwritten ones.

He was still shorter than me, and was still hitting the weights. His arms and chest were huge.

I came out with the regular greeting you give

people when you bump into them like this. 'Fucking hell, I heard you were dead!'

He didn't answer. He just advanced on me with his arms wide open and banged himself into me for a big bear-hug. Then he stood back, still holding me by the shoulders. His eyes were level with my nose. 'Fucking hell, mate, you look a bag of shit!'

Fair one: I probably did. Gaz had to be in his early fifties now, but looked much younger. His black sweatshirt was soaking wet, front and back. It had started out with long sleeves but they'd been ripped off, leaving the threads hanging over the top of his big tanned Popeye arms. He'd been in the Light Infantry before the Regiment, and still had a faded tattoo of his old cap badge on his right biceps. Only now it looked more like an anchor.

'Thanks, Gaz, good to see you too. How long you been here?'

He was jumping up and down, speaking with his hands. 'Six months. It's fucking brilliant, know what I mean?' He pulled his jeans up by their thick leather belt. A 9mm sat in a pancake holder at his side. 'Who you working for, Nicky boy?'

'Newspaper guy, American. He's still in Immigration.'

He grabbed my arm. 'Come here – come and see my crew.' All smiles, he dragged me towards the four guys lounging in the shade nearby, all dressed in his regulation jeans and T-shirt combo. I'd never seen Gaz firing on less than six cylinders: everything was always great with him. He'd been married more times than Liz Taylor and still loved every one of them. They probably felt the same about him.

He punched me in the arm. 'It's good to see you, mate. I didn't know you was on the circuit. I haven't heard about you since fuck knows when.'

Once I'd left the Regiment and started to work for the Firm, I dropped out of almost everything I'd known. That was just how it had to be.

The 'circuit' was the job market for the ex-military. Security companies snap up personnel for helping out in a war, VIP protection, guarding pipelines, training foreign armies, that sort of thing. There's a whole bunch of firms, British and American, some more reliable than others. The work is mostly freelance, payment always by the day. You're responsible for your own tax and insurance, which means that most blokes don't take care of either. It's called the circuit because you bounce from one company to another. If you hear of a better job, you drop the one you're doing and move on.

Gaz introduced me to a South African, a Russian and two Americans. I didn't bother taking their names – I wouldn't be seeing them again. We shook hands anyway. 'Me and Nick used to be in the same troop,' Gary announced, with evident pleasure.

The guys nodded a hello, then fell back into their own conversation. It was no big deal: I wasn't expecting a group hug. It's not as if we're part of some brotherhood – it's a business like any other. That's just how it is. This lot looked different from the guys working for the CPA. They were in it for the money, not the boom mikes.

It wasn't just transport out of here I wanted to know about. 'What's the score on getting a weapon – you got any spare?'

'Got 'em coming out our fucking ears. Where you staying?'

'The Palestine.'

I spotted the four Iraqi women further along, struggling with their luggage, shouting and hollering at each other.

'Great place. Fucking odd-looking – wait till you see it. Good protection, though. Tell you what, you're better off just getting them from one of the fixers. They've got shedloads, but they're tearing the arse out of the prices. Be a lot quicker than waiting for me to bring a couple round, know what I mean?'

I turned back to Gaz. 'I'll do that. So what you doing here, mate?'

'Fucking brilliant. Money for old rope, mate. Training the police. They're using AKs, but we're showing them how to use the fucking things properly. I get my training in twice a day and then I head out on patrol with the boys.'

I wanted to keep up this pretence of being on the circuit. 'How much a day you on?'

'Three fifty, plus expenses. Better than last time we were fucking about here, eh?'

In those days it had been MoD pay of about

seventy pounds a day. Three hundred and fifty for freelancing sounded about right. Where middle-management guys in London talk about the rise in their house prices at dinner parties on a Saturday night, guys on the circuit talk about their daily rate. Nine times out of ten they're bullshitting. Anyone who says, 'Six or seven hundred,' is lying through their teeth. As far as Gaz was concerned, three hundred and fifty pounds a day was the dog's bollocks. He was just happy to be there, and had probably even paid his own fare.

'I'm staying as long as they want me, Nick. There's a bit of drama now and again, but fuck it. It's Baghdad, innit?'

It was wonderful to see him; it added to the good feeling I was already getting. I didn't know about the Canadian woman, but for me it was definitely like coming home.

I didn't want to be with Gaz when Jerry turned up, but I had one last question. 'Do you know how we get out of here? We're trying to get into town.'

He was apologetic. 'I'd give you a lift if I could, mate, but we're waiting for PC Plod. Some superintendent from the Met. The poor fucker's been seconded here for a couple of years. I can't wait to watch him trying to teach ethical policing, know what I mean? The boys we're training were lobbing RPGs [rocket-propelled grenades] at American tanks five minutes ago.'

The South African spotted their passenger and went to pick him up.

Gaz gave me another big hug. 'Listen, boy, really good to see you. There's a coach that takes you into town. Follow them women, they'll know.' He nodded at the Iraqi quartet, then spotted someone behind me. 'You with this dickhead?'

Jerry couldn't wait to answer in the affirmative. 'Yeah. Hiya, I'm Jerry.'

Gaz finally let go of me and shook Jerry's hand. 'What the fuck for?' He pointed over at a group of guys in waistcoats, hunched over their MP5s. 'You'd be better off with that bunch of tossers. At least they look as if they can do something.' Then I got yet another bear-hug. 'Only joking, boy.'

Gaz's mates had got PC Plod by their 4x4s and into body armour and were now getting their own on. Gary started to move towards his wagons. 'That's it, time to go. If I'm near the Palestine I'll come on in. Can't call, fucking phones ain't working yet. See you later, yeah? Fucking brilliant.' He looked over at Jerry, a huge smile under his aviator sunglasses. 'Listen, mate, when he fucks up and you need a professional, give us a call.'

'I'll do that. You come across any Bosnians in the city?'

'They're fucking everywhere! Bosnians, Serbs, Kosovans, you name it. Course they're here – it's a war, innit?'

He dragged his body armour out of his 4x4 and pulled it over his head, covering the big sweat marks on his T-shirt. He wouldn't be dropping in to see me. His head would be full of something else in five minutes and by tonight he'd probably have forgotten we'd even met.

Jerry smirked at me like the cat who'd got the cream. 'Old friend from the advertising business?'

'Yeah, sort of.'

'Mother's maiden name? Yeah, right. Nick Stone your real name?'

'Yeah.' And before he could follow up I pointed at the women who were still gobbing off nineteen to the dozen. 'There's a bus that takes us into town. All we've got to do is follow the Spice Girls.'

27

The twenty-seater minibus was run by Iran Airways, even though they didn't have any flights into or out of Baghdad. Maybe it was a way of keeping the staff ticking over, and at twenty-five US dollars for a one-way trip of fifty Ks it was a nice little earner. There might be only one commercial flight a day, the one we'd just come in on, but there were plenty of NGO [non-governmental organization] people on the move.

More of us piled in than there were places for us to sit. The four Iraqi women ended up sitting on their cases in the aisle as we rumbled past the sandbagged and gannet-wired security cordon that circled the airport. The vehicle wasn't air-conditioned, and even with the windows open it was swelteringly hot. It was going to take us the rest of the day to unstick ourselves from the PVC seat covers.

The approach roads into the city looked unscathed by the war, although the Americans were making up for it now. All the bushes and palm trees that lined the road were being cleared back thirty metres or so by local guys with axes and bulldozers so that there was no cover for IEDs [improvised explosive devices] or manned attacks.

The roads were packed with a mixture of new Mercedes, 4x4s, minging old cars and trucks with the wings hanging off. The people inside them were mostly dressed in suits and chinos rather than the traditional dishdash. Quite a few women wore skirts short enough to show a fair amount of leg, and not many were fully veiled; most just had their hair covered. I'd seen more burkas driving through East London; not as many kebab shops, though.

White goods were piled up outside electrical shops, alongside shiny mountain bikes and racks of clothes. New billboards advertised perfume and washing-powder, and there seemed to be plenty of food and computer games for sale on the stalls. I'd seen South American cities that looked far worse than this. Everything seemed pretty normal, if you ignored the seven or eight Blackhawks that thundered over the rooftops on their way back to the airport.

Minutes later, there was no longer any doubt that this had been a country at war. Huge concrete blocks topped with razor wire channelled the traffic as we got nearer the Tigris. A convoy of high-back Hummers appeared. The roof gunners, all in helmets and Oakleys, nervously checked the buildings either side as they screamed past.

Somebody once worked out that enough AK47 assault rifles had been produced to arm every sixtieth person in the world. As we worked our way through the streets it looked as if most of them were in Baghdad. Nearly every shop and building was guarded by an Iraqi in sandals with one hanging off his shoulder, the very same weapon he'd probably been cabbying at American Hummers a couple of months ago. Others also had them slung over their shoulders, their hands full of shopping or their kids.

Some buildings bore strike and scorch marks, with half-burned curtains still hanging where window-frames had once been. Some were no more than heaps of concrete clinging to re-inforced-steel skeletons. One whole shopping mall had been flattened, then there was a run of three or four buildings that had remained intact, then more piles of rubble. But for all that, the city wasn't a wasteland: people were out and about, doing their thing, just as they had in Sarajevo, just as they do anywhere in the world when the shit hits the fan. These guys were just getting on with their lives as best they could. Customers from the teahouses and restaurants overflowed on to the street. News-stands were doing a roaring trade. I'd read there were nearly a hundred different papers in print now Saddam had gone.

As we fought our way on to a roundabout I caught my first glimpse of the great man. There was a tiled mural of him in the centre that had been used for some serious target practice. The small parts of his smiling face that remained had been painted a bilious yellow.

Drivers stopped at the roadside and kids filled up their tanks with black-market petrol from an assortment of plastic containers. It was Baghdad's answer to the Formula One pit-stop. They smothered every car that came within reach, checking tyres and cleaning windscreens like they were going out of style.

The minibus only had one stop, which was as near to the Iran Airways offices as the concrete and razor-wire barriers would permit. As we clambered out I could see our hotel, the Palestine, less than a hundred metres away. The driver got on to the roof and started throwing down cases. The four Iraqi women stopped gobbing off at each other long enough to give him some serious grief, and he gave back as good as he got.

A couple of AK-carrying Iraqis sauntered over and stood around smoking as we got ourselves organized. Jerry was in the back, passing bags forward. He started laughing.

'What's up?'

'Looks like the Spice Girls don't wanna be dropped here. They want the other side of town.'

I picked up my daysack, and waited for Jerry to emerge with all his kit. We went through the barrier and started up the street parallel to the hotel, past the shuttered-up Iran Airways and Aeroflot offices.

A line of huge generators chugged away on the

pavement, leaking diesel and feeding power to a row of seedy hotels. The road was full of potholes and puddles, and hadn't been cleared of litter since the days when Saddam still had a smile on his face.

28

The Palestine and the Sheraton were now part of a fortified complex at the end of a road sealed off by five-metre-high concrete sections. We'd just turned through a man-sized gap in the wire when we were spotted by a posse of little kids. They came running towards us, nothing on their feet, their arses hanging out of their trousers. They followed us silently, but we both knew better than to hand out cash in daylight. Help one, and about six hundred others will leap on top of you. If you're going to do it, you only do it at night, and well out of sight of the others. They'd gang up on whoever got the cash and steal it.

We followed the wall for about twenty metres until we joined the end of a queue of news crews, Iraqis, drivers and businessmen with their BG. Half a dozen different languages were being bounced backwards and forwards along the line. There was a makeshift guard post, in what looked like a B&Q garden shed. The checkpoint was manned by a family of Iraqis. Dad vetted the men, Mum the women, and a boy of about twelve was looking through the bags. They all had AKs. Sitting outside the shed on folding chairs were three US soldiers, eyes hidden behind sunglasses, sweating under their helmets and body armour, well-worn M16s across their laps. It looked as if they could all use a lesson from Gaz on community policing.

Once Jerry had finished talking Arabic to the dad, we filed through the gap and turned left between two huge, newly installed concrete walls. Directly ahead was the rear door of an AFV [armoured fighting vehicle], its engine rattling. In front of it was a solid line of nylon containers the size of skips, each filled with sand. Its .50 cal was manned.

We turned left again just short of it, down the road that separated the two hotels. This one was blocked by an M60 tank, also bunkered in behind nylon skips, with a cam net over the top to keep the crew out of the sun. It faced on to a huge roundabout, beyond which I could see the blue domes of a mosque.

I recognized the area at once from news footage. In the middle of the roundabout was a large stone pedestal, all that remained of the giant statue of Saddam that had been toppled symbolically at the end of the war. The roof had given a grandstand view of the shock-and-awe bombing of the government buildings just the other side of the river. Every one of Saddam's men had moved out of them long before, but it looked great on TV.

I could see now why everyone had got such great pictures: they hadn't even needed to move off their hotel balconies.

The secure area between the hotels was teeming with news crews jumping in and out of 4x4s, sweating buckets after a day in helmets and body armour. The word 'Press' was stencilled just about everywhere there was space.

The Palestine wouldn't have looked out of place in a Moscow slum. It was sixteen storeys high, rectangular and very plain. A few single-storey sections, probably ballrooms and restaurants, jutted out from the base. Every room seemed to have a balcony, no matter whether you were looking out over the Tigris, the garden or the roundabout, each protected by an ugly concrete section that looked like the wings on one of Darth Vader's imperial fighters.

Satellite dishes the size of flying saucers were mounted on the roof, and smaller ones sprouted from almost every balcony. Cables were strung everywhere.

A German news reporter in body armour was doing his piece to camera, with the tank, the mosque and the roundabout as a backdrop. A convoy of Hummers screamed round the roundabout, looking very warlike, machine-guns and M16s sticking out all over the shop. Jerry was wearing his bad-smell face. 'Look at this bullshit. Give me Nuhanovic any day.'

We followed the driveway up to the hotel and went in through a set of big glass doors, past the security, a couple of Iraqis with AKs. Not that they checked us. Maybe it was too hot for them.

Thronging the lobby were the guys you'd find in any big hotel in any trouble spot: the fixers. Drink, drugs, guns, cigarettes, women, you name it, they'd get it for you. At a price, of course.

The inside of the hotel was just as 1970s as the outside. The dark marble floors had seen a few years' hard polishing. I'd heard that during the sanctions all these places stank of petrol. It was much cheaper than water, and used to clean the floors.

US soldiers in uniform wandered in to buy cans of Coke. Others had their PT kit on, blue shorts and trainers and a grey T-shirt with the word 'Army', just in case we hadn't guessed from the M16s slung over their shoulders.

Overweight men in suits and khaki waistcoats had monopolized every available sofa, while their BG stood a discreet distance away. It looked as if it was pretty much business as usual in Baghdad. Soldiers, businessmen, BG, journalists: everyone was in on the act.

A sign on the desk announced that rooms were '$60 US' a night, no ifs, no buts. A deposit covering half your stay was required up front and always in cash. In this neck of the woods, it said more about you than American Express ever could.

Jerry counted out a week's worth of dollars in cash. I wanted to be on the first floor – a jumpable height if we needed to get out in a hurry – but everything was full. The closest to the ground we were going to get was the sixth.

We took the lift. Our rooms were next to each other, and whoever had stayed in mine had left about ten minutes earlier and not told the house-keeper. The place reeked of cigarettes and sweat.

There were two single beds. The veneer was lifting off every chipboard surface, and the carpet was scarred with cigarette burns. The walls had been sprayed with concrete and were now a lumpy, faded yellow. The tiny bathroom had a toilet, basin and shower. I tried turning on the tap. Nothing happened. Maybe later.

I dumped my kit on the bed, which was covered with old, mustard-coloured, furry nylon blankets. No sheets, and a couple of saliva-stained foam pillows without cases. B-and-B owners in Margate and Blackpool would have been proud of this place, charging so much for so little.

I went and pulled open the glass sliding door to the balcony and was mugged by the noise of the city. The Tigris lay in front of me, glittering in the mid-afternoon sun. Apart from the mosques and a few surviving government build-ings, all I could see was miles of middle-class housing, little blocks of concrete fighting for space among the towers. Further out, on the edge of the city, was the Baghdad I knew.

It suddenly felt like yesterday that Gaz, Rob and I had been mincing about on the north-eastern edge of the city during the '91 war. It was a slum, a massive township of crumbling build-ings, a world of poverty and shit. The Shia who lived there were forced to call it Saddam City.

Finding the fibre-optic cables that ran beneath it on the way from Baghdad to the Scud teams in the Western desert had been a fucker, but it had had to be done. If they weren't destroyed, the Scuds could still be fired into Israel. The Israelis would have joined the war, and the coalition's alliance with the Arab states would have been over.

I looked out into the heat haze beyond the city. It had been about this time of day that I would give my orders for the coming night's fuckabout, and my four-man patrol would start preparing. We would stay in the sewer under a market square until last light, then slip out to do the night's work. It was more or less the same each time, checking the power lines leaving the city, checking any communications towers still standing after the last twenty-four hours' air attacks.

When my patrol finally located the cables, it was almost an anticlimax. All they needed was one good tap with a two-pound ball hammer and that was it.

Looking down, I could see that the garden area was surrounded by a low wall and some pretty serious rush fencing. A couple of guys were drinking coffee inside a *cabana* in what looked like a small oasis. The war seemed a million miles away. There was even somebody cutting the grass with a petrol mower.

Then two Blackhawks came screaming across the river, so low I could have headbutted the pilots, but nobody took the blindest bit of notice.

29

One of the single-storey rooms jutting out from the ground floor seemed to have been taken over by CNN. All its windows had been sandbagged, and their logo hung from a small shed where the security guy was sitting. Just outside, on the grass, were a black leatherette sofa and chairs that would only get sat on once they were in the shade. The place was heaving with important-looking cables and antennae. Beyond it, a guy in shorts, T-shirt and trainers was sprinting along the bottom of an empty thirty-metre swimming-pool. Each time he got to one end he did a shedload of sit-ups, ran to the other, did some burpees, then back again for more press-ups. It was making me sweat just watching him.

I needed to check out our escape route, since jumping six floors wasn't an option. A green sign in the corridor directed me in Arabic and English to the fire escape.

A push-bar door led to a bare concrete stair-well. There were no lights, just slits in the walls, so fuck knows what happened here at night. The stairwell was littered with cigarette butts and old newspaper photographs of Saddam smiling and pointing at something in the distance. I'd always assumed it was a fucking great suitcase full of money. I wedged one of the papers between the door and the frame so it wouldn't lock on me if I needed to come back up.

Moving down the fire escape, I checked the doors on each floor. They were all locked from the inside. Even worse, on the flooded ground floor, the double exit doors that led out into the open were chained, padlocked and blocked by a mountain of rubbish. The only way out from the sixth was the lift.

I went back up and knocked on Jerry's door. He was busy sorting out the recharging equipment for the camera and phone. The Thuraya, about the size of a household mobile, was resting on the balcony ledge. He'd pulled the thick plastic antenna out from the side in an attempt to get a satellite fix.

No cell networks were operating in Iraq now the Ba'ath Party's had been obliterated. There was a system of sorts, but for the exclusive use of CPA officials. With a Thuraya it didn't matter if you were in the middle of the Russian steppes or on top of Mount Everest: as long as it could shake hands with a satellite, you could talk to anyone, anywhere, with a mobile or a landline. Where anyone got the money to run them, I didn't have a clue. You could buy a week in Greece for a few minutes on one of these things.

I went out on to the balcony while Jerry un-tangled several lengths of wire, one of which connected the phone to the camera so he could transmit images down the line. Jerry's plan was to download them to the *Telegraph* as soon as he got them, then wipe the memory card clean so there was no chance of anyone else getting their hands on them.

The guy in shorts was still bouncing back-wards and forwards in the pool. I picked up the Thuraya to see if it had a signal, but the five-bar indicator was blank. I carried it along the balcony a few steps, but still got nothing.

I went back into the room. Jerry was stretched out on the bed, hands behind his head, admiring his prowess with the electrics.

'No signal – the sat must be the other side.' I threw the Thuraya on to the bed next to him. 'The only way out of here is by the lift or jumping. The fire escape is blocked.'

'Don't worry, man, this place is as safe as Fort Knox. First things first.' He had cheered up a lot since the wait in Amman. Maybe he felt we were just that bit closer to Nuhanovic. He sat up on the edge of the bed. 'You get the beers. I'm going to need some local clothes if I'm going to do the brown thing right.'

We had already agreed that he was going to do the brown-man stuff and I would do the white.

'I'll call DC, then hit the mosque over the road in time for Asur and see what I can pick up. That's if I can get past that tank without them putting a bullet in my Islamic ass.'

I nodded. It was pointless just sitting around waiting for the source to come up with the goods: we had to get out there. Somebody had to know something. Jerry didn't want to quiz the journalists because they'd sniff a story and either clam up or lie. But there was nothing to stop me getting among the guys working on the circuit.

I checked Baby-G, my own black one this time. I'd left Kelly's behind: I needed to keep a clear head. Who was I kidding? Looking at my own just made me think about hers – and then about her. It had been wider than her wrist, and took her for ever to fasten.

It was just after three p.m. – seven a.m. Washington time. We'd missed a couple of nights' sleep. No wonder I was feeling knackered.

30

We took the small, nine-person lift down to the lobby. Jerry, as ever, was clutching his camera; I had my bumbag with my passport in it, along with just over three thousand dollars in cash. The lift stank of cigarettes and stopped at every floor with a disconcerting bounce. We were joined on the fourth by two Filipino guys with MP5s, dressed in black body armour like a SWAT team; on the third, by two military guys trying to look like civilians, which is pretty much impossible when you're sporting a whitewall haircut; finally, on the second, by two NGO guys with fat Filofaxes and even fatter beer bellies.

Everyone, civilian or military, seemed to have some form of ID round their neck, a nylon tape with a hook and a plastic, see-through cardholder. Were we supposed to have one? What the fuck did I know?

As the doors closed, one Filipino offered the other a cigarette and they both lit up. By the time we reached the lobby I smelt like I'd spent the night in a pub.

There were now maybe a few more Iraqis than foreign businessmen sitting and smoking on the sofas, all with identical thick black moustaches, trousers, shirts, plastic dress shoes and white socks. Whatever else had changed here, the Saddam look was still in.

A pair of Hummers was parked up outside. A group of sweaty soldiers were dumping their body armour and taking off their soaking wet BDU jackets; hot food and bottles of mineral water were being passed round from the back of a canvas-skinned truck.

I could see two or three civilians pacing up and down just beyond the Hummers, chatting away on their sat phones. They must have been staying on our side of the hotel.

The two shops in the lobby were doing a roaring trade in toothpaste, Saddam watches and banknotes, which were still in circulation. Saddam looked the same on the dinars as he did in any picture: big smile, big moustache, and out-stretched arm pointing at something we never got to see. You could also buy Arabic coffee-pots, maps, clothes; one guy was putting up a little Bedouin tent to use as a carpet stall. Even DHL were setting up a stand as we walked past – so people could jet their purchases back home in time for Christmas.

As Jerry headed out into the blinding sunlight, I spotted a group of fixers.

I was greeted by three big smiling faces. 'Hello,

Mister, what can I get you?' It doesn't matter where you go in the world, everyone in this line of business speaks English.

I shook each by the hand and gave them a smily '*Salaam aleikum*. I need twelve beers.'

The youngest was the first to answer. He looked very smart in his brand new jeans and trainers. 'Ten minutes. You wait inside?'

The other two left us, still smiling away. They had more than enough custom. I grabbed my boy by the arm as he turned towards the door. 'There's a couple more things.'

His smile got even bigger. 'You want girl? I get you young girl, European. Very new.'

'No, just two pistols, with magazines and lots of ammunition.' I didn't even bother phrasing it as a question.

'Sure. For you I have Saddam's own pistols, good price. You want rifle, I get you Saddam's own—'

'No, mate, just two pistols. Saddam's or not, I don't care. Make sure they're semi-automatics.'

'Sure. For you, tomorrow morning. I bring here, OK. OK?'

I nodded and pointed towards the coffee area. 'I'll wait in there for the beers.'

He ran off before I'd had the chance to ask him about vehicles. Through the glass entrance I saw that Jerry had joined the other members of the Thuraya club and was waving his free arm about like a windmill. I hoped his source was coming up with the goods.

One of the soldiers who'd been eating outside

came into the lobby and homed in on one of the fixers. He spoke low and close up. There was a smile as the fixer showed him the size of the breasts he was about to get hold of. These two hotels were probably Shag Central for the grunts, for whom business would be conducted quickly in the toilets.

I left them to it; money changed hands as if it was a drugs deal.

Whoever had designed the café-bar area had opted for plastic banquettes and gone for the seventies, dark, sophisticated and moody look. They'd got the seventies, dark part of it spot on.

The carpet was threadbare and the air was heavy with cigarette smoke and country-and-western music. An old guy dressed in a red shirt and shiny plastic shoes, his hair immaculately combed back, was sitting flanked by a couple of speakers, an amplifier and a Casio Beatmaster. Apart from the Saddam moustache, he was a dead ringer for Johnny Cash's dad.

A few Iraqis sat half listening, drinking glasses of tea, as a couple of big white guys with flat-top crewcuts, one with a goatee, tried to do business with them. They exchanged a few words with each other in what sounded like Serbo-Croat, then switched back to something approaching English for the next stage of their mumbled negotiation. Their accents were so heavy, all they needed was a black-leather jacket each and they could still have been in the Balkans. I'd need to find out where exactly they came from before bouncing in and asking about a Bosnian. The war might have officially ended, but for a lot of these guys the Dayton Accord was only a piece of paper.

A small bowl of boiled eggs, a plate of cheese and some bread rolls looked rather tired on the bar top, carefully guarded by two guys in crumpled white shirts with elasticated bow-ties who were trying hard to look as if they were doing something useful.

One finally made it to my table. I wasn't going to drink Arab coffee so I ordered a Nescafé with milk, and a couple of the rolls.

He went away to put the kettle on.

A news crew came past, talking English but sounding French, with a couple of the local boys in tow. They sat down to hammer out what they were going to do tomorrow and how long they'd need the driver and interpreter. It wasn't long before everyone was nodding and one of the Frenchmen peeled some dollar bills from a wad and handed them over. The going rate seemed to be ninety dollars a day for an interpreter and sixty for a driver, paid in advance – and if the French wanted to go anywhere outside Baghdad it would be extra.

My coffee, rolls and a foil-wrapped pat of butter turned up as the two Balkan boys got up to leave. Their Iraqi companions had a little waffle among themselves, puffed happily away on their cigarettes, and went back to listening to Johnny Cash's dad.

31

I was half-way through my first mouthful when I realized I had competition. The oldest biker in town was making a beeline for the buffet. He was late fifties, early sixties, only about five foot five, but powerfully built, with big freckled arms and hands the size of baseball gloves. He ordered eggs, rolls and cheese with his Nescafé and, judging by the size of his gut, it wasn't for the first time: it strained under a black Harley Davidson T-shirt that shouted: 'Born To Ride, Born To Raise Hell'. The image was completed by a long grey beard, jeans, and a big black belt with a Harley buckle. His head was totally bald, and he'd been out here for ever, by the look of it. He was nearly as brown as Jerry.

He was certainly pretty pleased with himself. He waved at the French, who were now in a smoking competition with the Iraqis, as he settled himself on a stool a few down from me, and treated me to the sort of nod that said, 'Later, we'll talk.' I treated him to one that said I was in no hurry, but I had a feeling it wouldn't be long before we were best mates and he was offering me the use of his house, car and wife next time I was in the States.

I'd just filled my second roll with butter and shoved it in my mouth when the baseball glove appeared in front of me. 'Howdy, I'm Jacob. How's it hanging?'

I swallowed fast but my reply still emerged in a shower of crumbs. 'Fine, how about you?'

'Good, real good. Big day tomorrow. My son's in town.'

His T-shirt should have said 'World's Proudest Dad'. None of his worldly goods heading my way, then.

'Here in Baghdad?'

'Sure. He's in the 101st, up north. Ain't seen the boy for months. I'm kinda excited.'

His food turned up and he started to make himself an egg and cheese roll. I finished my Nescafé and ordered another. Why do Arabs only serve the stuff in thimbles? 'So, you've come to Baghdad to see him?'

His gut quivered with laughter as he sliced the eggs. 'Hell, no. I work in power – been getting the juice back on for five months now. I've got another son here, too – Apache pilot. Pretty cool, eh?' He beamed. 'Yep, he's west of here. I'm gonna go see him some time soon. He can't get into the city.'

A group of American squaddies came in, looking as if they should have had schoolbags over their shoulders, not automatic weapons. Shit, I used to look like that. They unloaded their belt-kit and body armour and dumped it beside the sofas.

Jacob smiled at them and they smiled back. He got back to his roll and coffee. 'Yep, been following my boys about since Grenada.' He chuckled so hard his beard threatened to slide off his chin. 'My boys destroy the power, their daddy gets the contract to fix it. Kinda neat, ain't it?'

I was seeing the United States military industrial complex at its lowest binary level. 'Sounds like the perfect family business.'

He roared with laughter. 'Where you from?'

'The UK. I'm looking after a journalist.'

'You one of them snake-eaters? Hey, I got two myself.'

'By the look of you, you're one of the few people around here who doesn't need them.'

He liked that. But it was true. 'You know the companies, they gotta look after their people. It's Crazyville out there. But I was in the service myself. Nineteen years in the 82nd. Damn proud of it.'

I thought this might be a good time to get on and do the white thing. 'Reminds me of Bosnia . . .'

He wiped some crumbs from his beard and shook his head. 'One gig I never got to. There wasn't that much work for us.' He nodded towards the French. 'Them cheese-eating surrender monkeys got most of it.'

I smiled as he shoved another lump of cheese into his mouth. 'Well, it looks like the Bosnians are about to level the score. I heard they're here in force. You bump into any along the way?'

He shook his head. 'Not in the reconstruction game.' He gave me the sort of wink that used up most of the muscles in his face. 'Some other kinda game, maybe? You got a special interest there?'

I didn't answer. The Casio sparked up a bit, and Johnny's dad began to knock out the theme tune to *Bonanza*. War or no war, a man had to feed his family. He plucked away, eyes closed as if he had the music tattooed under his lids.

'Say, how long you staying here?'

'Dunno,' I said. 'A week or so?'

'Cool, maybe we'll crash into each other. You can meet my boy.'

Two bullet-headed MP5 slingers headed in our direction. All they needed was the boom mikes and they could have gone into partnership with the CPA Action Men at the airport.

Jacob lifted a hand as they reached our table. 'Hey, boys, nearly ready.' He finished shoving egg slices into his last roll and squashed it into his left hand, then stood up and held out the other for me to shake. 'Good to meet you. Say, I didn't catch your name . . .'

'Nick,' I said. 'Good to meet you too. I hope you get to see your sons.'

He nodded away. 'Yep, I hope so too, Nick. Maybe catch up tomorrow.' His eyes twinkled. 'I'll look out one of those little Bosnian ladies for you . . .'

He joined the two BGs and slapped each of

them on the shoulder. 'Come on, boys – let's go make some juice.'

He disappeared to the final chords of *Bonanza* and I threw down the last of my Nescafé. Jacob might be right, this was Crazyville, but I'd definitely made the correct decision coming here.

32

Ten minutes for the beers, my arse. I went and joined the Saddam-lookalike competition on the settees; I just didn't bother trying to smoke myself to death at the same time.

Faces flowed constantly in and out of the hotel, and I recognized one. It was Rob, on his way out. He was on his own, with no ID laminate round his neck but an old semi-automatic on his hip. The Parkerization had worn away, exposing the dull steel beneath. In his hand was an unloaded AK, Para version. It had a shorter barrel than the normal assault rifle and a collapsible butt. Great for close-quarters work or in a car. That, too, had seen a few years' wear and tear.

He caught my eye and smiled. Things were different now: we were on our own. I hauled myself off the settee. 'Hello, mate, I thought you were dead!'

His big nose crinkled into a grin. 'What's going on, you on the circuit? I thought you'd dropped out years ago.'

'Sort of. I'm working for an American. A journalist. He's here for maybe a week to get a picture – a Bosnian guy, here in Baghdad, if you can believe that.'

He could. 'There's plenty of weirder stuff going on here – listen . . .'

Three German ex-Paras were singing their regimental song by the newly erected Bedouin tent as two Russians loading AK mags chatted to each other about the noise. Going by their crew-cuts, tattoos and scars, they'd spent longer in Chechnya than in Moscow.

'What about you? What firm you working for?'

'None of those wankers.' Rob had always wanted to go his own way. 'I work for an Uzbek – he's in the oil business.'

'Staying here?'

'No, the al-Hamra. Famous for its swimming-pool, chilled beers and dancing girls. Allegedly. It's not as well protected as this, but he's a private sort of guy, and it's not like he's not used to a bit of drama, if you know what I mean. That's why I've been looking after him for the last three years. He's a good man, as it happens.'

'Even better. How long you here for?'

'Four, five days? We're not too sure. But no more than a week. I came to pick these fucking things up.' He hefted the AK. 'Three fifty they wanted for this heap of shit.' His nose crinkled again as he had a thought. 'What you doing tonight? CNN are having a pool party here.'

'Without water?'

My fixer arrived with the beer. It had a

Bavarian-looking label, and was probably brewed just up the road. There'd never been a problem with alcohol in Muslim countries like this, even in restaurants. You just brought your own and asked if it was OK to drink it.

I gave the guy fifteen dollars instead of the five he'd asked for. The ten was to make sure he came back in the morning with the weapons. As he left I turned back to Rob. 'What time's kick-off?'

'Eightish? You're here anyway.'

We shook hands and I watched him loading a mag on to his AK as he headed for the door.

The best part of an hour must have passed back on the settee before I heard the sudden sound of a heavy machine-gun, then short bursts of 5.56, both from less than three, four hundred metres away.

Jerry came through the main doors as if his tail was on fire. 'You hear that? Fuck . . .'

I stood up. 'Any luck at the mosque?'

'Nope. Nothing at all. I'll try again at Maghrib.' His eyes scanned the activity in the lobby. 'I got no news from DC either. I'll keep on calling. I know if he finds out we'll find out.'

'So, come on, you can tell me now. We're here, so it doesn't matter. What paper does he work for?'

His eyes locked on to mine. This was going to be the last time he told me. 'Look, Nick, you know the score with sources. I can't, and won't, say zip. He'd lose his job, man, everything. We gotta respect that shit.'

He was right, of course. But it didn't stop me wanting to know.

He had an afterthought. 'You want to use the phone?'

I shook my head.

'What are you, Billy-no-mates?'

'Something like that.' I held up the beers. 'Here, for you. I ain't touching this shit.'

He took the bag off me as we headed for the lifts.

'You staying in all night to drink those?' I hit the lift call button. 'Or you want to come to a party and maybe find Nuhanovic?'

33

There was a knock at the door. It couldn't be Jerry. He had left ages ago for the mosque to catch Maghrib at around last light. I opened it to find two old boys, cigarettes in their mouths. One handed me a sliver of soap and a hand towel. The other gave me some thin sheets that had gone grey a few hundred wash cycles ago. Everything stank of cigarettes.

I tried the shower tap and got a trickle of cold water, so I jumped under it before it ran out. The 1970s radio set into the Formica bedhead was tuned to American Free Radio and pumped out country-and-western.

The sun was going down when I emerged. I switched off the radio and turned on the steam-driven TV, which was tuned to a snowflaky version of CNN, but at least I had decent sound. The only other channel was showing a football game.

Not wanting to be the object of tonight's target practice, I turned out the lights before I went on to the balcony and looked out over the thousands of satellite dishes that sprouted like weeds from the rooftops.

The rattle of automatic gunfire came from somewhere in the distance. A few more rounds of heavier automatic fire, probably 7.62 short from AKs, were met by a huge amount of fire from the Americans' lighter 5.56 ammunition. Then a stream of heavier-calibre stuff was unleashed, probably .50 cals, and this time I saw tracer bouncing up into the last few minutes of dusk from the other side of the Tigris.

It stopped as quickly as it had started, but the lull didn't last long. Two Apache gunships thundered overhead, their shapes deep black against the evening sky. Somebody was going to wish they'd had an early night.

They swooped over the river and, moments later, one of them opened up, strafing the river-bank. It felt strange to be spectating from the very place that most of the shock-and-awe footage had been shot, watching the same area taking hits all over again.

Below me, preparations for the pool party continued as if no one had a care in the world about what was happening the other side of the rush fence. Either they felt immune to attack or wanted to believe they were. Plastic tables straight from the same B&Q as the garden shed were being dragged into the grass and round the still empty pool, and a couple of big oil-drum barbecues were on the go.

Another brief contact rattled round the city

somewhere, followed closely by an explosion. Nobody stopped doing what they were doing. Nothing mattered beyond the garden wall and our American protection. The Palestine was a little oasis, a bubble of safety.

I looked around the sky. There was no tracer, and I couldn't see any smoke. It was time for a brew.

The lift bounced at every floor as it took me down to the lobby.

From a mug the boys had found behind the counter, I took a heat-testing sip of Nescafé. There were just a couple of Iraqis left in here, maybe because all the eggs and cheese had been eaten. The Casio and guitar stuff was still in place but the player wasn't to be seen. Shame: Johnny Cash's dad had grown on me.

I heard Jacob before I saw him, coming up the stairs saying goodbye to his BG. He saw someone to talk to and gave me a smile. 'Hey, Nick, they glued you to that seat?'

I stood up and we shook hands as he asked for three coffees at once – unless they had another mug?

'How's your half-day been, Jacob?'

'Oh, just had to go check up on a few things. Kinda got to keep on top of them. Say, where's your reporter fella? What's his name? He treating himself to an early night?'

I thought he was going to treat me to another of his winks. 'Jerry. No, he's gone to the mosque.'

The waiter brought the first two coffees over and started to pour in the milk. Jacob lifted a hand. 'No, fully leaded when the sun goes down.' He turned to me. 'Well, I've been talking to a few people for you. Ain't heard nothing about no Bosnians. They kinda should have – it's a mighty small town in some ways.'

Jacob had an asbestos mouth. He'd already picked up his second cup as the waiter brought the third. 'Anything else I can do for you, you just let me know, y'hear? Maybe I can make some connections for you.'

I was starting to get an uncomfortable feeling about Jacob. He was being a bit too helpful. 'To tell you the truth, I don't give a fuck about the Bosnians. We're just throwing out a net and seeing what gets dragged in.'

The third cup was about to be killed. 'Tell you what, I'll keep my eyes open. What room you in, just in case you decide to unglue yourself from here?'

I told him and we shook hands. 'Thanks, Jacob. Appreciate it. Have fun tomorrow with your son.'

'Sure will. We'll talk later.'

I left him to it and walked down into the lobby to wait for Jerry. He might have bumped into his ayatollah in the mosque, but I wasn't counting on it. Tonight I'd see who was about on the circuit. A Bosnian would certainly stick in their minds.

34

A huge amount of automatic gunfire kicked off close by. From where I was, near the main entrance, tracer seemed to bounce straight up into the sky. It wasn't necessarily a contact. After all, it was Thursday night. I went out into the garden to see if anyone had arrived early. There was no music yet but a couple of guys were preparing the barbecue. They weren't remotely interested in the firefights as they tipped charcoal from paper sacks into two sawn-off oil drums.

I wandered over to the pool. I couldn't see the bottom of it from where I was, but I could hear a chorus of grunts and the rhythmic slap of running feet. I went right up to the edge and looked in, just as another burst of tracer shot skywards. I saw a headful of sweaty, short, wiry ginger hair training in the semi-darkness. The last time I'd seen Danny Connor was in Northern Ireland in 1993 – in a gym, naturally.

He pounded up and down the pool, totally focused on the job in hand. I watched him for several minutes, wondering whether to interrupt. He ran to one end, did twenty press-ups, spun round, ran to the other and did some sit-ups. I started to grin like an idiot. Connor's motto had always been: 'I train, therefore I am'. Well, after he got married it was. Before that it was 'Training + lots of = women pulled'. He had to do a lot of training in those days to be in with a chance. His face was covered with acne scars; it looked like someone had been chewing it. His accent did him no favours either. He came from the bit of Glasgow where everyone sounds like Rab C. Nesbit on speed. Connor hadn't been born, he'd done star jumps out of the womb. I worked with him on and off in the late eighties and early nineties. In all that time the sum total of any conversation from him was, 'You done yours yet?'

'Oi, Connor! You're getting a bit of lard on!'

He stopped running, but dropped to do some sit-ups as he looked up. I stood there and smiled, but he didn't react. He sprinted to the other side and started to do some burpees.

I shouted, 'Connor, you knobber. It's Nick!'

'Yeah, I know, don't wear the name out. You done yours yet?'

I sat down on the edge of the pool, dangling my legs, as he thundered up and down.

We were together in an OP once, overlooking a farm. PIRA had an arms cache in one of the barns. Our information was that in the next eight days an ASU [active-service unit] was coming to lift the weapons for a hit. There were four of us in the team, and we'd been lying there for five or six days. One man was always on stag, watching the target; another was always protecting the rear. Two would be resting or manning the radio.

The success of these jobs depended on being honest with each other, not macho. If you were tired and you needed a rest, you just said so. Better that than bluff it and fall asleep on stag just as the ASU appeared. It was no bad thing to turn round and say, 'Can someone take over for a bit, because I'm fucked?'

We were in a dip in the ground in a forestry block, no protection apart from our Gore-Tex sniper suits and M16s. Connor was doing his two hours on stag, covering the target. I was lying behind him, weapon at the ready, but resting. I felt a boot make contact with my shoulder, and looked up to see him gesturing for me to come up alongside while he kept his eyes on the barn. I thought he'd seen something, but he hadn't. 'Take over for half an hour, will you?'

No problems about that. I took the binos and moved into position behind the GPMG [general-purpose machine-gun]. Connor crawled backwards and I assumed he'd either got his head down or was taking a shit into a handful of clingfilm – we never left anything behind to show we'd been there – so when I heard his muffled grunts I didn't even bother to glance behind me. Ten minutes later he was still going strong: the fucker was doing press-ups. He carried on like that a full half-hour, then slid up next to me, sweating but happy. 'I had to get some in.' He gulped in oxygen. 'It's been nearly a week.'

Twenty minutes later, he climbed the ladder to ground level. His running vest and shorts were soaking wet. His body might have been a temple, but the rest of him wasn't exactly a work of art. He couldn't reverse the damage years of working in the Middle East had done to the pale skin that comes with ginger pubic hair. The skin around his eyes and mouth was more creased than the bartender's shirt. Mrs Connor called them laughter lines, but nothing was that funny. Not to him anyway.

I stretched out my hand. 'All right?'

He gave me the once-over. 'You're in shit state. You still getting it in?'

'Nah, been busy, mate.'

'Hey, my boy's nineteen, at university now.'

I was taken aback. Connor had gone off message. Maybe he thought I was a lost cause when it came to the god of training. 'That old?'

'Yep. I'm only getting it in twice a day.' That hadn't taken long, then. He was on a twenty-second loop. 'I'd rather be swimming but the fuckers won't fill the pool. They can, you know – I've heard other hotels have, but the fuckers here won't fill it.'

I was dying to tell him the al-Hamra had a full pool but I'd be here all night listening to him honk about it.

'Who do you work for?'

'CNN. It's a good team. I've been with them since Christmas. We came up from Kuwait with the Marines. It was difficult getting the training in to begin with, but there's no problem now. If the fucking pool was working I could get some decent stuff in.'

'What's it like here?'

As if in answer, another burst of AK rattled around the streets somewhere beyond the safety of the garden.

'Belfast times ten. The Yanks out here, I feel sorry for them. They haven't got a fucking clue what they're doing. They're not trained for all this shit.' He stood with his hands on his hips, panting away. 'Even during the war, we'd be harbouring up for the night and they wouldn't send out clearing patrols. Then they'd honk in the morning that they were getting hit. For fuck's sake! I took two American patrols out myself, just to make sure we were secure.'

There was a massive wave of AK gunfire just the other side of the wall. This time, everyone ducked. Then we heard the warbling of the women. It was OK. It was a wedding.

35

Connor thumbed towards the noise. 'The Yanks still haven't worked out Thursday nights yet. The wedding opens up, the Yanks think they're firing at them, and they open up in return. The wedding guests get pissed off, they start firing back, and soon everybody's got their heads down. I'll tell you what, watch yourself here – nobody knows what the fuck's going on.'

Connor was still honking about the Americans, something he had always liked doing. I wondered if it was because they couldn't understand his accent.

'The Yanks reckon the militants are stringing cheese wire across the roads to chop their heads off as they scream through in their Hummers. But you know what? All that's happening is the locals are running cable from the parts of the city that have power, and shoving them into their houses. Decapitation, my arse – they just want to get the fucking kettle on!'

He roared with laughter as more tracer zipped

across the horizon, followed a split second later by the rattle of gunfire. 'There they go again. The party will start soon. Any cabbying after that will be the real gear.'

'There's a no-firing-till-after-the-confetti rule?'

'Is there fuck. They don't even know the twenty-minute rule. I had to tell them yesterday, while we were filming them.'

One of the rules of urban guerrilla warfare is that if you're static for more than twenty minutes, guerrillas will have time to react and get an attack going.

Connor laughed. 'I should be paid more, I'm training the US Army! Bet they've got a full-on gym.'

The clatter of tracked vehicles came from not many streets away. Armoured troops were on the move. 'I bumped into Rob Newman and Gary Mackie. Not together, but they're in the city.'

'Yeah, fucking Mackie, the bastard. He's got a gym. All I've got is the bottom of this fucking thing. Still, at least I don't get zapped in it.'

That seemed to be the end of the conversation for Connor. He turned to walk away, closing one nostril with a finger and clearing the other on to the grass.

'You heard about any Bosnians in the city?'

'Aye, the fuckers haven't lost any time bringing their tarts over. They got the whorehouses sorted out already. Those dirty fat NGO bastards will be spending their money soon enough.'

'It's a Bosnian ayatollah called Nuhanovic I'm thinking of.'

'What the fuck does a Bosnian ayatollah want to come here for? They got enough of their own.'

I shrugged. 'Just what I thought. You going to the party later?'

'What the fuck for?'

Of course. He'd be going back to his hotel room to knock back a few pints of orange juice or whatever the new fad was, and get his head down.

'See you, Connor. I'm staying here if you hear anything.'

'Yeah. Don't forget to get some in. Sort yourself out, for fuck's sake.'

The night's festivities were slowly getting under way. Some speakers were being rigged up in the garden area and the barbecue was blazing. I walked back into the lobby.

It wasn't just military contractors and security companies that made money after an army had done its stuff. The bars and whorehouses sprang up like mushrooms in shit. It was nothing new – even the Romans had camp followers – but the set-up for these girls would be very different. They weren't self-employed prostitutes, here to make some fast cash for themselves and their families. It was an open secret in the Balkans that people-trafficking rings ran through Montenegro to Bosnia and Kosovo.

The white girl the fixer had said he could get me was probably some poor kid who'd been kidnapped or duped, then smuggled in and forced to 'repay her debt' to her owners. It was just as easy to get these girls now as it had been during the war, when both sides had sold their female prisoners. Ads in the papers in places like Moldova or Romania spoke of well-paid waitressing and bar jobs in the Balkans. When the girls arrived at their new places of work, they were lifted. Their passports were taken off them, and the next thing they knew they'd been sold as sex slaves. It looked like the Bosnians were spreading their wings and going global instead of sticking to Europe.

No sooner had I got to the bar than the main doors burst open. A crowd surged through, chanting and clapping, all the women doing their Red Indian yodel.

Next in was the bride, done up to the nines in a big fluffy white gown. She was young and very beautiful. No wonder the groom beamed beside her, looking very smart in his shiny suit. The bridesmaids were in pink and looked like little princesses, tiaras and all sorts in their hair.

They surged off to the right and down a corridor, probably heading for one of the conference rooms. The women were all in trouser suits or dresses, the men in suits or leather jackets. It could have been a wedding anywhere in Liverpool, except this lot were unarmed. They'd probably had to leave their AKs in the B&Q garden shed.

Jerry came in at the end of the conga, clapping and smiling away with the best of them. 'Great, huh?' He grinned. 'Life goes on.'

We headed to the lift.

'Any luck?' I checked out his Baghdad market

gear: polyester trousers and shiny plastic shoes. They went down a treat with the lime-green shirt. He looked like one of the wedding party. 'At the mosque, I mean. I can see you had none at the clothes shop.'

'Yeah, funny. I'm not too sure. But I tell you what – he's definitely here.' He looked about him at the others in the lift. 'Later.'

We got to the sixth floor. For once we were on our own. 'He's here, Nick. No one said anything, but you know when they can't quite look you in the eye. The fucker is here somewhere. I had to leave kinda quick – some of the guys weren't too happy that someone was asking questions. Any questions. What about you?'

'I talked with one of the military contractors and a couple of guys I know. Maybe I'll find out at the party. You coming?'

He looked me up and down. 'Of course. Big question is, do you think the beer will be cold?'

'Don't care, I won't be drinking it. Not on a job.'

36

From where I stood on Jerry's balcony, Baghdad was now a patchwork of light and dark. On the other side of the Tigris, entire neighbourhoods were pitch black; I imagined them criss-crossed with cables so the locals could get their kettles on. Next to them, a few streets had lights that flickered, then whole sectors were reasonably well lit, probably thanks to generators like ours that droned on the back of an artic trailer with a sign saying 'A gift from the people of Japan'.

'You fashioned up yet?'

I'd drawn the curtains behind me so I wouldn't be someone's warm-up shot before a night's sniping at any soldier who stood still long enough.

Jerry was changing out of his local 'look at me, I'm one of you' clothes. 'Nearly. I'm dying for a beer, but the fridge is fucked.'

I looked down. Either the party had split into two or there'd always been rival events. The grassed area was full of people, and about twenty or so were congregated round the barbecue near the pool. Johnny Cash's dad had moved out of the bar to serenade a group of Iraqis and whites sitting round a plastic table, and the Balkan boys were doing a meet-and-greet.

The raffia *cabanas* and fencing now made sense to me. They hadn't done it to make it look good: it was to stop outsiders having an unrestricted view and therefore a good arc of fire into the compound. It obviously worked. Everybody looked very relaxed, even though a random cabby into the fencing might take any of them out. But fuck it – as Gaz would say, 'It's a war, innit?'

Quite a few more people wandered around the pool as Bob Marley sparked up from the speakers and went into competition with Johnny's dad, but neither of them was making much headway against the rumble of conversation and laughter. The whole lot got drowned out as a helicopter swooped low over the rooftops just the other side of the hotel.

Jerry came out and watched it go as he clipped his bumbag round him. 'Must be the cheese-wire patrol . . .'

As we headed for the lift I wondered if Rob would turn up. I hoped so. Seeing these people again made me feel as if nothing had changed, and I liked that. It wasn't as if Rob and I'd been in and out of each other's houses during our time together in the Regiment, but whenever we met up we connected – mostly because we were the sad fucks who hadn't scored down town all night and were still trying to chat up women at the Chinese takeaway on the way back to camp.

The lobby was still heaving. Loud Arab music drifted out of the wedding reception and the women were warbling big-time. They'd be knackered by the morning.

Outside, a crowd had gathered round the far end of the pool, waiting to collect food from the barbecue. The necks of beer bottles stuck out of big bins of ice like the spines of frozen hedge-hogs. An Apple PowerBook had been rigged up to a couple of speakers, its screen displaying the music menu. The Wailers were fighting hard to make themselves heard over the country-and-western.

Jerry swayed to the beat and pointed at the strings of fairy-lights in the palm trees. 'This could be the Caribbean, man.'

'Must be what makes it so popular,' I said, as I made my way along the pool side. 'And I bet the Yardies don't have many of those.' A tracked vehicle screeched noisily down the road just the other side of the wall and helicopters clattered across the sky.

The guests were mostly Brits and Americans and seemed to know each other. The news agencies always did have a pretty incestuous set-up, with the same crews moving from war zone to war zone. None of their protection was carry-ing: the guys all had their party kit on, lurid Hawaiian shirts and Bermudan shorts. It was fun time, and we were the right side of the fence.

They outnumbered the women by about sixteen to one, and hovered round the few available like flies round shit.

Jerry picked up a beer for himself and a Coke for me and we gave the place a good scan, me keeping an eye out for Rob, him for anybody who looked like they might know the secret of the Bosnian ayatollah. We must have looked like the proverbial spare pricks.

Sporadic gunfire punctuated the hubbub of conversation, but it was obviously too far away to worry about. I wondered how they defined too close for comfort. A hundred metres? Fifty? Or wait till someone drops? That really would be effective enemy fire.

A huge contact sparked up nearby. This time everybody did look up. An amazing amount of heavy .50 cal tracer stitched hot dotted lines across the sky. Every pair of eyes followed its trajectory, but once they realized it wasn't going to fall on our heads, their owners got back to their chats and beers.

I was just treating myself to a swig of Coke when I got a huge slap on the back that made my teeth bang against the bottle.

'Wanker!'

I recognized the broad Geordie accent even before I turned round. I'd known Pete Holland for years, but thankfully not that well. He was one of those guys who had an opinion on everything, and a lot of them disappeared when you held them up to the light. Built like a prop forward, he was known in the Regiment as a good

Bergen carrier, a strong back you could depend on to get kit from A to B. So strong, in fact, he could make the muscles in his back bulge like bat wings. His nickname was, of course, Lats-Like-A-Bat.

We shook hands. 'All right, mate? How's it going? This is Jerry.'

It wasn't long before Jerry made his excuses and left, probably so I could start quizzing Lats about Nuhanovic. But I'd need to be pretty fucking desperate before I went that route. He'd want to know why, where, when – and how much I was willing to pay him for answering.

Pete had a beer in one hand and a spare in the other, what he called 'having one on the loading tray'. He'd been in the Artillery before the Regiment. That was his problem: once he'd started on the beers, the loading tray was as busy as a factory conveyor belt. He could have given Ezra a lifetime's work.

He nodded at the two Balkan boys I'd seen in the coffee-bar area, who had just joined a group at the end of the pool. The one with the goatee had a huge smile on his face as he offered round his pack of cigarettes. 'Not working for them cunts, are you?'

I shook my head. 'A journalist. That guy Jerry. You?'

He stuck out his jaw and pranced around on the spot as if he was sizing up to throw a punch. 'Doing me own thing. A wee bit of freelance. I'm on a good number, BGing some Japanese. Five hundred a day. Champion.' He took a hefty swig of free beer.

How did you answer that? 'Five hundred. Good for you, mate. Listen, those flat-tops. They Bosnian, Serb, what?'

'Fuck knows. I fucking know what they're up to, though.' He pointed at the others in the group with his bottle. 'Don't these cunts know what they're doing? Some of them are younger than my two girls.'

It clicked. These two were part of the Balkans' globalization campaign. It didn't sound like they'd be spending much time with the ayatollah.

He took another swig, not that he needed it, and I realized what the posturing was all about. He was trying to keep his balance. No wonder he was on his own. Anybody working for a decent firm and found drinking on a job would be thrown out, no exceptions, no second chances. And word flew round the circuit quicker than tracer. He wasn't an independent by choice. No one would vouch for him. It was a big deal to do that. If the guy you vouched for turned out to be crap, that meant so were you. It was just the way it was.

I hoped he hadn't come over and slapped me on the back because he thought I was a kindred spirit. 'You and the Japanese in the hotel?'

'Aye, I'm here and there. You know how it is.'

I didn't. I hadn't a clue what he was on about.

37

The Canadian woman floated into the pool area with Mr Gap in tow. He looked as if he'd stepped straight out of the shop window, only tonight his polo shirt was green. She was in a black cheesecloth dress that she knew made the best of the buttons she had left unfastened between her breasts.

Lats couldn't keep his eyes off them as she joined the bunch by the barbecue. He put down his empty bottle and kicked into the next as he fished in the bin for another. 'I'm gonna fuck her. She with that dickhead in green?'

'Don't know, mate.'

'I'm going to give her the old special-forces chat-up. Know what I mean?'

This time I did know what he was on about. 'Well, good luck, mate. I've got to go talk to my man about tomorrow.'

It was a mistake shaking the hand that had just come out of the ice bin. As I walked away I felt like I'd just had a close encounter with the living dead.

Jerry hadn't wasted any time. He'd hooked up with a guy who looked a bit like a New Age traveller. Randy was a TV cameraman, though I wondered if he'd remember that come the morning. Waccy baccy was probably as easy to get hold of here as beer and Randy had been making the most of it. 'I've been here seven fucking months, Jerry,' he drawled. 'Ain't no Bosnian Messiah here, no way, my man.' So much for not talking to the media. 'I came in with the Marines—' He stopped and looked up as three helicopters screamed overhead, one after the other. We couldn't see them: they were unlit. Randy staggered backwards and pointed up, shouting, like a driver with road rage, 'Quiet! For fuck's sake, be quiet – it's my fucking birthday.'

Once he regained his balance he had a fit of giggles, then leaned an arm on Jerry's shoulder. 'I got a way with choppers. See, they get off my case pretty damn sharp, man. It's those fucking tanks I have issues with, man.'

Over Jerry's spare shoulder, I saw Rob coming into the pool area from the lobby. He looked as though he was heading for a different kind of party. There were sweat stains on his T-shirt from where he'd just removed his body armour, he had a pistol on his belt and an AK in his hand. I didn't think he'd be staying long.

'Good to meet you, Randy.' I had a crack at trying to shake his hand, but he was too busy waving at another burst of tracer. 'Jerry,

I've got to go – Rob's here. See you later.'

Randy tried to focus his eyes on mine, but gave up. 'Yeah, me too. I've gotta get out of here. Right out of fucking Iraq. Seven months, man.'

Rob was searching the crowd. He smiled as I approached. 'Sorry, mate. I'm not hanging about. Ten minutes and that's it.'

'You with your man?'

He shook his head as his eyes scanned the party. 'At the al-Hamra. Thought I'd come and say hello. How's your search for the Bosnian getting on? You have a name for him?'

'Nuhanovic. He's their answer to Mahatma Gandhi. You heard anything?'

'Nah. It's just a picture you want?'

'Jerry, the guy I'm with, says he's going to be famous one day.'

'For what?'

'World peace, mate. Putting us out of a job.'

He held out his hand and pointed at nowhere in particular. 'Just don't tell that to any of the Serbs on the circuit, will you?'

'You want a Coke?'

'No Coke, thanks – water will do.' Sweat streamed down his face.

I grabbed a bottle from one of the ice bins. He twisted the cap and threw his head back. It would have made a great commercial if I'd really been in the advertising business.

A couple of AKs sparked up the other side of the fence and a tracked vehicle rattled along the road. Rob listened to the chaos and shook his head. 'Close my eyes and I could be back home.'

'Fuck me, Rob, I know Coventry can be bad at times but—'

'No, mate, Uzbekistan. They're my people now. It's the same sort of situation out there.' He jerked his head roughly in the direction of the outside world. 'Indiscriminate body-count stuff. There's got to be a better way, don't you think?'

I shrugged. Why Uzbekistan? From the little I knew, it was in a shit state. It had got independence from Russia in '91, but was still state-run. The government decided everything, from what food you could buy to what TV you could watch. I'd been slumped on the settee not long ago watching a documentary about human rights. Uzbekistan had the sort of record that made Pol Pot look like Mother Teresa. One of their favourite tricks was boiling people till their skin peeled, then scrubbing them down with disinfectant. 'Know what, Rob? I try really hard not to think about it too much.'

He held his bottle in his right hand, weapon in the left. 'We're fucking up here, exactly like the French did in Algiers. History repeats itself, but nobody learns.'

I scratched my head. 'Well, I've only been here a day, mate. I haven't taken much notice.'

He pointed at the media crew the other side of the pool with Jerry. 'The French used to report stuff exactly the way those wankers over there are reporting this. Telling the world things are improving. Are they fuck. Demonstrators killed in Fallujah – so what? Not worth reporting. An American goes apeshit with a full mag and drops some kids in Mosul – who cares? Iraqis slaughter each other by night, but come first light, everyone's blind.' He lifted the bottle to his mouth.

I suddenly felt as tired as he was. 'You're right, mate, but that's how it's always been. We know it's all bullshit. We're never going to be told the truth.'

Rob finished the bottle and placed it alongside a collection of empties on a low wall. Randy was arguing over the Apple with a guy in a hat with Mickey Mouse ears. He didn't want Bob and the Wailers any more and, after all, it was his birthday. I didn't think Mickey had a problem with switching the music: he'd just had enough of Randy slobbering over his keyboard.

Rob was still grappling with the big picture. 'It's not as if I'm all bitter and twisted. I understand what's going on, and the reason why. I just can't help feeling there's got to be a better way. Back home my man listens to Al Alam radio. It broadcasts out of Tehran, but it's the only station with up-to-date news of what's really going on in Iraq. Isn't that bizarre? The closest we get to the truth, and it's coming from the latest axis of evil.

'The Western news agencies are just reporting whatever the CPA tells them to: "There's a little local difficulty here, nothing that can't be sorted." But the boys on the ground know different. Two Americans get blown up here. Six Brits get shot there. You know the US isn't even covering the funerals now? The White House doesn't want sobbing families and coffins draped in the Stars and Stripes on TV.'

He glanced again at the partygoers around him. 'Know what, Nick? They've got to pull back, start telling it like it is, otherwise everyone at home will think things are great. They won't demand action, we'll lose this war, then we're fucked. Because it won't end here, mate. It'll spread.'

38

Randy was really starting to piss Mickey off, especially since he was now pouring beer over the keyboard because he wasn't getting his own way.

'If other countries get it into their heads the Americans can be humbled by strategic resistance, why should they give up their own struggle?'

'You talking about Uzbekistan?'

'It's a fucking nightmare there, mate. Our esteemed president, Karimov, has made himself Dubya's new best friend.'

I knew courtesy of the Discovery Channel that Uzbekistan had one of the best tables in the Washington Good Lads Club: it had let itself be used as a base for US forces during Operation Fuck Off Taleban, and they'd stayed on as part of the war on terror. Of course, the guardians of freedom and liberty hadn't jumped up and down too much about their host's misdemeanours: he'd handed them a strategic position at the heart of Central Asia, the reward for which was a full-dress White House reception and a couple of hundred million dollars in aid.

It was just another load of bollocks. Fuck it, who cared? Well, Rob did, by the sound of it. 'We've got Shi'ites bombing and shooting their way around the fucking country, trying to replace Karimov with an Islamic caliphate. Karimov doesn't want that. The White House doesn't want it. Nor do most Uzbekis. But it's that fucker Karimov who's causing the drama. He's crushing religious freedom – creating the very fundamentalism that he and Bush think they're fighting.'

Rob was having one of his famous intense moments. I generally tried to avoid them: they used up far too many brain cells. 'He's closed down nearly all the mosques. Clever move in a country that's eighty per cent Muslim. There's just a handful still open in each city for state-sanctioned Friday prayers, but worship anywhere else, any time, and you're banged up. It's a fucking nightmare, and if we lose this war here it's only going to get worse back home – in fact, anywhere that people are pissed off. Got another water?'

I fumbled about in one of the bins. Most of the ice had already melted.

'The Algerians perked up when they saw France getting annihilated in Vietnam. They thought, right, if they can fuck them, so can we. Here? Just take out the French and insert the Americans and Brits.'

He took the water and shoved it into the map pocket on his cargoes. 'One for the road, mate. I've got to get back before curfew.'

I hadn't known there was one. 'What time does it kick in?'

'That's the thing, no one's really sure. Some say ten till four thirty. Others say ten thirty till four. Who knows? Anyway, I've got to get back. '

Rob fished into his back pocket for the thirty-round curved mag for his AK. A gale of female laughter erupted on the other side of the pool. Pete Holland had his shirt off and was flexing his lats for the Canadian woman. It was his party piece.

Mr Gap was laughing too, but I bet he was really pissed off that a drunk was getting all the attention after he'd been doing all the spadework.

Rob just ignored him. 'I reckon this great coalition had better start learning from the Algerian experience, because those fucking oiks out there in the desert, they have. And if we don't sort this situation out we're going to be here for years and the problem will spread. The Stans are ready to rock for a start – Turkmenistan, Uzbekistan, whatever – they're all up for it.'

I hoped the lecture was over. Rob could be like a dog with a bone. 'You been eating those history books again, haven't you?'

He squared up to me. 'No, mate. I'm just getting a huge education from my man. There's a few who are talking about a different way, using a different weapon, rather than these things.' He pushed the front of the mag into its housing on the weapon and it clicked home. 'What about you, Nick? You interested in finding a different way?'

An agonized gasp from the Canadian saved me having to answer. It was just as well. I didn't have a clue what he was on about.

Every man and his dog spun round to see what was happening. Lats was trading punches with the flat-tops. He wasn't coming off best. Goatee was trying to stamp on his head as he got pulled away by do-gooders.

'That fucker hasn't changed, has he?' Rob never had liked him.

'They're slavers.'

'Here already? He's doing something useful for once, then, ain't he?'

Rob and I shook hands. There was more gun-fire from a few blocks away. Rob racked back the cocking handle and made ready the AK, his right thumb pushing the safety catch on the right-hand side of the weapon all the way up. 'Tell me I'm not right. There's got to be a better way. There's no rich kids out there tonight fighting this war. It's all soft cunts like me and you were fifteen or sixteen years ago. See yer soon. I'll call by, see if you find Mahatma.' He turned and disappeared into the lobby.

Jerry came over as the brawlers were pulled apart. 'Any luck?'

'Fuck all.'

'I see that Pete guy's doing his bit for inter-national relations. They're Serbs, apparently. Know what it was about?'

'Maybe he tried his special-forces chat-up line on them and they didn't like it.'

He was waiting for the punch line. 'And?'

'"Please give us a fuck. I'm special forces. I'll be in and out before you know it."'

At that moment Lats broke free from the do-gooders and charged at the Serbs again. 'Actually,' I said, 'I think he's pissed off with them because he's got daughters of his own.'

'Slavers?' Jerry knew the score. 'They're not wasting any time, are they?'

'Nope, let's hope he goes apeshit and kills them, eh?'

He headed for reception to shop for toothpaste and stuff and I went to watch a blizzard on CNN.

39

Friday, 10 October

I turned over in the single bed, still more asleep than awake. The balcony door was open and I could hear the odd vehicle on the move. It was still dark, but a bird down in the garden hadn't cottoned on. I checked Baby-G—06:31.

I dozed a few more minutes, then began to hear a new yet familiar sound, the rhythmic slap-slap-slap of running feet. They went a short distance, stopped for several seconds, then started again. I threw off the hairy nylon blanket and went and turned on CNN; the picture was still shit, but at least the sound was good. According to the world weather round-up it was a scorcher in Sydney.

I went into the bathroom and twisted the tap. There was a gurgle and some water spluttered out, a bit brown at first, then clearer, but a long way from hot. I put a glass under the cold tap, drank, then filled it again. I'd never been one for only drinking bottled water when you got to these places: the sooner your gut got used to the real stuff the better.

After turning the room light off, I scratched my arse and head, as you do of a morning, and padded out on to the balcony with my second glass. It was chilly outside, but the sun was just peeping over the horizon. Soon there was enough light to make out Connor in the empty swimming-pool getting some in.

A diesel generator sparked up nearby, startling a small flock of birds out of their tree. I followed their line of flight out over the Tigris and a couple of boats that chugged their way upstream. At first I thought the dull bang off to my right was the generator backfiring. Then I saw a flash of light and a small plume of grey-blue smoke rising from a pair of burnt-out tower blocks three or four hundred metres away.

I ran back into my room just as the RPG thudded into one of the floors below. A split second later there was an explosion, and the whole building shuddered.

I fell to the floor and covered my head, braced for a second hit. I thought it had come, but it was just the bathroom mirror falling off the wall and shattering. Plaster dust trickled from the joists above me.

Another round hit the building, and this time it was a lot closer. There was a loud thud and the floor beneath me trembled. My ears rang.

Still naked, I jumped up and ran into the corridor. The middle of the building seemed the best place to be: for all I knew, they were attacking from both sides. I couldn't go down the fire escape and the lift was a no-no. Everyone would be trying to jam into it, and a power-cut was almost inevitable.

There was another explosion and the lights flickered. A bunch of other guests rushed past me, shouting at no one in particular, just panicking big-time.

Another RPG punched into our side of the hotel. A woman screamed above the din. Two men stumbled and fell and the people behind them just kept scrambling over each other, trying to get away, if only they could work out where to.

I banged on Jerry's door. 'Jerry, for fuck's sake!'

A heavy machine-gun sparked up on the opposite side of the hotel. Then the tank thundered a round into something out there.

The door swung open. Jerry was naked, dazed. I could smell waccy baccy.

More people swarmed out into the corridor, leaving their doors open behind them. The lifts weren't going anywhere; some hammered the buttons and scrabbled at the doors, others made a run for the fire escape.

'It's safer out here,' I yelled. 'Come on, fuck the clothes!'

There was a sustained rattle of machine-gun fire, then another RPG round thumped into the building.

'Fuck me.' Jerry fell into the corridor. 'We came here to get a story, not be fucking part of one.' He ran back into his room.

'What are you doing? Get away from the outside wall!'

He reappeared with his camera in his hand,

and started shooting the confusion in the corridor.

There was a sudden silence. The seconds ticked by. People were holding their breath. Still nothing. Audible sighs of relief, then excited chatter.

Jerry nodded at the open doors opposite. 'Let's check that side of the building.'

'And get shot by the fucking troops? They'll be sparked up. Just stay here. Let them contain the area. You'll get plenty of pictures soon enough.'

It had gone in one ear and out the other. Jerry shot across the corridor. Next thing I knew, he was hanging over the balcony, pointing his camera in the direction of the tank.

There was a sob to my left. A young Iraqi, naked, dazed and covered with blood, was coming down the corridor, staggering under the weight of the young woman in his arms. I could see shards of glass sticking out all over her. Her arm swayed in time with his steps. They got closer. I recognized them. They'd only been married about twelve hours.

40

He looked down at his bride and couldn't stop
sobbing. There was a huge rip in her face. Her
cheek had been split almost as far as her ear,
making her mouth twice its original size. I
couldn't tell if she was dead or alive.

I pushed him into my room.

He resisted. He didn't know what I was saying. I grabbed hold of the woman.

Jerry was still hanging over the balcony. 'Get in
here – I need you!'

The husband screamed and tried to prise her
off me as I backed into my room.

I put her down on the carpet, shouting at
him, 'The lights, get the fucking lights on!'

Of course he didn't understand. I jumped up
and pushed him out of the way. He fell on his arse
on the bed as Jerry came in. I pushed him towards
the husband. 'Shut this fucker up!'

The main lights didn't come on. I hit the bedside lamp. It didn't do much, but it was better
than nothing.

I knelt down beside her, my face nearly touching the bloody mess that was hers. I couldn't feel any breath on my skin. Her chest wasn't moving. I lifted one of her eyelids. No pupil reaction. Nothing anywhere to show she was alive.

I turned her on to her side, opened her lips and dug my fingers into her mouth. I scooped out a couple of broken teeth, then a big plug of mucus and blood that was blocking her airway. Fuck wasting time finding out if she had a pulse. I needed to breathe for her, fill her lungs with air. Even if her heart was still pumping, it was doing nothing without oxygen.

I rolled her on to her back again, tilting her head back to open the airway. The poor bastard jumped up and grabbed my wrist, pulling it away from his wife. 'Jerry! Get him back on the bed. Tell him she'll die if he doesn't stop fucking about!'

She was warm, but that didn't mean much. She was probably already dead, but I had to try. The only real dead body is a cold one.

I freed my arm, then eased her head back to open the airway once more. I pinched her nose shut with my right hand and held together the rip in her cheek with my left. Her husband hollered: he was so distressed he still didn't understand what was going on. Jerry tried making soothing noises.

I filled my lungs and put my mouth over what was left of hers, tasting the metallic tang of her blood. I breathed into her – I could feel some of it leaking through the rip in her cheek, but her

204

chest rose a fraction. I tried again, but it was no good. My left hand was slipping on her blood-drenched skin. I couldn't keep a good enough seal. Her blood spat out of my mouth as I yelled at Jerry. 'Get over here! Keep this fucking rip together.'

He came and knelt beside her and gripped the rip with both hands. I took a breath, got a seal, exhaled.

Her chest rose. She was taking in oxygen. I breathed into her again.

The husband started tearing at me. Fuck knows what he thought I was doing.

I jumped up, grabbed him by the ears, and headbutted him hard. I didn't have a choice. My head spun and my eyes watered as he fell back, arms flailing, on to the bed. Blood poured from his nose. I shoved Jerry in his direction before dropping back down on the floor. 'Jump on the fucker. Keep him down.'

Tilting her head back, I pinched her nose and gripped a handful of ripped cheek as best I could, forcing the air in harder now. Ten big breaths to get her inflated, spitting out her blood between each one. I could still feel air leaking through her cheek, but it was working. My head was swimming. Jerry and the husband screamed at each other above me, somewhere in the distance. My brain was crying out for oxygen too.

Ten done. I checked for a pulse. Jamming two fingers into the side of her neck, I checked her carotid. Nothing. She was still only getting oxygen from me, and her heart wasn't pumping

any of that oxygenated blood around her body.
Shit.

I hoped nothing was fractured in her chest area, because if it was, what I was going to do next might finish her off.

41

I pulled away the bigger shards of glass from between her breasts, gave her two more breaths, then put the heel of my left hand on to her sternum, and my right on top of that. I leaned over her, straightened my arms and started pumping steadily, counting off the seconds in my head.

Thousand and one, thousand and two, thousand and three, thousand and four . . .

I spat out another mouthful of blood and started to call it out loud: 'Thousand and six, thousand and seven . . .'

I yelled across at Jerry, 'Tell him her heart's stopped and she can't breathe for herself. I'm trying to do it for her.'

The husband struggled and yelled something back.

'Tell him to get downstairs and find some help. Ambulances, medics, whatever . . . But fuck him off, I need you here.'

Jerry gave him a torrent of Arabic, pulled the blanket off the bed and wrapped it round him, then virtually pushed him out of the door.

'Squeeze her face together again – we need that seal.'

He dropped to his knees.

I got my mouth round hers, pinched her nose, and breathed hard. Fuck knows how long it had been since her brain had last had oxygen.

Her lungs fully inflated this time. Once. Twice. Then it was back to fifteen pumps over her heart.

'Thousand and one, thousand and two, thousand and three, thousand and four . . .'

It was a whole lot quieter now the husband had gone. I could even hear a bird singing on the balcony.

'Thousand and six, thousand and seven, thousand and eight . . .'

I pumped away, squashing the heart to move that oxygenated blood round her body on its own. A fair amount of red stuff was oozing out of her, but it wasn't as bad as it looked. If you drop a bottle of Ribena on your kitchen floor it looks like breakfast turned into the Texas chainsaw massacre, but it's only one bottle.

'Start breathing, for fuck's sake! Thousand and thirteen, thousand and fourteen, thousand and fifteen . . .'

Jerry and I bent down and I started to fill her again, one, two, big breaths. Each time, her chest fully rose and fell.

Another fifteen pumps. I checked for signs of life. Nothing. Not a flicker.

Head back, two more breaths.

'Thousand and one, thousand and two,

thousand and three . . .'

Jerry and I exchanged glances. Was there any point?

'Thousand and four, thousand and five . . .' I shouted it louder, as if that might help.

Helicopters careered overhead, then came back in to hover.

'Thousand and fourteen, thousand and fifteen . . .'

There was a small tremor in her good cheek.

'She's pumping, she's fucking pumping!'

I jammed two fingers into her neck as Jerry's face broke into a grin. 'Good things, Nick. Good things.'

Her carotid was quick and weak, but her heart was beating. All I had to do now was carry on the breathing for her – she would tell me when to stop.

I did two more breaths and checked. Her eyelids flickered.

Another two, and she coughed. A trickle of blood spilled from her mouth. Jerry was so excited his hands slipped. 'Keep the seal closed, keep it closed.'

I'd just started to give her another ten short breaths when her hand came up and tried to push me away. She moaned softly, like a baby. She was in a lot of pain, which was a good thing. If she could feel pain, her brain was working.

I opened an eyelid and the pupil reacted. Not a lot, but enough.

'Talk to her, Jerry. Make her answer. Try and keep her going. Wake her up.'

42

She was still only semi-conscious but uttered another low moan as I turned her on to her side, so her tongue would fall forward and not block the airway.

I rolled away and sat on the floor just a couple of feet away, completely exhausted. Jerry leaned over her, talking into her ear in Arabic, brushing back her blood-matted hair. She moaned a bit louder.

I looked down at my naked body. I was covered in her blood; my hands were slippery with it. I'd also picked up a fair amount of glass from her – I could see slivers of it glittering in my palms. I looked over to the left. The TV had been knocked off the sideboard and was lying sideways on the floor. The picture was almost perfect now, but the sound had gone.

I tilted my head to watch as they broadcast pictures of the outside of the hotel. One RPG had hit a balcony, and all the fancy *Star Wars* concrete had been blown away. The camera zoomed in on another scorch-marked hole, less than a foot in diameter, where the RPG's explosive charge had punched through into the building. These things were designed to pierce armour so they could fuck everybody inside the target. Anyone the other side of the hole would have been hit by a storm of flying glass and masonry.

They cut back to the reporter in body armour and early-morning, post-party, sticky-up hair. The tank had been hit. The scene behind him was a blur of soldiers, smoke, ambulances and medics.

There were voices in the corridor: American, male, macho. 'Anybody injured? Anybody there?'

Jerry ran to the door. 'In here! In here!'

A uniformed medical team hurried in, trauma packs on their backs. Jerry started to say something about her husband being downstairs to look for them, but they weren't listening. They were already on the floor, running their checks.

One looked at me. 'You OK, man?'

'Yeah, fine.' I held up my hands. 'It's hers.'

I got up and moved over to the bed to get out of their way. CNN's cameras were now focused on the tank. It had taken a mobility hit: one track had been blasted off and lay flat behind the vehicle on the tarmac. The militants had had a good morning's work.

The bride's moans turned to sobs as the pain caught up with her. I went over to the balcony. The sun was nearly over the rooftops. I wiped my face free of her blood and started to pick the glass out of my hands.

Tracked vehicles surged up and down the streets. Fuck knows what they were hoping to achieve. The horse had well and truly bolted.

The sound of sirens filled the air and more ambulances screeched up outside. Down in the garden, groups of reporters and cameramen were doing interviews as if they were the only ones on the scene.

I looked across at the RPG's firing point. It was about three hundred and fifty metres away; they were good for up to five hundred at a stationary target. The tower-block windows were missing and it had been burned out long ago. Maybe it had been a Ba'ath Party HQ. Now it had a big fresh fuck-off tank shell hole, and was peppered with .50 cal strike marks around the sixth or seventh floor. RPGs are great weapons, but they have a massive signature: a big flash, then a plume of grey-blue smoke. Once you've pulled the trigger, you've got to be quick on your feet.

It was all over and done with. They'd had a cabby at us, we'd had a cabby at them. I just felt sorry for the bride. She was going to have to go through the rest of her life with a face like a patchwork quilt. Then again, at least she was alive, and that made me feel quite good, I supposed.

There was a bit of a commotion down on the ground. The balcony that had taken the hit directly overlooked the pool. The huge slab of concrete had gone straight down, and a small group of people were now gathering round the remains of the madman who'd been getting some in beneath it.

I didn't feel that good any more.

43

The medics were still working to stabilize the bride. I gathered up my clothes and daysack as her blood started to dry on me, and climbed over the bed to follow Jerry to his room. The corridor was flooded. Water seeped from under a nearby door.

Jerry tried a bath tap and it produced a small trickle.

'After you, mate.'

He jumped in and soaped himself. I went straight to the balcony.

Danny Connor was being lifted on to a table-top by six or seven Iraqis who were all shouting at each other, trying to keep the thing level so he didn't slip off and back into the pool. His body flopped about like a large rag doll. There wasn't much blood on him; his sweat-covered training kit was covered with concrete dust.

I really didn't know what to think. He got paid to be here, he knew the risks. At least he'd died doing what he liked best, I supposed. But it felt like a waste.

I thought about Danny's kid. Last time I'd seen him he was a pug-nosed, freckly minger of nine or ten. He always seemed to have a tooth missing after a mishap on his bike or skateboard. Now it was his dad that was missing, and the gap was going to be permanent. That wasn't going to fuck up his university studies much, was it? Maybe Rob was right: there had to be another way.

I came back inside and sat on one of the beds. Jerry's version of CNN was even snowier than mine had been before the attack, and the sound was just as bad. Larry King seemed to be on with a couple of talking heads, but I didn't have a clue who they were or what it was all about. Then a girl breezed on and started to sing.

Jerry came out with a towel round his waist just as the attack, the bride, Danny, Rob and his history lesson started to rumble around in the washing-machine inside my head.

'What now?' He was quite subdued, as you often are when the odd RPG has been kicked off in your direction.

I got up and ripped the sheet off the bed. 'First let's try and get another room. Then I'll see if I can track down any more guys on the circuit. What about you?'

'I'll give Renee a call – she'll see this shit on the morning news. After that I'll check in with my guy in DC, and do a trawl through the local papers.'

Rather him than me. I went into the bathroom while Jerry got dressed.

He'd left the water in for me; it looked like

weak Ribena. I turned the tap but it seemed we'd had our ration. I took what was left of the little sliver of soap and tried to work up a lather. My hands stung. 'Listen,' I called, while picking a couple of glass fragments out of my palms, 'I got a fixer to get me a couple of weapons. You want one?'

'Count me out. I wouldn't know what to do with it anyway.' He started to chuckle. 'I've never worked in advertising.' He disappeared back into the bedroom, buttoning his shirt, a red Baghdad special.

After a while he said, 'Nick, we did well, didn't we?'

I tried to work the soap into my hair but there wasn't enough to dislodge the blood from the roots. 'Yeah.'

Danny Connor was dead and the bride wouldn't want to spend too much time in front of a mirror now, but things could have been a fuck of a lot worse. And doing this sort of shit somehow made a fuck of a lot more sense to me than mincing round the States on a road trip.

The soap still wouldn't lather, so I gave up. A good day's sweat would sort it.

I got out of the bath and dried myself with the sheet.

Jerry was out on the balcony with a camera, snapping away at the block of flats the tank had taken a chunk out of.

Once I'd got my clothes on, Jerry took his Thuraya off the charger, then gathered up his camera and bumbag. The corridor was shoe deep in water now. My door was open. The carpet was dark with blood and the beds had been stripped bare. The sheets must have been used to wrap the not-so-happy bride. I closed the door and locked it, even though there was nothing there to nick.

When the lift finally came we found ourselves crammed in with a whole lot of people who'd suddenly decided that maybe the Palestine wasn't the safest place to stay after all. Everybody had their bags. I wondered where they thought would be safer.

44

Chaos reigned at the reception desk. About fifty people wanted to get their money back and check out. Jerry went off to make his calls while I got into the scrum and eventually worked my way to the front. Even then it was like trying to attract a busy barman's attention. One of the guys finally pointed to me. He was a happy old Iraqi with the full Saddam, and what had probably been a white shirt until an hour or so ago.

I leaned over the desk, trying to shout into his ear: 'What about a discount? The rooms are damaged.'

He smiled. 'Ah, yes.' This was looking promising. 'Room is sixty dollars a night.'

'No, no – the corridor's flooded, my friend's room has holes in it, everything in my room is smashed up. We want to stay, we're not like all these other people.'

'I know, it is terrible, very terrible. I would not wish to stay here.'

'So we get a discount?'

He smiled in agreement. 'Yes, room is sixty dollars a night.'

I was banging my head against a brick wall. 'What about a different floor? Can we get two rooms on the first floor?'

He smiled and ran his finger down a ledger. People were hollering and shouting, many of them Iraqi; I recognized some of the leather jackets from the wedding last night.

The Canadian woman and Mr Gap, still in the green polo, emerged from the lift together, heading for the exit. He was carrying her bags. He'd finally won through. I was proud of him. Maybe she'd thought the earth was moving just for her this morning.

Another desk manager joined my new mate and checked the ledger. They had a chat, probably about bloody foreigners who wanted discounts. Didn't they know there was a war on?

'Nick!' Jerry was at the back of the scrum, working his way through. 'How's it going?'

The desk guy gave me a five-star smile. 'We have one room on the first floor. The man is dead. You share?'

I looked at Jerry. 'Is that all right?' He didn't care. 'Excellent,' I said. 'That's only sixty dollars, so we get some rebate because we've already paid for two rooms.'

The guy's smile got even wider. 'Oh, no. Sixty dollars each.'

I gave up. He laughed, we laughed, and he handed me the key to 106. 'We'll drop off the keys to the other two rooms in a minute. Give the blood time to dry.'

We tried to make our way back to the lifts. The place was flooded with news crews in helmets and body armour.

Back on the sixth floor, Jerry went to pack and I did a final check that I hadn't left anything behind. I wondered if we were about to move into Danny's old room. I'd forgotten my tooth-brush, and as I retrieved it I heard the door open. 'That didn't take you long, mate. You got my daysack?'

I turned to see three US military policemen. Two had their M16s pointing at my head. The one in the middle, a Puerto Rican sergeant with a pencil moustache and dark wraparounds, had plasticuffs in his hands ready to lash me down. 'Get your hands up!'

The guys with the M16s were young and looked nervous. One had his safety catch off. I wasn't going to argue.

The sergeant pointed to the bumbag round my waist. 'You got any weapons in here?'

'No.'

'You sure you're not lying to me now? You got no weapons in that fanny pack? Just tell me now, just tell me now.'

'Only a passport and cash. No weapons.'

'OK, fella, down on the bed, hands behind your back. Real slow.' His tone told me he'd done this job many times, and he was happy in his work.

I did as he said, ending up face down on the

bed. The plasticuffs went on, a little too tight, my bumbag was ripped off, and several sets of hands set about frisking me to see if I'd been lying. I could smell sweat and grime; the uniforms were well worn, and a few rips had been repaired in the material. I was treated to a blast of minted breath as I was pulled backwards on to my feet. 'Slow now, fella – don't make us hurt you. Just do it real slow. Let's get this done sensible.'

They turned me round and dragged me out into the corridor. A bunch of white guys and Iraqis were waiting by the lift; they averted their eyes, not wanting to get involved.

I couldn't see Jerry anywhere. Had they lifted him? Had he escaped? Or were they just coming for me?

45

They bundled me out through the lobby. Straight out through the main doors, into dazzling sunlight, then into the back of a Hummer. The driver gunned the engine. A group of fixers were staring in after me, smoking themselves to death. My boy was there with a sack in his hand: Saddam's pistols had arrived.

It's more cramped than it looks in these things. There are only two seats front and back, and a raised square section of steel, covering the drive shaft, running down the centre. One of the MPs jumped in next to me; his belt-kit pressed me hard against the raised section. I leaned over to my right, trying to relieve the pressure.

The dash-mounted radio crackled. Another MP jumped in from the other side. He kicked me out of his way with a scuffed and scabbed-up desert boot. He was aiming for the turret, to man the roof-mounted machine-gun, and needed my bit of cover to stand on.

I had webbing and a body to my left, boots and

legs to my right. I wasn't going anywhere. The sergeant was still outside the vehicle. Were we waiting for Jerry? I hoped we weren't. If he could avoid getting lifted, maybe he could help me out. Then again, it would be comforting to know I wasn't the only one in the shit. How much in the shit I didn't have a clue, but I was sure going to find out soon enough. The best bet was to keep quiet with these boys: it was pointless resisting or protesting. They were here to lift me, and that was it, no matter what I said or did. Keep quiet, keep passive, keep uninjured.

The hotel doors opened and Jerry was heaved out past the fixers. He hadn't come quietly. Blood streamed from a cut on his forehead. 'Where are you taking me?' He looked at the crowd. 'Remember me if I disappear. Remember what happened here. I'm an American.'

Why didn't the fucker just shut up and get in the back of the wagon? If they were going to kill us, they would hardly have done this in broad daylight, in front of half the world's media.

The sergeant leaned in and produced a length of cloth. I got a kick from one of the boots level with my right shoulder.

I closed my eyes to protect them as the blindfold went on. The cloth wasn't fit-for-task. Daylight still got in: I could feel it through my lids.

The doors slammed, the engine roared and the Hummer started to move. The sergeant got on the net to tell whoever wanted to know that he was on his way with two 'pax', while the gunner shouted at whoever was within reach to get the fuck out of his way. The MP next to me adjusted himself in his seat, forcing his belt-kit deeper into my ribs. 'What you been doing, pal?' I couldn't tell where the accent was from.

'Dunno. I was hoping you could tell me.'

The sergeant's voice boomed from up front. 'Shut the fuck up, both of you.'

I lifted my head a little and opened my eyes as much as I could behind the blindfold. I could see just a sliver of reality. The inside of the Hummer, like any military vehicle during operations, was in shit state. To the right, the other side of the roof gunner, was a blue plastic cooler box, probably full of ice, mineral water and Coke. Candy wrappers and empty bottles littered the floor. The driver gripped the wheel with his left hand and a Beretta with his right. There was a Walkman on the dash. When the guys got bored I guessed they'd treat themselves to a blast of Eminem.

The matt green paintwork had been chipped, rubbed and worn down to bare steel and aluminium. Danny Connor was right: American troops hadn't been prepared for the sort of war they were fighting now. Someone had secured sets of body armour to the doors. Before that, there'd have been just a thin sheet of steel between them and the enemy.

These guys had been prepared and trained for a fast, mobile and aggressive war, not the guerrilla action they were being treated to round here. As Danny Connor had said, it was like

Belfast, only worse. I almost felt sorry for them, driving these big vehicles down narrow streets, open to attack every inch of the way. They had no protection at all against RPGs and only sandbags in the footwells as some kind of barrier to the IEDs. There was so much rubbish in the streets they were impossible to spot.

As we drove I tried to make it look as if my head was bouncing around like everybody else's, so I could get a decent view of where we were going. I thought it might make me feel better if I could get a rough idea of where I was.

I wasn't scared, just pissed off.

I caught the glint of sun on water, and recognized the silhouette of the bridge over the Tigris. I'd looked at it often enough from my hotel room. Shit, it was hot in here.

46

We piled past queues of traffic. The collapsed shopping mall came into view, then, a minute or so later, the large colonial building with shuttered windows and a big fuck-off Union Jack on top. British soldiers in desert camouflage were on stag: a line of Warrior AFVs were parked up amid walls of sandbags and rolls of razor wire.

My shirt was soaked with sweat and stuck to the PVC seat cover. I could feel the body heat of the MP beside me. My hands were swelling beneath the plasticuffs, and I tried to lean forward to relieve the pain. Each time I did, the MP pulled me back.

We passed an American checkpoint. Helmets and sunglasses. M16s. Sandbags. Wire. The river was on our right, a wall topped by short railings on our left. Beyond it was a mass of palm trees. Against the brilliant blue sky they looked more Beverly Hills than Baghdad.

The driver stood on the brakes and took a sharp, ninety-degree left. I lifted my head: we were passing a run of low, rectangular concrete buildings with flat roofs. Some had been destroyed; the walls of others had been covered with tarpaulins. There were US military vehicles everywhere. Green army towels and BDUs hung from makeshift washing lines. Sat dishes pointed skywards. I could hear generators.

We rounded another corner and passed a row of Iraqi tanks with their turrets hanging off, and a bunch of other scorch-marked vehicles that had been given the good news.

Iraqis were being herded off a line of trucks that had been backed up against a series of blockhouses with small, barred windows. My heart sank.

The wagon stopped with a jolt and rusty iron gates creaked shut. The Hummer's doors were thrown open and the sergeant and MP next to me jumped out.

I heard a 'sssh'. I knew what was about to happen. Shutting my eyes and clenching my teeth, I got my head down and tensed myself.

Hands reached in and grabbed me, dragged me out of the vehicle and immediately let go. I dropped to the ground.

They didn't speak. All I could hear was laboured breathing and grunts as I was pulled upright.

Jerry was somewhere behind me. 'I'm an American citizen. Check my passport.'

I heard a dull thump as the punch landed, then the sound of him retching. A mouthful of vomit splashed on to the sand.

They dragged me away, my feet only just touching the ground. The grip on my arms didn't relax as we entered a building. It was suddenly cooler. I opened my eyes again and peered below the blindfold. The soles of worn desert boots squeaked either side of me as I got marched across not-so-recently polished black and white tiles.

The grip on my arms was now almost as painful as the plasticuffs on my wrists. I tried to keep the balls of my feet in contact with the ground, to take some of the pressure. I heard Jerry moan and try to catch his breath.

Another door opened and we went through. There was still an echo, but no more squeaking soles. We were on green carpet now. We stopped abruptly and I was swung around. My legs hit a chair and I stumbled backwards. The MPs grabbed me and forced me down.

Time to close my eyes, tense up and grit my teeth.

My hands were agony. I tried leaning forward, but somebody behind me grabbed my hair and pulled me back.

Jerry groaned. 'Why are you doing this? I'm an American. I've done nothing wrong.'

The blindfold was ripped off. I'd been transported into a Hollywood fantasy version of eighteenth-century France. The walls were gilded. In front of me was an enormous, ornate gilt desk with a red leather top. Scattered around the room were plush velvet sofas. One had a big slash in it.

Eight guys in soaking wet T-shirts stood at the ready, poised to climb aboard us if we did something stupid.

Jerry looked at me, wide-eyed. 'Nick, what—?'

I turned away. I hoped he'd switch on soon and shut the fuck up.

I took in some more of the room. The new owners had done it up a bit, but it had obviously taken a bit of a pasting during the war. The odd bit of plaster still hung off the ceiling, tiles were still missing from the wall, and fluorescent lights dangled from exposed wiring, but that's what happens when Mr Paveway comes to visit.

To my right, a small window had been patched up with perspex. I couldn't help but grin when I looked through it. I could see a tower of some sort out there, with the usual picture of Saddam waving – except that his face had been replaced by a big yellow Smiley. I caught the eye of one of the guys standing guard and he smiled too.

'Why am I here?' Jerry was getting more and more agitated. 'I'm an American.'

Nobody replied because everyone knew it. He'd said it enough times. Besides, they were here to enforce, not answer questions, and they wouldn't hesitate to make him vomit again if he got boring.

47

'Jeral, I know you are.'

The Texan drawl came from behind us, near the door. 'And if you keep quiet, this won't take long.'

I didn't turn round.

'I'm an American journalist. I have a right to know why we're here.' Jerry was doing too much talking and not enough listening.

Two men in uniform came and leaned their arses against the desk in front of us. Both were in their mid-thirties, and had identical, Brylcreemed short-back-and-sides with the kind of parting you can usually only get with a fretsaw. Their BDUs were so perfectly pressed they could have stepped straight out of a Chinese laundry. I looked down at their boots. They were broken in, but they weren't scuffed and fucked like the MPs'.

These guys were remfs. You can tell one from twenty paces, in any army, in any country in the world. No scabby boots, no sweaty T-shirts.

The only things that get worn out are their pencils and the arses of their trousers. Remfs are from command. Rear echelon motherfuckers. They wouldn't have looked out of place in Costco with baskets in their hands.

They had a buff-coloured folder that they passed between them as if they were reading our medical notes. I couldn't tell what unit they were from. Americans wear badges like the Russians wear medals. It's hard to know where to start.

The Texan broke the silence. 'We're all busy people. Let's move this along.' He sounded like a bank manager.

Jerry still wasn't quite with the programme. 'Why have we been brought here?'

The bank manager was getting a little frustrated. 'Jeral, please, don't make this hard on yourself. Just listen to what we're about to say, because it's only coming your way once.'

He pointed to me. 'You've been asking military contractors about Bosnians in Baghdad. Correct?'

What was the point of lying? 'Yes.'

'Why are these Bosnians here?'

I was racking my brain, trying to remember exactly what I'd said to Jacob. I'd leave the ayatollah part out of this conversation. 'We don't know. It just sounded like a good story. You know—'

Jerry couldn't help himself. 'We're journalists and covered the Bosnian war and I heard about a—'

The bank manager didn't bother glancing at him. 'Jeral, was I talking to you?'

'No.'

'Therefore continue, Nick.'

Thank fuck for that. Jerry would have given them chapter and verse.

'The way we saw it – Bosnians coming here, from one war-torn Muslim country to another. We covered that war, and thought, Why not see if we can get the next chapter in the story? What brings them here, that sort of thing.'

'You know their names?'

'Not a clue. That's why we're just sniffing about.'

As his mate jotted notes in the folder, he thought about what I'd said. 'You telling me you decided to just turn up and see what they had to say?' He tapped my passport on the palm of his hand. 'Don't mess me, now. Remember, you're in my world.'

'Well, OK, we thought maybe they might have something to do with the sex trade. The papers love that stuff. We heard there's a few in town.'

He smiled at me. He'd got what he was after. 'That accent of yours doesn't sound much like home to me.'

'I'm from the UK. Moved to the States a year or so ago. The date's in my passport.'

He took a breath and adopted the kind of expression you'd use if you were about to refuse an overdraft. 'Well, people, I'm going to level with you. My job is to be the clearing-house for you kinda guys. We just don't like freelancers that maybe turn out to make us look bad. What we like are stories about getting the lights back on in the city. Even better, stories about the water supply being restored to a grateful local population. What we like most of all are stories about Iraqi children being cared for in American-supplied hospitals.

'So . . .' He paused, looked at Jerry, then back at me '. . . both of you are to leave Iraq today. I don't care how you do it, but go. Be advised: if you fail to do so, the consequences of your actions could be fatal. It's a real bad world out there. Upon this subject, gentlemen,' he focused on Jerry for this one, 'I do not jest.' He levelled a finger at Jerry. 'Understand?'

'Oh, I understand. Sex trafficking's a sensitive issue, especially after the shit hitting the fan in Bosnia last year. You remember, Nick – US executives buying underage girls for playthings. Some of the fat fucks even got involved with selling them on as part of a deal. No one got prosecuted, just big payoffs to keep everyone quiet. The same corporation's now been awarded contracts here in Iraq?'

I didn't know what he was on about, but it must have been true. The two remfs didn't say a word.

'I'm right, aren't I? Well, fuck you.'

This wasn't the best way to the bank manager's heart.

'We'll go north.' I didn't just say it, I shouted it, so loud a couple of the guys by the door reacted and moved closer. 'We'll go north,' I shouted again. 'We'll drive to Turkey today.'

'Thank you, Nick. Jeral, please . . .' The Texan

pointed at Jerry's wedding ring. 'It seems you have people back home who care for you. Think about that. I'm trying to get you both out of a dangerous situation that, quite frankly, is of your own making.'

They both stood up. I kept my eyes down and watched four very clean and unscuffed boots until they disappeared behind me.

48

As he cut through my plasticuffs with a pair of scissors, the guy I'd shared a smile with spoke to the back of my head. 'You got a ride waiting.'

Rubbing our wrists, Jerry and I were escorted out into a palatial corridor. We walked past carved stone columns, under vaulted ceilings and fluted domes. If the arches hadn't been sealed off with plywood to make office space, and the walls and marble floors hadn't been covered by miles of metallic grey duct tape, wires and cables, I'd have expected Louis the Fifteenth to appear at any moment.

We approached a large pair of double doors next to a ping-pong table. Two soldiers jumped up from the ornate chairs they'd been sitting in and opened them wide.

We stepped out into the sun. I had to squint to protect my eyes. Heat bounced off the top of my head. With a soldier either side of each of us, we were guided to a Hummer and ushered into the back. This wasn't one of the MP vehicles. It belonged to Captain D. Frankenmeyer. His name was stencilled on the right-hand side of the windscreen, as if it was a jazzed-up P-reg Ford Escort. Our kit was already inside. I checked my bumbag. My passport was safe. The rest of it didn't matter, but I was happy to find the three thousand-odd dollars in twenties and smaller.

The soldier behind the wheel wasn't wearing body armour and his helmet rested on the steel hump between the front seats. There was another helmet on the spare front seat, with two rank bars. The captain it belonged to jumped in and threw on his Oakleys. As he slammed the door, I saw the very long nametag on his breast pocket. It was the Hummer's owner.

The driver threw the engine into gear and we set off past the Smiley face. Frankenmeyer swivelled round to face us. 'Kinda cool, ain't it?' If he'd been a few years younger, Frankenmeyer could have come straight from playing college football. Big shoulders, toned body, white teeth, golden tan: he should have been in films. I smiled back at him – or, rather, at the reflection of myself in his mirrored lenses. There was no point in being surly. These boys were just doing the best they could.

He pointed up at Smiley. 'You know what? We got fifteen of them painted around town before we had to pull them down. What you guys do to get people so pissed?'

Jerry took a breath and I put a hand on his arm to shut him up. 'I think we were asking the wrong sort of questions. He's a reporter.'

Frankenmeyer turned back towards the windscreen. 'We get a lot of them here. You been told to leave town today?'

I nodded.

'You're the third this week. Those guys like to keep things sweet around here. I just wish they'd do the same for us. They said we were going to be here no more than four months, period.' He punched the driver's arm. 'How long ago was that, Davers?'

Davers didn't bother to look at the captain: he was busy checking a junction left. 'Fuck, that was Christmas, sir. And I joined the National Guard for the dental plan, not this shit.'

Davers wasn't on his own. A lot of small-town America joined the National Guard for the medical insurance and education credits. Most saw the weekend training camps as a box to be ticked before they got to the real benefits. No one really expected to get sent away to war, let alone for a year or more.

That wasn't the only problem. The National Guard deployed as independent units. The guy who ran the corner store back home might now be your commanding officer on operations. Everybody was a part-timer, and that always spelt trouble for command and control, and the standard of professionalism in contact. That was why most other countries integrated their part-timers into regular units.

We passed the tank and vehicle graveyard. Off-duty soldiers mooched around in the shade of their half-bombed homes. Davers turned a corner and passed a café furnished with an assortment of tables, sofas and chairs. The original Arabic sign had been crossed out and replaced with 'Bagdad Café' in crude white paint. The Whoopee Goldberg painting on the wall wasn't much better. A couple of Hummers and AFVs were parked outside, alongside men and women drinking water and Coke, relaxing in the shade. Their body armour, helmets and M16s were piled on the ground at their feet.

'Where we going?' The fact that Frankenmeyer and the driver hadn't bothered with their body armour and we were both in one vehicle had already given me the answer, but I thought I'd ask anyway.

He wiped the sweat from his shaved blond head with both hands. 'Back gate, and that's it – end of your ride.'

'No chance of a lift back to the hotel?'

''Fraid not, man – you have to hail yourselves a taxicab!' He liked the sound of that.

The driver gulped on a can of Minute Maid with such relish it made me feel thirsty. But there was no icebox in this wagon. There wasn't even body armour on the doors, just sandbags on the floor.

We drove through the gate and turned right. The Tigris was to our left and the sandbagged sangar at the checkpoint was about two hundred metres ahead and on the river side of the road. Beyond that was the main drag, crossing the river via a big metal bridge.

The sangar looked like a square igloo built

from hundreds of sandbags. As we approached I could see the rear entrance more clearly. Inside, three, maybe four soldiers were hurrying to put their belt-kit back on. They were supposed to keep it on at all times but that was a real pain in the arse. They probably just grabbed it whenever they saw a wagon coming; I'd done the same enough times.

Traffic boomed across the bridge. Trucks, cars, motorbikes stuck behind a military convoy, everyone hooting. They knew better than to try to overtake.

A watchtower rose maybe fifty feet in the air just short of the sangar. It looked like something out of *The Great Escape*: four wooden pillars with crossed bracing and a little pillbox on top. Whoever was on stag up there wasn't protected by sandbags, which seemed strange. They'd be a sitting target for any line-of-sight weapon, whether it was an AK or an RPG.

The Hummer kicked up the dust and rattled and groaned its way from pot-hole to pot-hole, so the first I knew of the attack were the dull thuds as three or four rounds slammed into the side of the cabin.

The radio crackled. 'Contact, contact, contact!'

49

We swerved and everybody ducked. I hoped Davers wasn't ducking as much as the rest of us when he hit the gas.

Frankenmeyer fumbled about, getting his helmet on. 'Get to the checkpoint!'

Seconds later the wagon screeched to a halt by the sangar. I opened the door and pushed myself out on to the hot tarmac, checking for Jerry. 'Get inside!'

The fire was coming in from the other side of the river. Soldiers poured out of the sangar, heading for the bank. Jerry slowed up and tried to pull the camera out of his bumbag.

'For fuck's sake, come on!'

The Americans opened up from behind a three-foot-thick wall as more rounds poured in from across the water, maybe three hundred metres away; long, sustained bursts, then individual shots. I could make out the distinctive heavy crack of the AKs' 7.62, but couldn't see any muzzle flashes coming from the jumble of six- or seven-storey tower blocks and concrete squares.

Jerry was still fucking about behind me, trying to get his camera working. I ran back, grabbed him and dragged him into the sangar. I saw immediately why the boys had needed to get out into the open: unbelievably, the place had been built without firing ports overlooking the water. They only covered the road to the bridge with a .50 cal.

For some reason, the floor was sandbagged. We threw ourselves flat as a couple of rounds thumped into the ones around the entrance. I looked out at the chaos along our side of the riverbank. The squaddie who'd been at the top of the watchtower was dropping down like a submariner from a conning tower. If there'd been a fireman's pole they'd have been on it.

Frankenmeyer was trying to take control. 'Can you see 'em? Can you see 'em?'

It didn't matter: everybody seemed to be cabbying away regardless. The squaddie reached the bottom of the ladder. Frankenmeyer shouted, pointing to the sangar, 'Get the fifty! Get the fifty!'

Jerry had his bumbag open. 'Bastards! They've taken my memory cards!' He scrabbled in his jeans for replacements as more rounds thwacked into the sandbags. The .50 cal was above him, its barrel facing the main, with the legs of the tripod straddling the firing port. It would have been useless even if it had been pointing the right way. The tripod was unsupported; it should have been weighted down with sandbags. If they

241

started firing it, it would bounce all over the place and fall off the sill.

The soldier from the watchtower was coming full pelt towards the sangar, head down, M16 in hand. Her brown hair was long and had been up in a bun, but had now mostly fallen across her face and neck. There was a guy, a zit-faced nineteen-year-old, hot on her heels. I moved out of their way as they plunged through the entrance, pouring sweat, kicking Jerry's camera out of his hands, as more bursts hit the sangar and the Hummer. She yelled at Zit-face as they tried to lift the .50 cal at the same time as shouldering their own weapons. It wasn't going to happen: the slings weren't slack enough to fit over their helmets.

I wanted these two out of here. They were flapping; their barrels banged together as they fucked about and there were too many made-ready weapons flying about in this tight space for my liking. 'Cradle your weapons, hold the fifty by the tripod. Get the fucking thing out there!'

More rounds thudded into the sandbags and they flinched as they dragged out the heavy weapon, one holding the barrel, the other the tripod. They half ran, half stumbled with it towards the riverbank, the belt of thirty or so rounds on the weapon dragging behind them in the sand.

The command radio in the sangar was going apeshit. Everybody was being stood to. Jerry was still reloading, cursing the guys who'd dared to confiscate his precious cards.

I watched them rigging the .50 cal. Hadn't they ever fired one of these things? They'd done their usual trick with the tripod legs straddling the wall.

I turned to Jerry as another barrage of rounds headed our way. He was lying on his side, camera pointing across the river like a weapon.

'Keep an eye on the .50. When that fucker starts firing you're going to get a great picture!'

50

A stream of tracer shot high over our heads. Now and again I saw a weapon flash inside a building.

The .50 cal responded with short bursts, its one-in-four tracer rounds curving just slightly over the river before making splash marks on the concrete and spinning away. The Humvee took another couple of rounds and so did the sangar. Whoever was manning the .50 cal was screaming and shouting, the voice so high-pitched I couldn't tell if it was male or female. 'Fuck you, fuck you, fuck you!'

The bursts got longer and the tracer started to clear the lower buildings. The tripod was moving backwards and the barrel was getting higher and higher. The gunner didn't seem to notice. He or she was too far gone.

Jerry kept his finger on the button. There was nothing I could do and, besides, this wasn't a war I was getting paid to join. I looked around and spotted a white polystyrene cool-box. Small half-litre bottles of water floated in melting ice.

I took two and held one out for Jerry. He waved it away. He had bigger things on his mind. He got to his feet and crouched in the sangar entrance, as if he was about to make a run for it. I grabbed hold of him. Tracked vehicles rumbled out of the camp gate. 'Whoa, whoa. We're not here for that. We're off to Turkey tonight, remember?'

Any reply he might have made was drowned by the roar of rotor blades, very low, coming from the bridge.

The .50 fired again, and so did an AFV moving up the road. Its turret gunner had a more stable platform and was getting rounds on target.

I watched the helicopter swoop towards the riverbank, heading straight over the precariously balanced .50.

'It's going to get hit! Get the picture!'

The .50 fired and there was a groaning sound, like the rolling of massive chains on a drum. The helicopter must have been at its very limits as the pilot took evasive action.

I looked out of the firing port. It had banked hard right, back over the bridge. Traffic was still crossing. The .50 cal was still firing, at least seventy degrees into the air. The gunner probably didn't have a clue how close he'd come to fucking up big-time.

Frankenmeyer was running around the team, screaming at the top of his voice. 'Stop, stop, stop!'

The radio burst back into life. 'Red Dragon four-one, we've got one hundred and fifty in contact. Repeat, that's one-five-zero *hajis*!'

Same as gooks for the Viet Cong, I supposed. It never took an army long to get derogatory about their enemies.

Jerry spun round. 'Let's get over there and have a look!'

I threw the water bottle at him. 'Dickhead, do you really think there's a hundred and fifty over there?'

He gulped from the bottle, letting the water pour down the side of his mouth. His eyes were glued to the chaos outside.

The attack seemed to have stopped. The loudest noises now came from the traffic and the command radio.

I looked out through the door. The soldiers behind the wall were getting to their feet, cheering with relief that no one had been hit. Now they could concentrate their energies on honing it into a good war story to tell the folks back home.

I took a swig of water. It was boiling in here and the sweat poured down my face. No wonder the guys had taken their belt-kit off.

There was a box of muesli energy bars in the corner and I helped myself to a hot, soggy blueberry one as about a dozen AFVs thundered past at warp speed to get over the bridge and in among the AK guys. They would have melted into the city by now.

I munched as Jerry put away his camera and zipped up the bumbag, then tipped the rest of his water over his head and down the back of his neck.

'You weren't serious about heading north, were you?'

The soldiers outside were shouting their versions of the contact to each other now, all claiming they'd made hits. Jerry dropped his empty bottle on to the sandbags. I stared at him as he packed his camera. 'You soft in the head or something? Those boys back there weren't fucking about. This isn't one you can stick your fingers up at. Fuck the pictures. Let's just bin it, and get to Turkey. All right?'

He didn't look up at me, just over-concentrated on packing his kit. 'I'm staying. It's really important to get to Nuhanovic. I mean, this guy's so cool, everywhere he walks there's a draught.'

The zip got closed on his bumbag.

'Come on, Nick, there must be a million things you want to ask him. I know there are, you're interested in him. Your face told me back in DC. I knew you were going to come. Seriously. Think about it. Wouldn't you want to ask him stuff?'

I threw my empty bottle at him. 'You're talking bollocks. But I'll stay with you.'

He grinned.

'We'll have to disappear, like Nuhanovic and the boys the other side of the river.'

'Booking yourself a few rapid tanning treatments?'

'No need.' I started to pull myself up off the sandbags. 'There's Rob.'

51

It took a while, but Jerry eventually managed to flag down a rusting Passat taxi on the main. The driver was in his fifties and spoke perfect English. He said he used to be a chemist until the sanctions bit and the economy started to collapse.

The al-Hamra was only a ten-minute ride away, and would be easy to spot from the main. Stark white and six or seven storeys high, it had a billboard on the roof that was big enough to read from several blocks away.

We turned off the dual carriageway and down a side road, past neat, concrete middle-class homes set in small green gardens. Security was more lax here than round the Palestine. A steel barrier blocked our route, manned by a solitary Iraqi with an AK in one hand and a cigarette in the other. Kids did wheelies on their bikes or ran in and out of the surrounding houses. A shop opposite sold fruit, bottles of water, buckets and mops.

The guard sauntered across and held the barrier open as we drove through. The pot-holed drive ran in a semicircle to the front of the hotel, which was surrounded by a high concrete wall. White soldiers with Australian flags on their uniforms patrolled in its shade, their Steyr assault weapons looking like something out of a sci-fi movie. I didn't have a clue what they were doing here, and they probably didn't either. They watched from behind their Oakleys as we got out of the cab.

A few fixers hung around outside the main entrance, hassling what I guessed was a news crew unloading alloy boxes and rolls of cables from three 4x4s. Inside the wagons I could see mixing consoles, laptops and satellite-phone sets. Two of the crew had been injured. One had fresh bandages around his arm. Another, the German gun stud, had one round his head. A wounded reporter? He was going to score big-time when he got back home.

Jerry gave the driver a five-dollar bill and we walked through the glass doors into reception. The lobby area was a lot smaller than the Palestine's, the ceilings lower. Wood veneer was still king, however, and a glass cabinet displayed the same kind of goods for sale, everything from packs of cards of the fifty-two most wanted, to Saddam watches and toothbrushes.

Jerry kept out of the way while I went up to the desk, which was manned by an Iraqi who smelt heavily of cologne and seemed more interested in his ledger than asking me if I needed help. A young woman was sorting out room keys behind him. I wondered if they were related. This had the feeling of a family hotel; they certainly had the same nose and eyes combo.

The news crew came in with their gear and headed straight for the lift, talking low and slow German. Just beyond, a pair of glass doors opened out on to a concrete terrace and I caught a glimpse of the end of a swimming-pool. Sunlight danced on the water. Danny Connor would have liked it here.

The young woman finished with the keys and looked up, her face creased by a big smile. She had long black shiny hair, parted in the centre, dark red lipstick and black eye-liner. 'Good day. Can I help you?' Her English was perfect; in fact, better than mine.

'I hope you can. I'm looking for Mr Robert Newman. He's staying here.'

She smiled and looked down at the book. They did have a PC but what was the point of using it when the power kept shutting down?

'He may be with a smaller man with thick black hair,' I added. 'He's a tall white guy with dark wavy hair and a big nose. Checked in yesterday?'

She flicked a page, trying not to smile too much at my powers of description. She looked beautiful in her crisp white blouse and black trousers, and it made me think of the bride. I wondered if she was still alive.

'Please, one moment.' She picked up a phone and tapped three digits. The Germans were back for a second load.

She put the phone down. 'Mr Newman is not in his room.'

'Never mind. We'll wait by the pool, if that's all right. Could you send someone to tell me when he comes in, or can you tell him someone's here for him?'

'Of course, of course.'

I headed for the doors near the lift. Jerry followed, and as we stepped outside we were slapped in the face again by a wall of heat.

The garden was another little oasis in the midst of Baghdad's chaos. Immediately ahead of us was an eating area with tables and chairs. The pool was down some steps to our left, its water turned blue by the tiling. Plastic sun-loungers, chairs and tables were dotted round the edge, under large blue canvas parasols that had been bleached by the sun.

Australian squaddies were on stag here too. One was in the shade of the perimeter wall. The old-style barbed wire had been unrolled along the top. The other guy was higher up, at the edge of the eating area.

We went down the steps and headed for the far end of the pool. It was still fairly early, and it looked as if there was some decent shade to be had at the tables. A few people were having a swim, the rest were lying under parasols. Most of them were white, but a few Iraqis sat sipping iced tea and ogling the women.

Gunfire rattled in the distance, maybe half a K away. The Australian in the shade got on his radio to report it. We walked past two women stretched out on their loungers, both reading chick-lit paperbacks as they hoovered up their morning dose of skin cancer. I could smell their sun cream.

The Australian was standing against the wall, paying a bit more attention to the sun-worshippers than he was to us. As we passed I gave him a big grin. 'War's hell, innit?'

I got a big smile back as we took a vacant table, and the moment his mouth opened it was obvious he wore dentures, only not during ops. Maybe he didn't want them damaged, or he'd sold them to an Iraqi.

We would stay in the shade here until the sun got higher, but there was another reason I wanted my back to the wall. I didn't want to miss Rob's turning to.

52

The menu was anchored beneath an ashtray. I picked it up as Jerry got out the phone.

'I'm gonna go and make a call to Renee.'

'Thought you called this morning?'

'Yeah, well, I did. But she was totally freaked out. Even more now, if she's seen the news. I just want to calm her down a little.'

'Better make this the last call for a while. The CPA might be waiting to see where that thing gets used again, and we're supposed to have left.'

He walked back to the steps and up on to the terrace. I lost sight of him as he rounded the corner.

People floated in and out of the door to Reception. I kept an eye out for Rob while checking the menu, and waited for the guy in the crumpled white shirt to come over with his little round tray. I wondered if he'd mind if I went in the pool wearing my very smelly and saggy boxers. A few birds competed briefly with the distant rumble of traffic.

A white guy in shorts with a towel over his shoulder sauntered past the two sun-worshippers, stopped, went back and settled himself on a chair next to them. He was a big lad, lots of brown hair brushed back. The moment he started speaking I could tell this Brit was a bit pleased with himself. He worked in documentaries, apparently. 'Yeah, been on a shoot this morning, actually – firefight just outside town.' He was the cameraman. Been in Baghdad a few days; came here straight from Cape Town. Couldn't work out which city was hotter. He was going to order a drink – did they want one? I didn't know what was funnier, his chat-up lines or that he'd been holding in his belly the whole time he'd been speaking.

The Australian squaddie looked on enviously. He must have been weighing up the chances of swapping a rifle for a TV camera. I was feeling the same way.

The waiter had been on his way to me but got waylaid by Cecil B. de Mille. I'd never had much restaurant presence, either. Maybe I didn't look the tipping kind.

I took off my greasy sun-gigs and gave them a wipe as I listened to their conversation – or, rather, his monologue. He'd worked with them all, you know – Simpson, Adie, Attenborough. He was interrupted when, from maybe a hundred metres away, either a car backfired or there was a single gunshot.

I was thirsty. I spotted another crumpled white shirt up on the terrace and got up. I walked past the Aussie and the two women, who'd abandoned their books to listen to their new friend. Shit, I wished I could waffle like that. They weren't good-looking, but that didn't seem to matter in this town. If you were young, white and had a pulse, you'd be scoring like a super-model. No wonder the Balkan boys were in town.

I managed to catch the waiter's eye by waving like a lunatic, showed him where I was sitting, then started back. Jerry soon followed. He didn't look happy.

'Everything all right, mate?' I held out my hand for the phone as he sort of nodded. 'I think I'll make one.'

'She saw the news and got totally hyped about me staying.'

Family shit: best keep out of it. Back in the shade, I pressed number history, but nothing was stored. Even the last number dialled had been cleared. Good skills.

'I hope you're clearing the history every time.' I did the whole pretend-dialling bit and held it to my ear.

'Yep. I don't know if those pinheads at the camp checked it, but they'd have got zip.'

I closed the phone down. 'No answer. Shame. It's my mum's birthday.'

As I watched the to-ing and fro-ing about the pool I tried to remember her birthday, or even how old she was. It wouldn't come to me. I'd sort of lost interest in that kind of thing when she lost interest in mine, when I was ten. My last birthday present was my first ever 99 ice-cream. The deal was me not saying anything to the school about the bruises on my neck and cheek.

My mum had been called in to explain. Was Nicholas being beaten at home? The ice-cream worked: I shut up as she told them how I'd fallen down the stairs. I nodded in agreement instead of saying her nice new husband had filled me in because I'd asked for a 99 when the ice-cream van came into the estate. Whatever. At least she'd come in handy for an excuse to see who Jerry had been calling.

The waiter turned up with two cans of cold Coke. Either he was clairvoyant, or I was fluent in Iraqi sign language. Or maybe this was all they stocked. He put them on the table and showed the kind of smile that could have done with renting the Aussie's teeth.

Jerry pulled back on his can and took two very thirsty gulps.

I picked up the menu before the waiter had time to decide he had better customers elsewhere. 'I'll have some potato fingers and a couple of bread rolls.'

'Yes, sir. Sure, sure, sure.' He didn't write it down, which was always a worry. It normally meant he wouldn't come back, or if he did, it would be with a boiled egg.

Jerry was checking his camera gear. 'I'll have whatever you're having, and another Coke.'

I looked up at the crumpled shirt. 'Two more Cokes, two potato fingers and tons of bread.

These soldiers here, do you know if they're allowed drinks?'

He didn't seem too sure.

'Give them a Coke each, will you? And make sure they're cold ones.' I handed the waiter eight dollars as Cecil managed to make the women laugh. Bastard.

Jerry was obsessing round his lenses with a little brush. 'You're getting generous in your old age.'

'Must be thirsty work listening to that bloke's bullshit all day.' I sat back in the chair and enjoyed the shade a while. I might even have dropped off for a minute or two.

53

'Sir?'

Crumply Shirt was back with the bowls of chips and bread rolls.

I showed Jerry the finer points of making a buttie with undercooked chips and butter so hot it had turned to oil. There was still no sign of Rob.

The place was filling up. One white guy stood out. He was sitting with another white guy and a couple of locals, all drinking tea from little glasses. His crewcut was just cropping out to show the grey on the sides. His face was peppered with small scars, as if he'd been blasted with fine shrapnel. Stubble only grew where the skin wasn't marked. But what made him difficult to ignore was that he was missing the little and ring fingers of his right hand.

Jerry had spotted him too. He leaned forward, grabbing some more bread out of the bowl. 'Bosnian Muslim? What you reckon?'

'Dunno, can't hear him properly.'

Jerry got up, still chewing a chip.

He skirted the two women, and went on past Three Fingers' table. A couple of paces further on he stopped, turned back, smiled and started talking to the four men.

He certainly looked old enough to have been captured by Mladic's mates. Cutting those two fingers off a prisoner really gave them a buzz because it left the hand in a Serb salute, sort of a Boy Scout thing.

The conversation lasted less than a minute. It didn't look promising. Jerry moved on to Reception, maybe going for a piss. It had to look like he was passing for a purpose.

The guys finished their tea and left before Jerry came back and helped himself to the two remaining chips.

'What you say?'

He sprinkled salt over the last one. 'He didn't speak English, but the other guy did a little. I just said I heard him talk, and wondered if he knew my old friend Hasan who I'd heard was in town. "I know it's a long shot but I'd really like to catch up with him." That kind of thing. But jack shit, man.'

I dipped a finger into a puddle of salt and chip grease on the table. 'What you reckon? Girl power? We got Muslims at this place, Serbs at the Palestine. We could have a war inside a war soon over who runs the knocking shops.'

Four cans of Coke and another round of chips later, the sun was a lot higher and hotter, and we were about to be in the firing line. I stood up and raised the parasol. Most people had drifted away from the swimming-pool and gone indoors.

'Midday.' Jerry was looking at his watch.

'Well, I guess I'm still an Englishman.' I sat back down and moved my chair a little to get right under the canvas with Jerry. 'So I guess that makes you the mad dog.'

I saw movement up by the doors. Rob stepped out on to the terrace, AK in hand. He squinted as he looked around for us.

'Heads up, mate, here we go.'

I didn't want him to come over to us. We'd be within earshot of the Australian, who was now standing in the shade of a big sheet of cardboard rigged up in the corner where the external wall met the building.

We got to him as he was coming down the steps. We shook hands. 'I need a favour.'

'Haven't got that much time, mate. I'm off again soon.' He paused. 'But what's all this about me having a big nose?'

He was wearing exactly the same clothes as yesterday, only now his shirt-tails were hanging out. They were probably covering a pistol in his jeans. His back and armpits were soaked. Sweat covered his face and chest.

Jerry shook his hand. 'I saw you at the party last night.'

'Yeah.' Rob turned back to me. He didn't know Jerry, so why talk to him? It's just how it is.

'Tell you what, let's go up.'

'Which floor?'

'First.'

Of course. I bet the crumpled shirts came to him without being asked as well.

A news crew, laden with cameras, cables and body armour, was waiting by the lifts, so Rob turned right for the stairs. 'I heard the Palestine got hit this morning.'

'Yeah, RPGs. Danny Connor's dead.'

'That's a shame.' His tone was matter-of-fact. 'At least his boy's a bit older.'

'Yeah. Nineteen, at university.'

'I hope he sorted his pension.'

'Connor? As if.'

And that was it, subject closed. There never was too much said about these things.

We got to the first floor and turned down a narrow corridor. The walls were covered with the same lumpy concrete finish as the Palestine, and painted white.

'What are the Aussies doing here?'

'Their consulate's just behind the hotel. They're here to make sure no one uses the terrace as a mortar baseplate. It's good for us because there's always a presence.'

We'd got to his door, and I followed Jerry into what was more like a small apartment than a hotel room. It didn't have air-conditioning, but it had everything else. A seating area with two foam settees with flowery-patterned nylon covers. A coffee table. The obligatory plastic-veneer TV, some kitchen units, a sink, a little Belling cooker and a kettle.

We dumped our kit and headed over to the settees. Jerry and I shared one, sitting with our backs to the wall of what I guessed was the bed-room. I could see a bathroom through the other open door.

Rob came and dropped his keys and AK on the worktop, then pulled the pistol from his jeans and placed it alongside them. 'Brew?'

We both asked for coffee and watched as he filled the kettle with bottled water. There was a little balcony, no more than a metre wide, the other side of french windows. Only one floor up, there wouldn't be much to look at anyway.

Rob messed with mugs and spoons and stuff, waiting for me to get explaining.

'Listen, mate, we need your help. We got our-selves lifted by the military this morning. They wanted to know why we've been asking about the Bosnians. They're flapping in case it turns out to be a bad story for them.'

Rob leaned against the kitchen unit, watching us silently as he unscrewed a small jar of Nescafé.

'They want us out of town – like, yesterday. I said we'd go north to Turkey. But we want to stay. Cards on the table, mate. We need a place to hide, maybe five days max, while we try to find this guy. It's putting you at risk, but we can't check in anywhere, and it's not as if we can doss on a bench. Even if I put on a bit of boot polish I'm not going to last long out there, am I?'

Rob over-concentrated on spooning Nescafé into multi-patterned mugs. 'Why are they pissed off? You mention Nuhanovic?'

'Nah, Jerry reckons they think we're trying to dig some dirt on reconstruction contracts.'

The kettle clicked and he poured boiling water into the mugs. 'I'm just going to ditch this.' He started unbuttoning his sweaty shirt as he headed for the bedroom.

Jerry wasn't happy with my intro. 'Why are you telling him all that? He might say no. Then what?'

I got closer, almost in his ear. 'If he's going to hide us he deserves to know what's going on. He's OK. Let me do the talking – I know him.'

Rob came back, pulling a faded blue T-shirt over his head. An armoured vehicle rumbled out on the main. A helicopter flew past, quite high. He said nothing as he tipped condensed milk into the coffees, gave them a stir, and brought the mugs over with a bowl of sugar. Then he sat down opposite us and took a deep breath. 'Nuhanovic is quite an elusive fucker, isn't he?'

54

Rob took a sip of his brew. 'Fixing an audience with Saddam might be easier.' He took a bigger one, then rested the mug on his thigh. His eyes were fixed on mine. 'We're looking for Nuhanovic as well.'

Jerry jumped in without an invitation. 'You know where he is?'

Rob glared. 'If we did, we wouldn't be looking, would we?'

It wasn't love at first sight.

'Let him finish, Jerry.' I got back to Rob. 'Why's he so hard to find, if all he's doing is spreading the good news?'

He put his mug down on the ring-stained table. 'Because every man and his dog wants to stop him. Unity is strength. Strength is trouble for everyone. He knows he's a target.'

Jerry was nodding eagerly, trying to join the club. 'That's why no one's managed to get to him in Bosnia. Baghdad's our best chance.'

Rob ignored him.

'Unity?' I kept Rob's attention. 'He must be quite a guy.'

Rob nodded. 'He's showing the people that you don't need missiles to win battles: you can use the coins in your pockets. If you do it together, you can have every government and corporation on their knees.'

Rob's eyes stayed fixed on mine, completely blanking Jerry. 'You hear about the Coke boycott in Pakistan? He showed the locals how they could wage cola wars instead of real ones.'

Jerry opened his mouth to speak, but I got in quicker. 'How did he do it?'

'First, he convinced businesses to sell Zam Zam, Mecca, all the Muslim brands. Then he preached his message.' He lifted a finger. 'To fight back against American imperialism, they didn't have to load their weapons, just their fridges. And it's working. Whenever a kid buys a bottle of Muslim-owned cola he knows a percentage of the profits goes to Islamic charities, not to some fat stockholder in New York.' He smiled. 'There are some great slogans. "Liberate Your Taste." "Don't drink stupid, drink committed." Every bottle's a protest – two fingers to the US.'

The windows rattled as some helis came in low and fucked about just above the building. The pilots were probably eyeing up the women on the sun-loungers. Rob waited for them to leave, then got back to the story.

'A couple of provinces in Pakistan have now even banned Coca-Cola altogether. Imagine where this could lead – if Nuhanovic does the same with electrical goods, cars, food, clothes. It's got people flapping. Not just corporations, but governments. Our man is a cancer that needs to be cut out before it can spread.'

'And what do you want with him?'

Rob picked up his keys. 'Look, I need to go down and get some cold ones. You coming, Nick?'

I got to my feet. Jerry stayed where he was. He was learning, slowly.

55

We took the stairs again. At the bottom, we went through the glass doors and on to the terrace. Within seconds, Rob was ordering some water from a crumpled shirt who'd appeared from nowhere. I watched two others trying to fish out a parasol the helis had blown into the pool.

We moved out of earshot of the Aussie as the crumpled shirts resorted to brooms and a lot of Arabic curses.

'I don't mind you both staying, but I'll have to get the OK from my man and tell him what's going on with you two. He's too good a guy to be kept in the dark.'

'We'll keep out of the way, whatever.'

The Aussies swapped positions, probably to relieve the boredom.

'You could be still out on your arse. I'll vouch for you, but if my man says no, there's nothing I can do about it. '

'Fair one.' The heat was unbearable. 'There's something I want to tell you.' I nodded over to a patch of shade near the building. 'Jerry doesn't realize this, but I know Nuhanovic – well, sort of. You remember the Mladic Paveway job? It was me you put the cache in for. Nuhanovic was there.'

Rob listened intently as I told him about that day, how Nuhanovic had fronted up to Mladic and saved so many people. Then I told him about Zina, and about the general surviving because Sarajevo had called off the strike. 'I don't give a fuck about Jerry's picture any more – never did.' I had just discovered something, and it had taken me by surprise. 'I want to meet him for myself.'

The waiter reappeared. Rob took a bottle for himself and handed me the tray. He liked the idea. 'I've got to go and talk to my man.' He headed for the glass doors.

'If you find him, I wouldn't mind being there.'

He turned, the bottle at his lips. 'Things might work out a lot better than just meeting him – if you're up for it.'

That was the second time he'd talked as if he was some game-show host. 'What the fuck are you on about? Start tree-hugging and stop drinking Coke?'

'You'll find out soon enough. We're leaving in about thirty, meeting someone who might know where he is. Maybe my man will let you tag along so he can explain exactly what I'm talking about. I'm just going to grab some kit, and have a word with him. See you here in a bit?'

He disappeared into the lobby.

56

Rather than bake outside I waited in Reception, sipping occasionally from the not-so-cold symbol of American imperialism I'd bought. Canned in Belgium, with information in French and what looked like Greek, it promoted the 2002 World Cup in Japan.

It was quiet; there was no one around apart from the two behind the desk. They exchanged the odd sentence in Arabic, and there was a clink now and again of tea-glasses on saucers as the serving staff made themselves sound busy at the back.

I sat there thinking about these Muslim colas. There were nearly a billion and a half Muslims, and it was the world's fastest-growing religion. No wonder the corporations were getting jumpy.

Fifteen minutes went by. Finally Rob came downstairs. He had a pistol on his belt, and the AK in his hands had a mag on.

'Jerry OK?' I asked. I put the Coke down on the floor by my foot, not too sure how Rob would react to the red can.

'He was on the phone – but shut down when I came in. Big secret?'

'He's got a source in Washington who thinks he knows where Nuhanovic might be.'

Rob sat down next to me. 'I've got some good news. You're staying. And my man wants to talk.'

'About Nuhanovic?'

'About work. Listen, I vouched for you, explained your connection with Nuhanovic. He liked that. If my man's plan works, people like us are going to be needed back in Uzbekistan. If he likes you, there could be a job going. I'm not talking about this circuit crap. We don't need knuckle-draggers with no commitment. This will be doing something good. Don't you want to do that?'

'Sort of. Depends on your view of good, I suppose.'

'Have you been to the hospitals here?'

I bent down for the can, shaking my head. He saw it anyway.

'We went this morning. There's kids missing arms and legs. Some have watched their whole families being wiped out. My man is organizing medical supplies. Crazy, isn't it? A poor relation like Uzbekistan sending supplies to an even poorer one. Do you know why he's having to do that?'

I could imagine, but let him carry on anyway.

'Because there's still nothing decent coming from the CPA, and most of what does gets stolen anyway.' Rob was pretty worked up. He was having a pool-party flashback. 'Look out there.' He pointed through the door, towards the terrace. 'Look at that poor fucker.' The Aussie squaddie was taking off his helmet to wipe the sweat from his shaven head with a heavily tattooed forearm. 'Like I said, rich kids don't fight wars. There's no rich kids in that hospital. It's just the poor on both sides that get fucked over. My man wants Nuhanovic to stop all this shit happening in Uzbekistan.'

'How's he going to do that?'

'He'll tell you. If you guys like each other, you could come back with us. We'll even take Jerry off your hands, drop him off in Turkey for you. Interested?'

Of course I was: if something was good enough for Rob it was good enough for me. Besides, the grass is always greener; except there wasn't any grass. I took a swig of black stuff. 'Maybe.'

He smiled. Perhaps he wanted someone he knew working alongside him. Perhaps he wanted to cure me of my Coke habit. 'We're leaving in about fifteen. I'm going to clear the vehicle, then pick up my man. Remember, Nick, I've vouched for you so don't fuck up. Just listen to what he has to say.'

Rob handed me the key and headed for the doors. I went back upstairs. The door to the balcony was open. Jerry was on the floor.

'What the fuck are you doing down there?'

'Just testing the camera, getting some low light shots.'

I looked down. Rob was half underneath a

battered, dust-covered blue BMW 3 Series with the bonnet up, checking for any devices.

'What you call DC for?'

'What?'

'I said not to use it again. You know what could happen.'

'I know, sorry, but I thought I'd call one last time. See if he had anything.'

'And?'

'Nah, not a thing.' He got up and took a bottle from the tray. 'Life here's a constant cycle of hot drinks followed by cold ones, isn't it?'

'You tell him there's no more calls from you now?'

He nodded as I closed the balcony doors. His Adam's apple moved up and down as he got the fluid into him.

We sat and I took a couple of mouthfuls myself then brought Jerry up to speed. 'Rob cleared it with his boss. We can stay.'

'You get his name?'

'Didn't ask. Listen, I'm going to see Rob down-stairs again in a few. I might be going with them to meet someone – sounds like a friend of a friend.'

Jerry was up and heading towards his kit.

'Just me, mate. That's the way he wants it.'

He held the bumbag in one hand and the camera in the other. 'I should be there, Nick.'

'Hey, we're hiding from the fucking US Army, remember? We can't call your source again, and we're fucked without Rob. Let's hold tight here and see if these guys can find him. If so, that's when we talk to them about the picture.'

'And if they don't?'

'Then you don't get it and we all go home. Simple.'

It wasn't that simple for me any more, and I'd known it the moment I started telling Rob about that day at the cement factory. I really wanted to meet this guy. I didn't know what I'd say if I met him, but that didn't matter. I'd think of something.

I picked my sun-gigs off the coffee-table and gave them a wipe with my shirt-tail. Jerry still looked pissed off. 'Look, what does it matter?' I said. 'As long as we get the right result.'

'What if you get to him tonight? I should be there.'

I shrugged and slid the glass door shut. 'Jerry, it's not open for discussion. You stay here, don't go outside, don't get yourself seen. We're supposed to have left for Turkey, remember?'

'OK, OK.' He wasn't really listening.

I left the room, made sure my bumbag was done up securely, and took the stairs. Baby-G said it was 17:46.

57

I'd only seen him briefly, but I recognized the Uzbek – I supposed that was what they were called – at once. He was sitting in the lobby reading the waffle on my empty Coke can. Maybe he was a football fan.

He stood up as he saw me, and smiled. After seeing Nuhanovic close up in 'Chetnik Mama', and now looking at this man more closely than I had on the flight, I realized they'd been part of the same job lot. He was slightly built, maybe five six, and in need of a few fish-and-chip suppers. He was wearing a black linen suit, white shirt and blue Kevlar with a ceramic plate covering his chest. It was a wonder he could support the weight.

I went straight over and shook a small, bony hand. 'Hello, I'm Nick.'

His teeth were perfect behind the big smile, his eyes green and clear. Close up his skin was almost translucent; there wasn't a crease. It was difficult to work out how old he was. 'I know.' Still smiling, he motioned towards the main entrance. 'Shall we?' His accent was like a 1950s BBC newsreader's.

As we stepped into the heat I saw the Beemer, Rob at the wheel, wraparounds shielding his eyes. We both put our sun-gigs on. The windows were up; I hoped that meant the air was running.

The Uzbek opened the rear door and ushered me inside. Coolish air hit me. I glanced up just before my head disappeared under the roof and I could see the balcony doors were open again. There was a brief flash of light. Jerry was on the balcony. He was a professional, he understood the dangers, and it pissed me off that he wasn't doing as he was told.

Rob's boss got in beside me and closed the door. Rob's semi-automatic was tucked under his right thigh. He wore no body armour. I could see it in front of me, tucked into the right passenger footwell along with the AK. Maybe he was trying to blend in a little with the outside world as we drove around – not that it was going to happen unless he acquired a serious suntan before we hit the main.

I was going to have to grip Jerry when I got back. For all I knew, I might be in one of his pictures now and I didn't like that. Never had done. I didn't even like showing my passport at Immigration.

58

The scaffold bar acting as a barrier was lifted by the bored local on stag. Two Aussie infantry in the shade of a tree looked just as uninterested.

Nothing was said until we got to the main, where we had to wait for a convoy of tanks and AFVs to pass. One of the tanks looked like it had been attacked very recently. The side facing us was scorched all the way up to the turret. The Bergens and other kit strapped to the outside were burnt to a crisp, and anything plastic had melted and stuck to the steel.

'My name is Benzil.' He spoke calmly and quietly.

I smiled politely.

'While we all waited for the flight from Amman – wasn't that a wait? – Robert told me some quite amusing stories of your younger days in the army.' He leaned forward and tapped his shoulder. 'Isn't that so, Robert?'

Rob nodded and smiled in the rear-view mirror as we turned right to merge with the main. Even with all the dust covering the windows, a bunch of locals did double-takes. Three whites in a car wasn't an everyday sight. Doesn't matter if you're white, black, brown or yellow, if you're where you don't belong, there's always someone wanting to know what the fuck you're up to.

Benzil's head was turned towards me, but I couldn't make out where his eyes were behind his gigs. Pleasantries over, he was ready to get down to business. 'Robert has explained the situation in our country to you, and that we are here, just like you, to find Mr Nuhanovic. What I would now like to tell you is the rest of our story, including where Mr Nuhanovic, and you, if you wish, fit into it. I hope you will find it illuminating, so please indulge me.'

I made the right signs.

'Thank you.' He adjusted his jacket and body armour. 'These are dangerous times, Nick. What is happening in Iraq today could be just the beginning of an epidemic that will spread far beyond the Middle East. Including my own country.'

The car slowed, then came to a complete halt in snarled traffic. Horns blasted and drivers shouted. A girl of six or seven, covered in dust, walked the line of equally dust-covered cars, begging. Even in a country this fucked-up, people still managed to pass her a few pictures of Saddam pointing at whatever.

Benzil had turned his head and watched the child walk the line of vehicles.

'You're a Muslim?'

He smiled, eyes still fixed on the beggar. 'In spirit.' He sighed deeply as he looked out on the chaos around us. 'I am Jewish.' No wonder he was keeping a low profile round here. I binned the fleeting thought that he could have been Nuhanovic's brother.

'Most in my country are Muslim, but they are oppressed. We all are.' Benzil turned back to me and lowered his gigs. 'And, as always in these matters, it is the ordinary people who suffer. Ask Robert, he knows it to be true.'

He caught my eye in the rear-view again. 'For now, it's just the militants who're pissed off and doing something about it.'

Benzil gave a rueful little smile. 'Last week we experienced the worst violence in our short history as an independent country. There were gun battles lasting hours between the police and the militants. More than forty people were killed in bomb attacks.' He shook his head sadly. 'Miserable poverty combined with a total lack of solidarity is producing a social vacuum,' he said, 'and it's this vacuum that militant Islam is filling. If it goes on like this, one fine day ordinary people will simply pick up their weapons and go crazy. That's where Mr Nuhanovic fits into our story. He will stop that happening.'

'You're hoping he can repeat what I hear he's achieved in Bosnia?'

Benzil opened his hands. 'Why not? After that war, the political parties still tried to play the same old hate cards but, thanks largely to Mr

Nuhanovic, men of all faiths have learned that the only stable future for the country lies in unity. Many powerful people hate him for it, but they have been forced to adapt. We have been there and seen it with our own eyes, haven't we, Robert?'

'Yep, now he's here and in Pakistan. That's all good news for them. But we need him in Uzbekistan.' He was too busy trying to edge the car forwards to look back at me.

Benzil nodded in agreement. 'The truth is that because Mr Nuhanovic has helped build Bosnia into a functional state, it has been able to join the outside world. Unity among former enemies for the greater good. Quite an appealing concept, don't you think?'

'And he's hoping to do the same in Iraq?'

'In the entire Muslim world, Nick. His biggest problem, the biggest block to progress, is there's so much vested interest in dysfunctionality. It suits the outside world to see divisions. Divide and rule, one of history's major lessons.' Benzil smiled wryly as he tapped on his window. 'That little girl knows more than all the Iraqi faction leaders put together.'

59

Rob powered down his window and gave her two 250-dinar notes, about a dollar twenty. Light streamed into the car through the haze of the bug-stained windscreen. The sun was getting lower and would be dropping behind the building any minute. The air-conditioner worked overtime as we all started to get sticky.

'What Mr Nuhanovic is trying to encourage people to do, Nick, is to retake control of their own destinies from those who think they have the right to dictate to other cultures.'

People were getting really pissed off now. The noise was almost deafening. At last the traffic crawled forward. 'You mean America?'

He turned back to the girl and waved gently at her as we inched past. 'In my country's case, not only the US. All the countries of former Soviet Central Asia and the Caspian have to sleep with the elephant.'

It was a good way of describing the Russian Federation. I'd try to remember that one.

The girl disappeared behind us as Rob cut up a few vehicles to keep moving.

'Already the elephant's dislike for unity lies behind Moscow's threats to launch bombing raids into northern Georgia, they say to pursue Islamic rebels.'

We took a sharp right down a side street, then started to take continuous right-hand turns. It was nearly dark, but Rob didn't have his lights on. I looked at him in the rear-view. 'Anything to be worried about?'

His eyes flicked rapidly from screen to mirror. 'Nah. Just seeing if anyone's on our arse. The guys we're on our way to see are a bit jumpy about having a meeting with whites in Sadr.'

'Sadr?'

'Yep. The Americans don't go there much – too risky. Makes it safer for us. But no one knows Benzil is Jewish, so keep it low, OK?'

We were heading for Shia world. Sadr City was its real name, but for years it's been called Saddam City.

Benzil wasn't worried at all. 'By 2050 our region will be the biggest oil-producer on the planet. And because of that we will feel American influence even more acutely. It's not just the military bases: it's the cultural intrusion.

'At the moment, our Muslim militancy is being stoked up deliberately so that the West has a reason to be there to protect what they consider to be their oil and gas resources. Maybe Mr Nuhanovic can work his magic, and then everybody will benefit from the oil wealth. Not just the Americans and the West, but everybody.

'It's a long-term plan, and to make it work we need to keep Nuhanovic alive. My plan is to persuade him to come to Uzbekistan, where he can be safe with me while he develops his message using my country. Once people understand they have power in unity and power in their pockets, it will not have to worry about its government, America, the elephant, or even our neighbours.'

The road led us to the outskirts of Sadr. A line of dead T52 tanks, their barrels drooping to the ground and being used as washing-lines, had become slum housing. The scorch-marked hulls had been painted red, yellow and pink, and flowers stuck out of pots where the fuel tanks had been. Women cooked from fires built over the engine grilles, and kids kicked footballs against what was left of the track wheels.

'We can stop the tension in the regions as the oil cash flows in. The West will have no reason to station troops there, and we can get on with our lives. Does that make sense to you, Nick?'

It did, but I knew there was more to come. He hadn't talked about how I fitted in yet.

'Where are we going now? To see him?'

He gave a gentle laugh and pushed his gigs further up his nose. 'Unfortunately not. I know people who have had contact with him, and have been trying to impress on them that I need to see him. He knows I'm here. I have had indirect contact with him in Bosnia for nearly two years, through one of his intermediaries in Sarajevo. Is that not so, Robert?'

'Nuhanovic is testing Benzil's commitment, Nick. In Bosnia, he only deals through a guy called Ramzi Salkic. You remember that big old mosque in the Turkish area? You know, Gazzer something?'

I nodded but, like him, I couldn't remember the name.

'Salkic almost lives in there. That's where we meet him. But Benzil can't go inside the mosque. They'd smell him. So I go. I'm really good at all the prayers now.' He was quite proud of himself.

Benzil looked at me over the top of his dark glasses. 'But now I fear Mr Nuhanovic may have already left for Sarajevo, earlier than expected.'

We worked our way through a market selling vehicle parts, American uniforms, weapons, and some of the drugs that should have been in the kids' hospital they'd visited that morning. The skeletons of Iraqi military trucks were everywhere, along with the twisted remains of the odd Hummer and a burnt-out AFV.

'I hope we can meet. I know I can convince him it's the right thing to do. He's a target for so many people. The West want him dead because he can unite Muslims, the corporations because of the boycotts, the fundamentalists because he's preaching the wrong message.' He nodded out towards the crush of people in the market. 'Some of his enemies are here, just the other side of this glass.'

He removed his gigs and leaned back against the door. 'I have talked enough about our situation. But what about you, Nick, what is your place in the story? Would you like to be part of something different? Would you like to be part of keeping him alive?'

Soon the market was behind us. We bounced along pitch-black, deserted streets and Rob hit the lights.

Both of them were silent now. I didn't know if it was because we were nearly there, or they were giving me time to think.

Benzil must have been reading my mind – or was it showing on my face? 'No need to rush your decision, Nick. We have time.'

There was a heavy, dull thud. The front of the vehicle lifted. The windscreen shattered. The car rose up and over to the right, then bounced back down. Rounds rained into the bodywork, punching through the steel.

Rob lunged for the footwell, scrabbling for the AK. Two rounds thumped into his neck, spraying the interior with blood. His head lolled from his shoulders, held by just a few ligaments.

I shoved the door and rolled out on to the road. Glass showered down on me. Petrol spewed out of the vehicle as more heavy 7.62 AK rounds ripped through metal.

I turned back, trying to grab Benzil, but I was too late. He was slumped in the footwell. The rounds poured in. I kept low, sprinted back to the junction, turned right and leaped over a fence. I landed in a garden.

60

Kids screamed. Dogs barked. My legs weren't moving as fast as my head wanted them to. It felt as if I was running in mud.

People peered from their windows and shouted when they spotted me. 'American! American!' A couple of women started the Red Indian warble.

There were a couple of long bursts from near the vehicle as I ran down a narrow alley between two tall breezeblock walls. Arab screams echoed behind me. A burst water main had left the ground slimy and I lost my footing. I stumbled over a pile of rotting garbage and fell face down. Scrambling on all fours to move forwards and get up, I saw headlights moving back and forth about seventy metres ahead. All I wanted to do was get there and turn, it didn't matter which way – anything to get out of the line of sight and fire.

I kept running, not bothering to look back. My feet kicked old cans and newspapers. My hands were stinging like I'd fallen into a nettle bed.

I stopped about two metres short of the road, and had a quick check left and right. A few pedestrians hovered on the dark pavements. Some shops and houses had electricity, others just a flicker of candlelight.

I was covered in Rob's blood. My hands were soaked with it; shards of glass were sticking to it. My heart pounded in my chest as I tried to regain my breath.

There was a junction about twenty metres down. I stepped out of the alley and started along the pavement, concentrating hard on the weeds growing in the cracks between the paving-stones, keeping myself in the shadows.

A couple of people spotted me immediately and pointed. Somebody behind me shouted. I ignored it and kept going. All I wanted to do was get level with the junction and run across the road. They shouted again, this time more distinctly. 'Hey, you! Stop! Stop!'

I turned my head but kept moving. A Hummer patrol was parked on the same road, just too far up for me to be seen from the alley. With them were some Iraqi police, standing next to a new blue and white, carrying AKs.

The patrol challenged me again: 'Stop!' The police joined in, in Arabic. I looked to my half right and spotted an alleyway. I crossed the road and broke into a run.

'You – fucking stop! Stop!'

The Hummers and police revved up and started rolling. I reached the other side of the road and was into the alleyway. My mouth was dry and I fought for breath. Sweat diluted the blood on my face and hands. There were rough breezeblock walls either side of me again, only this time closer together. Light streamed through the shutters. I kept running as police sirens wailed behind me.

The blow to my throat was so swift and hard I didn't see who'd delivered it.

I lay on my back, gasping for breath, trying to get my Adam's apple moving as I listened to vehicles shrieking to a halt and pissed-off shouts coming from a house to my left, now in darkness.

American voices joined in, screaming at each other: 'Where the fuck is he? Let's go, let's go!'

As I pulled myself on to my hands and knees, I realized I'd run straight into a cable stretched between two buildings. The fuckers were getting their kettles on.

I got up and ran, stooped. I tried to suck in air but my Adam's apple was still glued to the back of my throat.

A powerful torch beam swept the alley. I hugged the wall to the right, crouching among piles of garbage and old mattresses.

61

I came to a turning. Fuck knew where it led to, but it would take me out of the line of fire.

I ducked down it and found myself in a crap-filled courtyard. There was no obvious way out. The shouts behind me were getting louder. The troops were on their way down the alley.

I ran into a washing-line and it snapped with a loud twang. Torchlight flashed along the walls. Orders were shouted in Arabic.

A couple of old pallets were stacked against the far corner. I lifted the top one and leaned it against the breezeblocks as a makeshift ladder. A vehicle drove past about twenty metres the other side of the wall, its lights flickering along the top of it. Grabbing an armful of washing off the line, I scrambled over. As I dropped, two shots rang out, heavy rounds, AK. The fuckers didn't even know what or who they were firing at, or why. American voices echoed down the alleyway. 'Hold your fire, hold your fire!'

If these Iraqis had been trained by Gaz, he deserved the sack.

I landed on firm ground and started running again. My hand went down to my waist: the bumbag was still with me.

I got to just short of the road and stopped. There was no follow-up behind me, just plenty of commotion.

I threw the clothes to the ground and ripped off my shirt. A damp T-shirt from the pile got what I hoped was most of the blood and sweat off my face and hands; then I pulled on an old stripy shirt that smelt nothing like washing powder.

I moved out on to the street and turned right, keeping in the shadows, moving quickly, head down. Checking out those weedy pavement cracks again, I gulped in oxygen, trying to slow myself. Sweat streamed down my face, stinging my eyes.

The shops were open, and bare bulbs hung from wires. People sat outside cafés, drinking coffee and smoking, engrossed in their conversations. There was a line of three parked cabs about fifty metres down. Two guys leaned against the first one, a rusty 1980s Oldsmobile with orange wings. I walked up to them with my best smily face on and gave them a thumbs-up. They smiled back. They were both young, hair brushed back, beards a week old. Their shirts hung out of their trousers and both wore sandals on bare feet.

'OK, let's go, let's go!' I jumped into the back of

the Oldsmobile before the driver had time to object. Dirty foam burst from slits in the seats, and roses evaporated from a bottle of car-freshener plugged into the lighter socket.

One of the young guys opened the driver's door and leaned in. 'You pay dollars?'

'Yep, dollars, no problem.'

He smiled, climbed into the driver's seat, and turned the ignition key. 'Where do we go?' His English was good, and he obviously wasn't fazed by having a white guy in the cab after a contact no more than two hundred metres away.

'The Australian consulate. You know it?'

He nudged into the flow of the traffic, then checked junctions left and right as we went along. Most traffic-lights weren't working, and even if they had been, nobody would have paid much attention. It reminded me of Africa. He turned his head. 'That's far away, Mister. It must cost a twenty.'

I smiled at him. He could have asked a hundred, for all I cared. 'No drama, mate.'

His face fell. He'd just realized he could have got away with a lot more. To console himself, he threw a cassette into the player and George Michael sparked up through the speakers. 'What you do here at night, Mister?' He turned his head again. 'No good one man. Big trouble.'

'I'm a journalist. The car broke down. They're trying to sort it out, but I've got to get to the consulate. I've lost my passport.'

He nodded and started singing along quietly with George. I kept an eye on the road for

Hummers and cars with flashing blue lights, but the only thing I saw was one of the red double-decker buses that operated in the city passing the other way. Sweat sluiced out of every pore as my body started to recover.

What the fuck had all that been about? Did the CPA want to suppress a Bosnian story so badly? That couldn't be it. Killing US citizens would have looked even worse on the front pages. So was Benzil the target? More likely; it sounded like anyone connected to Nuhanovic was on a hit list. But who had done it? In this fucked-up place, anyone from a cast of thousands. I bet Nuhanovic would know.

62

I slumped back into the seat, keeping as low as I could without making the driver suspicious, and started to pick the glass out of my hands. This was getting to be a bit of a habit.

The driver still hummed away to George belting out 'Faith'. 'Where you from, Mister?'

'Australia.'

'Oh. I go to London soon. My sister lives there. I go to drive taxis of her husband. Three more weeks!' He nodded to himself, very happy. 'You go to London, Mister?'

'Not if I can avoid it.'

We hadn't been in the cab more than twenty minutes when I saw the half-illuminated sign of the al-Hamra. Either Rob had really got into those anti-surveillance drills on the way out, or it had just been busy. 'I thought you said it was a long way?'

He smiled into the rear-view mirror. 'You lucky, Mister. Some drivers take you to the bad places for money. The bad people in Saddam City pay me fifty dollar like that. But I am good taxi driver. I am good London taxi driver.'

We were still on the main drag, just short of the turn-off for the hotel. 'You might as well drop me here. I'll walk.'

He pulled over. Huge artics rumbled by on their way into the city centre. I gave him twenty dollars, and an extra thirty to cover what he could have got in Sadr.

I turned left down the approach road to the al-Hamra. There was power on the hotel side of the street, but none on the other, where the shop was lit by candles. A bunch of barefooted kids in shorts and a collection of Premier League T-shirts kicked about in the gloom.

I bent under the scaffold pole and carried on to the main entrance. Two more Aussies were on stag in the driveway. As I nodded at the Iraqi on the door, I looked up at Rob's room. The light was on and Jerry was on that fucking phone again. He disappeared from view as I went inside. If the CPA were tracking it, we'd be in the shit.

The old man was chatting to a few locals at the counter, every one of them with a cigarette on the go. I got a cursory look up and down, but they'd seen enough blood and sweat in their lives not to be too concerned at a little more splashed about on some white guy. Through the glass door by the lifts, the underwater lights filled the air with a blue glow. The poolside tables were crowded. The world's media were back from a hard day at the office.

A good friend was dead, and what might have been the best job I'd ever be offered had been shot to fuck. But at least I was in one piece and Jerry was alive; I supposed I had done what Renee wanted me to – so far. We still had a way to go.

I got to the door and put my hand on the knob. It was locked.

'Who is it?' Jerry sounded worried.

'Nick. Open up, quick, quick!'

He fumbled with the lock and the door half opened. 'Fuck, what's happened to you, man?'

I walked in and closed it behind me. A fuzzy BBC World was conducting a silent interview with Blair.

Jerry's camera was on the coffee-table with the cable attached.

'Who you talking to? You sending pictures?'

'Just testing the kit. What the fuck's happened?'

'The car got hit. The other two are dead. Get your stuff together, quick. We're getting out of here before curfew. Test or not, you had the fucking thing on – they'll find us.'

63

This time, we had a forty-seater minibus to take us across the tarmac. Jerry sat next to me, his right leg sticking out into the aisle because I'd taken up too much room. I was knackered and wanted to lean against the window as I listened to *Now That's What I Call Mosque 57* playing on the tape-machine. The driver bopped away in time with the music as he spun the wheel with his elbows. I could just hear the rotors of two Blackhawks; I turned my head and watched them hover the last few feet before hitting the pan alongside about another eight of the dull green things. My hands, knees and elbows were scabbing up nicely after my tour of Baghdad's back alleys, and in a few days, I knew, I'd have a hard time trying to resist picking them.

Jerry hadn't said much since we left the al-Hamra. That was OK, I needed time to think.

The bus was full of self-important business-men checking their mobiles as they roamed for the new signal, and others holding their diplomatic passports firmly in their hands like some sort of talisman. I never knew why, but the people who have one always think it gives them better protection than body armour.

'Hello, General,' someone brayed behind us, in the kind of voice that could only have been shaped by Sandhurst, the Guards and a lifetime's supply of Pink Gin.

It got worse. 'Ah, David, old boy. Been back to the UK, have you?' the general boomed, as if talking from the far side of a parade-ground.

'Three weeks' leave. New father and all that. Got there just in time to see the sprog drop.'

'Splendid, splendid. I was a young major when the memsahib had her two. Away on exercise both times. Damned good thing, if you ask me. Boy or girl?'

'Boy. Nine pounds six ounces.'

'Marvellous. Prop forward in the making, what?'

They had a jolly good laugh, apparently oblivious to the rest of us, until one of the very important businessmen's phones went off in his briefcase. Instant red face as he dug it out: the ring tone was the theme tune for *Mission Impossible*.

'Anything cooking in my absence, sir?'

'All rather rumbustious – as per. Just been to Oberammergau. Meeting about a meeting, you know the sort of thing.'

If he didn't, I did. Guys like this could wring years out of meetings about meetings. A year or two of to-ing and fro-ing from Sarajevo would see him through to his engraved gold watch and lump sum.

Jerry gave me a grin. Either he'd spotted the look on my face or he finally felt within reach of the picture of a lifetime.

I gave him one in return, then went back to planning how I'd track down Ramzi Salkic, the man who might be able to get me to Hasan Nuhanovic, the man who might, in turn, be able to help me find out who had killed Rob.

Because when I did, I'd drop them.

64

We trundled past a line of Blackhawks. SFOR
was stencilled in black on their airframes:
Stabilization Force was what they'd christened
the military presence in Bosnia these days. There
were about twelve thousand troops on the
ground, mostly supplied by NATO. By the look
of it, most of the troops around here were
German. Their box-like green Mercedes 4x4s
were parked in neat lines outside their HQ at the
other end of the airport. The UN was also still in
Sarajevo, feeling as guilty as ever for having
stood and watched as the Serbs bombed and shot
its half-million inhabitants to fuck during the
siege.

The airport had been rebuilt since the last time
I was here, and the terminal looked as though it
had only just been unwrapped. There were a
couple of Ks of flat plain between the other side
of the runway and the mountains, dotted with
newly rebuilt houses amid a patchwork of
freshly cultivated fields. During the war, the only

way in or out of the city had been via this runway and up into the mountains. The Serbs had sealed off everything else.

I gazed across to what had once been an 800-metre sprint to avoid getting dropped by Serb snipers or caught by UN troops and sent back. The Serbs killed or injured over a thousand people along this stretch of tarmac. They certainly knew how to shoot: the majority of their victims were running targets at night, like Jerry and me when I was trying to get us back into the city.

We'd been thrown together when I'd thumbed a lift in one of the wagons trying to make it back into Sarajevo. I was on the road south of the enclave after the second Paveway job. Jerry recognized me from the hotel bar and persuaded his driver and another journo to pull in and pick me up. Dried blood covered the back of the car and was smeared down the tailgate window. It wasn't an unusual sight around here, but these three were miserable enough to make me think that whatever had happened had happened pretty recently.

I sat in the back with Jerry. No one said a word as the front two smoked themselves through a packet of Marlboro and we all hoped the Serbs didn't decide to use us for target practice.

About an hour from the city we got stopped. It looked pretty straightforward, a VCP manned by three bored-looking Serbs, one of them puffing on some waccy baccy. Usually, the best approach was to give them a few packets of cigarettes, smile a lot and take their picture. But that didn't look like it was going to work today. They wanted us to roll down the windows. Then they wanted our cameras. I was the first to hand mine over: they were more than welcome to the pictures I'd taken.

Jason, the front passenger, put up more of a fight. He gabbled at them in Serbo-Croat, but eventually his went the same way. Jerry, however, had other ideas. A few weeks in the field, and he thought he could just get out of the car and start blustering and bluffing his way through. Then he went ballistic when one of the Serbs pulled the film out of his camera. Not a good move. The long and the short of it was, he was going to die. Everybody knew it but him. What the fuck did he think the Serbs were doing when they started slipping their weapons off their shoulders?

I didn't care if he got himself killed. But it wasn't just Jerry's life at stake: we would all be witnesses.

I got out of the knackered Golf too, still grinning like an idiot. One of the Serbs stepped forward and it wasn't the hardest thing I'd ever done to grab his weapon and drop all three of them. As Jerry and I stood there in the mud surrounded by dead bodies, a Golf sped down the road away from us. Fuck 'em, as far as I was concerned, it was safer on foot – I should have stuck to that from the start. We'd got stopped in this VCP, so it was odds on the VW would get stopped at the next. As word of what had happened here spread, the Serbs would open up on every vehicle that moved.

Jerry had left everything but his camera in the car: money, passport, press pass. That didn't worry him as much as the rolls of film he'd lost, but it should have. There was no way he was going to get back into Sarajevo without UN help. He was fucked.

So we'd spent the next seventy-two hours cold, wet and hungry, working our way round Serb positions and down to the free sector to the south of the airport. The last stretch, the sprint across eight hundred metres of exposed runway, took us five lung-bursting minutes. We must have had at least a couple of mags emptied at us.

Once we'd got to the other side, Jerry went to find himself a new set of documents and I leaked back into the city. I saw him a couple of times afterwards in the Holiday Inn, but kept well away. I couldn't stand him trying to thank me. He couldn't get his head around the fact that I'd been saving my own skin, not his.

His stuff never made it back, and neither did Jason and the driver. I passed their two charred bodies and the burnt-out wreck of their car on the road about two weeks later.

The bus driver turned the wheel sharp left and Jerry's head jerked to the side, but his eyes never left the runway. He had shrunk into his own little world. I could see him gazing across the tarmac, maybe picturing the razor-wire entanglements, the sandbag sangars, the white APCs full of UN troops trying to stop us, and the Serb fire arcing towards us under the floodlights. But we weren't going to go over all that now. Sarajevo was still too tense for talk of politics and war and, besides, the general and his sidekick were taking up too much oxygen as it was.

New Dad turned to the young woman beside him.

'General, have you met Liliana? Ministry of Internal Affairs?'

'Oh, yes, rather.' Liliana's brown linen trouser suit must have cost her a packet on Fifth Avenue, and as far as the general was concerned, it was worth every penny. I could just imagine him leering at her over the tray of Ferrero Rocher at the ambassador's cocktail party.

'You're with SFOR, General?'

'Paddy's military adviser, for my sins.'

No wonder the peace process had been like wading through treacle.

'It seems to me that only the British are carrying out the captures,' Liliana said with a coy smile. 'You're so very good at it, how come you haven't yet captured Karadic?'

The general chuckled. 'These chaps are jolly hard to ferret out, you know. Always on the move. But maybe that's no bad thing, my dear. It's best not to start with the most indigestible item on the menu. Go for something light to start with, what?'

I switched my attention back to Jerry: his eyes still hadn't left the other side of the runway.

65

Monday, 13 October 2003

The bus hissed to a stop outside the terminal and we all filed off. The plebs, which included Jerry and me, herded themselves towards the one passport-control box that was open. The general and his chums with the blue diplomatic passports went straight through the Diplomats and SFOR channel. I hoped his luggage was still in Oberammergau.

As we joined the queue my eyes started to close; they felt like they'd been dipped in grit. It had been a long journey. The drive from Baghdad to Turkey had gone OK, apart from the moment our fixer tried to overtake an American armoured convoy. He'd realized his mistake when he received three warning shots across the bonnet.

At the airport in Istanbul, I'd binned the washing-line kit, bought some new clothes, and cleaned up while Jerry called his source and the *Sunday Telegraph* to explain the change of plan. We'd taken a flight to Vienna, then caught a connection here. Jerry's card had taken a real beating, but the paper was going to pay him back, so what the fuck?

Once through the terminal, we looked for a taxi. An old man conjured up a newish red Vauxhall Vectra from the line about fifty metres to our left. As it left the front of the rank, the drivers behind moved their vehicles forward three or four metres without starting their engines, pushing on the window pillar and steering through an open window. After years of war shortages, old habits died hard.

The Vectra pulled up with the world's largest man in the driver's seat. They were all big in this neck of the woods; there must have been something in the water. He jumped out to fiddle with the windscreen wiper and show off his crewcut and black-leather bomber; it was the jacket of choice around here too. Most of the boys in Sarajevo had looked as if they should be in the Russian mafia. Maybe they were now.

The Bosnians had their own currency, the Konvertible Mark. We hadn't been able to get any in Vienna, so we made a deal: thirteen euros for the trip to the hotel – far more than the eight-K journey was worth. During the war it had been Deutschmarks everyone wanted. Now, it was euros. This had to be about the only area of the world that wasn't much fussed about the dollar.

Justin Timberlake was getting it all on as we headed for the hotel. Jerry's gaze seemed to be fixed on the mountains that hemmed us in on

both sides. These days, they looked like something out of *The Sound of Music*, but ten years ago
the Serbs had used them to bomb the shit out
of the city.

Sarajevo sat in a wide valley shaped like a
soup spoon, with the handle cut off, just a little
way down by the airport runway. A fast-flowing
river, the Miljacka, ran through the middle of it.
Before the war tore it apart, the city had probably
been beautiful: the guide books had gone on
about modern high-rise towers nestling side by
side with elegant Austro-Hungarian mansions,
which nudged up in turn against the Ottoman
heart of the city. But that was a lifetime ago. The
Serbs, or aggressors as they were known around
here, laid siege to the city from May '92 until
February '96. In some areas the front line was
actually inside the city, the two armies separated
by just the wall of a house. The Serbs killed over
ten thousand people in the longest siege in
history.

The houses facing the airport were still standing; some had been replastered, but many looked
as if they belonged in Berlin at the end of the
Second World War. The taxi driver kept glancing
at Jerry in his rear-view.

'Where you from?'

In this town I didn't have to worry about Jerry
opening his gob and putting us in the shit. He
knew very well what to say. 'America.' The Brits
and Canadians weren't liked that much round
here: their troops had had to stand on the side-
lines during the slaughter because they were

under the command of the UN, who didn't have the remit to intervene.

He waved his thumb in Jerry's direction. 'You Muslim?'

Jerry nodded, and got a smile of approval.

It was my turn. 'You American?'

'Australian.'

Satisfied, he went back to working his way on to the main.

66

We hit the main drag that paralleled the Miljacka. The broad dual carriageway was heaving with vehicles, and every other one was a VW Golf. Volkswagen had had a factory here before the war, and every man and his dog seemed to drive one.

The driver tore along Vojvode Putnika as if it was still Snipers' Alley and he knew he was in somebody's sights. The Serbs had enjoyed a good arc of fire from the high ground. Hundreds of Sarajevans had been killed in crashes as they drove through the city at 120 k.p.h.

Jerry was still in his own world as we drove past a host of new construction sites alongside bombed-out reminders of the past. One was the concrete skeleton of what had been a brand new old people's home. The first pensioners had only just moved in when the Serbs started lobbing shells at it. It looked exactly the same as it had when I last saw it; even the recently erected bill-boards couldn't cover up what had happened.

Despite everything, I liked Sarajevo. I always had. Like Baghdad, it was a grown-up place. It had been here for centuries. There were winding streets, and hundreds of dead ends and small alleyways that went nowhere in particular. Minarets poked up into the sky everywhere you looked, from small wooden mosques, brick ones the size of bungalows, and great big fuck-off ones as big as palaces. The majority of the city's inhabitants were Muslim, these days, but there was still a scattering of Jews, Orthodox Christians, and even a few hippies who had forgotten to go home in the sixties.

We passed the UN compound. Lines of white Land Rovers and Land Cruisers were parked outside a square block of concrete and glass. This part of the main had bristled with steel hedgehogs, X-shaped obstacles, placed in the road to prevent the Serb army's two hundred and fifty or so tanks screaming into the city. Sometimes I'd been able to hear them revving from down town. The hedgehogs hadn't been the only obstacles you had to try to avoid as you drove towards the airport. There was also any amount of falling concrete, burnt-out vehicles and, now and again, a body or two.

About a K ahead, a bombed-out tower block – what had been the parliament building – loomed above the city centre.

'Nearly there, Sunny Side Up.'

Jerry said it as I thought it.

I couldn't help but smile. I hadn't heard that saying for nearly ten years.

We hadn't talked about Rob and Benzil at all. But then, there wasn't a lot to say.

The taxi pulled up outside the large yellow cube with a Holiday Inn sign. Last time I was here the ground had been covered with snow, and its nickname was born. It still looked much the same, just a whole lot quieter than when four thousand shells and mortar rounds a day were raining down on the city. To me, it brought back good memories of great chips, and sometimes even sausages when they were on the menu. At least until a sniper got the cook on his way to work one day.

67

The Holiday Inn had been forced to close before the war because it was bankrupt, but as all the other hotels in the city were bombed out one by one, it reopened. Even though the prices rose higher and higher the longer the siege went on, it was never short of guests. It didn't seem to matter that its upper floors were constantly hammered by Serb artillery, rocket and mortar fire: just like the Palestine, it existed to make cash, and it remained the HQ and doss-house for the world's media.

Sometimes the power was on, sometimes it was off. Sometimes the rooms were freezing cold, sometimes they were too hot. Whatever, it had to be the only hotel in the world where the most expensive rooms were those without a view. The golden rule of survival was: if you see the sniper, the sniper sees you, and he wouldn't necessarily be a Serb. This war had attracted weirdos from all over: the neo-Nazis, anyone else who didn't like Muslims, and the ones who just liked killing people. They all came for a bit of war tourism, were escorted into fire positions on the high ground, and had a crack at anything that moved. There was even some avant-garde Russian writer caught on camera, sniping into the city.

The Firm's operations room above the café was about twenty minutes' walk away – in peace time – but as much as two or three hours during the siege if the snipers were active and people were backed up on the street corners, waiting for the courage to make a run for it.

When we checked in, the guys behind the desk took our passports as security, just like in the old days. I'd always hated that. I always wondered if it was going to be the last time I'd see it.

The décor hadn't changed much: still lots of grey ersatz marble covering just about every surface. Even the reception staff still behaved as if a smile of welcome would get them carted off to the gulags.

The Holiday Inn was a lot quieter now that no one was getting shot at and no artillery shells were landing in the lobby, but just as busy. I wondered if it was still a haunt for journalists. Probably not. Sarajevo wasn't that sort of place any more. There were new wars, new stories. Most of the people milling around looked as if they were here on business. Germans and Turks on cells headed for the lifts, wheeling their smart carry-ons behind them.

A coffee area covered most of the ground

floor, with square leather-and-chrome chairs huddled round low tables. In the far corner, the coffee-cum-drinks bar was trying hard to look like a large tent with a stripy canopy above the cappuccino machines and bottles of whisky. The hotel was hollow in the middle. All the rooms were built around the outside walls, so the ten-floor atrium looked like the inside of a state penitentiary. It reminded me of a trip I'd taken to Alcatraz with Kelly.

We got into the lift and pressed for the first floor. Jerry and I were sharing a double this time. The only available singles were on the top couple of floors.

Jerry was still in his own world as we got out and followed the landing. He had to start talking soon.

Room 115 could have been any room in any chain anywhere in the world. It had been re-decorated since the war, but dark-wood veneer was still king. And, just like the old days, I found myself looking straight out on to the wreckage of another burned-out building. Not too far beyond it lay the green slopes of Mount Trebevic, the sky above it a flinty blue.

Before the war, Sarajevans used to escape the city heat by cable car to picnic on the mountain-side. Then the Serbs came, and they covered Trebevic in land mines. Either I'd read this or seen it on the Discovery Channel, but I knew that most of it was still off-limits. It was known as 'the lost mountain'.

Jerry threw his new Istanbul bag on to the

bed nearest the door. The canvas holdall was a lot smaller than the one he'd arrived with in Baghdad, that was for sure. His bumbag followed.

I stretched out on the other and thought about finding this Ramzi Salkic guy.

68

At last, Jerry opened his mouth. 'This may sound crazy, but the stuff Benzil and Rob told you about Nuhanovic – it's kinda made me even more determined to get these shots. Maybe he really can stop some of the madness.'

I looked down at the burned-out building. 'That's worrying. Last time you went off taking pictures in this place it nearly got me killed.'

Jerry looked sheepish. 'I know, I fucked up majorly. But it was worth it. We got to save someone's life.' His expression darkened. 'Don't you ever want to know what happened up there in the enclaves?'

Not really. He had tried to tell me enough times nine years ago, on the way back into the city. I'd already known as much about the atrocities as I wanted to. I'd told him to keep it for his grandchildren.

I helped myself to a Coke from the minibar. 'You went up there because the papers were offering a hundred grand for a picture, right?'

What the fuck? He obviously wanted to tell me, so why not listen? At least he was talking.

'Yup, a hundred grand. Fuck, I'd have run all the way naked with a rose up my ass for that kind of dough. Soon as we heard, Jason and I got a driver and set off north.

'That road was seventy-five Ks of Dodge City. Two relief workers driving trucks had been killed a couple of days before on the same stretch. We were kinda hyper.

'Three miles south of the enclave, we hit a Serb checkpoint. Jason was cool at that sort of stuff. He just pulled out a carton of two hundred and did some trading.

'The village we came into had been totally fucked, man. I mean, every house had been hit. The Serbs had been pounding these guys for months. It was getting dark and we really started to freak, so we tried the UNHCR.'

I collapsed back on my bed and Jerry sat up on the edge of his to keep eye-contact. His face was alive for what seemed the first time in many days.

'We found some nurses. A Frenchwoman, Nicole, was in charge. We expected to be fucked off with all the usual shit about UN regulations and journalists, but they were cool.

'They told us the UN had tried parachuting food and medicine into the place at night. The women and children would hear the chutes open and run outside, waiting for the food to land. It was dark and they had tin cans on sticks with candles burning inside them. The Serbs just picked them off, firing at the lights.' Jerry shook his head sadly. 'Fuck, man, there was a story every way you turned.

'In the morning Jason and I walked down into the village to look at their hardware. These Muslims were fighting back with anything they could get their hands on. Guys were fighting from trenches in gardens, from cellars. They were like ants, everywhere. I got sixteen rolls that morning.

'Then all hell broke loose. We were walking back up the hill to the house when we started taking incoming. There was this young boy, no more than ten, just staggering about, bleeding and crying. His mother had a huge chunk of shrapnel in her back. The grandmother was trying to help.

'Jason ran to fetch Nicole while I went to see what I could do. Not much, as it turned out. She was dying.

'The boy had shrapnel in his hand. Nicole and her team did what they could for the two of them, but even I knew the mother needed surgery, and fast. Nicole wanted to take her to the UN base a couple of Ks away down the road. We had a vehicle, they didn't. How could we just stand by and do nothing?

'We got to the house, carrying the woman between us. The driver was up for it so we threw the back seats down and got her in. Jason and I got in with her; the kid and the grandmother sat in the front.

'We'd only driven a mile or two out of the

village when we ran into a Serb patrol. They told us to turn back – this lot were all of "fighting age", even the grandmother. Luckily there was one carton of cigarettes left, and Jason did the deal.

'Within half an hour, we were at the base. The boy's name was Fikret, and he wanted to play for Manchester United when he grew up. He was a good kid.'

By now the empty Coke can was resting on my chest. His voice faded, and I turned to see him staring at the floor. 'That it?'

'The doctor said the mother's only chance was to get to a proper hospital. She'd have to be evacuated in one of their APCs, but Fikret and the grandmother couldn't travel in the APC as they weren't wounded. UN regulations. Fuck that. He could have allowed them to travel if he'd had the balls.

'I didn't have the heart to tell Fikret. He was busy. His mother was swinging in and out of consciousness, and he was holding her hands, stroking her hair.

'The APC turned up, and that UN fuck still wouldn't let them travel with her. I gave him a hug. He cried on my shoulder for a bit, then he got himself together and explained what was happening to the grandmother.

'As soon as the APC had left, we were all escorted off the base. We couldn't drive them back to the village because we had nothing left to trade if we ran into the Serbs again. He knew that, and just took his grandmother's hand and headed home. My last shot was of their backs as they walked up the road.'

I threw the Coke can at the waste-bin and just clipped its edge. In the old days I'd have lobbed it to the nearest Muslim so he could make a hand grenade. It seemed a waste of metal to follow UN regulations and crush it so that I didn't break the arms embargo. 'And that's when you picked me up?'

'Yup. And I know you don't want to hear it, but I need to say thanks for saving my life.'

'Thank-you accepted.'

He smiled. 'I know you don't mean it, but it makes me feel better. You want a coffee or something? I'll go down.'

Jerry strapped on his bumbag. One of the downsides of being a photo man is the kit always has to be with you.

'Yeah, why not? Frothy, no sugar.'

I watched him leave, and as the door closed behind him my eyes were drawn to the emergency-information sheet pinned to the back of it. I got up and studied the diagrams, but none of them seemed to show me what to do if I needed to run away from people armed with AKs. I dug around for my room card and went out on to the landing.

The coffee area was hidden under its stripy canvas canopy, but Jerry hadn't got there yet. He was pacing up and down just outside the main doors, the Thuraya against his cheek. He wasn't just testing for a signal, he was talking. The conversation ended and he disappeared under the tent.

I was back on my bed, channel-hopping for CNN or BBC World, when he came back with a cup and saucer in each hand. His coffee was black, with several sachets of sugar sitting in the saucer.

'You sure that's healthy?'

'Few extra calories never hurt anyone.' He handed me mine.

'I meant all that phoning. You're going to end up with a brain tumour.'

'Just a quick one to DC. He's got nothing new.'

It was eleven forty-three. The second prayer of the day was some time after midday. Times changed, depending on where you were in the world and daylight saving, all that sort of stuff. 'Maybe we could make Zuhr?'

Jerry called down to Reception. They'd know prayer times, which would probably be in the papers anyway. Even if we missed the Salkic guy this time round, we could hang about, have a brew and something to eat, and try again during Asr.

Jerry got off the phone as I checked my bumbag. 'One twenty. Plenty of time.'

We tuned the TV to a German soap with Serbo-Croat subtitles, put the Do Not Disturb sign on the door, and headed for the lifts.

I looked down into the atrium. A group of five American troops were sitting by the coffee shop, getting into their brews and cigarettes. In this part of the world, they wore green BDUs and were part of SFOR. They'd probably been stationed in Germany before being posted here, and counted themselves lucky. Going by the size of them, they had a KFC at the camp gate that only sold family buckets. They didn't look like their lean and mean mates who were getting the good news in Baghdad.

69

The air was crisp outside, just cold enough to see a little vapour as we breathed. We were going to need coats.

We picked our way across the wide dual carriageway that used to be Snipers' Alley. Traffic careered along the outside, and trams moved fast down the middle. Instead of turning left to the city centre, we were going to cut straight on down to the river, less than two hundred metres from the hotel.

Some of the trams rattling past looked as though they were left over from the war. Jerry read my thoughts. 'Least they don't have to be dragged along by trucks, these days.'

We passed the burnt-out shell of the parliament building I'd been looking at from the hotel. The underground car park was obviously still usable: two policemen were on stag at the entrance, checking cars in and out.

Nearer the river, we found ourselves among older, grander, more lavish Hungarian-style buildings. They were still inhabited, but had taken a fearsome pounding. The other side of the Miljacka, less than forty metres away, was where the Serb front line had penetrated this part of the city; even the wired glass protecting the balconies was still splattered with strike marks. Lumps of grey plaster had been blown away, exposing the brickwork beneath.

As far as I could tell, the only difference between then and now in this part of town was that the roads were no longer covered with rubble, or blocked off by trucks and sheets of corrugated iron to provide cover from sniper fire. I remembered seeing four wooden cargo containers at the bottom of this very road, piled on top of each other to create a screen. The Serbs still took random potshots into the woodwork, and occasionally managed to drop the odd pedestrian who just happened to be legging it behind.

Every bit of the city had been a danger zone. Bridges and crossroads were particularly vulnerable if you were on foot, and it paid to be a sprinter – but at least you knew what you had to do. In other parts of town, you were never sure whether to walk fast or slow. Were you going to walk into a mortar round as it impacted, or was it going to land on your head anyway because you weren't moving fast enough? Signs saying 'WATCH OUT – SNIPER' had been painted on pieces of cardboard or UNHCR plastic sheeting, or just chalked on the walls. To a lot of Sarajevans, and me, UNPROFOR's most important role was providing APCs to shield us from sniper fire as we crossed the street.

I felt myself break into a smile as we passed another bunch of fucked-up buildings facing the river. One night some madman had painted a big yellow Smiley face on the wall, and 'Don't worry, be happy!' underneath. It got annihilated the following day. I was never sure if that meant the Serbs had got the joke or not.

Walking beside me, Jerry also seemed to have disappeared into the past again, back to the days he'd spent dodging from one piece of cover to another as he tried to get a photograph to pay the bills.

We hit the river by the Vrbana bridge, and everything looked familiar except the little monument that had been erected exactly half-way across it. Jerry pointed at the bunches of fresh flowers arranged below it. 'I was here when it happened.'

He leaned his shoulder against the glass panel of a brand-new bus shelter, behind which a poster told us that if we bought a bottle of Coca-Cola Light, we could win an Audi.

'Romeo and Juliet?'

'Fucking nightmare, man. I was with Jason before the enclaves blew up. We were just cruising, looking for something different to shoot. But everywhere you went in Sarajevo was the same, wasn't it? We decided to check out the front line a bit before going back to the hotel.

'There was a stand-off, city guys against a group of Serbs just over there. This Serb tank appeared from nowhere and started firing. We ended up with the city guys. Next thing I knew, one was yelling at us to get our cameras. He was pointing at a young couple running towards the far side of the bridge.

'They got the guy first. The girl was just wounded, and I got a shot as she crawled across to his body and put an arm round him before she died. Turned out she was Muslim, he was Serb . . .' He had the sort of expression I probably showed every time I caught myself thinking about Zina or Kelly. 'Fucked up or what, man? It was the first time I ever cried doing this shit. First time I ever wanted to put down my camera and pick up a gun.'

It was business as usual these days. Cars crossed the bridge, people walked around with bags of shopping. On the steep rising ground immediately the other side of the river, all the roofs were shiny, and all the mosques had new minarets. There seemed to be one every two hundred metres or so. It was easy to spot a Muslim house: its roof was pyramidal while the rest were gabled. Satellite dishes sprouted from just about every wall; these guys must have been as keen on *The Simpsons* as the Iraqis.

Just to the right of the bridge, flags of every description fluttered over a new steel and glass building. I pointed it out to Jerry. 'That must be where our friend the general takes his meetings about meetings. I wonder how Paddy puts up with him.' The Right Honourable Lord Ashdown was the UN's High Representative in Bosnia. It was the sort of title you only expected to find in Gilbert and Sullivan, but in effect he ran the country.

We turned left and followed the river towards the city centre, but we hadn't gone far when there was the dull thud of an explosion up on the high ground.

Everyone in the street looked up. A small plume of grey smoke floated above a square of trees, surrounded by rooftops. Two old women coming towards us, weighed down with carrier-bags, tutted to each other as if this was an everyday annoyance.

'What do you reckon, Nick? A mine?'

'Had to be.'

When the Serbs withdrew, they left hundreds of thousands of the little fuckers in their wake. There was no need for Keep Off the Grass signs in Bosnia.

70

There was some reconstruction in progress along the riverbank, but most buildings still hadn't been patched up. A few of the places immediately facing the Miljacka had all but collapsed. Others had done so long since, their rubble cleared to make room for muddy car parks. At least the river was nice and picturesque these days. The last time I'd seen it, there'd been bodies floating downstream.

A tram stopped just ahead of us, brand new with a sign announcing it was a gift from the people of yet another guilt-ridden country that had done fuck-all to help when it was really needed. Passengers jostled to get on and off with their shopping, a very few in headscarves, some in grey raincoats, briefcases in their hands and cellphones to their ears.

Soon we couldn't move for people and cafés. A coffee shop seemed to have sprung up every ten paces, but these were indigenous. George would have given Sarajevo the thumbs up: there wasn't a Starbucks or skinny *latte* in sight. A lot of them had outside tables with canopies and butane heaters so the punters didn't have to stem their nicotine and caffeine intake even when the temperature dropped.

Most of the buildings were still peppered with shrapnel and bullet scars, but at street level it was all plate glass and stainless steel, bright lights and rap. We even passed a Miss Selfridge, where women were holding up the new season's collection against themselves, and teenage girls lounged around in Levi's, smoking and listening to their Walkmans.

Our first stop was to buy us each a coat. We didn't think that the *Sunday Telegraph* would stretch to Versace so we headed into one of the old local boys' shops. I settled for a brown three-quarter-length number that didn't look or feel remotely like leather, despite what the salesman said. But, then, what can you expect for about twelve dollars? Jerry spent about the same on a waterproof with a fleecy lining. We looked like dickheads, but at least we were warm.

Sarajevo isn't big, but it's teeming with different ethnic neighbourhoods. We moved into another Hungarian quarter. The pedestrian area, once cratered by mortar rounds, was now paved with flat stone.

The old black and red board was still where I remembered it, inviting us to visit the Café Bar Muppet. The Firm had had a room above it, which was very apt, I'd always thought. There was an archway through into a very small square, and the café was just off to the right. Even at the height of the war it had felt protected. A direct hit wouldn't have been too healthy, although it would probably have been better than a bullet in the back. I'd preferred the Bodyguard Café up the road, for the simple reason that it was in a cellar. But you had to be quick, because every other fucker wanted to get in there too.

The smell of *cevapcici*, grilled sausages served with pitta bread, drifted through the streets, signalling that we were coming into the old Turkish area, Bascarsija. The Gazi Husrev Bey mosque, or 'Gazzer something' as Rob had called it, was the largest in the city, and now close enough to spit at.

71

When a mortar round explodes on a hard surface like a road or pavement, it creates a characteristic pattern. We came across a lot of strike marks that had been filled with red cement as a memorial to whoever had died on that spot. Bascarsija, a warren of narrow cobblestoned streets, alleyways and dead-ends, had more than its fair share of 'Sarajevo roses'. The Serbs had been particularly fond of busy places like markets and shopping arcades.

The area was dotted with mosques and lined with tiny interconnected one-storey wooden shops, selling leatherwork and brass tea-sets, postcards of bombed-out buildings and pens to write on them made from spent .50 cal cases. I didn't see any tourists haggling with the owners. Most customers, when there were any, seemed to be in uniform with SFOR flashes.

We turned a corner and the massive Gazi Husrev Bey mosque was suddenly there in front of us, pristine and white. They'd really gone to town on the renovation. Elevations had been re-rendered, strike marks in the stone had been removed, and there were brand new his'n'hers washrooms in the courtyard area.

The arched entrance was protected by a stone portico. Big carpets were laid out beneath it, perhaps for those who wanted a quick prayer without going inside, or to cater for overspill when the mosque was full.

There are different lengths of prayers for the different prayer times, and shorter prayers if you're travelling or ill. They can be said alone, or in congregation. It's pretty much a pick 'n' mix affair to suit the individual. You can even combine a couple of prayer times, like some Catholics do on a Saturday night to save them having to get up early the following morning.

A lone man in his mid-sixties, wearing jeans and an Adidas windcheater, was kneeling and offering Salah [prayers]. His shoes were tucked into the racks provided. We made our way towards the side door, past a small shop window decked out with a lifetime's supply of Qur'āns and other religious paraphernalia and two stone shrines to a couple of high-rankers in the Muslim world. Jerry couldn't remember exactly who they were and actually blushed with embarrassment because he felt he should: after all, this was the most historic mosque in Europe.

We took off our shoes before going in. Non-Muslims are welcome in mosques; they don't like you trying to take part if you're not one of the faithful, but you can stand at the back and watch if you want, it's no big deal. The two religions I had most time for, Judaism and Islam, both managed to create this sense of everyone being part of one big family.

The interior was cavernous, with a dome at least twenty-five metres high. Chandeliers hung down on cable and chain. The walls were decorated with beautiful framed quotes from the Qur'ān. The entire floor was covered in intricately woven Oriental carpets.

Four old women had their backs against the wall to our right, heads covered and mumbling to themselves. I smiled, gesturing for their permission to enter. They smiled back and ushered me in. They gave Jerry a strange look, which made me smile: in a world of Muslims, he was clearly the weird-looking one.

The moment we stepped out of the hustle and bustle of the street, there was a sense of tranquillity I could almost touch. People seemed to glide across the carpets; voices were hushed.

I looked down and could see my socks were leaving sweat marks on the highly polished tiles. I shrugged an apology to the women.

They all smiled back.

Encouraged, I moved closer to them. 'English? Speak English?'

They smiled even more, nodded and said nothing. I thought I might as well start asking about Salkic. I wanted as many people as possible to know we were looking for him. With luck, the bush telegraph would swing into operation. He'd either run for cover, or get curious and come looking.

'Mr Salkic? Do you know him? Ramzi Salkic?'

They looked at each other and gobbed off, then just smiled and nodded again.

I had another go, but got exactly the same response.

I shrugged my shoulders and thanked them, then started to back out with Jerry. We put on our shoes and left.

'You did well there, didn't you?' At least Jerry thought it was funny.

'C'mon, then, we'll go in the shop. Let's see you do better.'

It turned out to be little more than a table covered with a jumbled selection of books and cassettes and other religious bric-à-brac. Maybe this was where the airport's minibus driver had bought his greatest-hits collection. A guy with a grey beard stood behind the display, in a black tanktop over a white shirt buttoned all the way up his neck. He smiled at me and I smiled back.

Jerry tried his luck. 'Speak English?'

He looked almost offended. 'Of course!'

'I'm looking for Ramzi Salkic. We were told he prays here. Do you know where we can find him?'

He didn't even give it time for the name to sink in. 'No, no. I've never heard that name. What does he look like?'

'That's the thing, we don't really know.'

He opened his hands, palms upwards. 'Then I am sorry.'

'Never mind, thanks a lot.'

Dark clouds were scudding across the sky as we emerged from the mosque, and it had turned noticeably colder. 'We've got thirty-five till Zuhr.' I shoved my Baby-G under his nose. 'Let's get a brew. Pointless hanging around.'

We left the sanctuary of the courtyard and moved back into the hustle and bustle of the streets. A guy in a fluorescent vest was holding a fat hose over a blocked manhole while his truck sucked noisily. Paddy obviously hadn't got round to sorting out the sewers yet. It probably wasn't top of his list of priorities because, according to the waffle on its side, this shit-clearing vehicle was a gift from the German Red Cross. I wondered if they were being ironic.

72

There were cafés everywhere, and each one was a bigger lung-cancer factory than the last. Bosnians smoked like chimneys. Last time I'd been here the running gag was that if the Serbs didn't finish you off, the Drinas certainly would. Health and safety probably worked in reverse here, like so much else. If they found out you had an extractor fan or a no-smoking policy, they'd probably shut you down.

We walked into one with lots of glass and chrome, cutting through a curtain of nicotine. We sat down and ordered a couple of cappuccinos. Apart from the smoke, we could have been in London or New York. The spectrum was the same, from teenagers sipping hot chocolate and obsessively checking for texts, to old boys on their own trying to make a small coffee last a lifetime.

The brew finally turned up just as Adhan, the call to prayer, sounded across the rooftops. Quite a few customers got up and headed for the till.

We joined the queue, trying to get the hot liquid down us before we made the thirty-metre trek back to the mosque.

We walked through the wrought-iron gates, past men and women lining up in their separate, segregated areas. Little kids ran in and out of the legs of middle-aged men in business suits. Teenagers stood chatting to grannies.

Quite a few guys were already on mats in the drive-through outside, getting the prayers in early. Jerry and I mingled with the rest of the crowd, smiling at everyone as they waited in line at the washroom to perform Taharah, purification. You didn't have to wash at the mosque: it could be done beforehand. Some just chatted as their kids ran riot. I'd decided we should split up to cover more ground.

Most of the people I asked about Salkic responded with a little English and a big smile, but they couldn't – or wouldn't – help me. Jerry worked another section of the crowd about fifteen metres away. He looked like a bad impression of Inspector Clouseau, and so did I, probably. I caught his eye and shook my head. He did the same.

The Qur'ān vendor was standing outside his premises, watching the crowd hopefully. Maybe he was anticipating a big run on his religious merchandise today. Then I looked at him more closely and realized he was actually studying faces. He was looking for someone.

I decided to up the ante. I stopped a young guy in a black-leather overcoat. When I asked him if he could help me, he replied in very good English.

'I'm looking for a cleric, a man called Hasan Nuhanovic. Do you know what mosque he goes to? Is it this one?'

His smile faded and his eyes dropped to the floor as he shuffled past me. 'No, I don't know. I'm sorry. Excuse me.'

Jerry was near the washrooms now and I worked my way towards him, asking as I went. The next one I tried was a suited, briefcase-toting businessman who looked like he'd just come out of an insurance office. 'I'm looking for a holy man, a Hasan Nuhanovic. Have you—?' Before I'd even finished the sentence, he'd walked away without answering.

Jerry was immediately at my side, looking concerned. 'What're you doing, man?'

'Rocking the boat.'

I spotted the shopkeeper talking urgently to a young guy with brown hair, and not about the weather. There was a lot of pointing into the crowd.

Jerry was still agitated. 'Shouldn't we stick to the plan? We're here for Salkic first, right?'

I was already on my way towards the shop. The young man had a neat short back and sides and the kind of raincoat that wouldn't have looked out of place in DC. I closed on him as he headed for the main entrance. 'Ramzi Salkic?'

I knew it was him, the moment he tried to side-step me and didn't look up.

'No, no, no. I'm not—' His eyes never left the ground.

I found myself speaking to the top of his head. 'I need to get a message to Hasan Nuhanovic. Can you do that for me? Have I got the right person?'

He pushed past me and I decided not to create any more of a scene by trying to stop him. Instead, I followed him to the shoe racks, where he slipped off his smart loafers.

'Please leave me alone.' He had to talk loudly to make himself heard over the murmurs of the faithful. 'You have the wrong person.'

We were getting quite a few disapproving glances from the direction of the mats.

'My mistake. I'm sorry.'

Their attention switched to me as I turned and moved back against the tide.

I headed for the shop. When he saw me coming, the owner scuttled inside and turned the lights off. 'We are closed.' He disappeared into the gloom without a backward glance.

For some reason I'd been expecting Salkic to be a lot older. It takes time to build trust with a principal; the middle man is normally someone they've grown up with, a contemporary with shared history and experience.

Jerry joined me. 'What do you think? Is that him?'

'For sure. He didn't look confused, he didn't look at me. He just wanted to get away.'

'You fucked that up, then, didn't you?'

But that was the least of our worries.

'There's two guys over there by the wash-rooms.' Jerry kept eye-contact with me, as if I might take a look. 'They didn't look too pleased to see you. You're gonna think I'm crazy, but I think one of them was at the Palestine.'

73

We walked out of the courtyard together, smiling and chatting as if we didn't have a care in the world. 'What's he look like?'

'Remember the pool fight? With that Lats guy? The one with the goatee, I think it's him.'

We exited the gates near the two shrines, turned right, out of their line of sight, carried on down the road, then took another right to get us behind the mosque. The narrow road was lined with bars and cafés.

We sat down outside a *cevapcici* shop, on a long wooden bench under an awning. The doors were open and we were hit by a blast of warm air from the grill, where an old boy was frying meat.

I got Jerry to sit facing the shop because I needed a better view of the road. All the cafés were pretty quiet. It wasn't really time to eat yet.

Seconds later, the two flat tops rounded the corner. I looked at Jerry and smiled as if we were enjoying a joke. 'Both of them were in Baghdad.'

They were in pretty much the same kit, too; the

only additions were the black-leather bomber jackets. Goatee caught sight of us and they ducked into a bar more or less opposite.

'Won't be long before at least one of them comes to the window.'

'Why the fuck were you going public about Nuhanovic, man?' He managed to give me a big smile and a bollocking at the same time. 'That's what's got us in the shit. What we going to do?'

'Nothing, yet. Chances are it's nothing to do with Nuhanovic; maybe they just recognized us. I'd be curious if I bumped into someone here I'd seen in Baghdad.'

Jerry leaned forward. 'Me too.'

A waiter appeared with ears that stuck out far enough to have held ten pens instead of just the one, and we both ordered *cevapcici*. 'Five or ten piece?'

I asked for ten and Jerry nodded. 'You have any Zam Zam?'

The waiter looked puzzled.

'Or Mecca? You got any Mecca Cola?'

He looked as if he thought Jerry was taking the piss.

'OK, maybe Fanta?'

He nodded and walked away, shouting our order to the old guy who, going by the size of the jug handles each side of his head, must have been his dad.

Jerry was rather good at this acting-normal-while-really-doing-something-else routine. Maybe it was a photojournalist thing.

The Fanta arrived, complete with straws and

glasses. Jerry picked his up and held it in front of him. 'I just thought I'd liberate my taste – you know, "Don't drink stupid, drink committed." Those guys still in the bar?'

I nodded as I reached over and swivelled the can so he could read the manufacturer's details. 'See who makes it?'

'Coca-Cola. Shit.' He pulled back on the ring and poured it into his glass. 'Oh, well, I tried.'

I took a map I'd picked up at Reception from my pocket, put it on the table and pretended to play the well-known tourist game, Where the Fuck Are We?

The *cevapcici* turned up, ten sausage-type things the size of my little finger, made of kebab meat. I ripped open the pitta bread and shoved them in with a king-size helping of chopped raw onion. 'They've still got eyes on us.'

One bite took me straight back to the Hereford kebab shop with Rob, trying to impress women with our sophistication while our lips were covered with grease, and chilli sauce dripped on to our shirts. 'OK, here's the plan.' I kept on chewing. 'If Salkic is there during Asr, we hit him again.'

Twenty minutes and a couple of Fantas later, we were ready to roll. It was time to shop. Well, sort of: I wanted to see how the flat tops reacted. There was no point trying to lose them – there weren't that many hotels in town. Someone, somewhere, would know where we were.

Jerry paid the bill, all of about four dollars, and we wandered back across a small square where old men played park chess with giant pieces on faded black and white paving slabs. Weeds sprouted through the gaps and some of the original pieces hadn't survived. The missing ones were improvised with sculptures made from lumps of wood and plastic bottles.

Jerry and I weren't the only ones who had stopped to watch. Maybe the flat tops' surveillance drills were shit; maybe they wanted us to know that they were there. Either way, they never took their eyes off us.

Jerry was still switched on and avoided getting eye to eye with them. He walked and talked as if he was totally unaware.

The more I thought about it, the more I agreed with Jerry that the flat tops were on to us because of Nuhanovic. Like everyone else on the planet, they'd want him dead: a moral crusade would be bad for business – probably always had been, even during the war. I wondered if the girls at the cement factory had been held so they could be sold on, until Nuhanovic managed to get them released. Well, most of them. The bastards had still managed to keep hold of Zina and the other three or four.

A parade of small shops at the end of the square had a scary number of Sarajevo roses sprinkled across the pavement in front of them. A different pop or rap tune blared from each doorway and all sold either cellphones or hair-dryers. 'About half an hour left till Asr. What do you reckon?'

He had the correct answer. 'Coffee.'

We went back to the place we'd had to abandon our cappuccinos, and got a table. I couldn't see the flat tops through the windows, but I was sure they'd be out there.

I took one of the paper napkins and borrowed a pen from the waiter as Jerry delivered a sit rep. 'They're outside, still together. Standing in a doorway.' He turned back to me with a grin. 'Don't they know they should be watching our reflection in a big silver samovar? They obviously didn't see *Spy Game*.' He looked down at the napkin. 'What are you writing?'

'I want to make sure Salkic at least knows where to find us.'

74

Adhan sounded round the streets once more. A few people got up, but not as many as before. We lined up at the till with them and filtered out into the courtyard.

This time we didn't mingle with the crowd, but leaned against the courtyard wall behind the washrooms. We watched everyone coming in, waiting to get a glimpse of Salkic. I wasn't feeling hopeful. It was mainly an older crowd this time. The women grouped themselves together and moved under the portico. Several men were already praying at the drive-through.

This session had a sort of market-day feel about it. Everyone seemed to know each other. The Qur'ān seller appeared in his doorway and had an even bigger scout round than the last time.

Jerry scanned heads as people went into the male washroom. 'Flat tops – they're staying outside.'

I looked to my right. They weren't in the

courtyard, but out on the street, chatting and smoking.

Moments later, the man I'd pegged as Salkic entered the courtyard via the shrine gates. He seemed to be glancing warily around him as he walked.

'You gonna approach him again? Want me to do it?'

I shook my head. 'We'll go inside. We're going to pray with him.'

'Fuck me – you know what to do?'

Salkic disappeared into the washroom this time. He would be out within a few minutes: Taharah didn't take long. The routine is hands, mouth, nose, face, forearms, wet hands over head to the back of your neck, ears. Then, once your feet get the good news, you're ready to roll. It doesn't always have to be water, either. In deserts, Allah lets you use sand.

'Of course I know what to do – I just don't know what to say. You hum it, I'll play it.'

Salkic emerged with his shoes in his hands and a pair of flip-flops on his feet, and headed towards the carpetloads of kneeling men.

I checked my watch. It was exactly four thirty.

We waited for Salkic to rack his shoes and walk up the stone steps. Jerry drew a few odd looks as we followed and took our boots off, but at least he knew what he was doing once we were through the door.

The hushed tones around the drive-through had been replaced by the low, all-pervading rumble of people talking to God. There's no middle man when Muslims pray, no vicar or priest with exclusive access to God's cell number. Islam offers the worshipper a hotline to his creator.

Salkic had settled himself on one of the rugs off to the right, about half-way along a row of worshippers offering Salah.

Some stood with their palms upraised; some were already bowing; others were on their knees with their foreheads and noses pressed to the floor. Some were addressing Allah aloud; others mumbled quietly to themselves.

Salkic had his back to us and was standing with his hands open each side of his head. This was the first stage of Salah, I knew that much. Most of the guys around him were well into it.

I scrunched up the napkin in my hand and knelt on Salkic's right; Jerry did so on his left. He eyed us both but didn't look concerned: he just carried on with his devotions. He was very well dressed. The shirt looked Italian and expensive, and so did the silk tie and jacket.

Jerry's palms went up by his head. Salkic had finished that bit and lowered his arms to his sides. I followed suit and began to speak to him, keeping my voice low. 'We tried to make contact with Hasan Nuhanovic in Baghdad.' I checked to see if this was registering. 'I was with the Jew, Benzil, when he got killed. Nuhanovic knew he was in the city – does he know he's dead?'

Salkic bowed and muttered a few more things to Allah. His green eyes closed a little; he was trying to look as if what I had said meant nothing to him. But my words had struck home. He knew Benzil: we had the right man.

'Tell him we need to see him as soon as possible.' I turned to face him as he straightened up. 'Tell him I was at the cement factory. I saw it all, even what happened to the girls once he left. Does he know they kept some back? I saw what happened.'

Jerry leaned forward and shot me a quizzical look as I slipped the ball of napkin into Salkic's pocket.

'This is where we are. There's no time to test commitment – we're being followed by slavers. We might have to leave the city quickly.'

Salkic remained silent as he went down on his knees, then mumbled into the rug, 'Go back to your hotel and wait.'

There was no point staying: I'd said what I'd come to say. A few people glared at me as I eased my way out, but most were too bound up in what they were doing to pay much attention.

The flat tops were in here as well, over by the side entrance we'd used earlier in the day. They must have seen everything. Fuck it, so what? I had more than enough to worry about. Regardless of what he'd said, Salkic, the gate-keeper, would either pass on the message or not. It wasn't something I could control. And if Nuhanovic received my message, he'd either say yes, or he'd say no. I had no control over that either.

I'd find out soon enough. If Salkic didn't do the job, or he did and Nuhanovic didn't want to play, it was going to be a long, boring business trying to follow, cheat or threaten Salkic to find out where his boss was. Fuck it, I hadn't come all the way here for nothing.

Jerry was at my shoulder as we walked back towards the river. There were no flat tops in sight yet.

A couple of German SFOR 4x4s had pulled up on the pavement. The troops were haggling with a stallholder over some pirate DVDs.

We sat on a bench in a kids' play area, which butted up to a squat and ugly concrete block of flats thrown up in the seventies. If we were still being followed, we'd find out soon enough.

I could see two Sarajevo roses from where we were sitting, one near a set of swings, another near a curly slide. The Serbs always said that the children killed during the siege were the unintended victims of shellfire, but the Sarajevans knew better. Around two hundred and fifty kids were killed by sniper fire alone and there's never anything unintentional or uncalculated about what a sniper does.

The concrete facings were still scabbed up and covered in graffiti. Beyond the slide and seesaw was a mosque about the size of a two-bedroomed house, with a stone minaret.

Jerry put on his happy face. 'What was that about Mladic? Were you really there? The factory? Shit, I told you that story, but you knew all along?'

I nodded, checking again for company. I didn't

need to tell Jerry to do the same. His eyes roamed left and right.

'Is it true, you know, he saved all those people?'

'Something like that.'

'You get any film – shit, that would be amazing if—'

'No, no pictures. I'd had my kit stolen. I was trying to get back to the city and hid near the factory when I heard the wagons heading my way.'

It started to rain.

'No good sitting here now, we'll look right dickheads.' It would be obvious to the flat tops what we were doing. We got up and followed the river back to the hotel.

75

Jerry put the Thuraya and camera on charge while I looked in all the drawers for a *Yellow Pages* or directory, but there wasn't one. The Gideons hadn't been to visit, either.

The room was freezing so I kept my plastic coat on and pulled a couple of small bottles of Italian pear juice from the minibar. I looked through the rain-streaked window. Two Blackhawks hovered above the city, disappearing now and again into the grey clouds.

'Here's the score.' I lobbed a bottle at him and he gave it a shake. 'There are three things that might happen to us. One, we get a visit from Salkic, which hopefully will be with a smile. Two, we get a visit from the flat tops, and I imagine that won't be. Three, we get fuck-all visits, in which case we go and find Salkic at the mosque again tomorrow, and we follow him. If he doesn't turn to, we'll have to check phone books, ask around, try to track him down. Then we find out how he makes contact with Nuhanovic, and hopefully we find out where Nuhanovic is – then you get your picture and maybe I get to find out who killed Rob. After that, well, I'm going back to Baghdad. Maybe kill whoever killed Rob, then get a job on the circuit. Why not? Got fuck-all else to do.'

We twisted the caps off the bottles. Jerry had gone quiet again: maybe he didn't like me talking about killing. It was time to get off the subject.

'If we get lifted by the flat tops tonight we're going to have to think on our feet, big-time. There's no way out of here except by jumping on to the coffee-bar canopy, just like in those Jackie Chan movies.'

Jerry gave a nervous laugh. He didn't fancy plummeting straight through the canvas and ending up bent round the cappuccino machine any more than I did. But if the wrong guys came calling, it might be the only option. 'If we do get away and have to split, we'll meet in the car park by the Romeo and Juliet bridge, OK? Wait there for two hours. If I don't turn up, you're on your own. I'll do the same if I'm there first. You got that?'

Jerry nodded calmly enough, but I knew he was flapping. I patted his shoulder. 'Listen, I doubt that'll happen. If it's Nuhanovic the flat tops want, they'll wait and see if we lead them to him.'

I got up and went over to the window. It was now dark and headlights pierced the rain along Snipers' Alley. 'Well, I think the condemned men deserve to have their last meal, don't you?'

Jerry smiled and reached for the bedside phone. He ordered us both the house special, Sarajevo burger and chips, and loads of extra bread and red sauce for the butties.

'Tell them to call us when they bring the food up. Say we're both going to be in the bath, and you want to make sure one of us is able to get the door.'

The last thing I wanted was to open up for what we thought was room service, and get a trolleyload of flat top-with-Goatee instead.

Jerry rang Reception, found out the time of first prayers, and booked a five thirty call. I imagined we'd be the only ones there. Salkic hadn't looked the sort who'd be in the mosque before daybreak, but I could be wrong and we had to be prepared.

Both of us stayed as we were, fully dressed, boots on, kit packed and ready to go. I lay on the bed with my hands behind my head, staring at the ceiling. Jerry got up, grabbed the remote from the top of the TV and started to channel-hop. I watched the screen, not thinking about much, just picking at the scabs on my hand. I'd known I wouldn't be able to resist it for long.

Jerry rested the remote on his stomach as he pressed the buttons and the screen flickered from station to station. We finally settled for *Law and Order*, just the way we liked it: dubbed into German, with Serbo-Croat subtitles. We didn't have a clue what was going on. Everybody nodded a lot, pointed at dead bodies lying on the floor, and jumped in and out of cars by hot-dog stalls.

The phone rang and Jerry answered. The food was on its way.

I checked the spyhole and saw the waiter leaning over the trolley. No Goatee. I opened up. He came and laid everything out on the table, took the two-euro tip I offered him, and left.

We tucked into our Sarajevo burgers and chip butties, downed the Cokes, and went back to watching TV. Our favourite channel ran out of steam after midnight, and we lay on our beds reading. Jerry had a *Herald Tribune* he'd bought at the airport in Vienna. I just scanned the label on the back of my Coke can a few hundred times.

We put the lights out at about one in the morning but Jerry carried on channel-surfing. We watched Baghdad and Fallujah getting the good news from a few RPGs and a handful of suicide bombers on BBC World, then moved on to a German news quiz. I scored one point for recognizing David Hasselhoff in the picture round.

There was a gentle knock on the door. In the glow of the TV screen, Jerry and I exchanged a glance. Too late for room service to be collecting the dirties.

He turned the sound down with the remote, we both sat up and I hit the bedside light. His eyes were bouncing between me and the door, trying to see through it. He bit his lip. There was another knock, a little louder this time.

I got to my feet, checking my bumbag to make

sure it was secure round my waist. Jerry started to get his on as well.

Through the spyhole, I could see a couple of new, serious-looking faces dressed by World of Leather. Their heads were close enough to kiss the lens.

I glanced back at Jerry. He stood there, checking the zip on his bumbag one last time before nodding a 'ready'.

I hoped he was right: I suddenly had the feeling that he'd be better off strapping on some body armour and making ready a decent-sized assault rifle. Just because these were new faces, it didn't mean they belonged to Nuhanovic.

There was only one way to find out. I slipped off the chain and turned the handle.

I took a couple of quick steps back into the room, then turned and tensed, ready to take the hit. The horror on Jerry's face was plain to see. He fell back on to the bed and curled up in a ball.

I closed my eyes, clenched my teeth, and waited.

76

Nothing happened. I sensed rather than heard somebody walking into the room.

Then I heard a voice like a 1950s BBC newsreader. 'It's all right, Nick, it's me.'

I spun round and opened my eyes. The leather boys had stayed outside in the corridor, but Benzil was right there in front of me. His face was badly scabbed. It looked as if the slightest glimmer of a smile would crack the scabs and restart the bleeding.

He was wearing a black overcoat over a white shirt that was undone at the collar, and a white crew-neck vest. 'It is not the first time enemies of Mr Nuhanovic have tried to kill me, and I hope it will not be the last time they fail to do so. Robert's death, however, is a terrible price to pay.'

'I heard them firing into the wagon.'

He lifted his hands to the sky. 'That might have been them shooting at a very fast-moving target. By the grace of God, I got out of the car quickly and into a house. The people were very kind. It was so sudden – our security is always so tight. I believed you were our only link with the outside world, but Robert vouched for you – and, of course, you would hardly have wanted to ambush yourself.'

'No, no idea.'

I heard Jerry rolling off the bed behind me. Benzil's eyes moved over my shoulder. Jerry muttered, 'Hi.'

Benzil nodded. 'Jerry?'

'Yes.'

Benzil had more urgent things on his mind. 'We have to move quickly. Mr Nuhanovic wants to meet us both. The gentlemen outside are going to take us.'

'They with Salkic?'

'Yes. I just missed you at the mosque, but I know you attracted a lot of attention towards Mr Salkic today. As a result, I suspect that the Serb slavers have made the link between him and Nuhanovic. The situation here is dangerous now. If you could get your things together, I'll meet you downstairs.'

Jerry stepped alongside me. 'What about our passports? We coming back here?'

'I'm told that's all taken care of.' He paused and managed just a hint of a smile. 'Maybe you will get to take your photograph after all.'

The leather boys were anxiously scanning the landing as we came out with our kit. Their jackets were undone, pistol grips within easy reach.

Nothing was said as we walked to the lift. Jerry stared straight ahead, his hands on his bumbag, checking its contents as if he expected the camera gypsies to strike at any moment.

Down at Reception, there was another familiar face. Salkic presented us with our passports without ceremony or emotion. 'Follow me.'

Two midnight-blue Audis with smoked glass and alloy wheels were waiting outside, engines running. Benzil was sitting in the back of the lead vehicle, his window down. His fresh-faced driver indicated, with a wave of the small radio in his hand, that we were to get into the one behind. Its boot clicked open.

The leather boys also peeled away from us to go with Benzil, one in the back beside him, the other beside the driver. Salkic climbed into the front seat of ours as we threw our bags into the boot and got into the back. A driver in his forties was at the wheel. His crewcut was just cropping out to show the grey on the sides, and his face was peppered with small scars. His stubble only grew where the skin wasn't marked. As he ran his right hand over the wheel I could see that his index and ring finger were missing.

Jerry had recognized him too. But he didn't look round to acknowledge us, or make eye contact in the rear-view, so we did the same.

The rain had stopped, but the heating was on. The interior smelt of new leather. Salkic and the driver were gobbing off to each other at warp speed. There was a burst of radio mush, then a voice in Serbo-Croat. Salkic pulled a Motorola two-way communicator from his pocket, the sort skiers use to keep in touch with each other on the slopes. He mumbled into it as Benzil's vehicle pulled away and we followed.

The wet pavements glistened in the streetlights. Sarajevo was bright with neon and illuminated billboards, but appeared deserted. I couldn't help feeling the place was all dressed up with nowhere to go. I saw a tram, but there was no other sign of life as we splashed our way out of the city.

In the driver's footwell, tucked against the seat so it didn't get in the way of the pedals, was an AK Para version, the same as Rob's. A spare thirty-round magazine was taped upside down to the one loaded in the weapon. I just hoped it was there for comfort rather than necessity. There was nothing armoured about this Audi and I didn't fancy the idea of repeating my Baghdad experience as brass-coated lead rounds ripped the tin can to bits.

'It is a long journey.' Salkic spoke without turning round. He didn't sound happy with life. His eyes were glued to the road ahead, as if he was expecting an attack from a side junction at any minute.

I leaned forward between the two seats. 'Where we going?'

'It would mean nothing to you, and even if it did, I would not tell you. It's better that way. Everybody either wants to kiss Hasan or kill him. I protect him from both. Those men who followed you, they do not want to kiss Hasan.'

There was more mumbling on the net and he held up his right hand in case I was about to speak. Those little Motorolas were perfect for close-up comms. They had a range of a couple of Ks, beyond which they couldn't be listened in to, and because they didn't produce that big a footprint it was difficult to keep track of them.

He pressed the send button and gave his answer. The front car immediately took a sharp right, but we carried on past the junction and took the next left. Salkic saw Jerry's concern in the rear-view as the streetlights flashed by, strobing the interior. 'For our own protection.'

I leaned forward again. 'How long have you known Nuhanovic?'

Salkic stared ahead at the empty road. It took a while before I got an answer. 'Hasan is a truly remarkable man.'

'So I hear. Thank you for passing on our message.'

He stared through the perfectly cleaned windscreen, not a bug splash in sight. The Motorola crackled and he concentrated on what was being said before responding. 'I gave him your message. He was interested to hear about you being at the cement factory.'

'How did you come to work for him?'

He turned round very slowly and deliberately, and in the strobed light I could see that his face was set like stone. 'I do not work for him,' he said simply. 'I serve him. He saved me and my sister from the aggressor when the British, the French –

everyone – were just standing by and wringing their hands.'

He tapped the driver on the shoulder, waffled off to him, and he nodded and waffled back. It looked like they all felt a similar obligation.

'Nasir says it was a shock in Baghdad when you asked about Hasan. Nasir begged him to leave the city within the hour. He, too, is always worried about security.'

Salkic faced the front again.

I took the hint and sat back. Before long we were heading out of the city and up on to the high ground. Apart from our headlights, the only light was what spilled now and again from the houses dotting the road.

We were on a metalled single carriageway that snaked its way across the ridge and down into the valley the other side.

A couple of Ks later, I spotted tail-lights in the distance. They were static, and off to the right. Salkic got on the net and the lights began to move and rejoined the road. We soon closed up behind them.

I leaned forward. 'Benzil?'

Salkic nodded. 'I'm the only link to Hasan in Sarajevo. Nasir will take us only part of the way, then I alone will take you on to him.'

Nasir's seat creaked softly as his weight shifted. There was nothing out there but inky darkness, the headlights catching the odd tree-trunk and house at the roadside as we drove past. A couple of times a scabby dog rushed out from behind one to take us on.

Jerry was doing the same as me, peering out into the night. His hands rested on the camera in his bumbag, as if he was still worried the camera gypsies were about to pounce.

77

Tuesday, 14 October

We had been following the Audi's tail-lights at a distance for about an hour and forty when Salkic sparked up. 'We are nearly at the transfer point.'

I guessed the next stage of the journey wasn't going to be as comfortable. He dug down round his neck and pulled out two keys on a chain, the sort ID tags are attached to. With luck, they belonged to a nice warm vehicle. I didn't fancy tabbing through the cuds in this kind of weather.

'Everything you have with you will stay with Nasir.'

Jerry leaned into the space between the front seats. 'What about my camera? If he lets me take some shots, I'll—'

Salkic turned to him, his face steely. 'Nothing must be brought with us. Certainly no electrical devices. We will also search you. Don't worry, everything will be returned after you have seen Hasan.'

The front Audi's tail-lights glowed red, and

stayed on. As we closed, Salkic talked cautiously into his Motorola.

We were almost on top of them before we could see the problem. The way ahead was blocked by a dead cow, and her mates didn't seem keen to let us through. We couldn't drive round them because of the barbed-wire fences either side of us.

It looked as if the road ran past a farm. A collection of barns stood just off to the right, rough old things knocked up out of concrete blocks and corrugated iron.

Nasir braked to a complete halt, lifting his foot off the pedal when we'd stopped to kill the rear lights. Then he threw the gearshift into reverse and started backing up as the other driver and a leather boy got out to investigate.

Salkic held the radio near his mouth, his eyes fixed on where we'd just been. 'This is where we leave Nasir and his people. They will go back to Sarajevo. I will take you to Hasan.'

We stopped about a hundred metres back, lights off, and waited. Nasir was cautious: he knew his drills. A frantic voice screamed over the net. Nasir went for the AK as a huge, dark mass roared out from one of the barns behind blazing lights, bouncing cows out of its way as it aimed for Benzil's Audi. Jerry pushed back into his seat, transfixed by the mechanical monster's headlights.

As the truck bore down on them, the leather boys ran back to their car. One of them managed to pull an AK and the muzzle flared in the darkness.

Salkic hollered into his radio, for all the good that was going to do. There was another burst from the AK, but it didn't stop the Audi getting T-boned dead centre and being bounced back into the fence.

Nasir threw open his door and jumped out at the same time as I did, his AK at the ready, yelling at the other two. I grabbed at Jerry's coat as rounds started to puncture the bodywork. 'Out the fucking car!'

The barbed wire buckled as the wheels of Benzil's Audi dug into the mud for a second or two before it toppled over on to its side. Automatic fire rattled among the barns as the truck ground to a halt, its headlights spilling across the wreckage and the sharply rising ground beyond it.

Rounds hammered into the side panel, inches away from me. Jerry twisted and tore away from my grip. He screamed once and dropped to the tarmac like liquid.

Shit. I fell with him.

His body was still wriggling.

'I'm OK, OK.'

Nasir was to my right, static and firing at the muzzle flashes that tore through the darkness from the direction of the farm buildings. He was calm and controlled, taking short bursts, making every round count. I didn't look back, just got my head down and legged it towards what was left of Benzil's Audi.

More bursts from the right. They were moving positions so they could get rounds into the heap of tangled metal wrapped round the front of the truck. Rounds zinged off the tarmac.

Shit, shit, shit. Don't look, just keep going.

Another four, maybe five sustained bursts.

I was nearly at the wreckage. The Audi was lying on its left side, wedged against the truck's radiator grille. The truck driver was slumped over his steering-wheel.

'Benzil! Benzil!'

I peered through the Audi's mud-splattered windscreen. There was nobody inside.

'Benzil! Benzil!'

One of the leather boys had been crushed between the two vehicles. I felt about for his weapon among the mangled flesh and steel.

A semi-automatic opened up from the high ground behind me, punctuating the frenzied shouts in Serbo-Croat that echoed all around us. Who the fuck was who?

'Benzil!'

No weapon found. I lay flat in the mud, using the Audi for cover, wishing I could dig myself into the ground. More rounds ripped into it from the barn, and again from the high ground. One of the leather boys was jumping up and down, yelling to me to move up. Then, as he gave me more covering fire, his muzzle flash illuminated Benzil kneeling by his side.

Fuck it, deep breath. I legged it up the hill towards him, only to be catapulted back down into the mud by the remains of the barbed-wire fence. The more I tried to untangle myself, the more it cut into my jeans and skin. The leather boy shouted something at me before returning fire, as if he thought I was deliberately taking my time.

I kicked free and kept well to the right of him as he squeezed off burst after burst. I saw Benzil again in the muzzle flash, lying at his feet now, waving me over.

No time to be static. I ran over to Benzil and grabbed hold of his overcoat. 'Come on, up!'

The leather boy was changing mags, but he was an accident waiting to happen. He was failing to move after each burst; he was going to get hit soon and I didn't want us anywhere near him when it happened. I kept moving uphill and to the left, dragging Benzil, trying to get us out of the line of fire and back towards what I hoped was a surviving Audi.

I pushed Benzil into the mud as two endless streams of tracer sailed over our heads. The leather boy went ballistic, then stopped firing and crumpled.

'Stay here!'

I slipped and slid my way back down the slope, finally landing on my arse beside him. He was alive, but wouldn't be for much longer.

78

The wet, rasping sounds he made as he tried to suck in oxygen were those of a fast-dying man. I reached inside his jacket and felt warm blood pumping over my hand. I wasn't going to seal the hole: there wasn't any point. I was just looking for spare mags for the AK.

I was out of luck, but grabbed the blood-wet weapon anyway as the boy stopped breathing, and scrambled back up the hill. 'Benzil! Benzil! Shout to me!'

'Here, over here!'

As I joined him, there was a burst towards the barns from further along the hill, parallel with the Audi. It had to be Nasir.

I kept us on the high ground, paralleling the road, trying to confirm who was up on the hill. Benzil was losing strength and spent more time in the mud than on his feet.

'Nasir, Nasir!'

'Over here, over here!' It was Jerry. I still couldn't see them.

'Back in the car! Go, let's go!'

I started dragging Benzil downhill. Each step was clearly agony for him, but that was tough shit: he'd have to sort himself out later.

He stumbled again and cried out. I grabbed a handful of coat and yanked him forwards as rounds thudded into the ground where we'd just been.

'Come on! Come on!'

Three bodies closed in from my right. Salkic was with them as they scrambled downhill towards the car. The fire from the barns became more concentrated as they worked out what we were doing. Rounds hammered into the Audi's doors and tyres.

'Back up the hill!'

I was fighting for air, my clothes soaked with sweat, trying to climb and keep a grip on Benzil at the same time. Nasir was returning fire behind us. 'Stop! Stop! Stop! Save the rounds! Salkic, where the fuck are you? Tell him to stop firing!'

We carried on climbing. There were no trees, nothing to haul ourselves up on; just mud, grass and rock. I slipped and fell. The AK barrel crashed against the stone, but it would survive. These things were built to be used and abused. I wasn't so sure about Benzil.

There was still firing from below us, but the tracer was going high. They'd lost us in the dark.

I felt blood leaking down my legs after my tangle with the barbed wire. My throat was parched. I kept my grip on Benzil, kept pulling him upwards.

I yelled across at Jerry. 'Keep up! We've got to keep together.'

Jerry came close, chest heaving and breath rattling in his throat. 'Where ... we ... going?'

'Fuck knows. Salkic?'

There didn't seem to be anything leaking out of Jerry apart from sweat. 'For a second there, I thought you were down for good.'

'Bastards hit my fanny pack.'

Salkic appeared out of the gloom, fighting for oxygen and so angry he could hardly speak. 'You are responsible for this! They must have followed me here earlier, and waited.' He pushed me so hard in the chest I nearly fell over Benzil. 'You lead them to me!'

Benzil remained in the mud as Salkic started gobbing off to Nasir.

I wasn't too sure how this was going to play, so pushed down gently on the AK's safety. Salkic heard the click and so did Nasir. His weapon swung up into the aim. Salkic gently pushed the barrel until it pointed at the mud. 'God would not have let this happen if it were not for a reason. My job is to take you to Hasan. We serve him, so it will be done.'

I made sure they heard the safety click back where it belonged, then glanced back down at the hill. I could see torchbeams criss-crossing the ground. I waited a second or two for Nasir to calm down. 'You know what's the other side of this hill?'

Salkic thought for a second or two. 'No. Just more hills?'

I checked Baby-G. We had about two hours at the most before first light. If we were caught out in the open in this terrain we'd be fucked.

Benzil was still on his knees, almost sobbing as he gasped for air.

Jerry, too, sank into the mud.

'Salkic, ask Nasir if he knows.' It was time to get sorted. 'OK, I saw one man go down and there's one by the Audi. Anyone see the other guy? We still got someone out there?'

The one missing would have to fend for himself. I had control of the most important two.

Salkic gobbed off again to Nasir.

I lifted the AK and pushed the magazine catch forward to release the two taped-up mags. I pressed down on the top round in the first mag with my finger. It stopped about two-thirds of the way down: I had about ten rounds left.

Salkic and Nasir were still in dialogue as I turned the mags over and pushed down on the second. It was full, so I slotted it into the mag housing and eased back the cocking handle to check chamber. 'Anybody else got a weapon?'

Salkic translated. 'He also has a pistol and two extra magazines. And he says there is a cave the other side of these hills. The aggressors used it to store supplies.' Salkic took in another couple of gulps of oxygen before continuing. 'He said that he isn't sure which valley. It's been many years since he has attacked it.'

Nasir muttered a few more words to Salkic, who hesitated before translating. 'Do you know which man you saw dead?'

'No.'

As Salkic mumbled back to Nasir there was a sudden burst of voice traffic on the radio inside his coat. He pulled it out, maybe hoping it was our missing man.

The radio might have belonged to him, but the gravelly voice that came out of it didn't. Whoever it was started singing what sounded like a nursery rhyme. Then there was a short, piercing scream. The song continued for a moment, but was interrupted by more screams and the sound of sobbing.

Nasir went apeshit.

Images flashed through my own head of others I'd seen taken prisoner by the Serbs, men strapped to trees who'd choked to death on their own genitals.

Nasir started downhill as the fading screams were replaced by mocking laughter.

'Salkic, turn that fucking thing off and get him back here!'

I didn't care what the fuck he wanted to do down there, but now wasn't the time. We needed a steady pair of hands on a weapon. Salkic ran ahead of him and held up a hand. I saw Nasir's shoulders heave as Salkic took a step forward and wrapped him in a hug.

For several minutes they talked to each other in gradually gentler tones. The rest of us kept our distance. At least it gave Benzil time to rest.

The torches below us were still on the move. A vehicle emerged from one of the barns, manoeuvred its way past our Audi, and headed back towards Sarajevo.

Salkic still had Nasir in his arms. They mumbled some more to each other. Both men were crying.

At length, they turned and came back up to us. Nasir carried on uphill a little way before kneeling. There was silence; no one spoke.

I stood up, and helped Benzil to his feet. 'We need to get going and be over this high ground before first light, out of their line of sight.'

Exhausted as he was, Benzil's only concern was for others. 'Is Nasir all right?'

'He will be,' Salkic said, 'but give him time. The man they just killed was his youngest brother.' He paused. 'And my brother-in-law.'

79

Nasir was lead scout.

Benzil was next. He was in a bad way, but we had to place him up there so we could keep an eye on him and go at his pace. He tried his best; Jerry, Salkic and I took it in turns to hitch his arm round our necks to help keep him upright.

Nasir was a totally steady hand. He was an old sweat, doubling back from time to time to mutter an encouraging word.

Benzil would just nod and agree. 'Yes, yes. Thank you.'

After ten minutes or so, he had to stop again. 'I'm so sorry, Nick. I'm so sorry.'

'Don't worry about it. Just try and keep going the best you can.'

There was a burst of fire in the valley below us as they cabbied at shadows.

Wind buffeted the summit, clawing at my face, cooling my sweat. At least the plastic coat kept it at bay as we started to slip and slide downhill.

The line was starting to get strung out, and not

just because of Benzil. Jerry and Salkic were feeling the pace. Nasir was still up front, slowing down at regular intervals for the rest of us to catch up.

The valley gradually took shape before us as first light seeped into the eastern sky, and what I saw was not good news: next to no cover, just mud and stones. There wasn't even a road.

I stopped and waited for Salkic to draw level with me.

'We're going to be fucked out here on open ground.' I nodded at Nasir. 'Ask him how far to the cave.'

We were in shit state. My jeans were in shreds; my legs shiny with blood and sweat. Everybody was caked in mud.

Salkic and Jerry were still struggling to keep Benzil upright as we stumbled downhill.

Nasir's eyes narrowed as he scanned the landscape below us. I could see he was getting worried, and so was I. I didn't want to use a cave: it was obvious cover, and would probably have only one point of entry and exit. If they followed us, they would check it out for sure. But as I looked around us, I realized that if we couldn't outrun them, it was probably our only option.

Nasir started gobbing off. Salkic nodded and turned back to me. 'Not far, near the bottom. I know the cave he is talking about now. My father also fought there.'

This side was much steeper, and we stumbled after Nasir as he picked his way through the mud and rock, trying to find an easy route down. He stopped after another couple of hundred metres and pointed east. I followed the direction of his finger and could just make out a dark shadow on the side of the hill.

A second later, there were two high-velocity cracks above us. I looked up and saw the first of our pursuers crossing the skyline. Fuck it, the decision had been made for us.

80

It looked like it had been a natural cleft in the rock that had been given a makeover with several crates of Serb high explosive: the mouth was now big enough to take a truck. Rubble was piled up on each side, and the tyre ruts in the track leading to it were smothered by grass and weeds.

The interior was cold and dank, but at least it gave us shelter from the wind. The walls glistened with slime and puddles of water splashed around our feet. Two rusty old cars and a skip full of wood had been abandoned just inside the entrance.

The further we went inside, the more it stank of mould and decay. The darkness and a couple of mounds of rock spoil, debris from the blasting operation that had widened the cave, gave us cover, but this was going to be as much of a tactical nightmare as I'd feared: a confined space and the only way out the way we had come in.

Benzil was suffering big-time. Jerry and Salkic lowered him on to the floor behind one of the mounds and tried to make him comfortable. He hardly even had the energy to apologize.

'Don't worry.' I crouched beside him to move some stone away from his head. 'It's OK. Just rest.'

There was no reply. His breathing was shallow and worryingly fast.

Salkic collapsed the other side of him in the gloom. Jerry just dropped where he was and fumbled with the clips of his bumbag. I crawled up the rock pile and looked through the cave mouth, about forty metres away, at the brightening sky. It was still dark this far in, and should stay that way. My eyes were already adapting.

Nasir had put himself on stag at the top of the pile to my left, and was also staring intently towards the entrance. I looked around at the other three. It's natural for people to bunch up in situations like this, and they were tearing the arse out of it. I got them to spread out a bit. If rounds started bouncing about in here I didn't want the flat tops getting two hits for the price of one.

'Fuck.' Jerry showed me what was left of his Nikon. A round had entered the left-hand corner and exited top right. He tried the power button. Not that that would help, even if the battery pack was OK. The lens was shattered.

'The phone, Jerry – is the phone OK?'

He nodded slowly, but I could see it wasn't much consolation.

Nasir started gobbing off and I could see

movement on the hill a couple of hundred metres or so from the cave mouth. 'Here they come.' I turned back to the others. 'We got five.'

Jerry scrambled up to me. 'Coming this way?'

'Not yet.'

I felt it; the look on Nasir's face said it. We were fucked.

Nasir settled himself into a fire position, scooping away some of the stone to make room for the curved magazine of his AK. The magazines on these things were so big and long that when you lay down you couldn't fire them from the shoulder. It was part of the doctrine according to Dr Kalashnikov: the AK was intended to be gripped in front of a hero of the Soviet Union as he leaped from the back of an APC and charged gallantly forward on full automatic.

Nasir's eyes never left the men on the track. He gobbed off something to Salkic.

'What's he getting so excited about?'

'Nasir said I must never tell anyone where Hasan is, or his brother's death would be in vain. He also wants to kill the aggressors.'

Nasir got the drift of what was being said and grunted. They were both grim-faced. As far as these boys were concerned, the war had never really ended.

I leaned into my pile of rocks, digging a space for my own magazine. 'Ramzi, you're the only one who knows?'

Salkic was taking deep breaths; Jerry slid back down to help Benzil into a more comfortable position. 'The only one here.'

Nasir muttered something and I looked out. 'They're coming.'

I slithered down too.

'Jerry, you got any idea how to use a pistol?'

He didn't bother looking up, just nodded.

'Good. Ramzi, tell Nasir to give him it.'

Nasir handed it over, along with a couple of mags. I couldn't see the make, but it didn't matter at this stage, as long as it went bang and Jerry knew how to point it and reload. Whether he had it in him to kill a fellow human being was something we'd be finding out soon enough. As for me, I'd always managed to be pretty calm at times like this, maybe because I could accept when I was in the shit, and had never been particularly bothered about dying. I just wanted to make sure I took as many of the fuckers with me as I could.

Nasir started muttering and I crawled back up my pile. The guys on the track had disappeared.

'Where'd they go?' I murmured to Salkic. 'Ask him where they went.'

Salkic did so. They'd gone off to the right, into dead ground.

The Motorola sparked up. 'Ramzi Salkic! Ramzi Salkic!'

The gravelly voice echoed round the cave.

I looked at Salkic for clues. His face was stony, but Nasir's was contorted with rage. He immediately started shouting back, then he turned and yelled at me too, so vehemently that flecks of spit showered across my face. If the flat tops hadn't known we were in here, they certainly did now.

Nasir rammed his weapon into his shoulder and fired off a burst.

I had to scream above the firing. 'For fuck's sake, stop! Ramzi! Get him to stop!'

Spent cases rattled on to the stones. The air was thick with cordite. Salkic tried to calm him down and at last he succeeded. Benzil stared up at me, eyes wide as saucers, trying hard not to look scared.

Return fire ricocheted off the walls as the flat tops shoved their automatic weapons around the edge of the cave and squeezed off. There was nothing any of us could do but curl up and hope.

Apart from Nasir, who yelled at the top of his voice and sprayed half a mag at nothing in particular.

'For fuck's sake, stop firing! Save ammo.'

Another long retaliatory burst came our way, filling the cave with sound heavy enough to feel.

Salkic shouted at him and tugged at his trouser leg, but I knew Nasir wasn't listening: blind hatred had taken over from common sense. If only he'd kept quiet, we could have let them come in and maybe been able to drop one or two.

It stopped as quickly as it started. I raised my head just enough to look over the top of the mound but saw nothing. Benzil was still curled up below me, Jerry half covering him despite my instruction to spread out. Salkic was below Nasir, who was up on his knees straining to find a target, still wanting to kill the world and his dog. He turned to me with wild eyes, and let loose another stream of angry words and saliva. His echo was as loud as their gunfire.

I ignored him and kept my eyes on the cave mouth. If he'd wanted to top me he would have done it by now. I wasn't sure what he was most sparked up about: his brother, me bringing the flat tops to Salkic, or that he wanted to kill everyone within reach. I hoped he still realized that if we were going to get out of here alive he'd need my steady pair of hands, as much as I'd need his not so steady ones. I waited until he'd finished and got his eyes back on stag.

'What's all that about, Ramzi?'

There was no answer. I turned and even in this light saw the glimmer of tears in his eyes.

Nasir tuned up again, venting his rage between Salkic, me and the cave entrance. Salkic reached up and put a hand on his leg, attempting to soothe him.

'What's going on, Ramzi? What the fuck is he saying?'

'He's blaming you because you led them to me in the mosque.' Salkic's face was a mask of pain. 'Not only is his brother dead, but now they say they are collecting his brother's wife, my sister, from Sarajevo. They have a family, two children.'

81

There was a few seconds' stunned silence as I slid down rocks next to Jerry and took the Thuraya out of his bumbag. The little red LED glowed brightly in the gloom when I hit the switch. 'Your sister got a phone?'

He recited the number and I tapped the buttons.

'We'll need to get nearer the entrance for a signal. Can we call Nuhanovic to get us out of this shit?'

Salkic shook his head. 'He has no phones. I drive there each time we need to talk. I'm sorry, this is not all your fault. I was in too much of a hurry after meeting you and Benzil. They must have followed me to the farm. Now we all have to pay the price.'

I checked Baby-G and the Thuraya: 06:47 and no signal.

I pulled up the antenna and pointed it at the entrance. 'You up for it?'

He stood, without a flicker of fear.

'Stay to the right, hugging that wall. If there's trouble, just turn and run back. Whatever you do, don't move into the centre of the cave.'

I held out my AK to Jerry. 'Can you handle one of these?'

He didn't look too sure, but he'd probably photographed enough guys using them to have a vague idea of which end was which.

'Ramzi, tell Nasir what we're doing. Tell him, if he's got to fire, to use single rounds and aim. We must save ammunition. Got that?'

He nodded and started to gob off in Serbo-Croat while Jerry took the AK.

'There's one in the chamber. You know how to work the safety catch?'

To my surprise, he immediately looked in the right place. The safety on an AK is a long lever on the right-hand side. All the way up is safe; first click down is fully automatic; next click down is single shot. Old Soviet doctrine: lots of firepower and not much aiming.

I took his pistol, a 9mm semi-automatic made in South Korea by Daewoo, the car people, and told him not to fire unless Nasir had a stoppage or got dropped. I didn't want to be in more danger from Jerry than the bastards outside.

'OK, Ramzi, you ready?'

Benzil gave a bit of a good-luck wave. Salkic nodded to him. 'If God wants me to die today, then so be it.'

'Enough of that fucking Muslim fatalism.' I meant it. 'Just have a quick word with him now so you stay alive and get us to Nuhanovic, all right?'

He patted my arm. *'Inshallah.'*

We bent low, trying to become part of the rock. After ten metres we had to get down on our stomachs and crawl through the puddles and chunks of rubble.

I checked the Thuraya every metre. One bar would be enough. Sweat poured down my face, despite the cold. And my twelve-dollar coat was no barrier to more stagnant water and mud. Sharp stone chips cut into my elbows and knees. The pain would come later.

I could hear them outside now, just to the right of the cave mouth. I stopped, Thuraya in my left hand, 9mm in my right, trigger finger out straight over the guard, thumb on the safety catch. No way was I giving myself the slightest opportunity to have an ND [negligent discharge] as we moved forward.

Still no bars, maybe ten metres short of the entrance.

'Salkic! Salkic!' It was Motorola voice again, followed by that mocking laugh.

Nasir screamed back. Whether they knew it or not, these guys were doing us a favour. The more noise they made, the more cover it gave us.

We inched forward. About two metres from the end, a bar appeared in the display. I stopped and motioned Salkic to come up level with me. Even Jerry joined in the shouting now. Nasir might be angry, but he wasn't stupid.

I hit Send on the number and passed the Thuraya to him. Then I held the pistol out in front of me, left hand supporting the right, aiming at about chest height, safety off and first pad of my finger on the trigger.

Nasir and Jerry were still letting the guys outside know what they thought of them at top volume, but they weren't getting much in return. Maybe the flat tops were becoming bored. Then I heard a roar of laughter. Whatever was being said, the flat tops thought it was pretty funny.

I hadn't heard Salkic say a word. I felt a tap on my arm and he passed me the phone. He didn't look happy. I listened; it was still ringing. I hit the button and leaned over so I was speaking right into his ear. My eyes were still forward, pistol out, pad on the trigger, safety off. 'You definitely know where we are?'

He nodded slowly. With my left hand, I fished around in my jeans for the Holiday Inn card and tapped in the number. 'Tell the hotel we're being robbed. They're armed. We need SFOR.'

I pressed Send and handed it over. While I concentrated on the entrance he muttered quietly into the mouthpiece.

Someone outside bellowed Salkic's name again and he took advantage of the noise to repeat the information more loudly.

The barrel of an AK poked round into the cave at about waist height. I took first pressure on the trigger of the Daewoo, my eyes glued to a point just above the muzzle.

I caught a glimpse of cheekbone and pulled the pistol up until I had the clear and focused foresight centre mass of the target. The rear sight was out of focus, just as it should be. The first pad of my forefinger squeezed the trigger a couple of millimetres, until I felt the first pressure stopping me moving it back any further.

Salkic was still mumbling into the phone, but I shut every ounce of background noise out of my head as I watched the cheekbone grow into a face, which half turned so its mouth could shout more efficiently into the cave. I could see the veins in its temple swell with effort as spit flew from its lips.

Then he turned to fire.

The weapon's foresight was level with his upper lip as I took second pressure. The pistol kicked in my hands and the boy crumpled. Another AK, attached to a pair of hands, appeared and fired. I could feel the pressure waves of the rounds above me, then a volley of single shots rang out from behind us.

When the AK finally stopped, I pushed myself up against the rock, kept my head down, and started to run.

Heavy 7.62 short rounds started to bounce off the walls again but there was nothing we could do about it. We just had to keep low and keep moving.

As I scrambled over the rock piles into cover, Salkic was at my shoulder, still firing.

'Stop! Stop! Save the ammo!'

I grabbed the phone from Salkic and switched it off. 'What did they say? They understand?'

His chest heaved. 'I think so. And they must have heard the firing.' He slumped against the rock pile, trying to catch his breath.

Nasir and Jerry had stopped firing. The only sounds now were our breathing and the shouts that echoed from just outside the cave mouth.

Jerry took back the phone. 'Maybe she was out at the shops. Maybe they couldn't find her . . .'

Salkic looked up, his eyes full of concern as he looked beyond us for Nasir. 'We'll see.' His voice was far too calm. It was that fatalism shit again.

82

We lay there for another hour, Nasir and me on the rock piles with our AKs, the other three on the ground below us.

Mocking flat-top voices kept echoing round the cave, with the odd aggressive insult or a line or two from a song thrown in. Nasir couldn't restrain himself. Each time, he'd give as good as he got.

I eased my way down to Salkic. 'What's Nuhanovic going to do now we haven't turned up? Come looking?'

'I don't know. This is the first time I've failed.'

I put on my happy face. 'Let's try and make sure it stays that way. First up, we've got to keep eyes on the entrance at all times. Since he's already there, Nasir might as well take the first hour.'

I wanted to get a routine going. A routine gives a sense of purpose and meaning. It kids you something productive is happening.

Salkic gobbed off and Nasir nodded, then cleared his nostrils into the rocks.

'Ramzi, get that radio of yours on, just in case Nuhanovic sends some of your guys out and they get line of sight with the cave.' There was a chance anyone trying to raise us would just scroll through the frequencies.

Benzil was still in a bad way. His face was etched with pain and concern. The scabs on his cheeks had cracked and started weeping again. 'Do you think SFOR will come?' His throat sounded like sandpaper. He needed liquid. He wasn't the only one.

'Absolutely. Sure of it.'

He pulled me so close I could smell the sourness of his breath. 'Nick, what we talked about in Baghdad ... the offer is still there. I know Rob would want you to take his place. We still have a purpose. I'm sure this is just a temporary setback that you will overcome for us.'

'Let's talk about it later, yeah?'

I crawled back up the rock pile to check on Nasir. He indicated with a shake of his head that nothing had changed, but wouldn't look at me. Fair one, I'd be pissed off, too. I knew I'd have to watch him when we got out of here. When he reckoned he no longer needed me, that AK of his might be pointing my way.

'What do you think, Nick?' Jerry crawled to the bottom of the rocks. 'They still there?'

'You're welcome to take a look.'

I slid down alongside him and put my lips to his ear. 'Keep that weapon of yours handy and watch Nasir. He's fucked off with us. We need to look out for each other.'

'Ramzi! Ramzi!' The gravelly voice from the cave mouth was now calm and controlled. Whatever it was saying, I liked it even less than when it was in mocking mode.

I moved back up to Nasir. Way in the distance, I could see a 4x4 making its way along the track. I watched it disappear off to our right. Salkic joined us. As Nasir filled him in, the look in his eyes told me all I needed to know.

'Your sister?'

The radio crackled in his pocket. I made out a gravel-voiced 'Ramzi! Ramzi!' Then Salkic pressed the button and spoke. I couldn't see that he was crying, but I could hear it. He was doing his best to make sure that whoever was at the other end couldn't do the same.

Nasir mumbled away to himself, then started to rant at no one in particular.

Benzil's eyes widened again. 'What is it, Ramzi? What do they want?'

'To know where Hasan is.'

Before I could say anything, a piercing scream echoed round the cave. Nasir ripped the radio from Salkic's hands and cracked it against the rock, but the screams and begging continued from just beyond the cave mouth.

Salkic lay with his arms over his head to try to block out the world. I knew exactly how he felt.

Nasir scrambled over the rocks and ran towards the light.

'For fuck's sake!'

I picked up my AK and started after him, flicking the safety down to full automatic. He might want to kill me once this was over, but I needed him alive if we were going to have a chance of getting out of there first. He kept left, weapon in the shoulder, oblivious to me behind him.

Fifteen metres to go and the moans and cries outside were drowned by the crunching of our feet on the rock chips. I checked safety again.

We only made it another five metres before another barrel appeared in front of us and fired a long burst into the cave. Nasir stood his ground and got some rounds down as I moved to his right and joined in.

Nasir didn't need any shouting at. We were on autopilot. He turned on the spot, ran back a few paces, stopped, turned and fired. I followed suit as we fired and manoeuvred back to safety. I could taste the cordite as empty cases clinked off the walls.

I turned for the last time to see Nasir and Jerry firing from the rocks. As I ran and hurled myself over the pile between them, I could feel the pressure waves of Nasir's AK against my face as they covered me in.

Everything fell silent, apart from the hissing of my barrel as I put it on the ground and it made contact with a puddle. Nasir slapped me on the shoulder as we both climbed back up to our vantage-point. It seemed as if I was in his good books at last, but I wouldn't stop watching my back.

We kept our eyes on the entrance as we both changed mags. I only had thirteen rounds left; I fed them all into one mag.

I heard a whimper then a shout behind me, and took a moment to work out where it came from. Nasir shook his head and pleaded with Salkic. The Motorola had survived his attempt to destroy it, and Salkic wanted to listen. His sister was sobbing, but defiant.

Salkic tried to mutter a few words of comfort but ended up in tears. His tormentor mocked and jeered as her sobs turned into rhythmic cries of pain.

Nasir ripped the radio from Salkic's hands, hurled it to the ground and stamped on it, but it brought them only a few seconds' respite. We could hear her outside, closer now, and Salkic retreated into a dark place of his own as his sister's agony filtered into the cave. 'She told me to be strong, and I will be,' he murmured to himself. 'The most important thing is protecting Hasan.'

Nasir sparked up, shouting at the top of his voice. If my guess was right, it had less to do with anger than drowning sound.

We all went quiet, apart from Nasir, who carried on trying to keep the cries at bay.

83

Everything went quiet. No more screams, no more shouts, not even from Nasir. Benzil insisted he did his share and went on stag above us, muttering a quiet prayer to himself.

Unless our call was taken seriously and SFOR appeared, night was going to be our only hope. I checked Baby-G: 11:14. If we could hold out until dark, we might be able to break out and make a run for it, especially if the cloud cover held.

'Oh, God! Oh, God!'

Benzil was no longer praying: he was in shock.

Nasir was the first one up the rocks to join him. I was close behind.

The silhouette swayed in the cave mouth, then staggered a couple of steps to one side. Nasir could not suppress a gasp of anguish.

Salkic and Jerry came up to join us, just as the girl started to stagger in our direction, like a drunk coming down an alley. She lost her balance and bounced against the wall. Nasir pulled his weapon up into the aim as she called out for her brother. 'Ramzi? Ramzi?'

One hand now against the wall for balance, she took a few more unsteady steps and groaned. Nasir still had his AK up, butt in the shoulder. Tears streamed down his face as he begged Salkic. They argued, and Nasir handed him the weapon.

Like me, Jerry didn't need a translation. Either before or after the rape, she would have been drugged, then rigged up with explosive. It had happened all the time during the war. Mothers were rigged up and pushed back towards the trenches where their sons, husbands and fathers were holding the line. Serbs or Muslims, it didn't matter, each side was as bad as the other. Now it looked as if the guys outside had decided that if Salkic wasn't going to give Nuhanovic away, there was no point keeping him alive. Then again, maybe they just wanted to see how he'd react, and have a bit of fun.

She was no more than twenty metres from us and something needed to happen. But this was family shit and I was keeping well out of it. One of them would have to drop her.

Jerry dragged Benzil down to explain the score as Salkic begged her to stop, choking on his tears. Nasir joined in, but her only response was to hold out her arms, lose her balance and fall to her knees.

Now would be a good time: she was a static target. It would be a cleaner kill.

Salkic's eyes were on Nasir's, begging his

brother-in-law for help. He couldn't raise his arms.

Benzil had just worked it out. 'Oh, God, he is telling him to shoot her . . .'

Salkic finally lifted the weapon into the aim as she tottered to her feet, calling out to him like a child. 'Ramzi . . . Ramzi . . .'

Nasir urged him on, but the stock just collapsed off his shoulder. Nasir turned his attention to his sister-in-law, pleading with her to stop.

She came a few steps closer. In the gloom, I could see that her nightgown was ripped and she was covered with blood. She was totally spaced out.

I couldn't see a line behind her.

Maybe she wasn't rigged up. Maybe this really was just their idea of a good day out.

Nasir screamed at her. The sound reverberated round the cave and she stumbled against the wall, disoriented. She took another couple of steps. I still couldn't see a line.

Salkic brought the AK into the aim again but it wasn't going to happen.

She continued to stumble forwards. This had to be done or we'd all be dead.

Fuck this. I got my butt in the shoulder and pushed the safety all the way down to single shot. All the shouting and screaming around me became background noise.

I lined up the rear- and foresight so they were centre mass of her head. She'd be dead before she heard the round fired.

There was a shot from my right and some

of the back of her head slapped against the wall.

I turned. Jerry had the 9mm up in the aim.

She was on the ground, but still moving. Nasir grabbed Salkic, pulling him behind the rock pile. The flat tops might detonate her now she was down.

Jerry fired again but his tears and shaking hand got in the way of his aim.

He didn't miss with his third round. Her body quivered, she gave a low moan, then nothing. I scrambled over, grabbed Jerry, and we joined the others behind the mound.

He took fast, shallow breaths; his whole body was shaking. I eased the weapon out of his hands, applied safe, and put it into his pocket.

We waited, but there was no explosion, only Salkic's chilling sobs of grief. I wished there had been. It would have made us all feel a lot better to know Jerry had done the right thing.

There was a chorus of laughter and catcalls from the lip of the cave. Nasir held Salkic's head into his chest. His eyes drilled into me. Benzil crawled back up the rocks.

Salkic pushed Nasir away, dug under his shirt and pulled out the two keys. He handed them to me, fingers caked with mud.

Benzil carried on praying above us as Salkic talked me through the approach to Nuhanovic's house, explained the whole security set-up. His voice was measured, almost robotic. 'I am now going to do the two things I wish most: protect Hasan and avenge my sister.'

Benzil protested. 'Enough people have died. Please, let's wait for SFOR.'

Salkic was scarily calm. 'I do not fear joining my sister in paradise, if it is God's will.'

Jerry and I exchanged a glance. More of that fatalist shit.

He told Nasir exactly what he had told us, and by the tone of the exchange Nasir wanted to go with him. Salkic wouldn't hear of it. Nasir had to stay with us. They embraced each other, then he nodded to each of us in turn and got to his feet. Hollering and shouting at the flat tops, he started down the cave.

He reached his sister and knelt down. His shoulders shook as he stroked what was left of her head.

Very gently, he turned her on to her stomach. Please, let there be a rig on her. I couldn't see anything. Salkic was in the way.

Then I heard the rasp of gaffer-tape. Nasir muttered in Serbo-Croat, but I got the gist. I watched as Salkic removed three egg-shaped hand grenades from her back. A string was attached to the middle one. The way she'd fallen must have prevented them detonating it.

'Jerry, she was rigged.'

Nasir looked at him and nodded. It wouldn't be much consolation, but he'd done the right thing.

Jerry looked stunned. Nothing had registered with him, one way or the other. He was probably still rerunning her death in his head video.

Salkic had much the same expression as he

wrapped a grenade in each of his hands and pulled out the pins. Then he scooped her into his arms. Leaning back to take her weight, he began to stagger towards the daylight.

We watched him all the way to the end of the cave, where he took a couple of steps to his right and disappeared.

84

We all froze. Would they drop him on sight?

Maybe ten seconds later we knew the answer. The first of the grenades kicked off, then the second. I was up and running before the echoes had stopped. I could only hope Nasir was close behind. Fuck knows what I was going to do if I found myself alone when I got out into the open. I'd just have to make the best of the confusion and take on whoever was left moving.

There was no time for anything fancy: just butt into the shoulder, a deep breath and out into the grey light.

I swung right and immediately saw movers – two, three, I couldn't be sure. Smoke hung low around the impact points.

I double-tapped into centre mass of a crawling flat top. A burst from behind me knocked another off his feet. Nasir was with me.

There was more firing behind us and to the right. Single shots, 9mm. Jerry was taking on the scabbed-up 4x4. The body at the wheel jerked and slumped. It was Goatee, the blood-drenched Motorola still in his hand.

I ran past Salkic. He was lying next to his sister: he must have dropped her and thrown the grenades at the wagon, then got dropped himself. He looked as though he might still be alive, but I didn't check: there was a runner down in the low ground beyond the 4x4, maybe a hundred and fifty metres away. I sat with my back against a wheel, brought my legs up, shoved my elbows into the sides of my knees to make a platform for the weapon, rammed it into my shoulder and took aim.

My first shot missed. Nasir knelt alongside me as I took aim again. His first round went high. The guy was nearly two hundred metres away now, following the line of the valley. I took two big breaths to oxygenate myself, squeezed first pressure and held the foresight about three body-widths behind him. One more breath, let it out, hold . . . I moved the foresight past him to the left until it was one body-width in front, then took up second pressure. The butt kicked back into my shoulder and this time he went down. His screams took a while to reach us. I watched for a moment as his legs thrashed on the ground. I could have given him one more but, fuck it, I might need the round.

Nasir raised his head suddenly and searched the sky. I heard it too: the throbbing of rotor blades.

I checked for Jerry. He was kneeling by Salkic, and it looked like the two of them were having some kind of profound moment. There wasn't time for that shit. He'd been sliced up by strands of steel-wire shrapnel from the grenades. He was in a bad way, but he was alive.

'Jerry, go and get Benzil!'

He looked up and shook his head. 'Wait.'

'No, now – no time! The fucking heli – go get him out!'

I shoved him out of the way and took hold of Salkic's head, making sure I got eye-to-eye.

Jerry stood up, pumping his arms as he started to run back towards the cave. The Daewoo was still clutched in his hand.

'Put the fucking safety catch on!'

He stopped, fumbled with the weapon, then disappeared into the cave mouth.

'Ramzi, listen to me. We're going to go and hide until SFOR have lifted you, OK? Ramzi, you hear me?'

I shook Salkic's head gently, trying to get him to listen. 'You take Benzil and Nasir with you, all right? Jerry and I will take cover until you've gone. You understand?'

He did his best to nod. I went and picked up one of the flat-tops' AKs and took off the magazine. He had no spares either. 'Nasir, Nasir!' I pulled him over to me. 'Ramzi, tell him what's going on.'

The helicopter was still hidden by cloud, but getting closer. If the cave was well known from the war, they'd be heading straight for us on GPS.

Salkic muttered some more stuff to Nasir and I ran back up the hill, my body wet with sweat.

Benzil was slumped just inside the cave, with Jerry doing his best to keep him going. 'Benzil, SFOR are coming. You go back with Salkic and Nasir, OK?'

He shook his head. 'No, no, I must see—'

'No time. You'll slow us down. Go back to the city, get sorted out, just lie your arse off about what's happened. We'll come for you after we've met him. If he wants to see you now, he'll still want to see you in a few days.'

The rotor blades were getting lower.

Benzil muttered something I couldn't make out above the din. 'Shut the fuck up!' Flecks of my saliva splashed on to his cheek. 'Listen to me! Make up a story. We'll get back to the city and we'll find you. Just don't tell them we're here, got it?' I pushed him out towards the entrance. 'And make sure you square the story with Salkic.'

He didn't have time to answer. Nasir appeared and started to drag him out. I wanted to thank him for firing at the runner and not me, but there was no time for nods or handshakes. It wasn't as if we'd become best mates or were now in some sort of brotherhood thing.

I grabbed Jerry and shoved him to the back of the cave to give him the facts of life.

We lay curled up as small as we could behind the rock pile and listened as the heli came into a hover just outside.

85

A second helicopter appeared about half an hour after the first, probably to ferry in more troops and pick up the bodies. The pilot landed about a hundred metres from the cave but didn't close down. The wind had picked up, hurling rain in all directions; he'd keep the rotor blades turning in case the thing didn't restart.

We listened to it for at least twenty minutes while the clearing party was at work. They were German, by the sound of it. One or two yodelled into the cave just to hear the echo. A couple ventured further inside, but nowhere like all the way to the back. Maybe they didn't like the dark; maybe they didn't like the idea of stepping on any mines or booby traps. About the only bit of luck we'd had in the last twenty-four hours was not tripping any of that shit ourselves.

I gave Jerry a shake the moment the heli had lifted off. 'Better go and get that wagon while we still have the chance.'

When we got to the cave mouth, I had to laugh.

The 4x4 had been cordoned off with blue and white scene-of-crime tape; it was practically gift-wrapped in the stuff. Some of the empty shell cases even had little flags stuck into the mud beside them.

The smile soon wiped itself off my face as we left the efficient German crime scene behind us. According to Salkic, the vehicle he'd have used to take us to Nuhanovic was parked in the biggest of the barns at the ambush site. The wind was bitterly cold and sliced into every millimetre of my exposed wet skin. I kept my arms tight against my sides and pulled up the collar of my coat to conserve as much warmth as I could. If I had to move my head I'd turn my whole body. I didn't want the slightest bit of wind or freezing rain down my neck.

We'd been going no more than twenty when I turned to check on Jerry and my foot slipped. I went down, and as my knees hit the rock they felt like they were on fire. I hoped I hadn't smashed a kneecap, but there was fuck all I could do about it. Black cloud cover was more or less total now. No wonder the heli pilot hadn't wanted to hang around.

Twenty more, and the wind was driving freezing rain straight into our faces. My eyes were streaming. All we could do was keep our heads down.

I stopped for Jerry. He shuffled up alongside me and stood so close that his breath merged with mine as it got whipped away by the wind.

The closer we got to the ridge, the stronger the gusts became. The ambient temperature was low enough as it was, but the wind-chill took it close to freezing. I was beginning to feel light-headed.

I realized I was suffering from the first stages of hypothermia. We needed to get out of the wind and we needed to get off the hill.

When we finally got to the top, the wind was so strong it nearly knocked me over. And what I saw through the sheets of rain down in the valley nearly finished the job.

A crane was lifting the Audis on to the back of a low-loader. SFOR troops swarmed around the wreckage of the truck, and they didn't look in as much of a hurry as I'd have liked. We couldn't go down there, but we had to get out of this fucking wind and rain. We had to go back to the cave.

We turned back uphill, leg muscles stinging as they tried to keep us moving. I made it to the top first, and looked down. Things this side of the valley weren't much better.

Jerry drew level with me. 'What's wrong?'

I motioned him down beside me and pointed. Three sets of headlights were closing in on the cave. They were probably going to pick up the 4x4, and maybe stick some more flags around the place. Whatever, we couldn't get back to the cave.

Jerry knew it too. 'What now?'

'Stay up here and get out of the wind. Soon as they leave, we go for the wagon. If it's still there . . .'

We moved back the way we'd come. The rain

made it almost impossible to see the farm and SFOR boys now, but that wasn't altogether a bad thing. Just like with the snipers during the siege, if we couldn't see them, they couldn't see us.

We ended up in what looked and smelt like an old sheep hollow, worn away over the centuries. But if it was good enough for them, it was good enough for us. We wrapped ourselves around each other, our faces just inches apart, trying to share what little body heat we had left.

Lifting my head, I couldn't see anything down in the valley now, just solid walls of rain. It came down so hard it felt like we were being attacked by a swarm of ice-cold bees.

'We'll wait until they've gone – or last light.' My throat was dry and rasping. I was wet, cold and hungry. What wouldn't I have given right now for a toasted cheese sandwich and a mug of monkey tea under the duvet, stretched out on the settee in front of the Discovery Channel?

Jerry's head moved, which I took to be a nod.

As the minutes ticked by, the ground itself seemed to become colder and soggier. I could feel his body warmth at the points where he was making contact with me, but the rest of me was freezing. Every time he fidgeted to get comfortable, I could feel the cold attack the newly exposed area. At least we were in cover. It's a psychological thing: get up against or under something and you begin to imagine you're a bit warmer. You're not, of course: you just think you are.

The wind howled against the lip of the hollow. The downpour was getting well into its stride, bouncing off my PVC coat like one long drum-roll.

86

At least two very cold hours must have passed with me listening to the wind and Jerry shivering and fidgeting constantly to get some kind of feeling back into his limbs. I wrapped him closer to me, for my benefit as much as his. 'Listen, with that camera of yours fucked, it's pointless you carrying on. Why not get down the hill to SFOR?'

He shook his head. 'Fuck, no. Why give up now, when we're so close?'

'You got no reason to go now, and you're in shit state.'

'So are you. Besides, I can still interview him. You ever thought I might want to know who killed Rob?'

'That's not the only thing I want to talk to him about.'

Despite his misery, Jerry managed a brief smile. 'What, like expenses?'

I looked down the hill. I still couldn't see the barns. I watched the top of his shivering head for a long time, wondering whether to tell him. But why change the habit of a lifetime? Even as a kid, I'd lied about where I'd been and what I'd done – not just to my mum; to everyone. I didn't want people to know things about me. It made me feel vulnerable. My stepdad would just use it as an excuse to fill me in. Why give people the rope to hang you with?

In the end, I just thought why the fuck not, as long as I left out who I really worked for. Perhaps if I carried on talking, I'd keep our minds off the cold. Jerry got everything, from the time I arrived in Bosnia to the time I left. I told him about the Paveway jobs. I told him about watching Nuhanovic at the cement factory, and listening to the screams of the girls being raped.

And, finally, I told him about Zina.

'She knew I was there, she just kept crawling those last few feet to the hide, her eyes begging me for help, but I couldn't do anything.

'I could have saved more lives than even Nuhanovic. At least he had the bollocks to intervene. All I did was watch, put the job first . . .'

'That's why you want to see him? You feel guilty?'

He looked at me for a long time, shaking and trembling all the while. 'You can't beat yourself up about that sort of shit. Believe me. I mean, do I grab the girl who's burning with napalm and try to put out the flames or do I take her photograph?

'When we were here in 'ninety-four, I was a kid: Mr Idealism, Mr Humanity. I told myself I was a human being first and a photographer second.' He gave an ironic little laugh as the rain fell down his face. His stubble had been washed clean. 'It took me three fucking wars, man, to understand the answer to that question. I'm the guy who presses the shutter, nothing else and nothing more. The world needs those images to jolt people out of their cholesterol-lined comfort zones. That's my contribution to humanity.' He leaned forward. 'You're no different, man. You had to keep your distance; if it had gone right you would have saved a lot more people than you saw killed. This making sense to you?'

It was, but it wasn't making me feel any better. I still wanted to square things with Nuhanovic.

'You remember that Kevin Carter shot in my apartment? You know, the kid and the vulture?'

I nodded, realizing that I'd just rubbed my soaking hair and sniffed my hands like some kind of addict. It was a while since I'd done that stuff.

'Three months after taking it, the poor fuck connected a hose to the exhaust pipe of his pickup truck and took a few deep sucks. The problem for Kevin was he wasn't able to tell the world if that girl survived. He was honest about it. He admitted he sat there for twenty minutes, just hoping the vulture would spread its wings. When it didn't, he took the picture anyway – then he sat under a tree, crying, talking to God, and thinking about his own daughter.

'When he got back to the States, he started getting midnight hate calls for not helping the girl. Even one of the fucking papers wrote – I'll never forget it – "The man adjusting his lens to take just the right frame of her suffering might as well be a predator, another vulture on the scene." The girl began to haunt him.'

I knew how he felt. I couldn't get Zina's mud- and blood-covered face out of my head, and I couldn't get the smell of Kelly off my hands.

'It wasn't fair to attack him. If I'm zooming in on someone dying, I'm composing an image, maybe even a work of art, but inside I'm scream- ing, wanting to go cry under a tree. Thing is, Nick, these suburban do-gooders, with their Gap and flat-pack lives, saw one little girl. Kevin was surrounded by a famine, and that kid, she was just one of hundreds he'd seen dying that day. If he hadn't taken that shot, not one of those fat fucks back home would even know where the Sudan was.'

We lay huddled a while longer as the rain lashed down.

'You know what, Nick? I wanted to get Fikret into the car and put him on a plane to the States – but what do you do when you see hundreds like him, everywhere you turn? I still think about that little fuck, wonder if he survived. Maybe he's playing soccer right now. Maybe he's lying in a mass grave. It tears me apart some days.' He took a deep breath. 'I think I can imagine what you went through, you know. Just don't beat yourself up over it.'

He placed a hand on my shoulder. 'The whole world is fucked up, man. You did what you felt was right. Hindsight is for those fucks who've never been out there, never had to make those kinds of choices. Since having Chloë, I've done a lot more thinking about that shit.'

'Tell me about it.'

He looked surprised. 'You got a kid?'

I rubbed my frozen hands together. 'Her name's Kelly.'

Maybe Ezra had been right. Maybe there was a right moment for everything to come out; maybe I couldn't have stopped it if I'd tried. It certainly felt that way.

I started to tell him everything.

'Her mother and father were my friends, my only friends. Her little sister was my god-daughter. Kelly was only nine when they were killed, in their house, just outside DC. I was too late to save them. Just by minutes. Kelly was the only one left. I didn't realize it at the time, but she was all I had left too.'

The rain started to ease a little while I fumbled my way through the day I'd discovered the bodies, and the weeks Kelly and I were on the run together afterwards, and how she'd ended up with Josh and his family in Maryland. 'He's a minister now in some happy-clappy church . . .'

I told him about me being shit at the job of looking after her, totally inconsistent, and how I felt a bit of me died when I signed her over permanently to Josh's care, convincing myself it was the best thing for her.

Shivering and shaking, Jerry seemed to understand. 'How do you ever recover from something like that?'

'She never really—'

I felt a hand touch my shoulder. It must have taken a lot to move it from the warmth of his armpit. 'I mean you, man. How the fuck do you hold it all together?'

Good question. Fucked if I knew the answer.

We lay there in the rain for maybe another twenty minutes. I checked Baby-G: 16:28. The rain had eased just enough for me to make out the headlights moving down the valley back towards Sarajevo. 'Not long till last light, mate. Maybe we'll get a fire going in the barn, even boil up some water. Then it'll be smiles all round.'

87

My clothes stuck to my freezing wet skin. My hands were so cold, it took for ever to get the key into the old brass padlock and give it a turn. Jerry shivered behind me, waiting until the lock came off and the double corrugated-iron doors creaked open.

It was a little warmer inside than out, but not much. I couldn't even console myself that we were out of the wet. It had stopped raining just as we got to the bottom of the hill.

'Go find the wagon,' I said. I wanted to keep Jerry moving.

I fumbled about for a light switch as he ventured further in, but didn't find one.

'Got it! Over here!'

Keys in hand, I stumbled towards the tapping noise he made against the bodywork. I eventually bounced off a high-sided wagon. I felt my way round the left-hand side and got the door open. The interior light came on to reveal a VW van and my vaporizing breath.

The van was one of the newer, squarer models but it was just as rusty and battered as any old surfer's Combi. The back was full of empty hessian and nylon sacks, lengths of baling twine and handfuls of straw. The cab floor was littered with newspapers, sheets of paper, pens, drinks cans, all the usual shit.

I jumped in and unlocked the passenger door for Jerry, then turned the ignition. The diesel engine fired after a few protesting shudders. I flicked on the headlights. The inside of the barn was high, with a corrugated-iron roof, and the floor would have been big enough to fit a dozen vehicles, if they didn't mind parking on piles of sacks and bits of old farm gear.

I pressed down on the cigarette lighter, then threw the gear shift into reverse, backing up so the lights covered as much of the place as possible. The fuel gauge showed half full. The cigarette lighter clicked back up. 'Check it, mate. See if we can get a fire going.'

I left it in neutral, engine running, the exhaust chugging against the concrete block wall. I was beginning to feel more energized as I jumped down on to the hard compacted earth. Fuck carbon monoxide – I just wanted to get the cab warm and be able to see my way around.

Concealed behind piles of cardboard and wooden crates, Salkic had promised, were six cans of diesel. I pulled away the crap until I found them, and lifted each one to check it was full.

Jerry gathered empty polythene sacks and

lumps of wood, straw, cardboard, anything that would burn. He made a pile big enough to give us some heat but not so high we torched the place, then ran back to the van. He got some newspaper going in the cab, and brought it over. We were soon warming our hands and faces and inhaling the stink of burning plastic.

I used a rusty old knife to rip arm- and neck-holes in a couple of the sacks and handed him a set. 'We need to get our clothes a bit drier, mate.'

I'd always hated peeling off wet things and exposing my skin to the cold, but the fibres had to be wrung out so they could do their job and trap a little air.

We ended up looking like Cabbage Patch dolls, but at least the sacking gave us an extra layer against the cold. By the time we'd put our clothes back on top, all the dirt inside had turned to mud, but at least it was warmish mud. The fire was helping.

There were enough combustibles lying around for us to have stayed all night drying kit, but I wanted to get on the road just as soon as we could.

'Have a look round for something to boil up some water. Be good to get something hot down us before we go. I'll fill up the tank.'

Jerry moved off into the shadows as I picked up my AK and both our bumbags.

I kept the engine on now. If I closed it down it might not start again, so why take the risk? I dumped the bumbags on the passenger seat, folded some cardboard into a cone and shoved it into the tank. After doing the smell and taste test to make sure it was diesel, I emptied in the first can.

It couldn't take all of the second, so I slung it in the back along with the three full ones. I was already fantasizing about heading up the road, the heater going full blast and a stomach full of hot water. What more could anyone want?

I went to the cab and leaned inside to check if the footwell heaters were doing their stuff. Nothing yet. The bumbags were just inches from my face, and through the nylon of Jerry's I could see what was left of his camera. Jerry had been lucky. The Nikon had probably saved his life. I unzipped the bag and pulled out the camera. Part of the lens fell on to the seat.

The round had ploughed through the casing. The body looked as if it was about to break in half. As I held it in my hands, that was exactly what happened. And, digital or not, I knew enough about cameras to see at once there was something inside this one that shouldn't have been.

I managed to slide a finger between the battery and its casing. The blue plastic disc was about the size of a 50p piece; it was cracked and chipped, but I could see clearly what it was, and it had nothing whatsoever to do with taking pictures.

My hands began to shake as I pulled out the Thuraya and powered it up. I pulled out the download cable and checked if anything else was in there that shouldn't be, then hit the menus.

This time, Jerry had fucked up with his opsec.

Registered on the call list were Salkic's sister's number and the hotel's, and one other, at least twenty digits long. It wasn't any source's land-line number in DC, Virginia or Maryland, or any normal cell number. They, too, have area codes.

Who the fuck had he been calling? I'd seen him in the al-Hamra with the cable attached. Had he been downloading pictures? Of who? Of what? To ID us for the attack?

Fuck the blue device for now. I could deal with that later.

There was a shout from the shadows. 'Hey, I got a can without a hole! It's gonna need one mean clean, though.'

88

I jumped out of the van, AK in hand. I pushed the safety all the way down and got the butt into the shoulder. Taking deep breaths to calm myself, I leaned into the weapon and aimed at the noise coming towards me from the darkness.

He moved into the van's lights, using them to inspect the tin can in his hands. His shadow danced along the far wall.

I stayed behind the headlights, waiting for him to get closer.

'Stand still. Hands up, both up.'

'Hey, it's me.' He held up the can, squinting into the beams. 'I got us a kettle.'

'The pistol. Where's the weapon?'

'My jacket. Nick, what's—?'

'Shut the fuck up. Drop the can. Kneel down and put the pistol on the floor.'

He did as he was told and I moved forward, weapon up, still in the shoulder, releasing first pressure.

'What's happening, man, what I do wrong?'

I came at him out of the beams, my boot connecting with his head before he had a chance to get up again. He hit the floor and I kicked the pistol away from him, then carried on kicking him wherever I could reach: head, arms, legs, back, anywhere he left exposed.

When he raised his hands to protect himself, I got him in the guts and he puked up blood-stained bile.

'You haven't been calling a DC source, have you?' I didn't give him time to answer, just kicked him towards the fire. 'You download from the al-Hamra to that fancy number?'

He tried to get to his knees again.

'That why the phone and camera were rigged up, was it?'

I kicked into the mass below me. He collapsed by the fire, falling into the embers and spreading them across the mud. He rolled back towards me, desperate to get away from it, and tried to curl into a ball. I could smell burnt hair.

'You got Rob killed, didn't you?'

Sweat poured off my face as I gave him another kick in the kidneys, then I got the AK butt back into the shoulder and dug the muzzle deep into his cheek.

I took first pressure.

'No, no, no . . .' he pleaded with me, his eyes made even more manic by the flames. 'I sent the shots, but there's no way they were connected with the attack. There wasn't time to rig anything up. No time!'

I could smell his fear and deceit: it was coming

off him in waves. 'I wanted to go with you, remember?' He sobbed. 'Please, Nick, please . . .'

I leaned into the weapon more; the muzzle dug deeper into his cheek. He fought for breath so hard through his split and swollen lips that he sprayed my face with blood and snot.

What the fuck was I doing? It was like an out-of-body experience. Someone else was controlling me, telling me to kill him.

'Nick, please . . . my family . . .'

I leaned more heavily into the weapon, felt the heat of the fire starting to burn my face. My finger held first pressure.

Then I stood up.

Jerry saw the safety click back up to safe, and rolled on to his side, his knees drawn up against his chest. He held the cuff of his jacket against his face as I went over to the pistol.

I picked up an oil-soaked rag and threw it towards him. 'Clean yourself up, for fuck's sake.'

He stuck it to his face and rocked backwards and forwards.

'You've been caught out, Jerry, accept it. You're in the shit.'

He tried to talk through the tears, the rag and the pain. I couldn't make out what he was saying so I knelt down beside him. 'Take that fucking thing away from your mouth. Who've you been talking to?'

He lifted the rag. I got a weak, snot-filled 'I don't know.'

This was going to be a long night.

But Jerry wanted to help. 'I don't know his name, man. I don't.'

'Did you use a number or a code or any of that shit?'

He shook his head slowly. Blood dripped down his face and on to his jacket. 'Just had to go see him in DC.'

'Where did you meet him?'

'An old building some place. I can't remember the street. The office was Hot something, Hot Black, something like that.'

It didn't have to mean anything.

For all I knew, lots of guys used the Hot Black business cover.

'What did he look like?'

What he said was mostly lost in the rag, but I heard enough to know the universe was caving in.

'He keeps calling me son. I'm not his fucking son. I'm no son of that asshole . . .'

'You're right, Jerry,' I said. 'He is an arsehole. Arsehole is George's middle name.'

89

'You know him?'

This was about me finding out what he knew, not the other way round. 'What's George got you doing?'

'He said you'd take care of me, help me find him. Once we did, I had to press a button on the side of the battery pack, then carry on with the shoot. I had to make sure the session lasted at least two hours. If we had to go early, I had to leave the camera.'

I started walking back towards the VW.

Jerry shuffled along behind me, trying to keep up so I could hear him over the engine.

'I know what he's got me doing, man. I'm not fucking stupid. It's some kind of tracking device, right? I press the button, they know where he is. They find him, they kill him. As soon as we got to the Palestine and then the Sunny Side Up I had to call him and press the button. That's all I know, man, that's all. I swear.'

He sat in the beam of the headlights, dabbing

the rag at his face, as if that was going to help.

'What did you tell George about Rob and Benzil at the al-Hamra?'

'He wanted to be on top of things. I had to tell him everything that was happening, every day. So when I called him about the military grabbing our asses, and then about Rob and Benzil, he wanted pictures. You gotta believe me, Nick, I only got the Beemer because that's where you guys were at. Can't have been anything to do with the hit . . .'

He let the rag fall from his face and his swollen, bloodshot eyes searched mine for help, forgiveness, anything.

'Why did you do it, Jerry?'

I reached into the cab and picked up the blue disc.

Blood dripped off his chin, making a small puddle in the mud. 'He said it would be one job, and all my problems would be over . . .' He coughed up some stuff from the back of his throat and spat it out.

'What problems? What's he got on you?'

Jerry had calmed a little. 'I fucked up.' He started dabbing again. 'I went to one of the training camps in Afghanistan with guys I'd met from Lackawanna. I got arrested when I landed back in Detroit.' He sounded almost angry. 'I'm no fucking terrorist. I was just chasing a story. They fucking knew that, but they still sent me to the Bay.'

'You were at Guantanamo?'

'Two fucking months, man, held in solitary.

Speaking to no one, nobody speaking to me. In the dark. Renee was totally out of her freaking mind – she didn't know where I was. Then one day this guy George turns up and plays the good cop, says he can get me out of there in a heartbeat – but I have to do something for him some time. Like having a favour in the bank. Well, he finally called it in. I told him I didn't wanna go, but I had to. He said if I didn't go find Nuhanovic, he'd kill Chloë.'

He crumpled, his face in his hands, sobbing into the rag, his shoulders heaving.

I pulled out the blue disc and put it on the van bumper. The technology had come on apace since the Paveway days. This wasn't just a tracking device. It was much more than that: it was a location device for time-critical targets. Once they're marked, they're hit. No need for man-in-the-loop technology. Now they had the Predator UAV [unmanned aerial vehicle], a remote-controlled aircraft about the size of a single-engined Cessna. They'd been around when I was here last, cruising at anything up to twenty-five thousand feet, but only used for what they were designed for, battlefield surveillance. They had real-time feed from infrared, thermal and normal cameras mounted in the nose; commanders could view the battlefield as easily as if they'd switched on the TV to watch a live traffic report on the Beltway.

Then, in around 2000, some boffin had had the bright idea of strapping an LTD to its nose alongside its surveillance package, and giving it a couple of hundred-pound Hellfire missiles to play with. So these days the operator just sat and watched a screen in the comfort of an operations room, until one of the sensors in the nose located the target – a tank, perhaps, or a carload of terrorists. All the operator had to do was splash it with the LTD then zap off the Hellfires, which would strike with an accuracy of plus or minus two metres. The only hard bit was identifying the target, especially if it was a single person. That had to be why George needed us here. It was back to the old man-in-loop technology again. Jerry would kick off the target indicator, which would start to transmit. The Predator would pick up the signal; the operator would home in the LTD and kick off the Hellfires.

I turned to Jerry and leaned against the front of the van. 'You've fucked up big-time. That's not just a tracking device. You're at the arsehole end of the detect, decide, destroy gang now.' I held up the blue disc in the light. 'This thing brings in missiles. George wants Nuhanovic dead . . . you and me are just collateral damage.

'We're in the shit, Jerry. He won't care that the camera's fucked. To him, the mission is every-thing. Believe me, I know the man.'

I clenched the device hard in my fist. The White House could have wanted Nuhanovic dead for any of about a dozen reasons that I could think of, from plunging Coke sales to Islam getting a bit more friendly with itself. But right now that didn't matter. What did was the bit about collateral damage.

Jerry pulled the rag away from his mouth. 'What we going to do, Nick? Call George? Maybe tell him what's happening?'

Jerry still hadn't quite got the hang of this. I paused. 'What was Salkic talking about back there, outside the cave? He say anything about Nuhanovic?'

He looked up, his face still creased with pain. 'No, just weird stuff, really. He wanted to thank me for killing the son of an aggressor whore. He said Nuhanovic would be happy – they were animals and not good for business, they messed up business . . . something like that . . .'

'What the fuck did he mean by that?'

'Dunno . . . he was pretty spaced out . . .'

I looked down at Jerry as he tried to clear enough blood from his nose to breathe. Why hadn't Salkic just said Goatee was the son of an aggressor whore, and leave it at that? 'You sure he said "business"?'

He didn't bother looking up. 'Yep, for sure.'

'Shit.' I took a couple of very deep breaths and threw the locator to the ground. 'You're not the only one round here who's fucked up . . .'

I dragged him to his feet. 'Come on, in the van. We're going.'

90

Frost glazed the fields and road and sparkled under a clear sky.

The heater was on full blast, but wasn't up to spec. It couldn't even demist the windscreen, let alone keep us warm. The back windows, though, were fine. The sacks and diesel cans were probably snug as fuck.

Jerry's breath billowed round his head as he leaned forward, teeth rattling, to wipe the glass with his sleeve.

I followed suit with my side of the screen. 'That Kevin Carter photo? The way no one looked past the vulture and the girl to the real story? I reckon I've fucked up and not seen the real picture of Nuhanovic.'

'The real Nuhanovic?'

'What if Nasir wasn't in Baghdad looking after Nuhanovic, but there doing business for him? What if he was doing exactly the same as that arsehole Goatee? The competition.'

'Nuhanovic? Come on . . .'

'Why not?'

'Even if you're right about Nasir, it doesn't mean Nuhanovic is involved.'

'Doesn't it? Remember what Salkic said? They don't work for him, they serve him. They do jack shit off their own back, they follow his orders. So just what the fuck was he doing in "Chetnik Mama"?'

'Fuck.' He slumped back in his seat.

'You got it. So what was I really seeing at the cement factory? Was he saving the girls, or trading them?'

'So . . . Zina . . .'

I nodded. 'Got it again. Tell you what, if I'm right I'll kill the fucker for you.'

The van lurched into a pot-hole; Jerry groaned and grabbed his abdomen. I didn't feel too bad about it. The pain would soon disappear. The damage to his face would take a lot longer.

Jerry pulled the rag away from his nose. 'Not seeing the whole picture . . .' He gave a deep sigh. 'That wasn't my family you met in DC. I don't know who the fuck the woman was.'

'So that was all bullshit too?'

He nodded. 'I am married to Renee. I have got a daughter. They just weren't the ones you met.'

He leaned back, trying to ease the tension in his neck.

'She knows nothing about this. She thinks I'm in Brazil covering the elections . . . What if I fuck up, man?'

'Listen, the only chance of Chloë surviving is if

you just do exactly what I tell you and George never finds out that I know. Once we're back in DC, you stick to the story – whatever that's going to be.'

I didn't add that for the rest of his life he must never tell anyone, not even his wife. Whoever she was.

For myself, I felt strangely OK about George stitching me up. I'd always known he wasn't one for loose ends. I'd become one the moment I wanted a bike instead of him. At least I knew where I stood.

What a set-up. I bet George had enjoyed rigging up the exhibition and the false family as much as any operation he'd ever prepared.

We carried on down the road and I couldn't help smiling as he told me about his made-up family. 'The woman didn't know how to change a diaper. I had to show her. Even then she wouldn't do it.'

Unless they knew George's previous, most people would find it hard to imagine that a man representing a western democratic government could act this way. But Jerry had seen a bit of shot and shell in his time, as well as the bullshit that surrounded it. He knew better. But it wasn't helping him. He just stared out at the frost glinting back at us, hands in his armpits, maybe trying to conjure up comforting images of his little girl. I looked across at him. 'Listen, just do exactly what I say, OK? Nothing's going to happen to anyone.'

He nodded thoughtfully. 'Would he really kill

a child, Nick? How's he get it done? He have some sick fuck on call or what?'

There was no way he was getting any of that kind of information from me. 'You don't need to know, because it won't happen.'

'Why? Why do it when I've fucked you over, man?'

I kept my eyes on the road. 'I used to work for George. That's why Kelly's dead.'

I could feel his stare drilling into the side of my head. 'George killed Kelly? Fuck.'

I turned. His eyes were glazed, as if he was elsewhere. I knew that look very well: I'd seen it in the mirror often enough.

'She'd been snatched by some fuck-ups. George was holding me back, not telling me where she was because he didn't want me going into the house and fucking things up for him. He knew they'd probably kill her, but the job, the fucking job came first. By the time I got there and found her, well . . .'

I felt a jolt in the centre of my chest. The image of her dead body I described to Jerry was as vivid as a photograph.

Jerry wasn't looking good. 'Oh, fuck . . .'

I rubbed my hair and cupped my hand over my nose. 'I took her body back to the States, and Josh and I buried her alongside the rest of her family. It was standing room only in the church.' I rubbed my hands on my soaked jeans, trying to get rid of the smell. I needed to get back into the real world. 'I don't know if she would have been proud or embarrassed.'

I wished I could have fished in my wallet and pulled out a photograph like any other proud parent, but the simple fact was that I didn't have one. Not one she would have been proud of anyway. Just the one from her passport: her face had been covered in zits that day and I'd had to drag her to the photo booth. There were others from her house, of course, but they were in storage. One of these days I'd get round to sorting all that stuff out.

'Fuck it, it's all history now.' I pushed the gearshift into third as we headed uphill. 'I don't want anyone else to have those nightmares. No one deserves them. Except George – but that'll never happen.'

We both just stared at the road as it was hoovered up by the headlights.

'Listen, I'm sorry for fucking up your face. I saw the location device, the phone number, the camera thing at the al-Hamra and my head just kind of exploded.'

He had bigger things to worry about. 'I deserved it. You know, Renee told me once that Buddha said we all have two dogs inside us, one good, one bad, constantly fighting each other. Which one wins depends on which one's fed.'

'You don't have to come, you know. Everybody gets scared when they've got things to lose. You've still got your family, all that gear – I've got fuck-all. I'll take you back to the barn and go on my own.'

'Nah . . .' He gave me as much of a grin as he could manage. 'It's just like old times . . .'

I checked the dial. Another three and a bit Ks and we should be hitting our first landmark. The frost was setting in with a vengeance: what had been a light dusting on the tarmac was now more or less solid ice. I just kept it in third and hoped for the best.

I thought about Renee's dogs, and I knew this was one whole can of chunky Pal I didn't want to open again.

91

Salkic had said the forestry block was just over two Ks long, and the next marker to look out for was a firebreak.

I glanced at Jerry, who was so close to the heating vents he nearly blocked off the supply. 'We're going to hit it soon, a group of "bomb-blasted" trees on the right.' I'd liked Salkic's description.

I slowed down and he wiped his side window with his wet sleeve, but there wasn't just a group of devastated trees, there were scores of them; some splintered trunks were five or six feet high, some no more than stumps. Salkic had been wrong – they hadn't all been blown up: most looked as if they'd been flattened by tanks.

We both spotted the break at the same time. I stopped just short of it so we could use the headlights to check things out. There was a rush of even colder air as Jerry opened the door. He was so frozen he hobbled rather than walked over to the treeline, and I knew just how he felt.

He waved me on, jumping up and down to try

to get some warmth into his aching limbs. I put the gearshift into first and chugged towards him. The narrow opening in the trees certainly wasn't a fire-break; it was just wide enough for a vehicle.

Jerry got himself back into his seat and we edged forwards. It was like driving into a cave. The trees were just a couple of feet either side of us and the canopy above shut out the stars.

Jerry leaned over the dash and did his best to look through the windscreen.

After a hundred metres or so the track opened up a little, and the van juddered as I put it into second. There was no frost in here: it was too enclosed. The ground was soft, and I hoped it wasn't going to turn muddy. The VW was a long way from being a member of the 4x4 club.

Jerry gave the screen another big wipe. 'What's this fucking guy live in? A tepee or a tree-house or something?'

I checked the instruments again. We'd driven about eighteen hundred metres from the road. Ahead of us, at about the two K mark, was a junction left. After bouncing through another couple of pot-holes, the headlights picked it out.

I turned and looked at Jerry's silhouette. 'Fuck knows what's going to happen now. We've just got to play it by ear.'

'Can't wait.'

We started down the track.

'If it gets really fucked up and we have to split, we'll meet up where we turned into the forest. For fuck's sake, don't go too far into the treeline – it could be mined. I'll do the same, see if we can link up. If that doesn't happen in six hours, we're on our own.'

Jerry nodded slowly. 'In the cave, I never thought I'd get this far, man. I'm still shitting myself.'

I delved into what was left of my PVC coat pocket. 'You still got the pistol mags?'

He nodded as I passed him the Daewoo. 'Seeing as your old mate Osama has obviously shown you how to use the fucking thing.'

Salkic's directions were spot on. Six hundred metres later, the track was blocked by two giant wooden hedgehogs. 'Heads up, here we go.'

As we got closer, Jerry spread both his hands on the dashboard. Good move. We wanted them in full view of any nervous people with weapons.

I followed Salkic's instructions to the letter; stopped, left the lights on, engine running.

The two hedgehogs had been laid out to create a chicane that would just about take the van between them. I couldn't see a thing ahead of it, just the track continuing a short way, then disappearing into the darkness.

Jerry stared into the void. 'What now?'

'Just as he said. We wait.'

I began to wind down my window. Before I even got half-way, there was movement in the treeline to my left. A powerful torch beam hit the side of my face. I kept my hands on the wheel and my eyes straight ahead.

'Ramzi?'

'No Ramzi. Nick Stone.'

The voice from the trees was immediately

joined by others, muttering a whole lot of stuff I didn't understand. I could feel the engine chugging away through the steering-wheel, and made sure my hands didn't move off it.

A group of men stepped out of the forest. They were dressed in a ragbag of uniforms: American BDUs, German parkas, tall leather boots, a variety of furry hats. Every one of them carried an automatic weapon.

Both doors were pulled open. We were hauled out of our seats and round the front of the vehicle, where they could have a good look at us in the headlights. But it didn't feel like we were prisoners: we were controlled rather than dragged.

I kept my arms straight out in a crucifix position, and started shaking with the cold as they removed my bumbag and ran their hands over me. I saw my AK lifted out of the VW. A voice kept talking to me in Serbo-Croat, but the only word I understood was 'Ramzi'.

I tried my best to explain. 'Hospital. Boom! Bang! Doctor.' I didn't know what the fuck they thought I was talking about, but I didn't want to risk any sudden movements to help make things clearer.

Jerry's pistol and mags were taken off him, along with his bumbag. My hands were pulled down by my sides and the guy who'd done it seemed to be telling me to relax. They were now containing, not controlling.

There were four of them. They were all much older than Salkic, more Nasir's vintage. They were old enough to have been through the war, and it showed. A couple had scars on their faces, and the sort of look in their eyes that said they'd seen and done things they didn't need to talk about. I wondered if any had fingers missing.

Their weapons were clearly well oiled and maintained; some AKs and a number of Heckler & Koch G3s, a 7.62mm assault rifle with a twenty-round mag.

One of them – who seemed to be calling the shots – had big curly hair that fell way past his shoulders from under his Russian fur hat. A Motorola crackled somewhere in his thick sheepskin glove. There was some quick-time gobbing off, with 'Ramzi' and 'Nick Stone' making regular appearances. Eventually he passed it over to me, and pointed at the pressle.

'Hello? Are you Nick Stone?' The voice was male, educated, authoritative.

I hit the pressle. 'Yes. I've got someone else with me, Jeral al-Hadi. The photographer.' I thought it sounded a bit better having a Muslim in tow.

'Where is Ramzi?'

Didn't they know what had happened?

'He's alive. So is Benzil. They're back in the city.'

I rattled through what had happened at the cave.

'Wait one minute, please wait.'

I hoped it wouldn't be much more than that. I was freezing.

I gave the radio back to the glove and just stood there, the cold biting into every inch of me. It was like being back in the sheep hollow. I stamped my feet together and so did Jerry. Whoever was on the end of the Motorola gobbed off at one of the crew, who disappeared as the long-haired one offered us both a cigarette. I'd never smoked in my life, but I was almost tempted, just so I could cup my hands round a match.

Two green German parkas were produced and neither of us needed to be told twice to get them on, hoods up. These boys knew what it was like to be wet, cold and hungry, and only wanted that for their enemies. They'd be taking them back before first light, then.

We stood there for another ten minutes or so before the Motorola sparked up again, then we were herded into the back of the VW, alongside the spare diesel. I'd been right, it was much warmer. The long-haired one got behind the wheel and manoeuvred us through the chicane.

The track went straight for a while, then bent to the right and led towards a dirty white wall, about three metres high. Set into it was an archway, blocked by a pair of heavy wooden coach doors that were opening inwards as we approached.

92

The van bounced to a halt. The long-haired one jumped out and slid open the side door. Light flickered on the other side of the archway and a small man in a long black coat, fur hat and sheepskin boots appeared, an oil lamp clutched in his hand. It was Nuhanovic. Although his face was mostly obscured by his collar and hat, I could see he'd binned the beard. It didn't seem to make much difference: he still came across like somebody's favourite uncle.

'Please come in.'

His eyes were bright and piercingly intelligent. The corners of his mouth were lifted in a half-smile, but I wasn't sure whether it was aimed at me and Jerry or his long-haired mate, who shepherded us in, then turned the VW back down towards the checkpoint.

We followed Nuhanovic through into a cobbled courtyard. He only came up to my chin, but there was no doubt who was in charge here.

'I have dry clothes for you, and hot water.

Once you are comfortable, we will eat and talk.'
He spoke slowly, in heavily accented but perfect
English, and chose each word with a lot of care.

Directly in front of us was a long, one-storey
building with a veranda that ran its whole
length. The place was in darkness.

He led us to the left, along the line of the wall,
to where another, taller building joined it, form-
ing an enclosed courtyard. We followed him and
his oil lamp up a very old and creaky external
wooden staircase on to the first-floor veranda.
Warm light glowed behind the blue-glass panels
in a door to our left.

He opened it and ushered us through. We
hesitated, starting to take off our boots before
crossing the threshold.

'Please, no need, just enter.' Nuhanovic took a
closer look at Jerry's face. 'That wound needs to
be cleaned.'

The room, maybe four metres by five, was
heated by a blazing fire. Logs were stacked
against the wall, and the air was heavy with
perfume and woodsmoke.

Our shadows flickered on the walls. An oil
lamp in the corner provided the only other light,
and lavender oil simmered in a little brass tray
above the flame. The happiest sight was the
steaming brews that stood on two brass trays by
the grate. I headed straight for them.

Jerry joined me, trying to kickstart his circulation in front of the fire. Above it, hot water
bubbled in a clay tank decorated with inlaid
pieces of coloured glass.

441

Nuhanovic stayed by the door. 'The water should be hot enough for you to shower. Please, change, be comfortable and then we can talk.' He turned to leave.

'I'm Nick.' I motioned with my hand. 'This is Jerry.'

That half-smile returned. 'And I am Hasan.'

He closed the door behind him.

Jerry didn't need any second invitation. He turned the small brass tap at the bottom of the tank and hot water streamed into a large clay jug beneath it. I poured out the brews. I was pleased to see it was tea rather than that Arabic coffee shite, although I would have gone for anything even half-way warm. I threw in a handful of lumps of crystallized brown sugar. The glass burned my fingers and lips as I started sipping.

Jerry filled the jug, and started to get undressed in front of the fire. I kicked off my boots, refilled my glass and took a look around. Two sides of the room were dominated by long seating areas littered with cushions. Some basic clothing had been laid out for us. There was no decoration on the dirty white plastered walls.

A slatted wooden door opposite the fire led to a toilet, a simple box with a hole in, with a washing bowl and hand towel alongside. There were no electric sockets or fittings that I could see. It was as if we'd been transported back two hundred years.

Jerry had ripped all his kit off and was busy drawing cold water from a barrel into a second jug. He obviously knew his way around nineteenth-century plumbing. He unhooked the chain that held the ornate brass bucket above the stone shower tray to the left of the fire. Letting it run through his hands until the bucket hit the shower tray, he poured in water from each jug until he was satisfied with the temperature.

I eased open the blue-glass door to check outside. The terracotta rooftops were covered with frost. Above them, a million stars glistened in a pitch-black sky.

The other side of the compound was in total darkness. The guys on stag must have been freezing. I could make out the shape of another building beyond the one-storey one, which was where the family would have lived. It was the usual Muslim set-up. Visitors would be kept this side. If they were here for business, they'd be confined to the ground floor. The first floor would be reserved for family guests, as they would be able to see into the private courtyard that separated the two areas. Weren't we the lucky ones?

These places were completely surrounded by thick walls, and were a nightmare to get into or out of. They'd even made sure the treeline was a fair distance from the walls to prevent any climbers.

I saw movement in the guest courtyard. A couple of bodies were standing under the veranda. Fair one; I'd have had eyes on us two full-time as well. They'd probably been there when we came in.

We needed to get ourselves sorted out if we

were going to be running around in the forest once we'd dropped Nuhanovic. We needed to get warm, dry and fed.

Jerry gasped. I couldn't tell whether that meant the water was too hot, too cold, or he just didn't like it hitting the bits I'd split open. I closed the door, went over to the shower and stood right next to him. Some of his hot water splashed over my face and soaked into my clothes. It felt great.

I murmured into his ear. 'Even if there's no electricity, the room could still be bugged, OK?'

He nodded.

I moved away to the fire as he cut the water before soaping himself down. I finished mixing my own as the water splashed in the shower once more with Jerry on rinse cycle, and got my kit off.

Less than twenty minutes later we were both dressed in baggy cotton trousers, white T-shirts, thin padded jackets and Turkish slippers. We finished off the brews as our kit steamed gently in front of the fire.

The smell now reminded me of the drying rooms in training camp. You'd come off exercise after days in the wet, and nine times out of ten the heaters didn't work and you'd have to wear the same wet gear until it dried out on you. When they did, we'd all be like pigs in shit, but no amount of lavender oil could have shifted the stench our kit left behind.

As I sat there in front of the flames, the stubble on my cheek rasping against my hand, my eyes started to droop. The drying rooms made me think of the Regiment, then Danny Connor, and Rob. I jerked them open and checked Baby-G. It was just after ten. Baby-G made me think about Kelly, which also made me think about Zina.

I tried watching Jerry patting his scabby nose with a towel, but my eyelids had a will of their own. Maybe I dozed.

There was a knock on the door, I didn't know how much later. Jerry jumped up and opened it. Nuhanovic remained outside this time, his lamp throwing shadows across the landing. Maybe he didn't like the smell. 'You will require your coats.'

I started to put on my kit, now just damp rather than completely soaking, over the clothes we'd been given. I'd decided to take everything except the sacks and my PVC special. Who knew how this eat-and-talk fest would end?

Nuhanovic said nothing as Jerry followed my example, just watched in mild amusement. We finished with our parkas, zipped up as tight as they would go. As we followed him back down the stairs, he explained the layout of the place as if we'd just arrived for a dinner party. 'It was built by a very wealthy Turkish trader in your sixteenth century. It hasn't changed that much.'

I couldn't see anyone under the veranda as we headed across the visitors' courtyard to a doorway where the two buildings met, but I knew they were out there somewhere in the darkness.

Inside, his oil lamp bathed the wide stone passageway with light, and his voice echoed as he carried on his pre-dinner-party waffle. 'The story is that the trader's wife was so beautiful he didn't want anyone to see her, so he built this house in the middle of nowhere. He was a jealous man, you see. But it still wasn't enough, so he also planted the forest to prevent even the house being seen.'

'That why you live here?'

He looked at me with that strange half-smile. 'I live for my work, Nick. I am not blessed with a beautiful wife . . .'

The door at the end of the passageway opened on to the family courtyard. The building facing us was flanked left and right by the exterior walls. Set in the centre of the one to the right were the coach doors. We followed him over the cobblestones, past another set of heavy doors. Ahead of us, a light glowed behind a window.

'But I am a nomad, Nick. I do not live anywhere. I move from place to place. Concealment is my greatest weapon, just as it is for the aggressors who avoid justice for their war crimes. It seems I have something in common with my old enemy, no?'

My eyes were fixed on the glow from the window. We stepped up on to the wooden veranda and he opened the door; this time he motioned for us to leave our boots outside. The threshold was two feet high. 'Mind your toes.' He lowered the lamp a little. 'These are designed to keep little children in the rooms, but they claim a lot of flesh from adult feet.'

We were in a large square room. Fragrant perfume wafted from a pair of oil lamps in each of the far corners. Here, too, low seating ran the entire length of two walls. A fire raged in the centre of the third.

Waiting for us in the centre of the rug-covered floor were three large cushions set round a big brass tray, on which were a coffee pot, glasses, and a medium-sized brown-paper bag.

93

We all took our coats off and hung them on the wall hooks to the left of the door. He was dressed in a simple black dishdash, black trousers and socks. My socks had dried like cardboard; it wouldn't be long before they warmed up and started stinking the place out.

This room was also very plain, decorated only with some framed verses from the Qur'ān. The light from the two oil lamps was enough to show that although Nuhanovic's skin wasn't translucent like Benzil's it was almost unnaturally clear and wrinkle-free.

The top panel of the door to our left was a decorative carved grille. We could hear the clanking of pans and the good-humoured murmur of people at work coming from the other side of it; even better, we could smell food.

Nuhanovic held out a bony hand to Jerry. 'Welcome.'

Then he took another step forward and shook my hand too. His grip wasn't firm, but it was quite obvious that, like Benzil, his strength was in his head; he didn't need it anywhere else. In this light, and up close, his dark brown eyes were even more piercing. They didn't roam, they looked where they wanted to look and stayed there until they'd seen enough.

'Nick, Jerry, please . . .' He gestured towards the cushions. 'Welcome.' He had his own teeth, but no teeth were that naturally white.

Jerry and I sat cross-legged with our backs to the door. He took the cushion opposite, the paper bag to his left, the coffee to his right, and started pouring the heavily perfumed brew, holding the spout right near the glass then lifting it away steeply. It was like watching some kind of ceremonial ritual.

I accepted a glass. His hands were still as perfectly manicured as they were in the 'Chetnik Mama' picture.

The coffee tasted just the way it smelt, so I added a couple more lumps of crystallized brown sugar.

Nuhanovic passed a glass to Jerry and once again glanced sympathetically at his damaged face. 'This has been an eventful time for you both. My people will discover what has happened to Ramzi and Benzil. I'm sure Nasir has taken care of everything; he normally does.'

He fixed us each in turn with his steady gaze, his eyes giving nothing away. 'But please explain to me again, in greater detail, the events that have beset you.'

For the next ten minutes his gaze only shifted once from my face, to pour more coffee for himself and Jerry. I gave him the edited version of why we'd gone to Baghdad, how we'd come to meet Benzil, seen Goatee, and what had subsequently led us here – Jerry for his picture, me because Nuhanovic found it interesting that I was at the cement factory.

He shook his head gently and listened while pouring again for Jerry. I left my glass a third full. Once you've emptied it, the host's duty is to offer a refill, and I'd had enough. I'd managed to avoid the perfumed shit for the whole of this job, and I wasn't about to get hit by it now.

I didn't want to waste any more time talking about things that didn't matter. I didn't know how much of it we had. 'Our passports, phone, money . . . Will we get them back?' I smiled. 'One of the curses of the West. We feel naked without them.'

He replaced his glass delicately on the tray in front of him, and dropped his hands on to his knees. 'Of course. When you leave. And of course you are free to go whenever you wish. I'm sure Ramzi explained that we do nothing here that might help our enemies to trace us. We use no electronics, no TV, no phones, no satellite technology. No devices of the kind that might bring a bomb down on my head.' He paused, and seemed to be reserving his little half-smile for me personally. 'You understand my concern, Nick, I am certain.'

I returned his smile as he picked up his glass.

'My people are not pleased that I wanted to meet with you. They think you could be here to kill me.' He took an appreciative sip and studied us both. 'I've told them that if that is God's will, then so be it. But the fact is, I wish to talk with you.'

He put his glass down, but his eyes never left mine. Was it true? Was I here to kill him? If I looked away, I knew his suspicions would be confirmed. 'But let us eat and talk a while. I'm sure you're hungry, after your long and eventful journey.'

His head tilted gently to one side. 'And you, Jerry ... Why is it that you wish to take my picture?'

Jerry looked straight at him as well. 'To help me, and to help you. To help me win a Pulitzer, and help you get on the front cover of *Time* magazine. I thought maybe you'd like that.' He sounded as if he was talking to royalty.

Nuhanovic arched an eyebrow. 'In what way?'

Jerry smiled wearily. 'I haven't got my camera any more, so it's academic.'

The side door opened and two men came in carrying a selection of bowls, which they laid out on the tray between us. I caught a glimpse of two others standing outside with AKs, paying a lot more attention to us than to what was happening in the kitchen. No way were we going to be able to hit-and-run this man.

The bowls contained hot rice, raisins, meat, chopped onions, and enough pitta bread for an invading army. Forks were offered, but we refused politely.

As the door closed again, Nuhanovic gestured

for us to eat. I ripped off a piece of pitta with my right hand and used it as a scoop to get among the meat juices. No doubt the two AK boys were now standing with their faces against the grille, just in case I tried to jam it down his throat and choke him with it.

The door opened and the waiters were back with glasses of orange juice and a brass washing bowl, jug and hand towels for later on. The AK boys hadn't budged an inch.

The door closed again.

'Hasan?'

He looked up and smiled, and I hoped my chin wasn't dripping gravy. 'What concerns me is that we might be the ones getting killed, because we know where you are.'

He glanced at the door and treated us to the full smile this time.

'They're simply for my protection. I do not kill people.' He took a sip of his coffee. 'Besides, you knew how to get here, and yet you have made no attempt to compromise me. I am happy for us to trust each other.'

He smiled again, but held our gaze for that extra second before continuing. 'When we have spoken about certain things, you will be taken back to Sarajevo.'

He put a piece of bread into his mouth and handed Jerry the paper bag. 'Jerry, I agree with you. I think being on the cover of *Time* would help me in my work.'

Jerry glanced inside and pulled out two cardboard and plastic disposable cameras, the sort you see waved about on hen nights.

It was as if a switch had been thrown. Suddenly Jerry was in Pulitzer mode. 'There's not enough light in here. Can we improve it?'

Nuhanovic nodded slowly, looking towards the decorative grille. 'I'm sure we can.'

Jerry ripped the cellophane wrapper from the first camera as he checked out the room for light angles or whatever photographers do.

Nuhanovic carried on eating, but I felt his eyes boring into me. The door opened and the two guys came in again, another oil lamp in each hand. Jerry showed them exactly where he wanted them, then adjusted them an inch or two for perfection as the boys chucked some more wood on the fire and left. The AK boys still stared at us from the other side of the door.

Jerry wound the first exposure into place. 'Mind if I move around, try some angles?'

Nuhanovic didn't look up, just nodded and finished chewing. Then, as Jerry began to fine-tune the lamp positions yet again and busy himself with even more photography stuff, he leaned towards me, his elbows on his thighs. 'Nick, I, too, want to talk about what happened in the cement factory. But first, please tell me, why were you there? And what exactly did you see?'

94

Flashlight bounced around the room as I told him everything, apart from the real reason I'd been there. Instead he got the camera-kit-stolen-and-had-to-hide-when-I-saw-the-trucks-coming version.

Jerry took shot after shot and the camera whined each time like a tiny jet engine.

I talked Nuhanovic along the whole timeline, from the moment I saw vehicles approaching to the moment he had his argument with Mladic. 'There was a group of girls held back after you'd left . . .'

His eyes never left mine.

'They were raped, systematically. One threw herself out of a third-floor window.'

What I was looking for was confirmation, but I wasn't going to get it just yet. His eyes went down and fixed on the rice. He took a few grains in his fingers and rolled it into a ball. Jerry still buzzed around us like a worker-bee with a mission.

'I found out much later that one of them was called Zina. She was only fifteen. After the other girl jumped, and they scraped her off Mladic's wagon, Zina made a run for it, towards the tree-line where I was hiding.'

He watched the ball of rice all the way to his mouth.

'The Serbs just laughed. Some of them were laughing so much they found it hard to come into the aim. When she spotted me, she looked confused. She stopped, looked round at the Serbs, then turned again. I can still see the look on her face. That was when she took a round in the back.

'She fell directly in front of me. So close I felt the mud splash. She crawled towards me, begging with her eyes. And I did nothing to help her as she died. I'll never forget her eyes . . .'

I ripped some bread and picked up another chunk of meat. 'For a long time, I used to lie awake at night, wondering what she'd be doing now if she was alive. Maybe she'd be a mother, maybe a model. She was a good-looking kid.'

Nuhanovic looked up slowly as he swallowed. Jerry pressed the shutter release and the flash made him blink. For a moment, he looked surprised.

'That's a very moving story, Nick, but one I find somewhat confusing. In fact, I was confused from the moment Ramzi told me about you.

'I had to ask myself, why would a Westerner have been in that part of Bosnia on that particular day? He could only have been a newsman, a soldier, or a spy. I was intrigued. Hence, my invitation.

'And I am still intrigued. You say you were a reporter, but I never saw a report about Mladic murdering Muslims that day. Why is that? No one in that line of business would have failed to exploit such a story. It would have grabbed world headlines.

'But no . . . no story. I think that is because you are not a reporter, Nick. Which means you must have been there as a soldier, or a spy. But let us not beat about the bush: the distinction between the two is irrelevant.' His eyes never left mine. 'Satisfy my curiosity, Nick. Why were you really there?'

Fuck it, why not? In any case, if I wanted more from him, I had to expect to trade.

I told him why I was there, how I just lay in my hide, waiting for the Paveway to come down on Mladic. 'I felt a lot of guilt for not calling it in sooner. I was haunted by the thought I could have stopped the killing. Lately, I've even been thinking that talking to you about it might help me. You were there, maybe you would have understood.'

Nuhanovic's face was set in a frown. 'Mladic?' He nodded to himself, as if working out the answer to his own question. 'Mladic . . . but they let him escape.'

I didn't want to talk about fucking Mladic. 'Someone explained to me I don't need forgiveness. I did what I thought was right at the time . . .'

Nuhanovic stared deeply at me, his lips pursed. 'I agree with your friend. He is very wise.' Then he added, without a flicker of a smile, 'He is obviously not a Serb.'

I lifted a glass of orange juice to my mouth and took a sip. Time to up the ante. 'I'm confused about something, too. Why were all the girls kept behind after everyone else had left? And why were a few of those kept by Mladic after you yourself had gone? Did you know about that?'

'Of course I did.' He seemed angry, but with what or whom I couldn't work out. 'The argument with Mladic was because he wanted me to pay the agreed price for the young women, yet keep some back for his men. We were arguing about cost, not lives. He is an animal. And yet he was allowed to live.'

'You bought the girls off Mladic?'

'The attack on you last night was not about ideology, just money. The Serbs are competitors in the market we both service.'

'Those girls were business?'

'I make no apology for that. What you saw wasn't just about buying those young women, it was also about saving the others. Their mothers, their brothers. That had always been part of every deal. The high prices I paid the Serbs reflected that. Does that disgust you?'

'Surprises me.'

'Some find what will soon be my past a little ... unsavoury. But I have saved many lives, including the very ones you could have saved. Mladic and his aggressors murdered many thousands. Five thousand at Srebrenica alone. Now, that disgusts me, Nick.

'And yet the West chose not to kill Mladic that day. They still seem happy for him to be at large. Why would that be, I wonder? I have told them where he is. He's in a monastery in Montenegro. But where are the bombs? Where are your special forces?'

I wanted to deflect his anger. We needed to stay best mates if Jerry and I were going to walk out of here. 'Jerry, you tell him.'

Jerry lowered the camera and explained about the international court. 'Simple as that. Looks like they decided to preserve a few big names to stick in the dock after the war.' He ripped the cellophane off camera two and waited for its flash to get up to speed.

Nuhanovic looked ready to explode. 'The criminals like Mladic and Karadic are still out there, yet I, not a murderer, am the target of so much hostility from the West . . . so much that I now have to move country to continue my work.'

Jerry took a chance and pressed the shutter release. The flash made Nuhanovic blink again. When he opened his eyes I could see the oil lamps reflected in their angry gaze.

'I, too, saw the horror on their faces as I left them to that terrible fate. But God will understand. I have Him on my side. What you have heard from Benzil, and no doubt elsewhere, is true. I can, and will, bring Islam together.

'The West and even Islam itself will try to stop me, but I have faith and commitment, the very qualities that make a mother become a suicide bomber, or a husband fly a 747 into a building. They also know that sometimes their own brothers and sisters have to die for greater things to come. It's a faith you will never understand.

'You look surprised again, Nick. You shouldn't be. Today's terrorist is tomorrow's statesman. If Ariel Sharon and Nelson Mandela can be accepted as leaders, then why not Hasan Nuhanovic, a man whose motives are essentially pure? God understands what I have had to do in order to continue and finance His will. I have done more for my Muslim brothers and sisters against the tyrannies and imperialism of the West than any terrorist bomb will achieve – and my work has only just begun.'

Jerry moved the lamps about again, trying to catch his subject's changing mood.

Nuhanovic nodded up at him. 'Jerry, if my face is to appear on a billion Muslim T-shirts, I suggest you just keep shooting. They will be the last photographs for quite a while. I am going to accept Benzil's offer of sanctuary and continue my work from his country.

'I thank God that Benzil is alive. His commitment, and the fact that God has chosen to spare him, has confirmed to me that taking up his offer is the right thing to do.'

'When are you going to Uzbekistan?'

'Soon, once Benzil and I have talked. The last few days have been very fraught – as I know I don't have to tell you.'

The door opened and the two AKs appeared.

One stayed where he was; the other went over to Nuhanovic and spoke quietly in his ear.

Nuhanovic looked at the two of us, his brow creased. He nodded at the AK boy and waved him back to his mate, then got up with an expression of regret, and went over to the bowl to wash his hands.

'Our meeting has come to end. It appears it is not only you two who are helping accelerate my schedule. There has been a lot of activity after the incident at the cave and Lord Ashdown seems to think that SFOR are closing in on Karadic or Mladic. I think he would be more delighted to discover I am in fact his target.'

The AK boys were making a show of checking their watches. Nuhanovic held out a clean hand. 'All I now ask is that you escort Jerry back to safety and make sure he gets his photographs developed. And publish my story. Tell your Western friends, whoever they are, that I know they let Mladic go free. They have blood on their hands.'

We shook. He turned to do the same with Jerry.

There was still one more question.

'Our bags, when do we get them?'

'In Sarajevo.'

The AK boys were looking even more agitated. Time for us to go.

95

Four clouds of breath hung in the cold, still air. The AK boys lit an oil lamp each, then we followed them across the courtyard to the passageway. The sky was still completely clear, the frost now hard underfoot.

Jerry had pulled up the hood on his parka, but I kept mine down. I wanted to take in as much information as I could. A vehicle was ticking over somewhere on the other side of the visitors' building.

Guided by the oil lamps, we went back along the passageway towards the guest courtyard. As we neared the door, Jerry quickened his pace to get level with me. His eyes stared out from inside the hood, shouting a silent question: 'What the fuck are we going to do now?'

The AK boys held the door open and motioned us through. The engine was the other side of the wall. 'Speak English?'

One nodded.

'Our bags? We came with bags. Will we get them back?'

'Of course. No problem.'

'When?'

'Later.'

We crossed the courtyard towards the archway. The vehicle the other side of the double doors wasn't chugging. It wasn't the VW.

They were pulled open and we were blinded by headlights. The wagon was buried in a cloud of exhaust fumes.

It appeared the AK boys weren't coming with us. They stayed where they were and gestured for us to climb in. We stepped into the cloud and discovered a Suzuki Vitara hardtop. The choke was doing overtime to fight the cold.

It was two up, both in front. I opened the back door and let Jerry get in first. I got in behind the driver. The cloud of cigarette smoke was as dense as the exhaust fumes outside.

There was no interior light but I could see the driver in the glow from the dash. Short back and sides, moustache, maybe in his forties. The passenger was the long-haired one. Between his legs, its muzzle resting dangerously against his chest, was a G3. I looked down. The plastic butt was the full-size, not foldaway, version. Much more important was what lay next to it in the footwell: our bumbags.

These guys had changed into black-leather jackets and jeans for the trip. Maybe we really were going back to Sarajevo.

The wagon lurched from side to side as we

drove down to the chicane, then the six hundred metres beyond it, before turning right on to the forest track. Neither of them said a word. The driver leaned across and flicked the radio on. It was local phone-in stuff.

We worked our way through the trees. Jerry had dropped his hood, but his eyes were still quizzing me.

I ignored him. I needed time to think. I stared down at the pistol grip of the G3. The safety catch was on the left. First click down was single-shot, fully down was automatic, the opposite of the AK. The cocking piece was also on the left, just over half-way up the stock and, like the MP5 and all the Heckler & Kochs of that era, had to be worked with the left hand. The mag was straight, not curved, and held twenty rounds.

There was no way of telling if it was made ready. I had to assume it wasn't.

Hairy lit two cigarettes and passed one to the driver before offering us one from the packet. I leaned forward a little between their seats.

'Bags?' I pointed into the footwell. 'Can we have our bags now?'

Hairy waved his hand testily towards the windscreen. 'Sarajevo, Sarajevo.'

The driver muttered something and worked the wheel. We bounced on to the frost-covered road and turned left, back towards the barns and the city. A press statement by Paddy Ashdown kicked off over the speakers: something to do with law and order, bringing evil men to justice, all the normal bluster, before the interpreter faded in over him.

The forestry block glided past on our left. I was going to have to do something soon. I leaned forward again and tapped Hairy on the shoulder. 'My friend needs a piss.'

He stared at me blankly.

'Piss?' I pointed at Jerry and simulated undoing my fly. 'He wants to go.'

He just waved his hand towards the windscreen again. 'Sarajevo.'

Fuck it, we were Nuhanovic's guests. We could give these guys orders. 'No, we stop! He wants to piss!' I poked the driver. 'Stop!'

While the two of them exchanged a few words, I sat back with Jerry. 'Get out, go down, stay down.'

I leaned forward. 'You stopping, or what?'

As the wagon pulled in at the side of the road, Jerry got out, unbuttoning himself as he went round the front, past the headlights, and towards the treeline, too modest to take his piss within view.

They looked at each other and rolled their eyes.

96

Jerry had been listening; he seemed to lose his footing, and fell with a shout.

I tapped Hairy and waved my hands urgently. 'Go help him! Go help him!'

Jerry wasn't going to get any Oscars for the moaning, but at least he kept doing it. Hairy muttered a curse or two, but opened his door anyway. As he climbed out, he put the G3 back in the footwell, resting it against the seat.

My eyes focused on the barrel. I wouldn't get a second chance at this.

I grabbed the muzzle with my right hand, yanked it back between the seats towards me and simultaneously pushed back, opened the door with my left and rolled out on to the tarmac.

I felt the butt bounce across the rear seat, and crash on to my chest as I landed.

My left hand grabbed the plastic stock, my right slid down on to the pistol grip. The road surface was hard against my back as I pushed away from the door.

Ignoring the shouts from the front of the wagon, I concentrated on getting my left hand on to the cocking piece, flicking it so it stuck out at right angles to the barrel, then racking it back. A brass round spun out of the ejection chamber as I let the working parts go forward and pick up another. I knew now that the weapon was made ready. The shouts continued as I got to my feet.

Butt in the shoulder, I aimed at Hairy, both eyes wide, needing to see everything.

Jerry lay stock-still on the grass. 'Jerry, on your feet – get him down, get him down!'

I kicked the driver's door and moved back at least three arm widths. 'Out! Out! Out!' If he didn't understand English, he got the drift. He came out of the car at warp speed, hands in the air, then sank to his knees and put them behind his head.

By now Hairy was on the floor too. I leaned into the weapon, safety catch off, first pad of the finger on the trigger. 'Jerry, get them together in the light.'

Jerry did as he was told and they soon lay together face down on the grass verge. I moved round so I faced the tops of their heads. I could get clear shots into them if they started fucking about. 'Search them. Make sure they've got no radios, no weapons.'

Long shadows were cast by the headlights as Jerry patted them down and rummaged in their pockets. Hairy had nothing on him apart from a wallet and cigarettes.

He moved over to the driver. 'What we going to do with them, Nick?'

'They stay here. Soon as you've finished, get them crawling into the treeline.'

We both followed as they shuffled to the edge of the canopy, their breath snorting out of them like racehorses'. The first line of trees blocked the Vitara's headlights, casting weird shadows into the first few metres of forest.

'Tie them up. Use their belts, shoelaces, whatever you can find.'

I kept them both covered as Jerry got them to sit against a tree. Then he had an idea, ran back to the Vitara and returned with the empty bumbags and a set of jump leads. He tied their hands with the leads, then clipped the bumbags round their necks and a tree. They didn't resist: they wanted to live.

I rested the G3 on the ground and pulled my boots and socks off. The frost-covered grass was freezing, but it was worth it. Fuck knows who might be within earshot, but I didn't want them spending the night screaming their heads off.

I put the damp boots back on and jammed a sock into each mouth. Then we shoved as much as possible of the bumbags into their mouths and tightened the straps around the tree-trunks so they were holding their heads and gagging them. If you don't fill the whole mouth void, sound can be produced and projected. With the void filled with a stinking sock, they'd be more worried about breathing and avoiding gagging than making noise.

Now they were sorted, we had to get back to the house. We ran to the Vitara and I grabbed the Thuraya.

'Do these things have silent alert or vibrate or what?'

Jerry shrugged as he shoved his passport and wallet into his parka.

I laid the G3 on the bonnet and powered it up while I retrieved my own docs. 'We can't risk using the wagon.' I kept my eyes on the phone LED. 'It's going to make too much noise on the approach and it might be compromised before we get back to the house. Go and park it in the treeline, take out the rotor arm and we'll keep it with us. We'll use it to get the fuck out. Don't forget the keys.'

I got the Thuraya on to vibrate. There were five bars on the sat signal and five for power. I scrolled down numbers called as Jerry jumped into the wagon. 'Right, that long fucker, that George's number?'

I took a couple of deep breaths and pressed Send as he headed towards the trees.

No answer. The phone just kept ringing. I gave it another twenty seconds before cancelling. That left only Ezra. I called the emergency number. Baby-G said 00:11. DC was six hours behind. Maybe he was still there, talking about trust to another of George's suckers.

I got the answering-machine. I talked slowly and clearly. 'It's Nick, Nick Stone. I need to speak to George, urgently. Tell him I know what's happening – tell him I will finish the job, but I must talk to him first. He must call me on the Thuraya. It's life and death, Ezra – don't think about it, just do it. Call him, go to him, whatever.'

Jerry had the Vitara in the trees, two long tracks gouged in the frozen grass behind it. The bonnet clicked open and Jerry climbed out. I went over to him as he bent over the engine. 'You get him?'

I put the phone and G3 on the passenger seat, took off the mag and pushed down on the rounds. It was full, apart from the round in the chamber and the one I'd ejected. I put it back on the weapon and removed my parka, keeping an eye out for the ejected round in the back of the wagon. 'Just a message.'

No luck with the round. I wrapped the parka sleeves round my waist. Jerry followed suit. 'That was one fucking amazing meeting. What you make of him?'

'Faith, my arse. He's just as fucked up as any suicide bomber, bin Laden without a beard.' There was a whole lot more I could have said, but it would have to wait. G3 in my left hand and the Thuraya in my right, I was ready to go.

I didn't give a shit about what he'd done to Coke sales, fucking about with the West's interest in dysfunctionality, or that he didn't paint his toenails red, white and blue. I had my own reasons for wanting him dead.

97

Jerry double-knotted the parka's sleeves round his waist. I put out a hand to stop him. 'Nothing's changed, mate, the offer still stands. You have a family, I've got fuck-all. Take the wagon, wait in the city. If I don't come back inside two days, you go home and try your luck with George – tell him you managed to escape or something.'

He had stopped tying his parka, but there was no reply.

I lifted the G3 between us. 'If George doesn't call, I'm going to have to use this thing. No need for you to be there.'

He was still thinking. 'Thanks, Nick, but no thanks. We both got the same job, for different reasons. I still gotta be there.'

'We'd better get on with it, then, before he fucks off with Benzil to Shangri-La. We can't go under the canopy until George calls. But we need to cover the road with the G3 to stop him leaving.'

I checked the Thuraya was still on, and we

started jogging along the verge, using the grass to give us a little grip on the frost. I could soon hear him panting behind me. I must have sounded pretty much the same after so many months of cheese and Branston.

The parka flapped rhythmically against my legs. Sweat leaked down to the small of my back. My hands and feet were boiling.

We had done maybe four hundred when the phone vibrated in my hand.

George wasn't one for small-talk. 'You have Nuhanovic?'

'Yes, but not for long.' I took deep breaths, wanting to be understood on the first attempt. 'Here's the deal. I'll mark the target with the sat phone. You get the fix, I'll talk the ordnance in, we get out and everyone's quits. No more fucking about with kids' lives, George, please.'

'Agreed. But you must personally identify the target.'

'We are about four hours out of Sarajevo. He's time critical. You got Predators?'

'I know where you are, I have you. There are three UAVs getting airborne now. Wait for a call from the operators. You will confirm the kill. I want him dead, son, not just a pile of rubble. Keep that sat phone on, they'll be calling.' The phone went dead.

I turned to Jerry. 'We got a deal.'

His knees nearly buckled with relief.

I turned and started legging it. It wasn't just because I wanted to get on to the road junction quickly. I didn't want to answer any questions about whether I thought George would keep the deal.

We made it to the track and moved off into the first line of trees. The grass was wet, not frozen. I put the weapon down while I shoved the Thuraya in my jeans so I could feel when it went off. I slid the parka back on as I explained what George had said, slowly and quietly, so he wouldn't miss anything.

'You can dump the keys and rotary arm here. This is our meeting-place if we get split, OK?'

Jerry nodded, and put them at the base of what was left of the nearest tree, then untied his sleeves and put his own parka back on.

'OK, actions on contact, on the way to target. You make your way back here. Pick up the wagon stuff and get away to the city. Don't waste time if it goes noisy. I'll try and get to target and get on with it. You'll be able to do fuck-all without a weapon.'

The Thuraya rumbled against my stomach. I got to my knees and pressed the green button. The cold soaked into me as I kept an eye on the darkness up the track, hoping not to see headlights.

'Who do I have speaking?' It was an American monotone, like a synthesized computer voice.

'This is Nick. You got a fix on us yet?'

'Say again, slowly, Nick – I can't understand you.'

'Do you have a fix on us yet?'

'That's an affirmative, Nick.'

I checked the display. There was no number. 'What's your number?'

'That's classified.'

'For fuck's sake, we're trying to carry out a fire-control mission here on a poxy sat phone. I need a number. We're not on target yet. You're going to lose the fix soon. I need to be able to call you once on target.'

There was a pause, then, 'Wait out.'

Jerry came up behind me, his face hidden in his hood. 'What the fuck they doing, man?'

I put my hand up to stop him. The monotone was back. 'I have a number.'

I tapped it straight into the Thuraya. It was another sat phone. 'OK, listen in. The target is about two Ks from this fix. It's a house complex in the forestry block. Roger so far?'

'That's affirmative.'

'You will lose this fix as we move under the canopy. I will call you once on target. Roger so far?'

'That's affirmative.'

'You on a ship?'

'That's classified.'

'We on the same side here? Just tell me how long you have to target.'

There was another pause. 'Time to target is one hour, thirty-four minutes. One hour, three-four minutes.'

'Got it. Wait out.'

I closed down and turned to Jerry as I zipped up my parka. 'One hour thirty-four.'

Those things travelled at about eighty m.p.h., so they would be on target too quickly to have started on a carrier in the Adriatic. Maybe they were from some remote airfield in Kosovo. The US had quite a large peacekeeping presence there.

He nodded somewhere inside the hood. I pulled it down. 'Get those ears working. We'll be seeing fuck-all soon. When we move, I want you to count the distance. I do about a hundred and sixteen paces for a hundred metres. You know your rate?'

'Not a clue.'

'OK, then, we've got two Ks in there before the track junction. You count my paces, and tell me when we get to eighteen hundred metres. We can't afford to miss that junction.'

I checked the G3's mag, safety, and that the Thuraya was secure in the parka's inside pocket. My feet were starting to freeze.

'You ready?'

98

He wasn't Nuhanovic any more, he was just a target. It had always been easier for me to think of people that way before I killed them.

Hood down, I set off fast along the track. If a vehicle came down the road I'd have to go noisy and take it on with the G3. If the target wasn't aboard, we'd have lost him for sure, but what choice did I have?

Fir branches scratched my face as I pushed my way through. Trapped water cascaded down on me.

Every ten paces I stopped, holding my left hand behind me until Jerry jammed into it. We had to keep together in the dark. Conditions were good underfoot: soft pine needles kept the noise down.

I did another ten metres and stopped, butt of the G3 on the ground, leaning forward with both hands on the barrel as I rested, taking deep breaths and waiting for Jerry to bump into me. I was soaked with sweat under all the layers of clothes, and it dripped down my face, making the scratches sting.

This time he got up close, his panting, minging breath across the side of my face. 'That's just over eighteen hundred.'

'We'll go a bit slower now; eyes open for the track junction on the left, OK?'

I closed my mouth, trying to get some saliva going to help my dry throat, and pushed myself upright on the G3.

A few minutes later I was at the junction with the track up to the house. I stopped again and waited. Now it was going to be his turn to smell my breath. It was eerily quiet, not a hint of wind to stir the trees. 'Count off five hundred this time, OK? After that we'll cut right and work our way through the trees towards the boundary wall. I want to box around that checkpoint.'

'Got it.'

We moved off again, keeping in the middle of the track. I had the G3 in my hands. There wasn't time to move tactically, weapon in the shoulder. I just moved with my head tilted to the right, keeping my ear pointed along the track. My eyes were hard right in their sockets, staring into the darkness ahead, trying to see any movement, any light, any indication of bodies.

I stopped and listened every five or six metres, trying to take deep, controlled breaths. Sweat poured down my face. Eventually Jerry came up, his mouth near my ear. 'Five hundred.'

I set off very slowly this time, weapon held at its point of balance in my right hand. The left reached behind for Jerry, making sure we had contact all the time.

About one fifty short of the checkpoint, I could still see and hear nothing. We could have played safe and cut right, into the forest, but that would have slowed us down even more. We'd just have to stay on the track for as long as we could.

Another twenty and there was a clanking of metal, forward and left. I froze. I could see nothing but black and then more black.

99

I held my breath and leaned forward, eyes closed, head tilted. All I could hear was Jerry breathing to my left.

Then there it was again, metal on metal.

I turned back to Jerry and pulled him slowly into the treeline. Fuck the mines. The target's people were under the canopy the other side of the track, so that was obviously secure. If they hadn't cleared this side, we'd soon get to know about it. If it was going to happen, it was going to happen. Maybe some of that fatalism shit had rubbed off on me after all.

I kept a grip on Jerry's sleeve. Even a few metres' separation could mean we lost each other, and it wasn't as if we could just call out to regroup. Now was the time to slow down.

It's so easy to lose any sense of direction in pitch dark, but I got a good marker from the occasional clank and snatch of conversation the other side of the track, which became clearer the closer we got. With luck we were going to hit the edge of the treeline soon, and there'd be a short stretch of open ground, then the wall.

I felt my way along, waving my left hand in front of me for obstructions, the right still holding the weapon. Jerry's hand gripped the butt to keep contact.

I stopped when a branch blocked my way, took a few paces back or sideways, tried to move round the obstacle and not make noise. Now that I'd slowed, I was more aware of the scratches to my face. My salty sweat made them as painful as wasp stings. My sockless feet had blistered in my boots. My whole body felt as if it was boiling under all the layers.

I stayed focused, trying to keep my sense of direction. An engine started up to our left. I guessed it must be further up the track, the other side of the hedgehogs. I hoped it didn't move. If it did, and up towards the house, I'd have to assume it was going to pick up the target. I'd have to get out of the trees and take it on. There'd be a gang-fuck with so many bodies about, and only nineteen rounds.

We came to the edge of the forestry block. I dropped to my knees and crawled the last two metres on my own. After the inky blackness of the canopy, the stars seemed as bright as the sun.

The wall facing me was the one running along the right-hand side of the compound as viewed from the track. The door into the family courtyard was about forty metres down it. Beyond the wall I could catch just the odd glimpse of terra-cotta rooftop. The three- or four-metre strip of rough grass between the wall and the treeline was white with frost. No vehicles or bodies had been along it tonight.

Somebody near the checkpoint had a bout of coughing. Maybe it was the exhaust fumes. The engine was still on, but the vehicle was stationary.

I moved back to grab Jerry, and together we followed the edge of the trees away from the checkpoint, towards the family entrance. We came level, and I inched forward.

I looked left. No movement from the checkpoint. Vehicle still stationary.

I moved over the grass, leaving sign in the frost. There was no gap between the doors, but maybe an inch and a half beneath them. I got down on my knees, then lay flat on the ground. The grass was icy against my cheek. I couldn't see any light or movement at ground level. There wasn't the perspective to see any higher up.

I got back on my feet and gave the doors a gentle push where they joined, just in case they were unlocked. As if.

I moved back to Jerry and knelt down next to him. We stayed like that, just inches apart, as I got out the Thuraya and powered it up, one hand cupped over the display.

100

I crawled forward a couple of metres, got a signal, and pressed Send on the new number. There was only one ring before the monotone answered.

I talked normally, but kept my voice low. 'It's Nick. Get a fix: what's the time to target?'

Monotone came back, 'Eleven minutes, twenty-two seconds to target.'

Slowly and, I hoped, clearly, I began to explain the set-up of the house to him as if he was walking through the guest doors – the guest courtyard with its one-storey building dead ahead, and two-storey guest accommodation to the left, with the passageway into the family compound where the buildings met.

I checked after each detail with 'Roger so far?' I got back, 'Affirmative,' each time.

'The target's last location was the far right corner of the long building in the family courtyard. Roger so far?'

'Affirmative. We have a fix on you. I repeat, we have a fix.'

'Roger that. Wait out for the fire-control order: I do not have a target yet. This is not a weapons-free zone. You understand?'

There was a second or two's pause. Then, 'Affirmative.'

'Roger that. Wait out.'

I kept the Thuraya switched on. I wanted to be able to pull it out, get a satellite, and start talking the moment we had the target. Until then, I didn't want some colonel, or whoever was watching the screens in the operations room and making decisions, to go and hit whatever he saw on the other side of the wall because he was flapping about fucking up.

We needed to be well away from here when the Hellfires came calling. The target had to die. There was no margin for error.

The operators in the AWACS would be watching their screens, running checks on the Predators' surveillance packages as Bosnia passed beneath them. The forward-looking infrared would be giving the operators a green negative of the landscape. Thermal imagers aboard the UAVs would be homing in on heat: the hotter the source, the whiter the image. Bodies would be picked out easily, even through the canopy. Just as important would be the LTD in the nose, and the feedback saying that the Hellfires were online and ready to go.

I crawled back to Jerry. 'Listen, they're here in about ten. The doors are locked. I need you to get over the wall and open them. I've got to stay this side. If that wagon comes to pick him up at the other doors, I'll need to get down there with the G3.'

He started getting to his feet. I grabbed him. 'When you get to the other side, you might not be able to open it, you realize that? It might be padlocked and then you're in the shit unless you can get back over. You understand what I'm telling you?'

There was no point bullshitting him. We'd come too far now and he needed to know.

He put a hand firmly on my shoulder and looked into my eyes. 'I'm already in the shit.'

He let go and started rummaging in his parka. 'I think I'd better split these up.' He handed me one of the cameras. 'Just in case. It'll make a little money for Renee. She's with Chloë, at her mother's in Detroit.'

I shoved it into my pocket.

'She's staying there until I get back from Brazil. You'll find her. Give it to her. She'll know what to do with it.'

We both started across the grass. I laid the G3 on the ground and got my back against the wall, eyes straining down to the right, towards the checkpoint. The wagon's engine still turned over in the darkness.

I bent my legs and cupped my hands between my thighs. Jerry stepped back a little, positioned his right foot in them as a launch pad, and jumped up. I kept contact with his foot, twisting myself round towards the wall and pushing myself up until it was past my face. Then I held it against the wall so he had something to push against. He hooked his arms over the top, and seemed to stay like that for ages. I didn't know if he was flapping, didn't have the strength to get the rest of his body over, or had spotted something.

A few seconds later, he started to scramble over the wall and his foot left my hands.

I picked up the G3 and put my ear against the door just as he landed with a bump the other side. Almost immediately, there was the gentle groan of metal being drawn across metal.

The door opened very, very slowly. I let Jerry do it: he was in control.

As I slipped through and into the courtyard, Jerry closed it again behind me. He didn't bolt it.

To my right, ten or eleven metres away, was the room where we'd last seen the target. The lamps were still burning.

Somewhere in the darkness, cooking pans clanged. To my left was the one-storey building separating the two courtyards. There were no windows this side of it. The first floor of the guest block, where we had showered, was completely dark.

I got the butt into the shoulder, flicked the safety on to single-shot, and positioned my trigger finger along the guard. Keeping Jerry behind me, I started to move towards the illuminated window. There was going to be nothing covert about this: there wasn't enough time. I had no option but to open doors and look through windows.

I knelt beneath the window, to the right of the

grime-covered frame. As I slowly raised my head, I could see the door to the left. I came up some more. The oil lamps were still burning where Jerry had left them. But the room was empty.

Even the meal things had been taken away.

I lowered myself, still butt in the shoulder, safety off, and began to follow the wall to the veranda and the door we'd gone through. No shoes outside; no target inside.

The kitchen noises were louder now, and joined by muttering in Serbo-Croat. The kitchen had to be behind one of the doors along the veranda.

My breath clouded around me as I stopped and listened. The muttering wasn't from the target; it wasn't that slow, deliberate, favourite-uncle voice. It sounded more like some old bottle-washer having a moan about the greasy plates.

I touched Jerry's arm and pointed towards the passageway and across the courtyard.

I'd taken just a few steps when I heard an engine. A vehicle was approaching the house.

Fuck the noise. We ran for it.

101

I grabbed the door handle and we legged it down the corridor. My left hand was out, ready to make contact with the door at the other end. I got there; took a breath, listened. There were voices the other side, four or five of them. The vehicle was static, but not in the courtyard.

Trying to block out the sounds of our breathing, I put my ear to the wood, my right hand firmly on the pistol grip, safety catch still off, trigger finger still across the guard.

The voices were urgent and low. None was the target's. Then his gentle tones sparked up, calming everyone down.

The engine noise got suddenly louder. The gates must have been opened.

'Stand by.'

I fumbled for the handle with my left hand. My fingers closed round it and I pulled back. The headlights were blinding.

I made out a mass of bodies in the beams, shrouded in their own breath and exhaust fumes.

From just two feet away a body loomed in front of me, weapon coming up. I fired; he went down. His AK clattered across the threshold.

There were screams and shouts from near the vehicle. The driver revved the engine. Weapons came up into the aim.

I just blatted away, single shots at anything that moved, then into the vehicle.

Shit, it started moving.

Rounds came back at us, taking chunks out of the plasterwork that sandblasted my face.

I turned and legged it down the corridor. Jerry grabbed the AK from the floor, its barrel dragging behind him as he wrestled with the butt. 'Back to the gate! Back to the gate!'

We burst through the door at the far end and headed across the family courtyard. Screams and movement under the veranda. It was a cluster of bottle-washers. They ducked when they saw us.

I was half-way across when we started taking fire from the follow-up behind us. I stopped, turned, and returned fire into the passage doorway.

Jerry was to my right. He ran past me as I fired controlled shots, trying to stop them leaving the passageway.

I squeezed off two more rounds at the door before Jerry started firing.

I turned on the spot and ran, got about four paces past him, turned again and started to fire. 'Move, Jerry! Move! Move!'

He didn't need to be told twice.

He stopped, turned, fired.

I turned, ran, stopped, fired.

As Jerry came past me I squeezed the trigger again. Nothing. Dead man's click.

I dropped the weapon and kept running. Jerry was already the other side of the door, using the frame for cover as he fired. I passed him, then headed down towards the checkpoint, hugging the wall. I couldn't see any moving lights. But there were shouts ahead of me in the darkness.

I pulled the Thuraya from my parka and held it to my face. 'Fire mission! Fire mission!' Fuck the signal: if I got one, it'd work. I had to get down there to see where the fucking wagon was.

Jerry was not many paces behind me when we started taking fire. The follow-up were through the gate and putting some down.

I swung left and dived into the treeline. 'On me, on me!'

I just kept going, crashing through the trees, trying to keep parallel to the wall. They ran down the gap, firing into the darkness, their muzzle flashes rippling across the tree-trunks.

We plunged on towards the checkpoint. With luck, the chicane was the only way out.

With no more than twenty metres to go, the follow-up got level with us. I stumbled and fell. Jerry stood his ground and opened up with long bursts. The noise was deafening. His white muzzle flash lit the darkness. Ejected rounds tumbled over my back.

I was still fighting to get up when Jerry let out a high-pitched scream. He collapsed on top of me, still firing, rounds going way up into the canopy before both he and the AK fell silent.

His blood was hot and wet on my face as I pushed him off me. The follow-up were still firing into the treeline, everywhere, anywhere; I grabbed him by the legs and pulled him deeper into the forest.

It wasn't far, but enough to buy me time. I collapsed next to him. His breathing was rapid and rasping, spraying me with blood at each exhalation.

I ran my fingers over his chest and found the entry wound in his stomach. No need to feel for the exit. My hand slid into it as I turned him over.

More screams from the follow-up.

Jerry gripped my head with both his hands, bringing me down to him with the last of his energy. 'Fucked up . . . sorry.'

I threw my arms round him and gripped hard as he jerked his last resistance. Seconds later, his body went limp. I checked his neck. There was no pulse.

The follow-up still fired blindly into the trees. They were covering the light I now saw moving out from the guest doorway.

I laid Jerry's body down and scrambled forward. A vehicle was just pulling out of the gates, guys running all around it, shouting at each other. It was chaos. One of the headlights was shot out.

I kept low and tumbled through the undergrowth to the left, down to where the treeline met the chicane.

The wagon was coming down towards me. I couldn't see if the target was inside or not.

It got closer and slowly negotiated the first hedgehog. The rear window was open. The target was talking to his protection as they ran alongside, even smiling at them as he pointed towards the follow-up. Then his head went back inside, and made itself comfortable against the headrest. The window powered up.

I looked down and checked the Thuraya. Fucking canopy.

102

I started legging it, paralleling the wall about twenty metres inside the trees. I needed to get out of the way, well past the family doors, right to the corner of the compound. I needed clear space.

I slipped and stumbled as I scrambled to make the distance. Torchlight now flickered between the trunks.

Fuck the follow-up. I got up and kept running. A minute or two later, I broke out from under the canopy and made my way behind the rear wall. Kneeling in the grass, gulping down oxygen, I checked the Thuraya. Five bars.

One more deep breath to slow myself down.

'Hello, this is Nick, this is Nick. Are you up there yet? Are you up there yet?'

Monotone came back. 'Affirmative, Nick. We see your contact. We see your contact.'

'In the forest, towards the metalled road – you have a vehicle. One headlight. You see it?'

It seemed to take for ever for the operator to

manoeuvre the UAVs thousands of feet above me, their surveillance packages scouring the ground for heat and light.

The phone was glued to my ear. My chest heaved, thirsty for oxygen. I worked my jaw, trying to conjure some saliva into my dry mouth, my head spinning with dehydration.

'I have it, Nick, I have it.'

'Roger that. That's your target. That's your target. Acknowledge.'

He still spoke as if he was ordering pizza or talking to his granny. 'Roger. We have a north-bound vehicle towards the metalled road.'

'Roger that. The activity at the front of the house, anything inside. Hit it, for fuck's sake, hit it now!'

'Roger that. You might wanna get your people back.'

'Too late. Look towards the back of the house. You will see me, I'm waving my left arm. Do you see me? Do you see me?'

'Roger that, we have you, we have you.'

'I'm the only one. Follow the right-hand tree-line. You see a body lying about twenty-five metres from the front of the house?'

'Yep. Roger that. We have a body. We have a body getting dragged out. That's three guys, three guys dragging out a body.' He paused. 'Target now free of the treeline, on the metalled road. Stand by, Nick. Here they come.'

I ran into the forest, then threw myself to the ground as two explosions rocked the front of the building. The shockwaves were soaked up by the buildings and the woods, but the ground trembled beneath me.

Then another, this time closer. Inside the compound.

The pressure wave pushed through the forest, bringing gallons of water down on me. My ears started ringing as I waited to hear a more distant hit on the vehicle.

Seconds later, it came, and another two seconds after that.

I hoped Nuhanovic was able to see a blur of red in the distant sky as the first Hellfire kicked off. He wouldn't understand the significance, but it would mean a fuck of a lot to me.

I got back on my feet and turned to head deeper into the forest. I switched off the Thuraya. Best conserve power till I got to the wagon and called George to confirm the slaver was dead.

Not that he would give a shit about that, now. But I would.

THE END

Andy McNab's stunning new
Nick Stone thriller,

Aggressor,

will be published in Bantam Press
hardback in November 2005.

Here's the prologue
to whet your appetite . . .

Prologue 01

The three of us clung to the top of the Bradley armoured fighting vehicle as it bucked and lurched over the churned up ground. Exhaust fumes streamed from its rear grille and made us choke, but at least they were warm. Tonight was a cold one.

My right hand was clenched round a grab handle near the turret. My left gripped the shoulder strap of my day sack. We'd flown 3,000 miles with this equipment. If I dropped it and it got smashed, there was nothing to replace it. The whole job would have to be aborted and I would be severely in the shit.

Nightsun searchlights mounted on our and three other AFVs bounced across the front of the target building as they also headed for its far right corner. The others were decoys; ours was the only one transporting a three-man SAS team. That was if we could all keep a grip.

Our AFV split from the rest, which stayed to the right of the target, their searchlights strafing the front of the buildings to blind anyone trying to see out. The driver took a sharp left to bring us along the rear of the target. Our beam jerked off-target, carving the night sky like a scene from the Blitz.

As team leader, Charlie wore a headset and boom mike, connected to the comms box outside the AFV, so he could talk to the crew. His mouth was moving but I didn't have a clue what he was saying. The roar of the engine and tracks put paid to that. He finished, pulled off the headset, and threw it on the grille. He gave Half Arse and me a slap and the shout to stand by.

Seconds later, the AFV slowed, then came to a halt. Our cue to jump. We scrambled down the sides, taking care our daysacks didn't strike anything on the way.

The driver swivelled the vehicle on its own axis, cascading us with mud before he headed back the way we had come.

I joined Charlie and Half Arse behind a couple of cars. We'd known they'd be obvious cover, but we'd only be there a few seconds – and if the searchlights had done their job, anybody watching from the building would have lost their night vision anyway.

We hugged the ground, looking, listening, tuning in.

The AFV's engine noise was now the other side of the building with its mates, their searchlights working the front of the target. And now that they were a safe distance from our eardrums, the loudspeakers mounted on each vehicle began to broadcast a horrible, high-pitched noise like baby rabbits being slaughtered. The noise had been constant for days. I didn't know if it was making the people inside crazy, but it certainly pissed me off.

We were about 50 metres from the rear of the target. I checked Baby-G: about six hours till first light. I checked the gaffer tape over my earpiece, and that the two throat-mike sensors were still in place.

Charlie positioned his own comms kit and taped over. A pressle hung from a wire attached to the lapel of his black corduroy bomber jacket. When he'd sorted his earpiece, he pressed it and spoke in a low voice, with a Yorkshire accent that few Brits could understand, let alone the American at the other end. 'This is Team Alpha. We clear to move yet? Over.'

He was talking to a P3 aircraft circling some twenty five thousand feet above our heads. Bristling with thermal imaging and infrared equipment to give us warning of any impending threat while we were on the job, it also carried an immensely powerful infrared torch angled down at us. I checked that my two-inch square of luminous tape was still stuck on my shoulder. The aircraft's IR beam was invisible to the naked eye, but the reflection off our squares would stick out like sore thumbs on their camera. If the thermal imaging failed, they'd still be able to keep track of our three squares.

The reply from the P3 came to my earpiece too. 'Yep, that's a free zone, Team Alpha, free zone.'

Charlie didn't bother to speak a reply; he just gave two clicks on the pressle. Then, after double checking the tape over his ear, he began to crawl. He'd know that I was second in line, with Half Arse bringing up the rear. Half Arse had a radio like us, but his ear piece was just shoved into his pocket. He was going to be the eyes and ears while Charlie and I worked on target.

The crawl was wet and muddy and my jeans and fleece were quickly soaked. The days out here might be hot, but the nights were freezing cold. I was beginning to wish I'd worn gloves and a couple of extra layers.

Like the other two, I kept my eyes on those parts of the target behind which the P3 couldn't penetrate. The windows. The slightest movement, and we'd freeze and hope we hadn't been seen or heard, but the rabbit noise and searchlights should keep the occupants' attention on the front of the target until we were done.

P3 were trying to be helpful. 'You've got thirty to target, Team Alpha.'

Torchlight flickered behind a curtain on the first floor window. It was directed inwards, not out at us. It wasn't a threat.

We carried on, and six minutes of slow crawling later we were on target. Soaking wet and cold, but where we wanted to be.

The flakey white, weatherboarded exterior wall was only the first of three layers. The building plans showed there were likely to be another two behind it. One was tar paper to help with insulation and to prevent damp, and then there'd be the interior stud wall, which would have a finishing coat of either paint or paper, or both. None of which should be a problem for the sophisticated gear we were carrying.

As planned, we'd crawled to a point between two ground floor windows. Set against the wall was a utility box the size of a coal bunker. It was an ideal location for the stuff we were going to leave behind.

Charlie opened the box with a square lug key and had a quick look inside, his fingers shielding the lens of his mini-Maglite.

Half Arse had his pistol out; he kept his eyes on the windows and his ears everywhere else. He'd had a buttock shot away during an operation a few years back, and I wondered if it meant his arse was only half as cold as mine was.

We knew that everyone in the command centres would be watching the thermal and IR imagery of us at work, beamed down to them by the P3. We wanted to make sure it was a job well done – Brit pride, don't mess with the best, and all that. But right now that was the last thing any of us was worried about; personally, I just wanted to do the business, and get away alive. This was my last job before I left the Regiment. It would be the mother of all ironies if I got dropped or injured now.

I eased my day sack off my back. A distant voice inside the building shouted out something but we ignored him. We'd only react if someone was actually shouting that they'd spotted us; otherwise, we'd be stopping and starting every five minutes. In any event, we'd soon know if there was a drama. Half Arse would be firing.

Charlie had worked out where he wanted to fix the device. He pressed a thumbnail into the wood at almost ground level and gave me a nod. From my day sack, I brought out a pyramid, seven inches high and made from alloy. Instead of a peak, it had a hole, and at each of the four corners was a fixing lug.

Guided by the beam from Charlie's Maglite, I positioned the pyramid so the hole was directly over his nail mark, and held it there while he put a battery-powered screwdriver to the first lug. Very slowly, very deliberately, the shaft of the screwdriver rotated. It took the best part of two minutes to screw it in tight. By the time the first three were in, my hands were freezing.

A different voice shouted from inside. It was closer, but it wasn't talking about us. He was complaining about the rabbit noise, and I couldn't blame him.

The sweat on my back was starting to cool and I could feel the wind fighting its way down my neck. At last, Charlie fixed the last lug and I gave the structure a wiggle left and right to test it was stable. He was the engineer; I was the oily rag. The rest was up to him now.

From his day sack he retrieved a drill bit half a metre long and seven millimetres in diameter. He threaded it carefully into the pyramid hole, oblivious to everything else that was going on.

He blew on his fingers to warm them, then eased the drill in further until it just touched the wood of the exterior wall. It called for a delicate touch, and Charlie was the best of the best at this sort of thing. Back in Hereford, they called him the CEO of MOE (method of entry). There wasn't a security system in existence that he couldn't defeat. If there was, he could always blow it up instead.

Next out was the power cable, which was connected to a lithium battery inside his day sack. Charlie plugged it into the pyramid. There was a moment's delay, and then the bit began to turn, so slowly it almost seemed not to be moving. Jaws inside the pyramid had clamped round the bit, and turned it to do its very precise work. The only sound was a barely audible, low-frequency hum.

There was nothing we could do now but wait as it started to work its way quietly, slowly, methodically through an inch of wood, a sheet of tar paper, and about half a centimetre of plasterboard. I moved against the wall to make myself as small a target as possible if anyone looked out of a window. My right hand lifted my fleece and came to rest on the grip of the pistol pancake-holstered on my jean belt. My left hand pulled the zipped-up front over my nose for warmth.

The drill was based on the technology used in brain surgery, which drilled through the skull but sensed when it was about to hit the cranial membrane and stopped. This one did the same when it was just about to break through the final skin of paint or paper. Meanwhile, it automatically collected the debris and dust so it left no sign.

The gentle hum slowed, and then the drill bit stopped. Charlie disconnected the power and pulled out the drill bit. He took out a fibre optic rod with a light on the end, very similar to the ones used in keyhole surgery. He moved it down through the pyramid, just to make sure he wasn't about to break through the stud wall. Everything seemed to be fine. He removed the fibre optic, re-inserted the drill, and re-connected the power. The gentle hum resumed.

It moved quicker as it hit the tar paper, then slowed again as it made way through the plasterboard. It stopped again. Charlie repeated the operation with the fibre optic.

I looked over at Half Arse, who was lying on his back with his feet nearest the wall. His pistol rested on his chest, pointing up at the first floor windows. He must have been freezing his arse off – or what he had left of it. I thought about all the Americans in the command centres, drinking coffee and smoking cigars while they watched our progress. Most of them were probably just wondering why the fuck we didn't get a move on.

It took nearly an hour before the drill stopped turning for the third and final time. Charlie checked it again with the fibre optic and gave us a thumbs-up with his eye still against the eyepiece. He removed the drill bit and put the screwdriver to the first lug. It began to turn anti-clockwise.

When that was done, Charlie dug out the microphone, which looked exactly the same as the fibre optic rod – in fact, it had a fibre optic cable on the end so it could be put into position correctly.

As all the gear came out I stowed it slowly and carefully back in my day sack. No point rushing it and making noise.

Charlie's final act was to connect the microphone fibre optic cable to the lithium battery and lay a metre-long wire antenna along the ground.

As soon as the power was switched on, I could hear the microphone rustling in my earpiece. The signal was being beamed to the command centre and then bounced back to us as a check before we left. We did that so we didn't have to get on the net to ask if we'd succeeded.

I heard the microphone brushing against the side of the hole as Charlie fed it gently through, stopping now and again and bringing it back a little, then pushing it through a bit more. It would be stopping just this side of the paint or paper, leaving a membrane well less than a milli-metre thick. If a mouse farted, the command centres would know about it.

The rustling of the mike became background noise as it got closer to the membrane. Women's murmurs took over as they comforted their chil-dren, and a man moaned in agony. It must have been the one who'd taken a round in the stomach on the first attack.

It was almost time to leave. Charlie closed and relocked the utilities box as I dug the wire into the earth and smoothed it over. Charlie did a quick final sweep of the area with his shielded Maglite, and we smoothed out a couple of footprints. Only then did we start to crawl back towards the cars to RV with the Bradley.

As we moved, I listened to the voices in my earpiece. A man mumbled quotes from the Bible, then a child whimpered that it wanted a drink of water.

We'd done our bit. Now it was time to hand the toys over to the Americans.

**Read the complete book –
coming in November 2005
from Bantam Press**

AGGRESSOR

Ex-deniable operator Nick Stone seems to be living his dream, not a care in the world as he steers his camper van round the surfing and parachuting centres of Australia. But when he witnesses on TV the massacre of children in a terrorist siege on the other side of the world, long-suppressed memories are triggered. Once more Nick is catapulted into working for the American secret services – only this time, of his own free will.

As events unfold on the bleak, medieval villages of Azerbaijan and teeming streets of modern Istanbul, it isn't long before Nick discovers the true objective of his mission. His talents are being misused by those who stalk the corridors of power . . . and this time he is determined to make a stand.

0 593 050312

COMING IN NOVEMBER FROM BANTAM PRESS

BRAVO TWO ZERO

In January 1991, eight members of the SAS regiment embarked upon a top secret mission that was to infiltrate them deep behind enemy lines. Under the command of Sergeant Andy McNab, they were to sever the underground communication link between Baghdad and north-west Iraq, and to seek and destroy mobile Scud launchers. Their call sign: *Bravo Two Zero*.

0 552 14127 5

'The best account yet of the SAS in action'
Sunday Times

IMMEDIATE ACTION

Millions of readers first came into contact with Andy McNab through *Bravo Two Zero*, but for Andy McNab, *Bravo Two Zero* was only part of the story. *Immediate Action* is a no-holds-barred account of an extraordinary life, from the day McNab was found in a carrier bag on the steps of Guy's Hospital to the day he went to fight in the Gulf War. As a delinquent youth he kicked against society. As a young soldier he waged war against the IRA in the streets and fields of South Armagh. As a member of 22 SAS Regiment he was at the centre of covert operations for nine years – on five continents.

0 552 14276 X

'One of the most extraordinary examples of human courage and survival in modern warfare'
The Times

REMOTE CONTROL

Nick Stone left the Special Air Service in 1988, soon after the shooting of three IRA terrorists in Gibraltar. Now working for British Intelligence on deniable operations, he discovers the seemingly senseless murders of a fellow SAS soldier and his family in Washington, DC. Only a seven-year-old daughter, Kelly, has survived – and the two of them are immediately on the run from unidentified pursuers. Stone doesn't even know which of them is the target.

0 552 14591 2

'Proceeds with a testosterone surge'
Daily Telegraph

CRISIS FOUR

In British military intelligence, deniable operations is the most dangerous tightrope you can walk. Ex-SAS man, Nick Stone, has no choice in the matter. He may be tough, resourceful, ruthless, highly trained, but he still must do what his masters want, whatever that might be. Sarah Greenwood is beautiful, steel-willed, intelligent, cunning – the only woman that Stone has ever let under his guard. And now he's been sent to hunt her down.

0 552 14592 0

'Pacy, gritty and full of surprises. Top stuff'
Maxim

FIREWALL
Helsinki, December 1999. Nick Stone, ex-SAS, is now a 'K' working for British Intelligence on deniable operations. Offered the lucrative freelance job of kidnapping a mafia warlord and delivering him to St Petersburg, it seems to Stone that his problems are over. In fact, they are only just beginning. Stone enters the bleak underworld of the former Soviet republic of Estonia, where unknown aggressors stalk the Arctic landscape.
0 552 14797 4

'Gripping stuff . . . Nick Stone makes Action Man look like a couch potato'
Daily Express

LAST LIGHT
Aborting an officially-sanctioned assassination attempt at the Houses of Parliament when he realises who the target is, Nick Stone is given a chilling ultimatum: fly to Panama and finish the job, or Kelly, the eleven-year-old orphan in his charge, will be killed. Stone is on the edge, struggling to pick up the pieces of his shattered life. By the time he arrives in Panama, he is close to breaking point.
0 552 14798 2

'McNab's great asset is that the heart of his fiction is non-fiction: other thriller writers do their research, but he has actually been there'
Sunday Times

LIBERATION DAY

A Zodiac inflatable slips away from a submarine off the North African coast. If he hadn't needed American citizenship so badly, Nick Stone wouldn't have agreed to do this one last job, but the CIA's offer of a new life in the United States, and the chance to share it with Carrie, the woman he's fallen in love with, is one he cannot refuse. The job seems simple enough for a man of his particular skills: infiltrate the hostile and violent republic of Algeria, kill a money-laundering local businessman, and bring back his severed head to the West.

0 552 14799 0

'McNab is a terrific novelist. When it comes to thrills, he's Forsyth class'
Mail on Sunday

DARK WINTER

When maverick agent Nick Stone is despatched to Malaysia by the CIA to assassinate a shadowy biochemist, he expects his mission to be a straightforward part of the fight against Osama Bin Laden's network of terror. Target neutralised, Stone returns to the USA – and a maelstrom of personal problems. Kelly, the fourteen-year-old orphan to whom he is joint guardian, cannot escape the ghosts of her traumatic past. He takes her to recuperate in England, but the terrible consequences of what happened in Penang are never far behind.

0 552 15018 5

'Andy McNab knows where his strengths lie, and it's not just in his biceps . . . Only people who have not read this book could suggest that he is not a fine writer. It is a heart-thumping read'
Daily Express

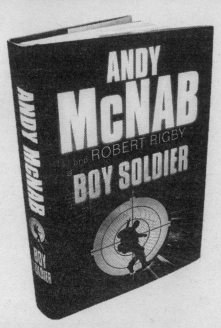

Purchasing and Supply Chain Management